# CHECKMATE

"Ye...ye Englishman," Megan exploded, bestowing the worst of all curses on him. "I should have never agreed to play chess wi' ye."

"Ah, but you did, my dear. And now you must honor your wager."

Slowly Rolf unfolded himself from the chair, stretching his sleek, muscular frame like a panther.

"Come here, Megan," he commanded softly, motioning with the crook of his finger. "I believe it is time to honor your wager."

Megan looked at him with wide eyes, her courage faltering. "N-nay," she whispered, her voice shaking unnaturally. "'Twas wrong o' me to make such a wager. I can't honor it. I simply don't think I could bear it."

"Bear what?" he asked sharply.

"Being kissed...by ye."

He frowned, raising his maimed hand. "You mean being kissed by a cripple."

She blinked in surprise, her brow drawing into a frown. "Nay, I mean being kissed by...by an Englishman." The soft burr in her voice deepened with anxiety. "I'm certain 'twill be most horrible."

Rolf stood deathly still before he suddenly began to laugh. "So that is what troubles you?" he asked. When she nodded, he shook his head in disbelief. "Come here, Megan. Let me show you what it is like to be kissed by an Englishman."

# THE THORN & THE THISTLE

## JULIE MOFFETT

**LEISURE BOOKS**  **NEW YORK CITY**

*To Larisa Silnicky*

*For believing in my abilities,*
*For advising me to get married,*
*For being a third grandmother to my son,*
*For being the best boss a girl could have,*
*For being a friend.*

*What a woman!*

LOVE SPELL®

February 2003

Published by

Dorchester Publishing Co., Inc.
276 Fifth Avenue
New York, NY   10001

ISBN: 0-8439-4263-0

The name "Love Spell" and its logo are trademarks of Dorchester Publishing Co., Inc.

Printed in the United States of America.

Visit us on the web at www.dorchesterpub.com.

# The THORN & the THISTLE

# Chapter One

*Glen Grudie*
*Scottish Highlands*
*November 1751*

Megan MacLeod hurried across the snow-covered ground, her long skirts swirling madly around her boot-clad legs. The cold wind howled through the pine trees, painfully snatching the breath from her lungs and causing her wool plaid of green, blue and yellow to stream out behind her like a banner. As she reached the bank of the frozen loch, she paused, drawing the plaid across her face, trying to shield her skin from the bitter cold.

Bracing her lambskin boot against a large boulder, she listenend to the sounds of the wintry glen—the fierce whistle of the wind and the groan of the barren branches heavily laden with ice and snow. It had begun snowing in earnest;

oversized flakes chased each other crazily through the air before settling on the ground, creating a thick white carpet. She could not see the water, for it was hidden beneath the snow and frozen beneath an inch of ice. It was the contrast of seasons. In the summer, hundreds of animals flocked to this spot to partake of the loch's sparkling clean water. But now, in the dead of winter, the river was still and game was scarce.

Today, however, she had not come to the loch's edge seeking food. Instead, she had hoped to hear the crunch of horse's hooves on the cold earth and the unmistakable murmur of men's voices as they returned to the camp. To her dismay, nothing other than the rush of the bitter wind disturbed the regal silence of the forest.

Anxiously, she glanced up at the sky, trying to determine the time. Although she suspected it was just past midday, the horizon was gray and full of clouds. Definitely a bad omen. It meant that the storm would continue and perhaps grow worse. Usually the weather didn't bother her, even the damp, chilling cold that was typical of Highland winters. She was accustomed to it, having lived all of her twenty years in the rugged splendor of the glen she called home. Yet for more than a week now the weather had been unusually frigid, and this day seemed the worst yet. The air was achingly cold, and Megan could feel the wind growing stronger. She knew full well that poor weather could interfere with, even hinder, the men's raid. They had been due back hours ago.

In frustration, Megan clenched her plaid tightly, the heavy wool bunching beneath her icy fingers. The raids against the English had become more than just an act of defiance; they were increasingly necessary to feed the many hungry mouths of clansmen and their families. Stripped of their rightful heritage, they had been forced to live in the hills like animals: stealing, harrassing and resisting the English with whatever methods they could employ. It was not a life Megan had envisioned for herself or her family, but it had not been a path willfully chosen.

Narrowing her eyes against the wind, Megan pictured Castle Kilcraig, the proud ancestoral home of the MacLeods of Gairloch. The enormous stone walls and the jutting twin towers had always been a place of security and pride for generations of MacLeods. But all of that had changed with the Jacobite Uprising and Scotland's crushing defeat in the fields of Culloden six years earlier. Despite the fact that her father had never openly supported the young Stuart prince's claim to the throne, the English had invaded their home anyway, ordering Robert MacLeod to sign an oath of fealty to the English King. When Robert refused, the English had cast him and his family from the land that had belonged to them for centuries.

Still, English interference did not stop there. King George had ordered the entire Highland clan system forbidden, outlawing the tartan and declaring that any Scot possessing a weapon be immediately punished by death. It was a barbaric madness that had become something beyond injustice. The English were destroying the very fabric of Highland life. And it was something the proud Clan MacLeod would resist as long as they could draw a breath.

Abruptly a strong gust of wind ripped through the forest, tearing the plaid from Megan's head. Long dark strands of hair whipped about her face, stinging the skin on her cheeks and bringing tears to her eyes. She knew she would have to return to the camp soon or freeze.

Clasping her hands together, Megan bowed her head and prayed. Snowflakes landed on the long sweep of her dark lashes, melting and trickling down her cheeks like tears. She stood there in silence, a small splash of color against the cool wintry landscape. Then, after a moment, she lifted her head and quickly disappeared into the forest.

Megan leapt from her seat near a blazing campfire when she saw her clansmen finally returning home. It was nearly dusk and the men rode single file and were strangely quiet. Concerned, she rushed across the snow to meet them. She nearly slipped as she skidded to a stop near her uncle, grabbing on to the reins of his horse to steady her balance.

"Ye're late, Uncle Geddes," she scolded breathlessly, the plaid slipping from her head. Snow swirled and settled on the dark strands of her hair. "Why, 'tis past nightfall and we've been worried sick about ye. What took ye so long?"

Geddes Kincaid looked down at his niece and exhaled heavily. His breath made a small cloud near his heavily bearded face.

"Megan, permit us to dismount," he said. "The men are weary and wounded."

She moved from his side, anxiously looking

about for her father's unmistakable black cloak. "Where is Father?" Megan asked when her uncle dismounted.

Geddes took one step and nearly collapsed in the snow. Megan gasped when she saw the blook-soaked rags tied around his thigh.

"My God, ye are injured," she exclaimed. Quickly she took his elbow, shouldering some of his weight. "Come, let me help ye into Father's tent."

Before they had gone two steps, a young man with flaming red hair and a curly beard rode up beside them. Muttering an oath, he slid off his horse.

"Could ye no' wait for me, Da?" he asked, wrapping a strong arm around the older man's waist. "Ye'll no' get far wi' only a wisp o' a lass to help ye."

"I'm no' a frail woman, Robbie," Megan countered heatedly. "I can help him just fine."

"Aye, mayhap ye could. But the snow is deep and ye've hardly a decent pair o' boots to your name. Dinna be stubborn, Meggie, and let me help him."

Megan stopped in her tracks, reluctantly releasing her uncle's arm. "All right, Robbie, but—" She broke off with a small cry. "Saints preserve us," she exclaimed, pointing at a deep gash in her cousin's arm. "Ye, too, have been wounded. What in God's name happened today?"

Geddes exchanged a quick glance with his son. A grim, unspoken message passed between them. "We had an unexpected skirmish wi' Edwin Farrington," Geddes answered, wincing in pain as he took a step. " 'Twas a trap. We were anxious to return before the storm and we got careless. Farrington caught us unaware."

Megan's eyes widened anxiously. "A trap? Blessed Virgin, was anyone else hurt?"

Geddes gently put a hand on her shoulder. "Megan, ye must be strong, lass."

She took a step back, clutching her plaid between her fingers. "What do ye mean? Just how many men have been harmed?"

Robbie sighed heavily, rubbing a bandaged hand across his lower jaw. "Eight men lost, Meggie. One o' them was your da."

She gasped, her face drained of all color. "Lost?" she asked dumbly.

"They're dead," Robbie said wearily. " 'Tis a black day indeed for the Clan MacLeod."

" 'Tis no' possible," she protested in shock.

Geddes exhaled deeply. "I wish 'twasn't true. But he is wi' us no more. Ye must be strong, Megan. For all o' us."

Megan only stared at him blankly, unable to comprehend the knowledge that her father was dead.

Geddes lifted an arm, pointing at his mount. "Your da's cloak is there, Megan. I saved it for ye."

Numbly she walked to the horse, reaching up and pulling down the bloodstained cloak. She held it in her hands for a long moment before burying her face in the soft, black pelt. "Nay, no' Papa, too. Och, my God, nay," she sobbed.

"Meggie, I'm sorry," Robbie said, exhaling a heavy breath.

She lifted her head from the cloak, tears rolling down her cheeks. "I don't believe ye," she cried. "He's alive. Ye simply left him there. He is

14

probably lying somewhere wounded and hurt. He needs our help."

Geddes shook his head sadly. "Megan, lass, listen to me. I buried your da wi' my own hands. I wish more than anything that I could say that 'tisn't true—that your father is alive—but, 'tis no' so. He's gone and somehow, we must go on without him."

For a moment Megan stood silently, the snow swirling furiously around her. Then with a heart-wrenching sob, she turned from the men and ran into the forest, her plaid streaming out behind her.

"Go after the lass," Geddes instructed his son wearily. "She needs ye more than I do now."

Robbie's brow drew into a worried frown as he strode purposefully into the trees after her. It broke his heart to see her like this, not knowing how to comfort her. Although a man of considerable strength and size, he always felt helpless when it came to his cousin. Megan had always been the more clever and strong-willed of the two of them. It was she who had led him and half the other bairns of the glen on one mischievous adventure after another. And it was she who had boldly talked their way out of punishment time after time. All of his life he had half-admired, half-envied her wit and poise.

And he had always loved her.

At fifteen, he had decided that he would make her his wife.

Robbie sighed at the memory, rubbing his knuckles against his bearded jaw. It worried him that to this day he had not yet been able to convince her to settle down. Before the English came, she had been a carefree spirit, not ready to bind herself to any man. It had both infuriated and terrified him when others paid her suit, but to his great relief, she had accepted none of them. Although she had not agreed to wed him either, he was comforted by the certainty that he held a special place in her heart. As children, they had been inseparable—as adults they remained confidants and close friends.

But now they were living like animals in the hills with little time for love and companionship. Sometimes, at night, he woke up in a cold sweat, fearing that she might never be his. Yet he clung to his cherished hope, believing that as long as he dared to dream, it might somehow come true. The English could be damned. His love for Meggie was one thing he'd not allow them to steal.

Robbie's frown deepened as he looked up at the dark sky, noting that the snowfall had increased and the temperature was dropping rapidly. Pulling the plaid tighter around his broad shoulders, he hunched over and plodded through the drifts.

Her trail was easy to follow on the snow-carpeted forest floor, and he soon found her sprawled on a log, sobbing into her hands. He knelt beside her, wrapping a possessive arm around her shoulder.

"Meggie, let's go back to the camp. 'Tis a great deal we need to talk about."

She lifted her grief-stricken eyes to his. "He's gone, Robbie," she whispered brokenly, tears streaming down her face. "He was all I had after J-Jamie . . ." She choked on her words, unable to finish.

A twinge of pain flashed through Robbie as he

thought of Megan's twin brother. " 'Tis a great tragedy that ye've had your family taken from ye. But take comfort," he murmured. "Ye should believe they are together in Heaven with your mum."

"But I have no one now," she sobbed. "I'm all alone."

Robbie drew her head into the hollow of his throat. Resting his bearded chin on top of her cold, windblown hair, he dared a kiss against the dark strands.

" 'Tisn't so, Meggie, and ye know it," he said softly. "Ye'll always have me."

She sobbed again and Robbie tightened his embrace, wishing he didn't feel so helpless. He had seen her behave in many different ways—wildly independent, brash and reckless. But he had never seen her this vulnerable and afraid. It frightened him and he didn't know what to do.

"Dinna cry, *mo graidh*." He whispered the Gaelic endearment, awkwardly patting her back with his large hand. "I'll take care o' ye. Ye know I will. Come wi' me; 'tis cold here."

Wordlessly, she stood and allowed him to lead her back to the large tent that she shared with her father. Robbie held the flap open, and she stepped inside. The tent was large—animal hides had been stretched across a wooden frame to make a space large enough to hold five men. A crude wooden table with two long benches sat in one corner. In the other corner were two piles of furs, one for Megan and one for her father. Robbie saw that Geddes had tossed the black wolf pelt onto Robert's bed and now sat despondently behind the table.

"Megan, lass," Geddes said when she stood

motionless in the center of the tent, staring at her father's bed. "Are ye all right?"

Megan blinked. "I'm all right," she replied in a shaky voice. "I just can't believe that hours earlier my da slept here peacefully, no' knowing what fate held in store for him. And now he's gone."

"I'm sorry, lass."

"So am I," she said softly. Fighting back a sob, she unfastened her own plaid and cast it to her pallet. "But 'tis no' the time for sadness. I must see to your wound." Pushing aside her grief, she dropped to her knees at his side.

"Saints preserve us, it looks as if it hurts something fearsome," she observed.

"Och, I've had worse," he answered, forcing a cheerful tone.

"Let me have a look at it then."

Nodding, Geddes moved his hand from his leg. "Megan, I'm truly sorry," he murmured as her hands skimmed across his leg, brushing the dirt and torn material away from the wound. "If ye only knew how much I wish 'twas me who would have fallen instead o' him."

"Don't say that," she answered. "Ye know that God has our lives planned out for us. 'Twas simply no' your time." She glanced up at Robbie, who stood silently in the entranceway. "Robbie, I'll take care o' your da now. There are others who need your help. Tend to them and I'll be around as soon as I can."

"But Meggie," Robbie protested. "Ye are in no condition to treat others."

"I'm fine," she replied sharply. "Now don't argue wi' me, Robbie Kincaid. Please, just do as I ask. Your da will be all right."

" 'Tis no' my da that I'm worried about."

"I'm no' about to fall apart just yet. Now, if your own wound permits, please, see to the others."

Frowning at being summarily dismissed, Robbie exchanged a glance with his father. When the elder Kincaid shrugged, Robbie lifted his hands in resignation.

"As ye wish," he said, lifting the tent flap and stepping out into the cold. A gust of cold air rushed into the tent and Megan shivered.

"Ye're hard on the lad," Geddes commented after Robbie was gone.

"I don't need coddling."

"He's in love wi' ye, ye know," Geddes said, wincing as her fingers deftly prodded his wound. "Ye canna blame him for wanting to comfort ye."

Megan sat back on her heels, wearily brushing a strand of dark hair from her forehead. "I know. And I don't blame him. 'Tis just that now is no' the time for grieving. We must think o' what to do without my father. The English must pay for what they have done."

Geddes was silent for a long moment before speaking. "Then ye plan to seek revenge? How long can we keep living like this, Megan?"

She looked up at him in surprise. "What is that supposed to mean?"

"I mean that we live in the forest like wild creatures. We are confined to uncomfortable tents in unbearable conditions. We are cold, restless and starving. The future is bleak for all o' us. Is this really the life ye want to live? Have ye forgotten that ye are a young lass wi' your life still in front o' ye?"

Megan's eyes flashed angrily. "I've forgotten naught. But that doesn't change anything. I'll resist the English as long as I have a breath in me." Pushing herself to her feet, she lifted her skirts and walked over to a wooden chest. Rummaging around, she pulled out a small pouch containing herbs. She measured out a small amount, and poured it into a wooden bowl with some water. "I have no intention o' giving up," she said, stirring the mixture. "I hope I speak for the rest o' the clan as well."

"Ye sound remarkably like your father, lass. Proud and stubborn to a fault."

She looked up, her mouth tightening with anger. "Are ye implying that our fight is no longer worthy?"

Geddes sighed deeply. "Worthy, 'twill always be. Wise, I'm no longer certain."

"Well, I'm certain 'tis the right thing to do," she said firmly, dipping a clean linen strip into the bowl. "I'd rather die than give up my land to the English without a fight."

"Have ye considered that it might come to that?"

Megan pushed a stray lock of hair from her eyes with the back of her hand. "What—dying? O' course, I've considered it. Do ye think I fear my own death, especially now that I've lost everyone I've ever loved? If ye do, ye are wrong. 'Twould be worse than death to live under the heavy hand o' the English."

"Ye understand so little, Megan. 'Tis oft the blindness o' the young. Life is precious."

She frowned fiercely. "Life without freedom is worth naught. I'll fight the English to the death if I must."

"And give Farrington the satisfaction of killing another MacLeod?"

She paused, a stricken look crossing her face. "Are ye saying 'twas Farrington himself who killed my father?"

Geddes sighed wearily. "Aye, 'twas him. His men caught us in an ambush. 'Twas little we could do. Robbie managed to wound two o' Farrington's men, permitting some o' us to escape, but they chased us anyway. I saw Farrington put a sword through your father in a clearing a wee bit from the village. But the man is a fool, he didn't know who your father was. After Farrington and his men left, I tried to help your father, but 'twas too late. He died in my arms."

Megan closed her eyes, tears trickling past her eyelids. "Farrington is the spawn o' the Devil himself. How has it come to this? We are forced off the land o' our ancestors, while those too poor to leave are starved into submission. Curse his black English soul—I swear by all the saints above that I'll make Farrington pay, Uncle Geddes. I will."

"And just how will ye do that, Megan? Your da is gone. Who will lead us in tthe attempt?"

At the sharp reminder of her father's death, Megan felt an aching stab of emptiness. Determinedly, she dashed the tears from her cheeks with the back of her hand, her eyes taking on a hard light. "I'll find a way. Did my father leave any final instructions? Had he ever talked wi' ye about what to do if something happened to him?"

Geddes shook his head sadly. "Nay, 'twas never the right time to discuss such a thing. Saints above, I wouldn't even let myself think such thoughts. But now I wish I would have. Och, what an old fool I am."

"Hush," Megan said, placing her hand on his shoulder. "Don't blame yourself, Uncle Geddes."

"At the end, he spoke only o' ye, Megan. Even wi' his dying breath, he was thinking o' your future. He made me swear I'd help ye and then asked me to take and bury his body so no one would know he'd been slain."

Megan looked up quickly, surprise evident on her face. "Bury his body so no one would know? 'Tis an odd request."

Deep lines of sadness stretched across the older man's cheeks. "Mayhap his mind was failing him in those last moments."

Megan withdrew into a thoughtful silence, setting the bowl with the salve on the table. "Perhaps 'tis no' as ye think," she mused aloud, her mind sorting though possibilities. "There may be a reason to his request to hide his body. 'Tis a rumor that the neighboring clans o' the Chisholms and the MacDonnells are near ready to join forces wi' us. But if they learn that my father's dead, they'll never agree to it. Perhaps my da was trying to tell ye that in order to unite the clans, we must keep his death a secret."

Geddes's mouth fell open. "A secret?" he choked out. "Have ye lost your senses, lass?"

She shook her head, a new light of determination flashing in her eyes. "Nay, in fact I think I have a plan."

"A plan? Just what are ye plotting, Megan MacLeod?"

She set her hands firmly on her hips. "I'm planning a way to outfox the English. But we must first swear our clansmen to secrecy about my father's demise—at least temporarily. Then we will negotiate for the support o' the Chisholms and the MacDonnells. If they ask where my father is, we'll tell them that he has gone to the Lowlands to gather support for us. We'll then present ourselves as his proxy, negotiating their aid on his behalf."

"His proxy?" Geddes exclaimed in horror. "Good God, child, I canna negotiate. I am a simple man. I've no' the words nor knowledge to do what ye ask o' me. I canna fill the shoes o' your father, no matter how I wish I could."

Megan gripped her uncle's hand fiercely. "But together we can. We can't give up, Uncle. At last our movement is gaining in strength and numbers. Words o' our deeds are spreading throughout Gairloch. People are once again beginning to have hope that mayhap all is no' lost for us. But what will happen if we let the legend o' the Black Wolf die wi' my father? 'Twill mean the end for all o' us. We'll live in fear in our own glens, subjugated to the whims o' English bastards like Farrington. I won't let it happen. No' while I have a breath o' life still in me."

"Megan," Geddes pleaded, "even if we wanted to, we could no' keep your father's death a secret forever."

" 'Tis no' forever that I am concerned about. I need only to bring a few other clans into the fold. Then we'll reveal my da's death."

"Saints preserve us, child, ye'll bring naught but strife to the clan," Geddes exclaimed in dismay. "Without a laird, t'will be a bloody struggle for leadership. 'Twould be different if your brother were still alive. But without a MacLeod heir, ye'll have your cousins from the Isle o' Skye

23

feuding wi' the MacDonnells and Chisholms for control o' the clan."

Megan took a deep breath, steadying her hands so they would not tremble. "When the time comes to reveal my father's death, I shall take a husband. 'Tis my right. As I am the last MacLeod o' my father's line, the man who marries me shall have the strongest claim to the lairdship."

Geddes's mouth opened in surprise. For as long as he had known Megan, she had avoided the issue of marriage. An independent spirit, she'd stubbornly resisted her father's every attempt to bind her into a union not of her choosing. For her to offer herself as a sacrifice for clan unity was as stunning as it was admirable.

He sighed, deeply troubled by her announcement. "'Tis a noble proposal, lass, but I still don't think we can do it."

"We can and we will," she replied firmly. "Until I marry, by all rights o' our laws, I am now legally the laird o' the MacLeod clan."

"And ye know full well that law was designed only to protect the clan line if the last surviving member was a female," he chided, frowning. "'Twould be expected o' ye to marry immediately."

"Mayhap under normal circumstances," she argued stubbornly, "but we both know that revealing the death o' my da at this time would only throw the clan and our entire effort into confusion. We must first protect our own and continue the success my da reaped as the Black Wolf. When the time comes, I shall take a husband. I promise ye that."

Geddes snorted in disbelief, running his fingers through his graying red hair. "Saint's mercy, Megan, do ye understand what ye are proposing? As laird, the responsibilities falling on your shoulders will be fearsome."

Megan lifted her chin proudly. "I'm ready for that responsibility. I think I always have been. I know that bringing the other clans into our effort against the English 'twill take some effort, but 'twill no' be impossible. I know every detail o' every plan o' my father's. I've watched him plot raids and learned strategy from him. He used to say that the English know little o' our ways. 'Tis this very thing that makes us strong, Uncle Geddes. I can be the Black Wolf in all ways except battle. In that manner, I'll defer to ye and Robbie. Ye must only trust me."

"Trust ye?" Geddes exclaimed heatedly, throwing up his hands. " 'Tis no' just a matter o' trust, lass. What ye ask o' me—what ye ask o' yourself—'tis sheer madness. By God, I implore ye to cease such foolish talk."

" 'Tis neither foolish nor idle talk. O' all people, Uncle Geddes, ye know that Father would have found a way to thwart the English. Search your heart and tell me that 'tisn't true. We must continue wi' our struggle. We canna give in to the likes o' Farrington. 'Twould only make the deaths o' Jamie, my father, and the many others of our clan but a mockery."

Geddes moaned, putting his head in his hands. "God's mercy, lass, ye talk circles around me, just like your da did. Ye surely share his gift for words."

"Aye, and 'tis what shall make us successful. Please, Uncle Geddes, do as I ask. We are family. My mother was your sister and her blood runs in my veins, as does yours. We cannot let the hopes o' our clans die here at the hands o' men who have no regard for our way o' life. We must fight back. Please, Uncle, I can't do it without ye. I need your help."

Geddes exhaled deeply, tugging anxiously on the thick curls of his beard. His gaunt face was troubled and tired. " 'Tis little I can deny ye, Megan. Ye are like my own child. And although 'tis against my better judgment, I will agree to help ye. I warn ye, though, that Robbie will no' like it. I only pray 'twill work. If no', may God have mercy on both our souls."

Megan threw her arms around her uncle, hugging him tightly. "He must have mercy, Uncle Geddes," she whispered fervently in his ear. "For He has no other choice. 'Tis little misery left for Him to allow us."

# *Chapter Two*

*London, England*
*December 1751*

A light snow swirled· and eddied as Rolf St. James carefully guided his black stallion along the darkened streets of London. He realized as the horse's muscles tightened beneath him that he should have summoned his carriage to take him to court in style. But he needed the fresh, crisp air to improve his mood. The cramped and stuffy space of a coach always made him edgy and tonight he didn't want anything to affect his humor.

Sliding a gloved hand beneath his expensive cloak, he lightly touched the parchment that contained the King's summons. His pulse quickened with anticipation. The request for an audience had been most mysterious, but Rolf was hopeful it was the beginning of something new

. . . or at least a welcome distraction. He only prayed that the summons meant he would be called upon to serve somewhere in a new venture that would take him away from London and its despicable court politics.

He frowned, the hard, square lines of his jaw tightening. God, how he hated this city. His court responsibilities were loathsome; the petty bickering of his fellow noblemen, intolerable. A soldier by training, he much preferred to meet honorable opponents on the battlefield than mingle with pompous idiots of the court. Being forced into discourse with them for any length of time was worse than taking a sword wound in battle.

Scowling, Rolf slapped the reins against his beast's neck, urging it on as the royal estate came into view. Upon entering the gates, he was barely given time to dismount and shrug out of his travel-stained cloak before being ushered in to see the King. Astonished, he realized that he was being led to the King's own bedchamber. As soon as he stepped across the threshold into the room, the servants withdrew, leaving them alone.

King George II, dressed for bed in a long gown of dark blue velvet, sat in a high-backed chair. His pudgy face was white and drawn, but he still wore a wig of thick brown curls that hung loosely to his shoulders. A blazing fire roared in a large hearth and the King had stretched out his bare feet to the warmth. The scent of hot spiced wine filled the air, and Rolf saw a pitcher and two goblets sitting on the table. Quickly, Rolf walked over to the King and knelt to one knee.

"Your Majesty, how may I be of service to you?"

King George waved a pale hand, urging Rolf to rise and sit in a chair opposite him. Rolf obeyed and settled himself on the rich, thick cushions.

"I received this parchment only hours ago," the King said in his thick German accent, pointing to a scroll that sat on an adjoining table. "It is yet another example of how many disloyal subjects I must contend with. The heathen Scottish refuse to obey me and I grow weary of their behavior."

Rolf nodded his dark head sympathetically. "It is a most difficult situation, sire. The Scots are a proud people. Their location makes it hard for us to regulate their activities as we should."

The King pressed a hand to his brow, the brilliant jewels on his fingers sparkled in the fire's glow. "Hard, indeed. Over the past six months, one man has exhibited positively odious behavior against the crown. He is a Highlander by the name of Robert MacLeod. Two years ago when he refused to sign an oath of fealty to me, I had him cast from his land. I wish now that I had taken his head." The King frowned deeply, and Rolf felt an immediate stirring of concern.

"The MacLeods of Skye?"

A grudging smile stretched across the King's face. "I can see you did not dally idly the last time I sent you to Scotland. No, Rolf, he is a MacLeod from the region of Gairloch. I am informed that the MacLeods of Skye are distant cousins. As far as I can tell, the clans are not particularly close. None of the other MacLeods stepped forward to help their cousin when I had him permanently removed from his land."

"What has this Robert MacLeod of Gairloch done, my lord?"

The King laughed harshly. "What hasn't he done? He calls himself the Black Wolf and roams the hills as if he owns them."

"The Black Wolf?" Rolf repeated with a raised eyebrow.

George nodded. "Apparently MacLeod wears a cloak made from the pelt of black wolves, a rare find these days in the Highlands. The villagers believe it enables him to change into a black wolf, giving him some sort of mystical, magical power over his enemies."

"Simple superstitions, certainly."

"Perhaps, but as the Black Wolf, MacLeod has harassed loyal English subjects in the area, stole from them, burned their houses and resorted to murder. Even more distressing, he seems to possess some rather remarkable diplomatic skills. In the past few months, he's brought together some of the fiercest clans in the area, including the Chisholms, who at one point swore fealty to me. I'll have no more of it, Rolf. This Wolf has become some sort of legendary figure to the local people and they seem willing to follow him, no matter how reckless such a venture may be."

Rolf swore softly. "The man is bold."

George nodded. "That he is. And I cannot take the risk that he may be able to organize them into some kind of effective fighting force. Our situation in the Highlands is tenuous at best, and I'll not have MacLeod among them stirring up trouble."

"What would you have me do?"

"You are one of my most trusted officers and

more importantly, you have valuable experience in Scotland. I want you to hunt down this Black Wolf and put an end to his activites. Then learn more about these Scottish heathen. Befriend them if you must in order to settle them down. You may offer them employment, help them rebuild their homes, or whatever it may take to gain their trust. But I'll have no more talk of insurrection, nor will I further tolerate flagrant disobedience of my laws."

Rolf digested the request with no small amount of surprise. This was certainly not what he had expected, but he felt honored the King had entrusted him with such a vital and important task.

George saw the surprise on Rolf's face and his voice softened. "I know that the past several months have been most difficult for you, Rolf. I've also noticed that lately you have appeared restless and troubled in your business about court. I speak as your friend now, not your sovereign, when I urge you to proceed with your life. It is time to put your tragedies behind you—that dreadful incident with your hand and, of course, the unfortunate loss of your wife. However, I feel compelled to remind you that the St. James estate needs an heir and it is your duty to provide one. I'm sure I speak as your father would if he were here."

A faint smile touched the corners of Rolf's lips. His father, Sir Percival St. James, had been a close friend of the King's family and had served with distinction alongside George during the Battle of Dettingen in Bavaria. The two men had been confidants and friends for many years

31

until Rolf's father had passed on just two years ago.

"Of course, you are right, sire," Rolf replied softly, "but I need a bit more time. Besides, I'm afraid this crippling injury and my wife's rather unusual death make me a somewhat questionable prospect for most young ladies."

"As far as I'm concerned, the matter with Caroline's death is closed," the King said firmly. He glanced down at Rolf's left hand. It was gloved and lay loosely on his thigh. "Your hand, however, is another issue. Does it still pain you?"

Rolf shrugged and then slowly pulled off the black glove. The fingers were curled inward toward his palm at an odd angle as if frozen in an angry clench.

The King was aghast. "My God, have you any use of it at all?"

Rolf's lips pursed dryly. "Practically none. I'm afraid my hand serves as little more than a dead weight."

"And the pain?"

"It occasionally bothers me, but I fear the sight of my injury is more disturbing to those who have occasion to witness it than it is to me."

The King sighed apologetically. "Forgive me, Rolf. I know that it has not affected your abilities to lead. That is why I asked specifically for you to handle this most delicate task in Scotland."

"I am honored by your faith in my abilities."

"You are a good and decent man much like your father. True, you have had some unfortunate luck, but that will certainly change. If you so desire, I shall command whichever woman you wish to wed you."

Rolf bowed his head gratefully, slowly replac-

ing the glove on his hand. "I appreciate your
kindness, sire, but that will not be necessary. I
am fully aware of my duty to wed again and shall
do so in good time. But at the moment I am most
intrigued by this business in Scotland. If you
will permit me to query, where do you wish for
me to begin?"

The King motioned toward the table with the
pitcher. "Pour us some wine."

Rolf arose from his chair and walked over to
the table where the wine and black goblets
stood. He poured the fragrant wine into one of
the goblets and offered it to the King before
pouring one for himself. The King waited until
Rolf returned to his seat before speaking.

"I am turning over MacLeod's castle and land
holdings to you. The locals call it Castle Kilcraig.
It is a bit of an ironic gesture on my part, and
one that I must admit gives me a devious sense
of satisfaction. There have been a variety of people living in it since being vacated, but I'll have
it cleared for your arrival. It is located on the
western coast of the country—north of the Isle
of Skye."

Rolf took a sip of his wine thoughtfully. "My
presence in this Castle Kilcraig shall certainly
capture the attention of the Wolf."

"As it is intended. You may also wish to con-
verse with a nobleman in the same area by the
name of Edwin Farrington. I sent him there myself two years ago after we were able to effectively appropriate the land from MacLeod and
the local heathens."

Rolf vaguely remembered hearing about the
bloody rebellions against the English in the
Gairloch region. He thought it remarkable that

in spite of their resounding defeat at the hands of the King's men, the Scots still refused to give in, fighting for an additional two years on little more than sheer will, pride and intelligence. The Black Wolf was certainly an enemy to be respected.

"Will I be permitted to take my men?" he asked.

"No more than sixty, I'm afraid, so choose well. I don't want it to appear as if the Black Wolf has us worried. I trust you, Rolf. You are a fine soldier, just as your father was before you."

"I will not fail you, my lord," Rolf said, setting his empty goblet on the table and standing.

The King stood as well, putting a friendly hand on Rolf's shoulder. "I have no doubt that you will succeed. Give yourself one week to put your affairs in order and then be on your way. I will see you are richly rewarded for your success."

"Serving you is reward enough, Your Majesty," Rolf replied softly, inclining his head slightly.

George laughed softly, his brown curls bouncing against his shoulders. "My God, if only all my subjects were as loyal as you, I'd be the happiest monarch in all of Europe."

He paused, and his face turned momentarily serious. "Just do one thing for your King, Rolf. Bring me the Black Wolf."

"You have my word on it, sire," Rolf replied firmly.

# Chapter Three

*Glen Grudie*
*February 1752*

Megan did not notice the bitterly cold wind as she rode into camp, her cheeks flushed, her eyes shining. Sliding off the horse, she handed the reins to one of her clansmen and entered the tent. A smile crossed her lips as she heard the shouts of victory. In excellent spirits, she unfastened her plaid, glancing up as Robbie entered the tent, a broad grin on his face. Striding purposefully the short distance to where she stood, he grabbed her around the waist, whirling her about in a circle before setting her down on the ground.

"God's mercy, ye did it again, Meggie. 'Tis the sixth successful raid we've had this month. We've got a half dozen o' Farrington's horses and enough fodder to feed them for the rest o' the winter. 'Tis nothing short o' a miracle. Ye have the luck o' the saints, lass."

Megan threw back her head and laughed. " 'Tisn't just luck. Ye know how I struggle wi' ways to outfox that cursed Englishman."

"And ye've done that and much more," Robbie said, his warm green eyes full of pride. "Ye've done everything ye promised. The MacDonnells and Chisholms have joined wi' us and the men are in better spirits than they have been in months. Ye've tricked the English in ways that would have made your da proud o' ye. Saints above, it makes *me* proud."

Megan carelessly cast her plaid to the bench, shaking out her hair. "Farrington is a fool and easily tricked. But we must be careful o' the new Englishman. Somehow I sense he is different."

Robbie frowned. "Aye, word is that the man is as evil as the Devil. I heard he lost a hand in battle and takes his anger out on his enemies, killing and crippling alike."

She paled slightly. " 'Tis true that a maimed man is oft dangerous, much like a wounded animal. But he'll no' catch us, Robbie. We've already proven to be too quick for him."

"So far, luck has been wi' us."

Megan whirled around to face him. "I told ye, luck has naught to do wi' it. We've painstakingly planned every detail."

"Aye, 'tis so, but ye canna stop me from worrying. Did ye know the Englishman even murdered his own wife?"

Megan gasped, taking a step back in horror. "Mary, Mother o' God, is that true?"

"Aye, Douglas MacLeary overheard talk among the English soldiers. We must take care wi' this man. 'Tis my belief that this Englishman would no' hesitate to murder our women or bairns if it suited his purpose."

Megan hugged herself tightly. "Well, I won't give him the chance. I'll no' let him hurt our people."

Reaching out, Robbie lightly brushed his fingers against her cheek. " 'Tis a fine leader ye've been, Meggie, but 'tis time we talk."

She stiffened defensively. "About what?"

Robbie took a deep breath. "It's been four months since your da died. Ye've achieved what ye wanted wi' the other clans. 'Tis now time to put aside your leadership and agree to become my wife. Let me take care o' ye, like a husband should."

"But 'tis not the right time yet," she protested heatedly. "Ye know that."

"And when will the time be right? Ye're just being stubborn, Meggie. Ye know we can't keep the death o' your father a secret for much longer."

"Why no'? My plan is working better than we ever anticipated. We are stronger now than we have been in months."

"And the last thing we want is to see it all come to naught by letting the clans know they've been led all along by a lass. The MacLeod clan trusts ye, but I dinna know about the others. We canna deceive them forever."

" 'Tis no' forever I intend. Just a while longer."

"Meggie," he growled with frustration. "Look at ye, dressed in trews and a shirt like a man. Ye need to end this deception. I urge ye listen to reason."

Megan sat down on one of the wooden

benches with an unladylike thump. "I am being reasonable."

"Ye'll put us all at risk because o' your stubborness. Dinna do it, lass."

She opened her mouth to protest and then shut it abruptly. "Och, rot!" she spluttered unhappily. "Must ye always be the voice o' reason?"

He blinked at her sudden acquiescence. "So ye think what I say is reasonable?" he asked cautiously.

"I do," she admitted.

He eagerly knelt beside her. "Then agree to marry me. Ye know 'tis the right thing to do."

"Don't rush me, Robbie. 'Tis too soon after my da's death."

Robbie threw up his hands in frustration. "What do ye mean, rush ye? I've been waiting all my life for ye, Megan MacLeod. I'd hardly say 'tis rushing matters. And we both know your da would have approved o' our joining."

Megan nervously wound a strand of her hair around her finger, knowing that Robbie was right. Her father would have approved. Besides, she knew that if she refused to marry her first cousin, she would only be postponing the inevitable. She had promised Geddes she would wed and in many ways, Robbie was the best choice. He was a kind and decent man and would be a good husband. They had been close friends since childhood.

So why did she hesitate? To be his wife meant a certain intimacy between a man and a woman that she could not imagine having with him. She didn't love him in that way and knew in her heart that she never would. But should that matter?

"Meggie, are ye listening to me?" Robbie asked softly.

Slowly she lifted her head to look at the face she knew so well. His thoughtful green eyes stared at her with a desperate intensity while his fingers anxiously tugged at the thick hair of his beard.

"Why do ye delay?" he continued. "Have we no' been friends all our lives?"

She reached out to cup his cheek affectionately. "O' course we have. 'Tis just that everything is happening so quickly."

" 'Tis one more reason why ye should marry me. 'Tis naught better than a family to provide stability and love. Think o' it, Meggie. Imagine the bairns we could have. We'd raise them to love Scotland as we do and cherish their mother and da."

She lifted her hands helplessly. "And raise them in this squalor and poverty? We are at war wi' the English, Robbie. Do we want to bring bairns into this world under such conditions?"

"I'll protect them, Meggie, just like I'll protect ye. I love ye. I always have."

His face was so earnest as he uttered the words, that Megan could not help but feel a stirring in her heart. "Och, Robbie," she breathed sadly.

He held her hand tightly against his face. "Say ye'll marry me, Meggie."

"I need more time. But I promise ye that I'll consider it seriously. 'Tis all the assurance I can give ye right now."

Frustrated, Robbie exhaled a heavy breath between his teeth. "Well, I'll no' wait forever. Nor will the clan. The matter needs to be settled soon, especially between us."

Before she could move, he fiercely drew her toward him, pressing a warm kiss against her lips. Surprised by his boldness, Megan did not resist and thought it a rather pleasant sensation. But when it was over, she felt none of the emotions that darkened Robbie's eyes and caused his breath to come faster. He leaned over to kiss her again, but she put a hand on his chest, stopping him.

"Good night, Robbie," she said firmly. " 'Twas a long day and we've another difficult day ahead o' us on the morrow."

He looked longingly at her lips once more before stepping back and nodding. "Good night, lass. Sweet dreams."

After he left, Megan blew out the candles and sat down on the furs, removing her heavy boots. Her muscles ached from the long ride and she rubbed her lower back with a groan. She was tired but not yet sleepy. The excitement of the raid and Robbie's proposal still rang in her ears. She would keep her promise and think it over— she owed him that much. Ignoring the aches in her back and legs, she crawled underneath the pelts and closed her eyes.

Was it her fate to marry a man of whom she was fond, but did not love in a romantic way? Although her mother had died when she was ten, Megan still remembered the shining look of love that passed between her parents. Their knowing glances, whispered secrets and hushed giggles were all things Megan longed to know and understand for herself. Yet deep in her heart, she knew it to be a dream beyond her grasp. Any chances for love and a stable life had long ago been taken away by the English.

Sliding her hands up behind her head, Megan stared into the darkness of her tent. Desires and aspirations were no longer attainable—life had more pressing matters to be resolved. Robbie was right—she was no longer a child. Life had been dictated to her by the forces of war and destruction. He deserved an answer and the clan deserved to know the truth about her father.

All right—it was settled. She would marry Robbie. That would serve two purposes. First it would strengthen Robbie's claim to the laird-ship, and second, it would ease her own fear of the future. It was a fear she had never contemplated in happier days—a future without her family and filled with crushing uncertainties. With Robbie she would be safe and loved. Perhaps that would be enough.

She pressed her hand against her eyes, a deep sadness filling her. It would have to be enough, for she no longer had anything more.

Rolf ordered his men to hug the shadows of the trees as they moved along the wooded path. He hoped his spies had been right. Two of them had managed to follow the Scottish raiders to an area not far from where he now stood. They had lost the Scots in the thick underbrush, but both men were certain that the camp was somewhere nearby. Afraid to continue searching on their own in case they accidentally stumbled upon the rebel camp, the spies had returned to Castle Kilcraig, where their lord was anxiously waiting. Upon hearing their report, Rolf had ordered forty of his men to saddle up. As a light snow fell down upon them, they had ridden out into the darkness.

If it were a trick or an ambush by the Scotsmen, Rolf knew that it might well cost many of them their lives. But it was a risk he was willing to take. Both he and his men were impatient to meet the elusive Scots who hid out in the mountains, using the cover of darkness to prey on the poorly protected holdings of the local English landlord, Edwin Farrington. For weeks Rolf and his men had plotted, chased and tried to trap the Black Wolf without success. Lately, however, the Wolf had become brazen and reckless in his raids against Farrington. In the past few weeks alone, the Wolf had struck at the Englishman six times, stealing horses, fodder and even cattle. Each time the Wolf had been able to outfox Rolf and his men. But not tonight. For the past two weeks, Rolf had altered his strategy, ordering several of his men to spread out and cover a larger perimeter of the area. Each night his men went out in the forest to pre-determined locations and waited, hoping the raiders would pass by their locations. For eleven nights, they had seen nothing. But tonight, on the twelfth night, they had finally gotten their first lead on the rebels. Rolf was not about to pass up the chance to meet his enemy face to face.

The night was bitterly cold, and even the moon was against them. It often slid out from behind the clouds unexpectedly, leaving Rolf and his men exposed in the light for long periods of time. Some way back, Rolf had ordered his men to leave their mounts and continue on foot. He knew the Scotsmen would have sentries, and did not want the noise of horses to alert anyone to their presence.

Rolf came to an abrupt halt beside a tree when he saw the winking lights of a few scattered campfires in the distance. Carefully he drew his sword, whispering back an order for his men to do same. Slowly they inched forward, stopping frequently to listen for any sounds of alarm. When Rolf believed they were mere yards from the camp, he gave his men a signal to spread out and surround the area.

Rolf felt a surge of excitement sweep through him. No shouts or cries came from the trees. So it hadn't been a trap after all. Rolf's heart beat faster, his grip tightened on his sword. Then a cry rang out abruptly to his left, splitting the deadly silence of the night. A Scottish sentry must have spotted one of Rolf's men and the alarm had been raised. Raising his sword in his good hand, Rolf charged forward, the clang of steel and the shouts of men filling the air.

As Rolf swung his broadsword with deadly accuracy, a faint smile crossed his lips. Tonight would be the night. On this bitterly cold Highland evening, he would finally fulfill the wishes of his sovereign and put an abrupt end to the Black Wolf's activities.

# Chapter Four

Megan was dreaming.

Single-handedly, she faced a band of marauding English soldiers, wielding a heavy Scottish claymore in her right hand. In her left, she held a metal shield, easily blocking the ineffective thrusts of the English lances. Their ineptness amused her, their frustration delighted her even more.

"Begone, ye English blackguards," she cried, swinging her sword at an advancing soldier. "Begone from Scotland forever."

She laughed again, throwing back her head. Her dark, unbound hair tumbled about her neck and shoulders in a protective curtain as if guarding her from the wayward attack of the enemy. The hefty sword felt unusally light in her hand as she swung it with little effort. A surge of power swept through her. She *could* not tire, she *would* not concede. She was invincible—and she

44

would vanquish the hated English on behalf of all Scotland.

She bravely stepped forward. The Englishmen began shouting at her, but she paid no heed.

"Ye shall rue the day ye ever dared to set foot in Scotland," she promised them, crossing swords with one of the soldiers.

Their cries became more strident and angry, but strangely, she was not afraid. Instead she felt with absolute certainty that she would prevail. Waving the claymore, she warned the soldiers to step back or she would do away with all of them.

Suddenly they did as she ordered, stepping back and lowering their swords. But they continued to shout and hurl insults until it became a loud thunder in her ears.

Then, seemingly out of nowhere, Megan felt the press of a hard, cool blade against her neck. It felt incredibly real.

*It was real!*

She opened her eyes abruptly. To her horror, she could see the dark outline of a man kneeling beside her, holding a knife to her neck with one hand and pulling the covers off her with the other.

"Too bad they want you alive," he muttered softly.

Quickly closing her eyes, she continued to feign sleep while carefully sliding her hand beneath her pillow. Pressing her lips together in relief, she felt her hand close around the handle of the small dagger she always hid there.

With a ferocious cry, she swung the dagger at his arm and then rolled sideways, safely away from his blade. Her attacker howled in pain and surprise, tumbling to the floor on one shoulder.

Coming to a crouch, she thrust at him again. Her second attempt was also successful and she heard an angry scream of rage.

Scrambling away from him, she thrust the dagger in the waistband of her breeches and groped for her boots. She shoved her feet into them, stumbling toward the exit. She could hear the screams and shouts from outside the tent and knew they were under attack. Swallowing her fear, she reached for the tent flap, but yelped when her attacker unexpectedly tackled her from behind, grabbing her around the knees. She landed against the floor with a bone-jarring thud. Kicking her legs viciously, she managed to free herself from his hold. As she struggled to her feet, she felt her father's wolf pelt bunched beneath her. Grabbing it in her hands, she stumbled to the tent flap, threw it aside and darted outside.

Throwing the pelt across her shoulders, Megan paused, aghast at the scene being played out in front of her. In the dim light of the moon, she could see the dark forms of her clansmen engaged in a fierce struggle with heavily armed attackers. Two of her men fell screaming while she watched in horror.

Panic swept over her. God help her, she was their leader. What should she do? She had to do something or they all would be lost.

*The legend!*

The answer came to her in a moment of startling clarity. The legend of the Black Wolf had always rallied her men, giving them renewed strength and determination. If she could invoke the legend of Black Wolf, it might create a diversion and permit her men to reorganize and regroup. Drawing the heavy cloak up over her head, she took a deep breath and howled at the top of her lungs.

*Aaaayooooo!*

The fighting ceased momentarily as all eyes turned toward her. The moon chose that moment to slide out from behind a cloud, casting a dramatic and eerie glow across the camp. Megan held up one hand in a silent salute.

*"The Black Wolf lives!"* someone shouted. *"Hurrah!"*

"Capture him!" came a shouted order from behind her. Whirling around, Megan saw her attacker, a young man, standing in the entrance of her tent, gripping his thigh with one hand. His hair was disheveled, his clothes torn, but he pointed at her eagerly as if urging his countrymen on to the kill. "Don't let him flee."

Taking a deep breath, Megan turned and dashed into the forest. Behind her, she could hear the English soldiers begin a furious pursuit.

She ran blindly, paying no attention to direction. Branches grabbed at her, scratching her face and hands and unraveling her hair from its tight braid. Her eyes watered from the angry lash of the wind and fear was nearly choking the breath in her throat. The wolf pelt was heavy and slowed her, but she dared not cast it aside for fear of freezing.

Gasping for air, she stumbled over a protruding log and landed straight on her face in the snow. Crying out in fear, she struggled to come to her feet when someone fell heavily on top of her from behind, painfully knocking the breath from her lungs.

"I've got him," someone shouted as she twisted furiously beneath the suffocating weight. "Bring me a light."

Her attacker grasped her arm in a painful grip and rolled her over. For a brief moment, Megan saw a flash of steel and knew that her demise was imminent. Clamping her lips together to hold back a cry of terror, she turned her head to the side, preparing to feel the cold blade pierce her skin.

Then a torch was thrust near her face and Megan squeezed her eyes shut at the blinding light. Still no blade sliced into her body. Time seemed to stand still before she finally heard her attacker speak.

"God's blood," he swore furiously. "It's just a woman."

"A woman?" she heard someone squeal, and then saw the angry face of the young man who had attacked her in the tent. "I swear, my lord, there was no one else in the tent."

Megan cringed as more Englishmen clamored about her in disbelief, cursing angrily. Her heart hammered fearfully, but she kept her lips pressed tightly together in defiance. She'd not beg for mercy. She'd go to her death honoring the memory of the many men who had died at the hands of these barbarians, including her father and brother.

"Christ, we've been tricked," her attacker swore, easing himself off her body and dragging her to her feet. As she stood facing him for the first time without the torch shining in her face, Megan felt a nauseating wave of fear sweep through her.

This man looked like a demon apparition

from Hell. His long, black hair swirled around his enormous shoulders and the front of his tunic was splattered with blood—undoubtedly the blood of her men. His dark, brooding face was framed with thick black eyebrows and his eyes gleamed coldly in the moonlight as he assessed her.

"Curse your foolish ruse, woman. Where is the Wolf?" he demanded, the controlled fury in his voice sending warning shivers of dread up her spine.

For a moment, Megan could only stare at him blankly. The Wolf? Why, he had already captured the Wolf.

She had opened her mouth to speak when an unexpected surge of elation swept through her. God help her, it hadn't even occured to these arrogant Englishmen that a woman could be the Wolf. Surpressing the smile of triumph that rose to her lips, Megan stared back at him coolly. Let him continue his search for the Wolf if he so desired.

"You came from his tent and wear his pelt," the Englishman repeated coolly. "So, where is he?"

Megan stiffened in defiance, refusing to answer. He scowled angrily at her and for a moment, Megan feared he might strike her. Instead, he released her with a disgusted grunt and turned to the young man who had attacked her while she slept.

"Andrew, are you certain there was no other person in the tent?" he asked the young boy sharply.

Andrew nodded vehemently. "I'm certain, my lord. She was alone. B-but it was dark and she came at me so ferociously with a dagger that I never even thought that she was . . . well, a woman."

The dark-haired Englishman crossed his arms against his chest, frowning. "She harmed you?"

The boy flushed, his expression one of moritification and anger. "N-not really, my lord. They are just flesh wounds and don't hurt . . . much."

The Englishman turned his speculative gaze back to Megan. "Well, I'm afraid we'll get little more from her now. But keep an eye on her. I'm certain she is someone of worth to the Wolf."

"Aye, Rolf, as you say," the boy replied quickly.

Megan's eyes narrowed as she heard the young man address the dark-haired man as Rolf. Undoubtedly this was Rolf St. James, the evil and maimed soldier King George had sent to the Scottish Highlands to capture the Wolf. Her gaze quickly fell to his hands. Both were gloved, the right one resting lightly on the shoulder of the man to whom he spoke, the other dangling loosely by his side. It was difficult to be certain in the dim light, but she thought his left hand was likely the infamous crippled appendage.

Megan shivered as she raised her gaze to study his shadowed profile while he spoke earnestly to a man holding a torch. He certainly looked dangerous and forbidding enough to have murdered his own wife. He had also proven to be clever by playing on her ego and trapping her in a foray such as tonight. Curse her rotten luck; she had been careless to underestimate him. It had cost her dearly.

Clenching her fists in frustration, she pressed them tightly against her side. In doing so, she felt the hard lump of the dirk in her waistband. A sweep of exhilaration shot through her. She hadn't been searched and no one had yet discovered the knife.

Megan slowly slipped her hand beneath the pelt, her fingers closing stealthily around the handle of the dirk. She might soon be dead, but perhaps she could take the infamous Rolf St. James with her. It would send a strong message to King George that the Scots would not be silent while the English starved and beat their people into submission. Closing her eyes, she summoned her courage by remembering the faces of her brother and father.

"For Scotland," Megan whispered as she moved toward Rolf.

Rolf heard the girl whisper something, and turned just in time to see a flash of steel reveal itself from beneath her pelt. His years of training as a soldier served him well. Instinctively, he raised his arm just as the dagger skimmed lightly across the skin of his forearm. Before she could move, his good hand shot out, clamping tightly around her wrist and pressing it hard until the dirk fell to the forest floor.

She fought against his hold like a tiger, clawing and struggling to get free. Andrew leapt to his lord's side, roughly grabbing Megan and pinning her arms behind her back. "God's blood, Rolf, she moved so quickly I didn't even see her."

Rolf nodded, examining his torn shirt and the shallow flesh wound she had inflicted. "Aye, if I'd been a bit slower, I would have felt that steel between my shoulder blades instead of across my arm."

Slowly Rolf brought his dark eyes up to the

girl's face, curiously examining her. Long strands of raven-black hair fell in a tangled mass about her shoulders, and her chest heaved with exertion. She met his gaze evenly, her eyes filled with defiance and most strangely, pride. Rolf felt a stirring of admiration for the woman. She had been clever in her escape and had forfeited her own freedom, and perhaps life, to permit the Wolf and several other men to flee unscathed. She was indeed a most intriguing woman.

Rolf knelt in front of her, placing his hands inside her boots and around her ankles before skimming his hands up the length of her legs. He was rewarded with a small cry of outrage from his prisoner.

"Don't ye *dare* touch me," she cried furiously, aiming a kick directly at his stomach.

He easily caught her foot and held it firmly. "Try that again and I'll have you tied both hand and foot while I check for weapons. You may rest assured that I have no intention of being skewered by another one of your hidden daggers."

By the look in his eyes, Megan knew that he was deadly serious. She immediately stopped her struggle and Rolf released her foot, letting it fall to the snowy ground in a temporary truce. Then he carefully felt along her waist and stomach, sliding his hand up both arms and her sides. He temporarily removed the wolf pelt and searched along the lining for any unusual bumps. Satisfied there were no more hidden weapons, Rolf wrapped the pelt around Megan's shoulders again. Megan gasped as the fingers of his good hand brushed lightly across her breasts, and then glared furiously at him as a faint smile touched his lips.

"All right, Andrew," Rolf said turning around, "she has no other weapons. Take her back to the horses, but see to it that her hands are tied and she rides double with one of the men. I'll take no more risks with this one. She has proven to be quite resourceful this night."

Nodding, Andrew yanked on her arm, pulling her into the forest. Rolf stood silently, watching Andrew remove the Scottish lass. She had shown spirit and remarkable courage in the face of astonishing danger. An odd mix of qualities for a woman, he mused to himself, wondering if all Highland women were as wild and untamed as she.

"Shall we search the woods for the Wolf?" a voice said eagerly, interrupting his thoughts.

Rolf turned around to face his trusted comrade, shaking his head. "Nay, Peter, it's too dark and the advantage of surprise is no longer ours. Have Henry round up the rest of the prisoners and bring them back to the castle. We'll see what information can be gleaned from them in regards to the whereabouts of the Wolf."

Peter nodded sharply and turned to bark an order at a nearby group of men. Rolf's eyes drifted back to the black spot amid the trees where Andrew had disappeared with the Scottish woman "An unsual lass," he murmured thoughtfully. "I wonder just what she was doing in the Black Wolf's tent."

# *Chapter Five*

The wind and snow howled around the riders in a white flurry, making the already difficult trek even more treacherous. Megan shivered with cold in spite of the heavy wolf pelt still draped around her shoulders. She rode double with the young man who had attacked her in the tent. He was furious, undoubtedly because she had managed to wound him. She had watched while he tied a strip of cloth around his thigh and arm, cursing the entire time under his breath. When he was done, he had roughly tied her hands behind her back and given her a rude push into the saddle.

Without hands to balance herself, the ride over the craggy terrain was arduous. Megan refused to lean against the young man for support, figuring he'd probably refuse aid to her anyway. Gritting her teeth together, she narrowed her eyes against the wind and concentrated on the direction in which they were headed. It didn't take her long to realize that they were almost upon Castle Kilcraig.

Two long years had passed since she had set foot inside her former home. It had been her dream, and the dream of her father and brother, that one day they would recapture the castle and return in triumph. But now they were dead, and Megan, the last of the MacLeods, was not returning victorious, but as a prisoner of the enemy.

Megan swallowed the bitter taste of bile in her throat, concentrating instead on the condition of the castle. The twin parapets loomed large in the dark and she could see candlelight gleaming through some of the windows. As they rode into the courtyard, Megan noticed that it had been swept clean and the stable roof, damaged during the eviction, had been repaired.

Andrew pulled her unceremoniously off the horse and she nearly fell, swaying slightly until she regained her balance. As other Englishmen rode into the courtyard, shouting orders and bringing more Scottish prisoners with them, Megan felt anger, strong and fierce, flood through her.

The English had no right to be here. Castle Kilcraig belonged to the MacLeods. It had been built with Scottish blood and sweat and the English had no right to occupy it.

How dare they even try, Megan thought, clenching her fists behind her back. She would get Castle Kilcraig back, she vowed silently. She would restore honor to the MacLeod name or die trying.

"Come on, lass," Andrew said, grabbing the

upper part of her arm and pulling her behind him.

"Don't touch me," she hissed, but the young man ignored her, tightening his grip on her arm. She clamped her mouth shut and suffered the indignity of being dragged into the place that once was her home.

Still, when they crossed the threshhold, Megan felt a twinge of homesickness. No matter who occupied Castle Kilcraig, this place would always be her home. She had been born here, grown up among these ancient stones and explored every corner. Her parents had been married in the Great Hall amid much fanfare. It was no use. Her heart was tied to this place as much as it was bound to the land in which she was born.

As they passed the Great Hall, Megan dared to pause for a quick look into the chamber. No candles were lit. It was dark except blazing fire in the enormous hearth. For a fleeting moment, Megan could picture its vastness lit by hundreds of candles and filled with long wooden tables covered with the blue, yellow and green plaids of the MacLeod clan. She fancied she could hear poignant strains of a bagpipe echoing through the room.

"Make haste," Andrew chided Megan, yanking on her arm and snapping her rudely from her daydream. He led her none too gently toward the staircase, guiding her up the stairs to the living quarters instead of down toward the dungeon where the rest of the prisoners were headed.

"What are ye doing?" Megan asked in alarm,

looking around. "Why am I no' going wi' the others?"

"Just do as I say," the young man answered. "You won't be harmed if you cooperate."

Megan swallowed her fear, attempting to keep her face emotionless as he continued to pull her along up the stairs and down a long corridor. Andrew stopped in front of a door which Megan immediately recognized as the small sitting room off her parents' bedchamber. Opening the door, he thrust her inside and stepped into the room behind her.

Megan saw there was a small divan and one chair situated close to the hearth. A fire had been lit and the room was fairly warm. The rest of the chamber was bare, most likely looted by the English, Megan thought with anger.

"What are ye going to do wi' me?" she asked softly as Andrew cut the rope around her hands.

"You will wait here," Andrew replied stiffly. "You will be dealt with in turn."

"Ye can't keep me separated from the others," she argued, rubbing her wrists. "I insist that ye take me to the dungeon wi' the other prisoners."

"You are in no position to make demands, woman," Andrew retorted. "God's blood, I should kill you right now for daring to attack my lord."

"He was foolish to think the Scottish would behave meekly."

Andrew's face flushed red with anger. "I warn you to have care how you speak about my lord. If it were not for the fact I've been ordered to take special care with you, I would gladly throw you in the dungeon with the others. But it was not my decision. So, I suggest you take this opportunity to rest and warm yourself by the fire. It will likely be some time before you are treated so well again."

Megan opened her mouth to protest, but the young man abruptly left the room, bolting the door firmly behind him. She watched him go, her own anger rising.

"Be quiet, indeed," she said, pressing her lips together. "That is highly unlikely, Englishman. Just ye wait and see."

"Release me at once! I demand to be taken to the dungeon."

Megan pounded her fists furiously upon the wooden door, her voice nearly hoarse from shouting. Finally she leaned her forehead against the door in exhaustion and frustration. She had been shouting for at least an hour to no avail. No one had answered her cries, no one had insisted she stop her shouting. She was simply ignored.

What they planned to do with her, Megan did not know. Apparently they would deal with her in their own time and in their own way. What they didn't know was that she hated being isolated from her men. She needed to know they were all right. She wanted them to know she would think of something to get them out of this mess.

Dispirited, she fought the urge to weep into her hands at her feelings of helplessness. "What am I to do?" she whispered, sliding down the door into a sitting position. She had no idea how an evil man like Rolf St. James would treat her. After all, Robbie had told her that he had murdered his own wife and most likely delighted in the torture and beating of women. She couldn't even begin to imagine the atrocities he certainly had planned for her. God help her, but she was probably better off not to even think about it.

Shivering, Megan pulled her knees to her chest, forcing herself to push aside her fears. She had to be calm and think. Her mind raced with a hundred thoughts, yet she could not come up with a single plan that would free her clansmen from this hated Englishman. Not yet anyway. She would have to face the dreadful man and learn what exactly it was that he sought from her. Then, once she had properly judged his character, she would be better prepared to make her own move.

"Ye may have captured the Wolf, but ye haven't won yet, Englishman," she promised grimly as she tightened her hold about her knees and closed her eyes. "Ye haven't won yet.

"What are you planning to do with the lass?" Peter asked Rolf as they stood side by side in the library. "She's been shouting for near an hour, demanding to be kept with the other prisoners in the dungeon."

Rolf glanced over at his friend, wondering if he looked as weary as Peter did. Peter was nearly six and forty, and had served Rolf's family for more than twenty-five years. Together the two of them had fought countless battles and shared much more than just a skill at fighting. Peter was the closest thing Rolf had to a friend and a confidant.

Rolf sank into a chair, wearily stretching his legs out in front of him. "Do you think me deaf, man? The entire castle has heard her cries. I simply wish to question her . . . alone."

"Do you think she knows where the Wolf is hiding?" Peter asked, moving over to the hearth to warm his hands.

"I'm certain of it."

"We searched the tent but could find nothing but her garments there. The Wolf left no trace of his existence," Peter said, rubbing his hands together. His thick knuckles were bloodied and bruised and every muscle in his body ached. The Scotsmen had put up a fierce fight.

Rolf slammed his fist down on the arm of the chair. "How could he have slipped through our fingers again? He has the wits of a fox and the luck of the Devil. It's no wonder people see him as a legend."

"Ease yourself, lad," Peter said soothingly. "We'll catch him yet. Our surprise attack today cost them heavily."

Rolf straightened in his chair, the muscles in his jaw tightening. "Yes, and I will take full advantage of that. I'm determined to catch the Wolf in one of his own traps."

"What do you think is the girl's role in all of this?"

Rolf's eyes darkened as he stood quickly. "I'd wager that she is someone of value to him. If we play our cards right, she could lead him right to us."

"Then I'd suggest we play those cards carefully. As we learned tonight, the Black Wolf is no fool."

Rolf nodded somberly. "He may be no fool, Peter, but he is still a man with pride. Mark my words. If I'm right, he'll come for the girl."

\*   \*   \*

When Rolf entered the sitting room from his bedchamber, he found his female prisoner huddled on the floor, apparently in an exhausted sleep. Although a peat fire blazed warmly in the fireplace and cushioned chairs beckoned invitingly, she appeared to have no interest in her own comfort.

Quietly he approached her unmoving form. Bending down on one knee, Rolf swept back a long strand of her midnight-black hair to examine her face. He was shocked by her pale skin and the tiny lines around her eyes. Hunger had clearly taken a toll. Her cheeks and neck were gaunt, her long, slender hands cut and swathed in dirty bandages.

Yet her features were remarkable in their own right, Rolf thought curiously. Her facial bones were delicately carved and she had a full and sensuous mouth. A square, determined jaw spoke of stubbornness, but it was offset by a short and charming nose. Although she was covered in dirt and grime, Rolf could tell that she had a wild, untamed sort of beauty about her.

Reaching out, he lightly cupped the side of her cheek, frowning when he discovered her skin was as cold as ice. For a brief moment, she sighed and pressed against the warmth of his hand. Then she stirred, her eyes fluttering open. Suddenly, Rolf looked directly into a magnificent pair of blue eyes. As recognition crossed her face, she cried out, pushing away from him.

"What do ye want?" she cried out, scooting back against the door. Pulling her knees to her chest, she wrapped her arms protectively about her legs, watching Rolf warily.

"I'm not going to hurt you," he said gently,

reaching out to take one of her bandaged hands. She immediately snatched it away, hugging it close to her body.

"Then why do ye keep me in this room apart from the others?" she demanded in a soft, lilting burr that Rolf found surprisingly pleasant.

"I want only to talk with you."

"Well, I'll no' be forced into discourse wi' an Englishman."

"I think," Rolf murmured softly, "that you have little choice in the matter. That is, of course, if you ever want to see your fellow Scots in the dungeon."

Her eyes narrowed, and Rolf could see that she did not take well to being threatened. "I won't be intimidated by ye, Englishman," she announced boldly.

Rolf smiled slowly. "I can see that," he said softly. "So how may I convince you to help me?"

" 'Tis naught that ye can say that will make me help ye."

"I'd like to have the opportunity to prove you wrong," he replied, crossing his arms against his chest.

Megan frowned, noticing that the Englishman had taken the time to wash himself and change from the blood-spattered tunic to a white shirt of linen with a round, flat collar.

He was wearing no coat or neckcloth, and his shirt was open at the throat and upper chest, revealing tan skin and a hint of dark chest hair. His body emanated heat, and Megan was surprised to catch the faint scent of oatmeal soap.

"Well, I have no intention o' giving ye that opportunity."

He made a small sound of disapproval in his

throat. "You know, I think we'd get along much better if we were to show a bit of mutual respect for each other."

"Mutual respect?" Megan exclaimed in disbelief. "Ye expect me to show respect to an English blackguard?"

"I believe respect will work better than insults," Rolf said, coming to his feet. Reaching down, he gripped her arm, drawing her to a standing position with his good hand. Once upright, she yanked her arm away and pressed back against the door, clearly trying to put as much distance as she could manage between them.

Rolf fought the urge to smile at her admirable defiance. He had half-expected her to swoon or beg for mercy. She apparently had no intention of doing either.

"Well, now that we have exchanged the proper pleasantries," he continued smoothly, "I insist that you warm yourself by the fire and get some rest. Unfortunately, not much of the night remains. I, too, plan to retire for the evening and give your countrymen some time to reflect on their fate. Perhaps they'll be more cooperative on the morn."

Megan shook her head vigorously. "Wishful thinking, Englishman. The Scots will never cooperate wi' your kind. Nor do I wish to remain here. Put me in the dungeon wi' the rest o' your prisoners."

Rolf raised a dark eyebrow. "Is this chamber not suitable for you?"

"I'd prefer the dungeon to your hospitality."

"Well, I do suppose my hospitality is rather lacking. I'm afraid that I was not expecting any guests and have no suitable chamber for you to sleep in . . . other than my own, of course."

A look of sheer horror crossed her face and a wry smile rose to Rolf's lips. "I trust you prefer the divan?" he asked.

"Aye," she answered quickly.

"I see. Well, there will be more time for us to talk. Tomorrow evening you will join me for a private supper."

"I will no'," she replied angrily.

"I'm afraid that was not a request."

Megan's body stiffened in defiance. "I don't care what it was. Ye waste your time wi' me, Englishman. I told ye I have naught to say."

"Well, as it is my time to waste, I don't see any harm in it," he said easily.

Megan felt her temper flare. "Why do ye play games wi' me? There are wounded men in your dungeon. I have the skills to help them. If ye have any sense o' decency at all, ye'll permit me to tend to their injuries."

Rolf calmly folded his arms across his broad chest. "I assure you that their wounds are being treated. You concern yourself needlessly."

"Needlessly?" She hissed at him furiously. "The lives o' those men may mean little to ye, but they mean everything to me. I know how to treat them so they heal properly. Now let me go to them."

Rolf stared at her in surprise, astonished by the clear ring of authority in her voice. He'd be damned, but it almost sounded as if she were used to giving orders and actually expecting men to follow them. She definitely warranted a closer examination.

"I'm afraid you look near death yourself," he

said firmly. "Your skin is as cold as ice, your garments in shreds. I'll not permit you to go to the dungeon at this time. I may, however, reconsider my decision after we dine tomorrow."

" 'Tis blackmail," the girl said softly, clenching her fists at her side.

Rolf shrugged. "Call it what you may. But you'll not leave this room until I'm convinced you can do so without dropping of exhaustion."

She glared at him fiercely, and Rolf shook his head in wonder. This Scottish lass was remarkably brave, perhaps even foolish to stand up to him. He felt a grudging admiration that she had not yet dissolved in tears.

Gruffly, he motioned to one of the chairs. "I assure you that it is in your best interest to seat yourself by the fire. I'll see that someone brings you food and water. Now, I will bid you a good evening or what's left of it." Turning on his heel, he strode to the door, stopping when he heard her call out.

"W-wait, please," she said, her voice wavering uncertainly.

Rolf stopped, his hand resting on the latch. "Yes?" he inquired, turning to face her.

"The women and bairns that ye took from the camp—have they been harmed?"

Rolf's dark eyebrows rose slightly. "Why do you ask?"

She bit her lower lip nervously. "I heard . . ." she began, and then clasped her hands in front of her anxiously. "I heard that ye delight in punishing women and bairns."

Rolf looked at her in surprise. God's teeth, had the rumors followed him all the way to Scotland? It seemed that he was not going to escape his past even in this godforsaken place.

His jaw tightened with anger. "The women were questioned briefly before my men released them and their children in the village," he replied curtly. "Contrary to your belief, I harmed none of them."

Visible relief crossed her face. "Thank God," she said faintly.

He pushed down on the latch, letting the door swing open. "May I ask you a question then, in return? If you've heard how much I delight in punishing women, why aren't you afraid of me?"

She shrugged, lifting her shoulders delicately. "Because I no longer care what happens to me," she replied softly. "Only to my people."

He nodded thoughtfully. "An admirable reply," he said, looking at her for a long moment before turning and leaving the room.

When Megan heard him slide the bolt across the door, she collapsed in a nearby chair. Despite her bold pronouncements to the contrary, she was very much afraid. As he'd done for her clansmen in the dungeon, the Englishman had given her time to reflect on her fate. When she refused to cooperate, would he resort to torture, or perhaps worse, to get what he wanted?

Shivering, Megan held out her hands toward the warmth of the hearth. The Englishman was right. She was achingly cold and exhausted from the night's foray. Her breeches were torn and dirtied, her hair a tangled mess. She had cut her right hand on her dirk, and it swelled and throbbed beneath the swaddled bandages on her palm. Still, she felt a stab of guilt that she could warm herself in relative comfort while her men languished below in the dungeon.

Her lips tightened in determination. She would sup with the despicable Englishman if that was what it took to be allowed to see them. It was her responsibility to get them out of this predicament. She had to stop being frightened and start using her head to outfox this Englishman. For now, her mind was the best weapon she had.

# Chapter Six

Dusk shrouded Castle Kilcraig in shadows as Rolf hastened his steps up the stairs. The day had gone slowly. After the encounter with his unusually stubborn female prisoner, he had snatched only three hours of sleep before rejoining his men in the dungeon for several unpleasant hours of questioning the Scotsmen.

From the beginning, Rolf knew that getting information from his prisoners would not be easy. The Scotsmen, and apparently their women, were fiercely proud and not easily intimidated. It was a realization that came to him with no small amount of regret. Although his primary concern in Scotland was to bring the King the Black Wolf, he was also under orders to ease tension in the area. Torturing men to get the information he needed about the Wolf would not be a helpful step in that direction.

Rolf sighed, rubbing the stiff knuckles of his

maimed hand. Now he had to pin his hopes on the lass. Unfortunately, getting her to cooperate did not present itself as an easy task. Here was a woman with a hostile disposition who was inclined to challenge his authority. She had yet to cry, swoon or beg for mercy as he had expected. Instead, she had boldly stood up to him, facing him as an equal.

Rolf frowned. Perhaps the fault was his. After all, his experience with women was mostly confined to pale, aristocratic English ladies who batted their eyelashes at him above a fan. The thought that even one of them could have survived a moment of what this girl had suffered was totally inconceivable.

A small smile came to his lips as he tried to imagine even one of the women from court living in a tent, disguising herself in the Wolf's clothes and leading an entire detail of the King's men on a merry chase through the forest. She would need a close watch kept on her.

He strode quickly through his bedchamber toward the barred door of the sitting room where she was being held. Drawing the bolt, he pushed open the door and stepped into the room. According to Abigail, the matronly housekeeper he had brought with him from London, the Scottish lass had eaten, bathed and dressed in a gown that had been found stashed away in an old trunk. Abigail reported that the girl had said absolutely nothing during the entire ordeal, only nodded her head when spoken to, following instructions without a word. A model prisoner.

For a moment Rolf thought the sitting room was empty, it was so quiet. But as he turned slightly to his right, he saw her standing in front of the fire, staring thoughtfully into the flames. She did not acknowledge his arrival, although Rolf knew she must have heard him enter.

"Good evening," Rolf said, surprised when his voice deepened unexpectedly. She had unsettled him, he realized. He had never met a woman like her and he'd be damned if knew what to expect from her next.

"Is it really, Englishman?" she asked softly, turning to face him.

Rolf blinked in sheer astonishment at the change in her. Beneath the dirt and grime was an astoundingly beautiful woman. Her skin was pale and smooth, and her startling blue eyes were framed with thick dark lashes. Clad in a simple gown of light blue that looked as if it had been made for her, she looked as lovely as a spring day. The rounded neckline of the gown was edged with lace, drawing his eye to the soft curves of her breasts. Tendrils of raven-colored hair clung to her cheeks while the rest cascaded down her back, bound loosely by a matching satin ribbon. Other than her painfully thin figure and the dark smudges of weariness evident beneath her eyes, she appeared utterly breathtaking.

"Well?" she asked, raising an eyebrow.

"Well, what?" he repeated dumbly. He was stunned by the sudden surge of desire tightening his loins, wondering if he had simply been too long without a woman. For a fleeting moment, he considered the consequences of sweeping her into his arms and pressing his lips to hers.

That would certainly encourage her to answer your questions, he thought wryly.

"I asked whether 'tis really a good evening.

Aren't ye weary from a long day o' torturing your enemies?"

The bitterness in her voice was as effective as a splash of cold water on his face. "We don't have to be enemies," he said slowly. "We could work together."

She laughed. "Now that's an unlikely happenstance. An Englishman and a Scotswoman working together."

"It doesn't have to be so unusual. Can we not put our differences aside for one evening and enjoy our supper?"

She put her hands on her hips in defiance. "The only reason I agreed to this supper is so that I may be permitted to visit the men in the dungeon."

"I am fully aware of your reasons for accepting my invitation," Rolf countered smoothly. "However, for now, will you permit me to escort you from this room?" He held out an arm.

For a long moment she simply stared at him. Then reluctantly, she walked toward him, taking his arm but barely touching him. Rolf led her from the room and down the stairs to the entrance of the Great Hall.

They stopped momentarily in the doorway and Megan felt her eyes fill with tears as she looked about the lit chamber, remembering the happy hours she had spent here with her family. So much had changed from those days. She had lost her home and everyone she had ever loved. No more gay laughter or squeals of delight would float through the corridors of her beloved castle; only the sounds of clanging swords and the heavy tread of enemy footfalls.

Now the magnificent tapestries that had once

adorned the stone walls were gone, as was the precious shield and crest of the MacLeod clan that had hung proudly over the hearth. There were no plaids adorning the tables, no musicians with bagpipes. It was a cold, empty place. It would never be the same. Never.

Rolf indicated with a brief gesture of his hand that she was to sit. Megan slid onto the bench, glad that he had seated them near the great stone hearth. She felt chilled from the memories as well as from the wicked draft that swept through the hall.

Rolf slid onto the bench beside her. His arm carelessly brushed her shoulder as he settled himself at the table. Megan sent him a quick, startled glance as she felt an unexpected warmth from the contact. For a moment, his eyes met hers before a knowing smile curved the strong lines of his face. She felt her cheeks warm with mortification as she slid sideways, giving him plenty of room to stretch his large frame without making further physical contact with her.

Examining the table with more interest, she realized that only two places had been prepared. A decanter of wine and two goblets were neatly arranged beside a flickering wax candle. Although she thought it absurd that only the two of them sat at a table that could seat a hundred, she noted with growing alarm that he had created a rather intimate setting.

Rolf reached across the table, picked up the decanter and poured them both a full glass of wine. Megan watched his movements, intrigued by his good hand. It was shaped as if sculpted from stone—long, taut fingers callused from the sword, yet deft and agile. His misshapen hand remained gloved and lay loosely on his lap. Occasionally, she saw him massage it with his good hand. She wondered if it pained him. In fact, she wondered if anything at all disturbed his poised demeanor.

Curious, Megan studied his face as he turned on the bench to face her. He actually was rather handsome in a dark sort of way. Heavy brows slashed low over an aristocratic nose. His lips were firm and sensual, his mouth curved slightly as if perhaps on the edge of a smile.

She thought he didn't seem like a very happy or reasonable man. In fact, there was something mysterious and predatory in the way he spoke and moved. Sleek, ruthless and dangerous. Aye, those were the words that fit him. A cruel man who'd killed his wife in cold blood and would not hesitate to cripple and torture those who crossed him. She wondered if it was his injury that had made him so bitter. Again, her gaze lingered on his left hand.

"Fascinated by my injury, are you?"

Megan flushed and quickly looked away. "I don't care a whit about your bloody injury," she snapped.

To her surprise, he laughed. "You're a poor liar. Why not satisfy your curiosity and ask what you are thinking?"

She raised her head to look at him directly. "All right, I will. How did that happen to ye?"

He lifted his injured hand and regarded it as he spoke. "In Wales during a skirmish. I fell off my mount and my opponent's horse tried to trample me. Fortunately only my hand was caught."

Megan shuddered at the thought. "Does it hurt?"

"Sometimes, especially when it's cold."

"Is that why ye hide it beneath a glove?"

He raised an dark eyebrow in suprise. "Would you have me display it?"

"And why no'? In Scotland, men wear their scars proudly."

Rolf smiled. "I'm afraid that Englishwomen have far more delicate sensibilities than Scottish lasses. Most would swoon if forced to look upon such an abomination."

Megan snorted unelegantly. "Somehow, that doesn't surprise me. Ye should know that Scottish women wear their scars proudly, too."

A flicker of interest sparked in his eyes. "Is that so?" he asked, leaning forward. "Have you any scars?"

She paused. "Only on my heart," she answered softly.

Rolf nodded thoughtfully. "A most intriguing answer," he murmured, lifting his wineglass to his lips.

Megan shrugged, looking around the room. "Why is no one else dining wi' us?"

"Because it is my wish to speak with you alone. Without the inconvenience of others listening to us."

"It makes no difference. I told ye, I have naught to say."

"Yes, well, we shall see," he replied, speaking no further when a servant entered the room carrying a large tray. Sweeping a cloth off the top, she removed two plates laden with fruit, meat, bread and cheese. Rolf thanked her as she set the plates in front of them and left the room discreetly.

"Before we eat, I have a request of you," Rolf said, the glow of the firelight dancing off his square jaw and shrouding his eyes in shadows.

Megan met his gaze, alert and wary. "What kind o' request?"

"I have yet to learn your name." A faint smile touched his lips. "It is the first time I have invited a woman to dine with me whose name I did not know."

Megan frowned slightly, her dark brows furrowing together. "What does it matter what I am called? Ye may call me whatever ye wish, Englishman."

Rolf was silent for a moment. "All right," he said at last. "Then I wish to call you Megan."

The look of sheer surprise on her face was enough to convince Rolf he had discovered her real name. So, the old man he had spoken with in the dungeon had been telling the truth about her.

"H-how did ye know?" she asked unsteadily, her heart quickening in her chest.

Rolf picked up a piece of cheese and popped it in his mouth, chewing slowly. After a moment, he took another sip of wine and studied her closely. "One of the men we hold in the dungeon claims that you are his daughter, Megan Kincaid. He went so far as to threaten me if anything happened to you."

"Kincaid?" she repeated dumbly. It took her a moment to fully comprehend his words. Then, for the first time since she had arrived at Castle Kilcraig, she felt a small spark of hope.

"K-kincaid . . ." she stammered. "O' course.

75

Has he . . . er . . . my father been harmed?"

The candlelight danced off Rolf's fingers as he absently caressed the stem of his goblet. "He took a cut in his shoulder during the fighting, but the wound was cleaned and bandaged. In fact, all the men have been well treated and fed. You see, Megan, we English are not all barbarians."

"I've seen nothing," she said, bitterness tingeing her voice. "If ye expect me to be grateful, ye'll have to let me see the men for myself."

Rolf shrugged. "It can be arranged. But first, I must insist you eat something."

Megan looked for the first time at the food on the plate before her. She couldn't remember the last time she had seen such a meal. Unwilling to appear weak in front of him, she bit her lower lip, convincing herself that she wasn't hungry. Unfortunately, her stomach chose that precise moment to growl loudly in protest. She flushed with embarrassment.

Rolf motioned to the plate with his hand. "Eat, Megan. I promise you no harm."

After a moment of indecision, she surrendered to her hunger. Picking up a piece of bread, she bit off a piece and chewed, closing her eyes at the wonderful taste of it. The bread she usually ate was so old it had to be softened in water before it was palatable. This bread was fresh and practically melted in her mouth. Reaching for her goblet, she washed it down with a sip of delicious red wine.

"Much better," Rolf said, smiling at her. "May I now speak frankly with you?"

Megan bit off another piece of bread, shrugging. " 'Tis your right to speak however ye wish.

I seriously doubt, however, that we have much in common to talk about."

"You're wrong, Megan. We could talk about the Wolf."

She permitted herself a small laugh. "Aye, I suppose we could. But I'm no' interested in discussing him wi' ye."

"I will capture him, you know," Rolf said softly, the certainty in his voice sending a shiver up Megan's spine.

She was careful to keep her face expressionless. "I think no', Englishman. Ye know little o' the Scottish and our ways. The Wolf is an excellent strategist. He'll no' be so easily caught in your paltry traps. 'Tis many tricks he still has up his sleeves."

Rolf rested his elbows lightly on the table, looking at her with interest. "It will take little time for me to break those in the dungeon. They will soon supply me with all the information I need to know."

Megan stiffened perceptively, her eyes blazing with scorn. "So, is this how ye English fight your battles? Torturing wounded men—interrogating helpless women? Is this what defines ye as a great soldier?"

Rolf's voice was low and purposefully calm. "Torturing men for information does not bring me pleasure, Megan. But it is you Scottish who are defying the law. Justice must be brought or else chaos will rule this land."

"Law? Justice? How *dare* ye speak such words. 'Tis ye English who take what ye want without cause, without right."

Unruffled, Rolf pulled a piece of bread from the loaf. "We have every right, Megan, and you know it. The Scottish were fairly routed at Culloden. Had they not committed treason by supporting your Prince Charles, perhaps we wouldn't be here discussing this issue today."

"Fairly routed?" Megan spluttered indignantly. "Ye slaughtered wounded men and then went into the villages, murdering thousands of innocent women and children."

Rolf's dark brows drew into a frown. "I was not at Culloden, but I do agree that General Cumberland's orders beyond the battlefield were most unfortunate. I do not agree with such tactics. It is my belief that every life lost in war is a loss for all mankind—the murder of innocents being the greatest loss of all."

Surprised, Megan heard genuine regret in his voice. "It doesn't matter what ye say," she replied, looking away. "The Scottish will never stop fighting ye."

Rolf reached over, grasping her hand firmly. "The war is over, Megan. It's time to stop fighting and start rebuilding lives."

She recoiled at his touch, but Rolf held on tightly. Eyes blazing, she met his gaze evenly. "Ye tell us to rebuild our lives under the heavy hand o' the English. But what kind o' lives can we have? We are not permitted to wear our plaids, bear arms to protect ourselves or even play the pipes. We will no' live a life that we despise."

Rolf exhaled deeply. "You are thinking only with emotion, Megan. How do you really think traditions are passed on from generation to generation?" When she didn't answer, he released her hand and reached up to touch his lips. "By word of mouth. By sitting in front of the fire and listening to parents and grandparents speak of those traditions they have always held dear. But if the Scottish continue to struggle—to war in vain against us—you will have little time for such activities. All your energy will be wasted on survival, leaving you no possibility for enjoying the very things that make you Scottish. This is what will destroy you in the end."

Her mouth tightened angrily. As much as she wanted to deny it, Megan saw a grain of wisdom in his words. "I don't care to have a history lesson," she replied stiffly. "I'd rather know what ye plan to do wi' me and the men ye hold prisoners in the dungeon."

Rolf sighed, leaning his elbows on the table. "They will be released to the village, once I have captured the Wolf."

"And once ye have captured the Wolf—what happens to him?"

Rolf's eyes hardened. "I'll not lie to you. He will be taken to London for execution. His crimes against the crown are severe."

Megan lowered her eyes, the gleam of hope she had felt fading. If she confessed to being the Wolf and was then executed, it would only lead her men to commit bloody retributions against the English. She knew they would fight to the death, every last one of them. And without a strong mind to lead them . . . they might all perish.

Megan no longer felt hungry. Hands trembling slightly, she pushed the plate away from her. "I've had enough," she said.

Rolf glanced at her scarcely touched plate and then at her face. The blood had drained from her cheeks, her expression drawn and worried. He swore silently at himself for having frightened her. Her intelligence had taken him off guard and he had momentarily forgotten that she was also a young woman who presumably cared deeply for the man he had just promised to see executed. He tempered his anger at himself with the knowledge that he was only trying to end this madness. Lifting the decanter, he poured himself some more wine.

"Megan, I know that a man called Robert MacLeod is the Wolf," he continued. "I assume you are someone of value to him or you would not have been sharing his bed. And there was only one bed in the tent." He lifted his gaze to her face as if expecting her to deny it.

"Sharing his bed?" she repeated dumbly.

"Well, there was only one bed," he repeated. "And your clothing was found there as well."

For a moment, Megan could only stare at him blankly. Then, with a dawning sense of understanding as to what he was implying, she also realized that her enemy had unwittingly offered her the first seeds of a plan.

Slowly, she raised her chin and met his gaze. "Aye, there was only one bed, Englishman. And ye are right that those were my garments ye found there."

Rolf reached for his goblet taking a sip of the wine. "I presume that makes you his mistress."

"Ye can presume whatever ye wish."

He stared at her thoughtfully. "Yes, I suppose I can."

An uneasy silence lengthened between them before Megan broke it. "So why do ye insist on keeping me here now that ye know who I am to him?"

"Perhaps he'll risk trying to rescue you."

Megan laughed. "Me? Do ye really think the Wolf would risk our cause for me?" When Rolf nodded, she shook her head. "Och, ye gravely underestimate the Wolf. I assure ye, there are plenty o' women waiting to take my place."

For some reason, her answer disturbed Rolf greatly. The thought that this remarkable woman could be so easily cast aside filled him with an unusual sense of anger. Yet there was something in her words that did not quite ring true. Rolf couldn't rid himself of a small nagging doubt that lingered in his mind.

Pushing away from the table, he abruptly stood. Megan looked up at him in surprise.

"Will ye take me to the dungeon now?" she asked hopefully. "I supped wi' ye as ye requested."

Rolf's dark eyes gleamed in the candlelight. "I haven't yet decided. Frankly, the evening looms before me and I'm rather enjoying our banter. Perhaps you would be so kind to join me for a brandy in the sitting room."

She looked at him warily. "Ye wish to drink wi' me? Your enemy?"

"We don't have to be enemies," he answered quietly. "To tell you the truth, I'm rather enjoying our discussion. You are a very intriguing and beautiful woman."

He reached out his good hand and lifted a tendril of her hair. She jerked away, a flash of panic crossing her face.

Rolf sighed. "You have nothing to fear. I won't harm you. My request is innocent enough. After dinner I often retire to the drawing room for a brandy and a game of chess."

"Chess?" she repeated in surprise.

"Yes. I don't suppose you play."

"But I do. In fact, I used to play often wi' my da. That is before he . . . er . . . before the English came."

"May I interest you in a game now?"

Suspiciously, Megan studied his face. His intentions seemed harmless enough, although she knew she should not underestimate him. Certainly he could have already taken advantage of her if that was what he really wanted to do. Perhaps he really did speak the truth and wished only to while away idle hours with her by engaging in a game of chess. She could hardly see how a game would be of any other value to him.

For her, on the other hand, it could be useful. Very useful. Her father had always told her that in order to conquer one's enemy, it was necessary to assess both their weaknesses and strengths. What better way than a game of chess to discover how his mind worked? If she could learn something of his approach to strategy, it might offer a glimpse into his inner character. It was an opportunity she could not permit to pass.

Slowly, she nodded, trying not to seem too interested in the prospect. "Actually, your offer does interest me. I am willing to meet ye across a chessboard, Englishman."

"Splendid," Rolf said, holding out a hand and drawing her to her feet. "It seems that this is going to be a most fascinating evening after all."

# *Chapter Seven*

Megan watched from the doorway of a small sitting room as Rolf arranged the furniture for their game. He dragged a small table near the hearth and then brought two heavy chairs, positioning them alongside the table.

She pressed her lips together, thinking he moved with surprising grace and elegance despite his injury. Although he appeared to use his left hand for little more than balance, his movements were so smooth and effortless that she hardly noticed the deformity.

He straightened, lifting his good hand and removing his neckcloth with one firm pull. Uttering an audible sigh of relief, he cast it to the back of one of the chairs and knelt in front of the hearth. Picking up the fire iron, he prodded several squares of peat until a small blaze burst forth. The distinctive smell of burning peat drifted through the chamber, both comforting

Megan and painfully reminding her of another time, when she had called this castle home.

Apparently satisfied that the chamber was ready, Rolf stood. "Shall we sit?" he invited politely, sweeping his hand toward one chair.

Megan walked past him, her bare shoulder brushing against his hand. As his fingers touched her skin, a flare of warmth shot through her and down her arm. Horrified, she felt a hot flush rush to her cheeks.

For a moment, he simply stared at her. Then a slow smile curved across his mouth. Megan sat down abruptly with a thump, arranging her skirts around her legs.

"Would you care for a brandy?" he asked.

"Nay," she answered firmly. She needed to keep a clear head around this Englishman.

Shrugging, he walked over to a side table, deftly pulling the glass top off a decanter of brandy. He poured a glass and lifted it to his lips for a taste. Satisfied, he joined her at the table and opened a wooden box, pulling out a board and several intricately carved chess pieces. Carefully he arranged all the pieces until they sat face to face, enemy to enemy, with naught more than squares on the chessboard between them.

Megan began the game, keeping her play solid and cautious. She had no idea what kind of player Rolf was and she wanted him to reveal his methods before she chose a strategy. It was difficult for her to restrain herself because she loved the game of chess. Her father had delighted in her unorthodox approaches to the game and her bold, brilliant forays into enemy territory. But now, she concentrated on a more staid and classical approach, waiting for Rolf to show his true abilities as a strategist.

As the game progressed, Megan felt a sharp disappointment. Rolf played more cautiously than she, apparently not even able to anticipate the simplest of her moves. In fact, he seemed to have no style at all; he tried simply to limit her damage. She watched him as he studied the board in concentration, his dark brows knitted together tightly. Shaking her head, she mentally judged his abilities as a leader and quickly came to the conclusion that his capture of her and the others had been sheer luck. This man sitting in front of her didn't seem to possess one ounce of strategic capability. All that talk about Rolf St. James being a brilliant soldier must have been just that—talk! In fact, if it weren't for his considerable muscles and brawn, he probably wouldn't have made a good soldier at all.

Tiring of the game, Megan moved forward quickly, achieving check mate in a relatively easy manner. Rolf looked up at her in surprise, inclining his head in a gesture of graceful defeat.

"I'm impressed," he said. "Your moves were well planned and executed. I learned a lot from just watching you."

Megan shrugged, embarrassed to hear him speak of her tepid play as something spectacular. Yet even as she dismissed his comments, her mind began to form a plan. If he were like most other men she knew, he would not back down from a challenge issued by a woman. Especially a Scottish woman. Using this to her advantage, she might yet be able to trick the Englishman into agreeing to take her to the dungeon. She mulled over the possibilities.

"Shall we play another game?" Rolf asked, returning the pieces to their opening positions on the board.

Megan smiled charmingly. "Aye, I'd like that. But I thought perhaps this time we might make the game a bit more interesting by wagering."

Rolf's lifted his head in surprise. "Wagering?"

Megan nodded. "Aye, whoever wins the game receives the reward of their choice. For example, if I win the game, ye must immediately take me to the dungeon to see the men."

His dark eyes flickered with interest. "I see. And what shall I gain if I win?"

Megan shrugged, doubtful of that outcome. "I have little to offer. Perhaps the promise that I will not try to kill ye again, at least while I remain here in the castle."

Rolf's hard features softened as he laughed lightly. "A paltry offer, I'm afraid. No, I think it will have to be something more."

Megan stiffened. "I'll no' speak again o' the Wolf nor o' our activities."

He lifted his hands innnocently. "Of course not, and I would not cause you further distress by making such a request." He paused for a long moment, seemingly deep into thought. Finally, a slow smile crossed his face. "Therefore, I ask for naught more than a kiss, given willingly to me this night."

All color drained from a shocked Megan's cheeks. "A k-kiss? From me? Ye must be in jest."

Rolf sighed. "Please forgive me. I can see that I have caused you distress. Let us forget about the wager and simply play the game for the mere enjoyment of it." He returned to setting up the pieces on the board.

Megan swallowed her surprise, watching him

carefully arrange the wooden figurines. Determinedly, she forced her face into what she
hoped was a reasonable expression, remembering that she had little to fear from such a player.
Besides, she argued with herself, if she won, she
would be able to see her clansmen tonight. The
thought of seeing them and making certain they
were all right was too tempting an opportunity
to pass up. And even if the inconceivable happened and she lost the game—she could suffer
through one kiss. Even if he were an Englishman.

"Nay, wait. 'Tis no' an unreasonable request,"
she said calmly. "I accept your terms."

Rolf lifted his head and his dark, burning eyes
held hers for a measured moment. "Then I accept your challenge," he answered.

For a moment, Megan wondered if she had
made a mistake. There was a new look in his
eyes, a kind of intense determination. She swallowed hard, feeling her palms become damp.
Taking a steady breath, she discreetly wiped her
hands on her gown beneath the table and leaned
forward to begin.

From the start, Megan moved her pieces with
none of the caution she had exhibited in the pre-
vious game. She was determined to finish as
quickly as possible and put an end to her cha-
rade. Yet after the first few moves, she realized
with growing concern that Rolf was making
equally bold and daring moves, forcing her to re-
think her strategy. Lifting her eyes from the
board, she looked at him in suspicious surprise.

"Ye are playing well," she said softly, almost
accusing him.

Rolf smiled, his lips curving sensuously. "I

find that playing for a valuable prize stimulates my mind."

A nervous flutter began in her stomach, but Megan pushed it aside firmly. She had to concentrate on the game. Her next several moves were a daring attempt to force his king into a corner. Yet in a series of advances that left her breathless, Rolf expertly countered her attack. Two moves later, Megan found herself checkmated.

Slowly, she pushed away from the table and stood. He had played a dazzling game of chess, using some of the most innovative moves she had ever seen.

"Ye knew all along how to play chess," she accused him, her eyes flashing with anger. " 'Twas naught but a ruse. Ye tricked me."

"*I* tricked *you*?" Rolf said with a significant lifting of his brows. "Was it *I* who suggested the wager against a player whom I thought I could easily best?"

"But ye played badly on purpose."

"Consider it a strategy—a lesson to take to heart. I didn't see you playing so expertly that first game either, although I could sense you held yourself back. If you must know, you are a most formidable opponent when you play to your abilities."

"Ye . . . ye Englishman," she exploded, bestowing the worst of all curses on him. "I should have never agreed to play chess wi' ye."

"Ah, but you did, my dear. And now you must honor your wager."

Slowly he unfolded himself from the chair, stretching his sleek, muscular frame like a panther. He walked to the hearth, bending over and adding another few squares of peat to the fire. Finally he straightened and turned to look at her.

"Come here, Megan," he commanded softly, motioning with the crook of his finger. "I believe it is time to honor your wager."

Megan looked at him with wide eyes, her courage faltering. "N-nay," she whispered, her voice shaking unnaturally. " 'Twas wrong o' me to make such a wager. I can't honor it. I simply don't think I could bear it."

"Bear what?" he asked sharply.

"Being kissed . . . by ye."

He frowned, raising his maimed hand. "You mean being kissed by a cripple."

She blinked in surprise, her brow drawing into a frown. "Nay, I mean being kissed by . . . by an Englishman." The soft burr in her voice deepened with anxiety. "I'm certain 'twill be most horrible."

Rolf stood deathly still before he suddenly began to laugh. "So that is what troubles you?" he asked. When she nodded, he shook his head in disbelief. "Come here, Megan. Let me show you what it is like to be kissed by an Englishman."

An odd flutter began in Megan's stomach. In a strange way, she was fascinated by the husky tone of his voice and the seductive caress of his voice when he said her name. A peculiar excitement raced through her, urging her toward him. Yet she could not bring herself to step forward.

"Are you going to honor your wager or not?" he finally asked when she did not move. His voice was soft and curiously undemanding.

After a long moment, Megan took a step forward. "I gave my word and I will honor it. But first ye must promise that 'twill be but a kiss."

Rolf nodded gravely. "You have my word," he replied, his gaze holding hers.

Murmuring a small prayer, Megan walked over to where he stood. He opened his arms and after a moment of hesitation, she moved into them slowly.

Gently Rolf drew her toward him until her hands rested lightly against his chest. He lightly fingered a loose tendril of hair on her cheek before reaching back and unfastening the ribbon in her hair. Raven-colored tresses spilled across her shoulders, like a dark river of satin. Leaning over, he breathed the feminine scent of rose soap and heather.

"Put your arms around my neck," he ordered softly when she remained rigid in his arms.

She complied, her arms shaking. With agonizing care, he cupped his fingers around her trembling chin, holding her still. He inclined his head, placing his mouth lightly against hers. He traced the soft fullness of her lips with his tongue, teasing the sensitive curves of her mouth.

Megan's determination to remain aloof during the kiss was shattered by the drugging sensation of his firm, hard mouth against hers. The feel of his tongue sent a shock wave spiraling through her entire body. Never had Robbie's kisses sent such a burning fire through her veins, causing her head to spin so dizzily and her knees to turn to jelly.

When she parted her lips, Rolf gently slid his tongue within her mouth, exploring the sensitive sides. Although she was startled by his invasion, another part of her shivered with pleasure at the delicious sensations flooding her body. Fascinated by the feelings, Megan tentatively touched her own tongue to his.

Rolf moaned with pleasure at her sweetness, surprised that she seemed so unsure of herself, almost inexperienced. As the mistress of the Wolf, she certainly would be no untried miss. Perhaps, he thought with a surge of satisfaction, the Black Wolf was lacking as a lover. Rolf was surprised at the acute sense of pleasure the thought gave him. As his tongue entwined with hers, his hand left her chin, gliding over her shoulder and down to the small of her back, where he pressed her tightly against him. God, she aroused him. Whether it was her soft feminine curves or her uninhibited responses, he did not know. He only knew that he wanted this kiss to continue indefintely.

Megan kept her eyes tightly shut, marveling at the feelings within her as if they had always existed there, unawakened. She had never suspected that a kiss could be so enjoyable. Heat radiated through her, warming her body in places she had never known existed and filling her with an indescribable ache for his touch upon her skin. Her fingers slowly unclenched. Tentatively, she began exploring the corded muscles of his shoulders and neck with sensitive, inquiring fingertips.

His response was to tighten his arms about her waist and deepen their kiss. Megan felt herself falling deep into a sea of pleasurable sensations. She tangled her fingers in his thick mane of hair, threading them through the dark strands and keeping his mouth on hers.

Feeling her hands in his hair, Rolf felt his desire increase tenfold. Lifting his lips from hers, he forged a trail of heated kisses from the corner of her mouth to the curve of her cheekbone. Brushing her silken hair aside, he kissed the soft skin of her neck, gratified when he heard a quiet moan escape her lips.

Pulling away slightly, he studied her face. Her eyes were shut, her mouth swollen from their kiss. Long dark lashes lay like a brush of dark silk on her skin and a warm pink glow suffused her cheeks. She was enjoying herself, Rolf thought with surprise. And God help him, so was he. The faint scent of the rosewater in which she had bathed lingered on her skin, beckoning him closer. Weakening, he battled the urge to slip his hand beneath her gown and cup the soft curve of her breast.

He wanted to take this further. Much further. But he had given his word to take a kiss and naught more. It might well kill him, but he would not rescind his promise. Regretfully, he pulled away from her.

She opened her eyes, an expression of wonder mixed with disappointment on her face. He hadn't been wrong. She had been enjoying herself. Rolf lightly traced the line of her cheekbone and jaw with his finger. He ached to take her back in his arms, but held himself to his word.

"You may now consider the wager fulfilled," he said gently in a deep husky timbre.

Dazed, Megan reached up and touched her lips, still tingling from his kiss. Her whole body was trembling, her legs weak. She was all too aware of just how much she had enjoyed his touch and the feel of his mouth upon hers.

Shame and self-loathing slammed into her

with the force of a tidal wave. Her cheeks blazed crimson and she stepped quickly away from him. Hoping he could not see how distressed she was, Megan forced herself to lift her chin and meet his eyes evenly.

"So what's next, Englishman?" she said, her voice cool. "Now that ye've humiliated me, are ye ready to return to the dungeon and resume torturing helpless men?"

Rolf's dark eyes turned flat and as unreadable as stone. "Humiliated you? If I'm not wrong, it seems to me that you just enjoyed that kiss as much as I did."

Mortified that he had so easily read her response, she felt the heat in her face intensify. "Well, ye were wrong. I hated every moment o' it."

His hand shot out unexpectedly, catching her arm and drawing her close. "I think you're a liar," he said softly. "Why deny it, Megan? I could tell what you wanted."

Megan yanked away, a sob catching in her throat. "Stop it," she demanded in a choked voice.

Perplexed, Rolf looked at her in surprise. "You are truly distressed," he said, frowning. He released her arm and she immediately turned her back to him, standing stiffly with her hands clenched at her side.

"So what's next, Englishman," she snapped harshly, but Rolf could hear the tremble in her voice.

"I believe it is time we retire for the evening," he answered quietly.

"Wh-what?" Megan gasped, whirling around to face him.

Rolf grimaced at the horror in her voice. "In separate chambers, of course. I've had Abigail prepare a room for you. I trust you will be comfortable."

She sighed with audible relief. "I don't need a room, Englishman. I'd be more comfortable in the dungeon."

Rolf shook his head. "I sincerely doubt it. But I will take you to see the men in the morning."

Startled, Megan glanced at him in surprise. "Ye will? But I lost the wager."

"Yes, you did." His voice softened. "But I hope you will soon learn that I am not a completely unreasonable man. Come now."

Megan was careful not to touch him as she left the sitting room. Her emotions were in a jumble. She knew full well that he could have tortured her or forced himself upon her before this, especially as he thought her to be the mistress of his enemy. Yet he had done neither. It was completely out of character with what she expected from a despicable Englishman.

She was disconcerted, and her brow drew together in an anxious frown. Lest she forget, this man was her enemy. If he discovered she was the Wolf, he would not hesitate to send her to London for immediate execution. She could never ever let down her guard with him again like she had tonight.

God help her. Rolf St. James had proved himself a worthy adversary and Megan knew she would have to be equally as stalwart. She realized all too well that the real game between the two of them had only just begun.

# Chapter Eight

*Blessed God above, it was a miracle!*

Megan couldn't believe her luck as Rolf ushered her into what used to be her brother Jamie's bedchamber. A fire had been lit in the hearth and fresh water placed in a basin on top of a wooden table. Other than the position of the bed and the absence of Jamie's personal belongings, the chamber was exactly as she remembered it.

Bittersweet memories flooded over her as she remembered her brother's handsome grin and the sparkle of blue eyes when he laughed. They had played in this room together as children—laughing, shouting and brewing up mischief. Later, when they had both grown, they'd sat in front of this very hearth, ferociously arguing politics until the wee hours of the morning.

A flood of sadness and regret crushed her. The MacLeod clan had never been one to agree on politics. When her father refused the call to arms for Prince Charles, Jamie had argued bitterly with him. Robert had had no love for the Hanovers, but had not believed Charles Stuart to be the man to lead Scotland out of her troubles. Megan had firmly backed her father's decision, and the rift had taken a painful toll on the family. But now she couldn't help but wonder if Jamie had been right all along. Mayhap it would have been more honorable to die on the fields of Culloden. For nearly anything would have been better than what she and her clansmen were reduced to now.

"Megan?"

"Aye?" she said, looking over at him quickly.

Rolf noticed her blue eyes were filled with sadness and wondered what had prompted such emotions. "I asked whether this room would be suitable."

A small, melancholy smile touched her lips. "Aye, 'twill be just fine." She walked over to the hearth, warming her hands by the fire. She stood there quietly, her shoulders erect, her black tresses glistening in the dim light.

Rolf watched her in fascination, marveling at the way she carried herself, proudly and regally. By the light of the fire, she appeared serenely wise and beautiful. Still, the demeanor of calm was slightly betrayed by the worried set of her mouth and the small frown furrowed at her brow.

"If you need anything—" he began, but she interrupted him softly.

"Good night, Englishman."

Frowning that he had somehow been summarily dismissed, Rolf bowed slightly and then left the room, shutting the door behind him. He firmly drew the bolt, spoke briefly to the guard and strode down the corridor to his own bedchamber, not to sleep, but to think. He had spent too much time with the girl and needed to turn his attention to discovering a way to lure the elusive Wolf into a trap.

Unfortunately, even after he had undressed and sat in front of the fire sipping a brandy, he found he could think of little other than the lass with eyes of blue Scottish fire. Somehow, after an evening with her, his problems with the Wolf seemed minimal in comparison to the mystery of this beautiful woman. He laughed at himself. By God, he must be mad to find himself attracted to a woman who only hours earlier had sought to kill him.

Thoughtfully, he set his glass aside and removed the glove from his injured hand. Methodically, he began to rub the twisted knuckles as he did every night. How odd that she had wished him to uncover it—to display this hideous deformity for the world to see. He had never met a woman so unusual and so utterly fascinating.

He blew out a deep breath. The truth of the matter was that he wanted her badly. He had foolishly thought a simple kiss would slake his curiosity and need. But he couldn't have been more wrong. It had done little to dampen his interest, and more to convince him that there was nothing simple or undesirable about this woman.

He'd be damned, but somehow his lovely captive had discovered a way to turn his own tactics against him. Now, instead of thinking of ways to capture the Wolf, he was becoming obsessed with the most intriguing woman he had ever met. What a jest it would be if that turned out to be the Wolf's strategy all along.

Megan did not ready herself for bed, nor did she rest beneath the soft quilts, for fear of falling asleep. Instead she waited by the window, judging the time from the position of the moon. When she was certain it was far past midnight, she walked over to the hearth. Running her hands down the side of the mantle, she groped for the latch that she knew would be there.

In moments she found it and firmly gave it a twist. With a groaning creak, a section of the fireplace moved outward, revealing a secret passageway. A dank and musty smell drifted out and Megan wrinkled her nose in disgust. Forcing herself to overcome her queasiness at entering the forbidding tunnel alone, she took a candle from the table and slipped into the passageway, pulling the fireplace door shut behind her.

The air was cool and damp and Megan shivered, wishing she had a cloak. Moving cautiously along the tunnel, she stifled a scream as a spiderweb brushed across her face. Saints above, how many years had it been since she'd last been in this tunnel?

"Too many," she whispered grimly, ignoring the strange rustling noises and the brush of something darting across her foot.

Determinedly, she tried to focus more on pleasant thoughts, like what the Englishman would think when he discovered the room empty and his prisoner missing.

"This time, 'tis checkmate to ye, Englishman,"

she whispered with a small smile of satisfaction.

Feeling cheered by the thought, she continued along the tunnel, guiding herself by keeping one hand on the cold stone wall. When she came to a narrow set of stairs leading downward, she knew that she was almost to her destination. Carefully, she descended the steps until she came to a door at the bottom of the stairway. Holding the candle closer for light, she searched the door until she found the turn-stone. Murmuring a small prayer that no one was waiting on the other side, Megan pressed on it with all her strength. With a rusty groan, the door swung open and she quickly slipped into her father's library.

The room was empty and Megan sighed a breath of relief. Turning, she closed the tunnel door behind her. Walking quickly across the room, she paused at the door to the hallway. With regret, she blew out the candle and set the holder on a nearby table. She would have to make the remainder of her escape without light. It would be too dangerous to do otherwise.

Opening the door a crack, she listened for sounds in the corridor. When she heard nothing, she slipped out of the room, making her way down the back stairs which were used by servants. She had no immediate plan in mind, but decided it was crucial to determine how well the dungeon was being guarded.

There was little choice, really. In order to slip out of the castle with the least chance of being detected, she would have to pass by the dungeon anyway. The long corridor leading to the dungeon also had a back door which led out to the courtyard. From there she would make her way to a part of the castle wall where, in their teens, she and Jamie had carved small footholds in the stone, enabling them to scale over it without a rope.

Summoning her courage, she moved stealthily along the dimly lit corridor, stifling a cry of pain when her shin slammed unexpectedly against the stub of a burnt-out torch someone had left propped against the wall. As the wood fell to the floor with a loud thump, Megan sank back into the shadows, listening for sounds of an alarm. When none came, she exhaled deeply, bending over and taking the wood in her hand. It wasn't much of a weapon, but it felt better to hold on to something.

When she finally reached the corner where the corridor to the dungeon intersected the hallway in which she was standing, she pressed herself against the cold wall. Taking several deep breaths to calm her pounding heart, she peeked slowly around the corner and took a cautious look down the long corridor.

Luck was with her. Only one guard sat in a wooden chair beneath a burning torch. He seemed very still, perhaps asleep, although she could not be certain. Clearly, the foolish Englishman felt secure within the confines of the castle walls. Megan smiled.

*Och, how little ye know o' us, Englishman!*

Pressing back against the wall, she contemplated the possibilities. She knew that as soon as she was discovered missing, Rolf would most likely assign more guards to the other prisoners. Therefore, the probability of her meeting just one guard again was slim, indeed. However, if she proceeded to disarm the guard now, she might be able to free the prisoners and escape with them over the wall before anyone even noticed she was missing. And if the guard was truly asleep, she would have the advantage of surprise.

She decided to risk it.

Her decision made, she stepped out from behind the wall and began tiptoeing down the long corridor. The guard did not move and with every step, Megan's confidence grew. As she drew closer, she assessed his chances for overpowering her. He was a big, burly man with thick arms. She knew that if she did not render him useless before he awoke, he would easily be able to subdue her.

Fortunately, his chest continued to rise and fall evenly in the steady rhythm of sleep. She was only a few steps from him when he suddenly snapped his eyes open, looking at her in astonishment.

"Wh-what in the bloody hell . . ." he stammered, his voice thick with sleep and confusion.

Frightened, Megan stepped forward, swinging the burnt-out torch with all her might. It connected solidly with the side of his head. With a groan of pain, the guard slid to the floor and lay motionless.

Leaning over him, she searched for a pulse and breathed a small sigh of relief when she felt it. She had no desire to maim or kill the man, just render him unconscious. A faint noise sounded in the dungeon. As Megan looked up, men clamored about the small barred window of their cell.

"Who goes there?" she heard Uncle Geddes call out.

Quickly, Megan felt through the guard's coat pockets until her fingers closed around an iron key ring. Straightening, she hurried over to the door and began trying the keys in the lock. "Hush, Uncle Geddes, 'tis only me, Megan."

"Megan?" Geddes said hoarsely. "My God, lass, how did ye manage to overpower the guard?"

"Never mind about that," she said fumbling with the keys. "As soon as I find the accursed key that opens this door, ye are to lead the prisoners to the west wall behind the dungeon. Near a thick clump o' bushes, ye'll find a series of footholds that'll permit ye to scale the wall without a rope. In case we are separated, we'll meet at our campsite from last spring. The English will no' think to look for us so close to the loch."

She heard Geddes hurriedly whispering her instructions among the prisoners. At last, she found the key that fit the lock. With a swift turn and pull, the door swung open. The men came spilling out, some being carried or helped along by the others.

"Blessed saints, did the English torture ye badly?" Megan asked in concern, seeing the numerous injuries. She carefully wrapped her arm beneath the shoulders of a young boy, Lachlan MacGee, whose entire middle was wrapped in bandages.

Geddes shook his head. "Nay, 'twas most strange. The English spoke wi' us but did no' resort to torture. The wounds ye see are the ones we received during the battle at the camp." He noticed Megan's fine gown for the first time and frowned. "How are faring ye, lass? Did the Englishman . . . er . . . harm ye in any way?"

Megan shook her head, but could not help the color from creeping to her cheeks as she remembered Rolf's kiss. "Nay, I swear that I have no' been harmed, Uncle. But that may change if we do no' get out o' here and quickly. Where's Robbie?"

Geddes grimaced as he limped forward. "He eluded capture thanks to ye, Megan. Your diversion permitted more than a handful o' the men to escape. I suppose he's been worried ill about us."

Megan's mouth tightened as she looked back over the prisoners. Their faces were drained and weary. Concerned, Megan began to wonder if they could make the climb over the wall at all. In an instant, she made a decision. She handed Lachlan over to Douglas MacLeary, a lifelong friend of her father's whose eyes were covered with bandages, and drew Uncle Geddes aside.

"That door at the end of the corridor leads to the courtyard," she said softly. "From there ye can make your way around the back o' the dungeon to the part o' the wall I told ye about. Take all the men who are fit to climb and scale the wall as soon as possible. Wait for us on the other side. I'll stay back with those who are injured to ensure that everyone makes it safely."

"Nay, Megan," Geddes gasped, aghast at her proposal. "Ye must save yourself."

Megan's blue eyes flashed proudly as she drew him aside. "And what kind o' laird would I be if I put my own safety before my men?" she whispered. "I'm ordering ye, Uncle, to lead the way to the wall. I want to free as many men as possible. Those who are fit can help the rest o' us o'er the wall. We will follow ye as quickly as we can. Besides, in this cumbersome gown, I'll no' be able to move as quickly as ye. Just get as many o' the men as ye can to safety." When Geddes still hesitated, she gripped his shoulder firmly. "I am your laird and that is an order, Uncle."

Seeing the determination in her eyes, Geddes reluctantly nodded. Turning, he gave a sharp command and swiftly led the way down the corridor. Those who could keep up with him followed. The rest stayed behind. Megan did a hasty head count. Four men left, plus herself.

"All right," Megan ordered briskly, taking Lachlan back from Douglas and wrapping her arm around the young boy's shoulders. "Let's go as quickly as we can. The others are getting in position to help us o'er the wall."

The injured men nodded as they began the agonizingly slow journey toward the door, Douglas holding Megan's other arm. They were nearly there when Lachlan begged her to stop.

"G-go on without me," he gasped, his face contorted with pain. "I dinna think I can make it."

Panting from the exertion of shouldering his weight, Megan leaned him gently against the wall. Lachlan was thirteen years old—still a boy, yet far too familiar with the responsibilities of a man.

"Go on ahead," Megan hastily instructed the other three men. "Joseph, take Douglas's hand and lead him out. Lachlan and I will catch our breath a bit and we'll be right behind ye."

Joseph nodded, guiding Douglas's hand to his shoulder. After a moment the three of them disappeared through the door and out into the courtyard.

Lachlan began to cry, tears streaming down his young face. "I'm scared, Megan. I dinna want to hold back the others, but I'm afraid to be alone."

"Hush," Megan said gently. "I'm no' leaving ye and ye're doing fine. Look, we are almost at the door. We'll make it."

"But I'll never be able to climb the wall," he sobbed. "I dinna want to die."

"No one is going to die," Megan relied firmly. "And no matter what happens, I'm no' going to leave ye. Come on, let's try to move a wee bit more."

At that moment, she heard the sound of thundering footsteps in the corridor. Megan's heart leapt to her throat in fear. Despite his cry of pain, she grasped Lachlan firmly beneath the arms. She dragged him to the door and pushed it open, pulling him into the courtyard.

Almost immediately, rough hands shot out from the darkness, seizing her by the shoulder and sending her and Lachlan tumbling to the ground. Englishmen charged into the courtyard, shouting and waving torches. Struggling to her feet, Megan saw one of the men swing a fist at Lachlan, who was bravely trying to sit up.

"Nay," she shrieked as the boy crumpled to the ground in a heap. Horrified, she rushed to his side, cradling his head in her hands. He appeared to be unconscious, but Megan noticed with relief that he was breathing. As she reached down to feel his bandages, someone grabbed a fistful of her hair, dragging her to her feet. Megan cried out both in surprise and pain.

" 'Tis the bloody wench who struck me," she heard someone shout. Twisting around, Megan looked directly into the face of the burly prison guard. Despite a purple bruise swelling near his left temple, he looked amazing healthy and frightfully mad.

"I apologize if I harmed ye," Megan said calmly as she could manage. "However, 'twas necessary to disarm ye in order to free the prisoners."

The men standing around guffawed in laughter at her statement. The guard's eyes narrowed angrily. "Disarm me? 'Tis a laughingstock you've made of me."

"Then I would suggest ye take a more vigilant approach to your duties in the future."

The guard's mouth dropped open in astonishment. "Ye heathen wench," he sputtered furiously, striking her hard across the mouth with the back of his hand. "I expect the proper respect from a woman." The other men surrounding him murmured in surprise, but none moved forward to stop him.

Megan's eyes watered from the blow and she could feel her lip beginning to swell. "Och, ye're a big man now, aren't ye? Well take this, ye English oaf." Doubling her fist, she swung with all her strength directly into the man's midsection.

The man gasped in astonishment, one hand clutching his stomach, the other still wound in her hair. "Ch-christ," he puffed. "She hit me again."

Amid the laughing, Megan shut her eyes, bracing herself for another blow. Instead she heard her attacker give a small squeal. She was released so quickly that she stumbled backward. Opening her eyes, Megan saw Rolf standing behind the prison guard, twisting his arm back behind the shoulder blades. Rolf was dressed in a dark cloak that swirled around his shoulders in the cool wind. His face was black with controlled fury, the muscles clenched tightly in his jaw.

"If any of you ever touch her again, I'll see you whipped within an inch of your lives," Rolf announced, his voice as chilling as a winter day.

The burly man trembled violently, visibly shaken by the sudden appearance of his lord. "M-my lord. The wench struck me while I was guarding the dungeon. I was only punishing her." He gave another cry of pain as Rolf applied more pressure on his arm.

"How was she able to strike you, Arthur? Were you too weak to stop the blow . . . or perhaps you were asleep?"

Arthur swallowed hard, his Adam's apple bobbing nervously. "F-forgive me, my lord. N-never again."

The depth of Rolf's bridled anger pierced the air as he faced the other men. "Why do you tarry here while our quarry escapes? Find me the prisoners *now!*" The men hastily dispersed, fearful of their lord's wrath.

Left alone with Rolf and Megan, Arthur whimpered pitifully. "Please, my lord, it hurts terribly."

With a grunt of disgust, Rolf released the man, pushing him away. Arthur stumbled forward, clutching his arm in pain.

"You will report to Peter in one hour," Rolf said to him in a cold, clipped voice. "You'll be given a mount, some food and the coin that you are due. Your presence here is no longer required."

"But, my lord," Arthur whined. "The girl came up on me—"

"Enough," Rolf thundered so loudly that even Megan took a step backward in fear. He raised one hand, pointing at the door. "Get out."

Arthur took one look at the harsh lines etched on Rolf's face and scurried through the door toward the dungeon. The door slammed shut with a loud final thump.

Megan stood shivering in the cold as Rolf turned his attention back to her. He said nothing but stared at her sternly. After a moment, she broke the gaze, kneeling beside Lachlan and resting her hand against his cheek. He moaned slightly and Megan bent over him, whispering soothing words.

The sound of hastily approaching footsteps caused her to look up as a shadowed figure emerged from the darkness. "We captured two more of the prisoners, my lord," a voice said breathlessly, "but the rest escaped into the forest on foot. Shall we pursue them?"

Rolf nodded. "Yes, Andrew. Make a thorough sweep of the surrounding area but do not venture past the river. It's too dark and they could lead us into an ambush. We can resume the search at dawn. The prisoners are weary and wounded. I doubt they can go far."

"Aye, my lord," Andrew said sharply, hurrying away.

As his footsteps faded across cobblestones, Megan rose facing Rolf directly. "The lad is gravely injured," she said quietly. "If we don't treat him immediately, he is going to die."

Rolf's eyes flickered over the boy. Without another word, he walked over and knelt by his side.

With ease, he reached down and carefully lifted Lachlan into his arms.

"Follow me," he said to Megan curtly.

He led her across the courtyard and past the stone arch entrance. In the distance Megan could hear shouts and see the flickering light of torches bobbing among the trees. She said a silent prayer hoping that Uncle Geddes had not waited for her and had instead successfully led the rest of the men to safety.

Without breaking his stride, Rolf walked up the gravel path that led to the entry hall of the castle. Tersely, he ordered one of the servants to bring fresh blankets, water and linen bandages to the tower room. After instructing Megan to take a torch, they climbed the narrow stone staircase to the tower.

Megan had been here many times as a child. Back then, the chamber had been something of a playroom with thick wool rugs and warm tapestries adorning the wall. Now, the room was cold and sparsely furnished. A small cot with a straw pallet had been pushed up against the wall. The hearth had been swept clean and several peat squares had been stacked neatly to one side. A thin woven rug lay on the floor and a single wooden chair had been placed near the fireplace.

Carefully, Rolf laid the injured boy on the cot. "The chamber will be warm once I have lit a fire," he commented briefly. Walking over to the fireplace, he arranged kindling and several peat squares on the grate, igniting them with flames from the torch.

Megan knelt by Lachlan's side, smoothing the hair back from his face. He had not regained consciousness, but moaned softly from the pain. As the fire began to lick hungrily at the peat, servants rushed into the room with quilts, water and bandages. Rolf lifted Lachlan from the bed while the servants hastily laid down the bedcovers. When they were finished, Rolf returned Lachlan to the cot. Megan immediately began removing the soiled bandages from his body.

Rolf watched her silently as she tended to the boy with remarkable gentleness. When the boy's wounds lay bare, she looked up at Rolf with anxious eyes.

"Have ye any healing herbs to make a poultice? His wounds have festered."

"You really do have healing skills," he remarked quietly.

"As I told ye before. A person learns a great many things after being forced into the hills to survive."

Rolf felt a twinge of guilt, but pushed it aside. Waving a hand, he instructed one of the hovering servants to bring some herbs and salve. The servant immediately disappeared to do his bidding.

"What about the others?" she asked. "May I be allowed to treat them as well?"

Rolf's eyes darkened angrily, his mouth compressing into a tight line. "I find you to be a most interesting woman, Megan. First you lead me and my men on a merry chase through the trees, then you try to skewer me with your blade. You manage to escape a locked chamber, beat and disarm one of my guards and free several of the prisoners. Now you ask for my favor?"

Megan swallowed. "I know ye are angry and ye have every right to be. Punish me as ye see fit. But don't harm the wounded men because o' my actions. I alone am responsible."

He crossed his arms against his chest, leaning back against the mantle. "Are you? How did you get out of that chamber?"

Megan sighed, realizing it was only a matter of time before he discovered her route of escape. "There is a secret passageway behind the fireplace leading to the library."

Interest flickered in Rolf's eyes. "And just how did you know about that passageway?"

She lifted her head quickly. "I . . . I used to play with the laird's bairns here in the castle. They showed it to me once."

"Ah, yes, the laird's children. Let me see, there was a son and a daughter, if I remember correctly. The son was killed, or at least that is what I've been told. He was shot by Farrington during a raid on his cattle. The daughter, I heard, was sent away for safekeeping to Ireland. How well did you know them, Megan?"

"Well enough," she answered shrugging. "They were . . . my friends."

"Interesting friends, indeed," Rolf mused. "Was it hard for them to look the other way while their father took on his children's playmate as his mistress?"

Megan flew across the room so quickly, Rolf was taken aback. Before he knew it, the crack of her open palm hitting his cheek sounded through the chamber.

"Don't ever speak o' the Wolf like that again," she cried. "I'll no' stand for it."

Rolf's hand shot out, capturing her wrist in a tight grip. His eyes had slitted into tiny dark irises of anger. One muscle in his jaw twitched furiously, the red imprint from her slap clearly visible.

"Have you no stomach for the truth?" he finally asked quietly, the calmness of his voice belitting the glitter in his eyes.

"I have no stomach for your depraved insinuations," she replied in a choked voice. "The Wolf is the most honorable man I've ever known."

Rolf let his eyes linger on her face, surprised that his words had wounded her so deeply. Her eyes shimmered with unshed tears, her color heightened not by exertion, but from real and raw distress. Her dark hair tumbled freely down her back like a river of black satin.

Slowly, Rolf dropped her hand. She met his gaze evenly, refusing to cower or step back from him. "So your plan was to free the prisoners and flee with them over the wall?" he asked quietly. "The escape was your idea."

"Aye, 'tis so," Megan answered honestly.

"Then why did the men put so little value on your safety? They left you behind, for God's sake. You are not injured, you had no reason to remain with those who were."

"I have healing skills. I knew that those unable to escape would need my help."

"I don't believe you are telling the truth. No man in his right mind would leave a woman at the mercy of his enemy."

Megan bristled. "Och, ye Englishmen know naught o' our ways. Scottish women are no' like your simpering English ladies who need to be rescued and coddled. We can fight, raid, even own our own land. Well, at least we could before ye English trampled o'er ever' tradition we held dear."

"Traditions the Scots jeopardized by supporting the Stuart Pretender to the Throne."

"No' all Scots supported him, damn ye," Megan replied furiously. "But I wish to God that we would have. Anything would have been better than what your precious King has reduced us to now."

Rolf's eyes narrowed angrily. "Have care to speak of your sovereign in such a tone."

"He is your sovereign, no' mine," Megan countered hotly. "I'll no' apologize for what I did tonight. I'll never stop fighting the injustice ye English have unleashed on my land, no matter what sort o' torture ye devise for me."

Rolf's eyes met hers for a tension-filled moment, neither willing to look away first. Their standoff was finally broken by the servant who rushed in carrying jars of herbs and salve.

"Here they are, my lord," the young woman said, suddenly sensing that she had interrupted something.

"Give them to the lass," Rolf said with a sharp jerk of his head.

Megan took the jars, quickly opening them and examining the contents. She knelt by Lachlan's side, whispering to him softly. Rolf leaned down to stir the fire once more before walking toward the door.

"You gave me your word once before and you honored it," he said to Megan in a coolly impersonal tone. "Was that a mere coincidence or do the Scots truly honor their word?"

Megan paused in her ministrations, turning

around to look at him. "If a Scot gives his word, then he means it."

He paused a moment, as if reflecting on her words. "So be it, then. You are to remain here until I have the tunnel in your room sealed. Those men who are re-captured may be sent here to be treated before they are returned to the dungeon. That is, if I have your word you will not try to escape again."

Megan looked down at Lachlan, whose eyes had fluttered open. The boy had heard everything that Rolf had just said.

"Nay, Megan, dinna promise anything to the Englishman," he whispered weakly before dissolving into a fit of painful coughing.

Rolf stood impassively at the doorway, awaiting her reply. His eyes were as dark and unreadable as the expression on his face.

Megan hesitated, torn by conflicting emotions. Finally, she spoke. "I give ye my word, Englishman."

Rolf nodded once and then disappeared amid a whirl of his cloak down the stairway.

# *Chapter Nine*

Megan placed her hand over her brow, squinting against the bright glare of the early morning sun. From her perch on the window seat, she glanced up at the clear winter sky. It was an unsually beautiful day for March—bright and sunny. Usually, clear skies meant good omens. But on this day Megan could not dare to hope that luck might be going the way of the Scottish.

Her eyes drifted back to the courtyard where she anxiously awaited sight of Rolf and his men. They had been gone for hours, making no secret of the fact that they meant to pursue her clansmen without pause until the prisoners were either re-captured or dead. Remembering their pale and weary faces when she released them from the dungeon, she knew they could not have gone far.

Berating herself for such thoughts, Megan clenched her fists at her side. Where was her

faith in Uncle Geddes and the men? It was true
that they were wounded, but no one knew the
forest like they did. They had to have escaped.
Besides, if it were not so, Rolf and his men
would most likely have returned hours ago.

Yet she could not ignore her feeling of apprehension that something had gone terribly
wrong. She forced herself to consider the possibility that Rolf no longer had any use . . . or
wish for Scottish prisoners. If that were to be
true, then all their lives would be worth nothing
to him.

"Nay," she murmured softly. It could not be—
it *must* not be. She determinedly pushed a
strand of ebony hair from her face and stood up.
Fear and exhaustion were taking their toll on
her. She had to be calm and think. But how
could she be calm when the nefarious Rolf St.
James was out hunting down her people?

Worriedly, Megan leapt to her feet and began
pacing the chamber anxiously. Her emotions
were in a tangled jumble—half of her daring to
hope that Rolf would return empty-handed, the
other half dreading what would happen to her
and the remaining three captives if he returned
without his prisoners. Closing her eyes, she
rubbed her fingers against her temples, willing
the pounding throb behind her eyes to cease.

She had to be strong. The Englishman had already discovered her biggest weakness—the
lives of her men. She could not allow herself to
be further compromised, knowing he would certainly try to break her whether he returned with
or without prisoners. She could not show him
that she was afraid.

A clatter of hoofbeats in the courtyard startled

Megan from her thoughts. In a mad dash, she
flew to the window, hastily pulling aside the
heavy velvet drapery. Her heart leapt uncomfortably as she spotted Rolf's unmistakable
form. He sat astride a black stallion, his cloak
hanging loosely over the side. He was speaking
rapidly with Andrew, the same young man who
had attacked her in her tent. Scarcely daring to
breathe, Megan quickly scanned the rest of the
courtyard for her men. A sob of relief slipped
past her lips when she saw there were none to
be found. Did she dare to hope that the rest of
the clansmen had escaped? Or had Rolf decided
that he would take no more prisoners?

As her mind tried to sort the grim possibilities,
Megan felt a gaze upon her. Turning her head,
she saw that Rolf had spotted her at the window.
Hastily, she stepped away, letting the drapes fall
back into place. Although she had only met his
eyes for a moment, Megan was certain she had
read a promise in his grim, serious expression.
Harsh punishment would be dealt for what she
had done. Leaning her head against the cold,
stone wall, she took a deep breath, readying her
courage. She wanted to be calm and composed
when she faced his anger.

But Rolf did not come. One hour passed and
then another before Megan finally heard the
heavy tread of boots in the corridor. She held
her breath as the footsteps stopped outside her
door. A low murmur of voices drifted in from
the corridor, but no move was made to slide the
bolt aside. Megan felt a keen disappointment as
the heavy footsteps moved on. Quietly, she sank
into a chair and waited.

Abigail brought her supper, but Megan had no

appetite for food and left the tray untouched. When the older woman came to remove it, she clucked her tongue disapprovingly, but said nothing.

It was early evening when Megan finally heard the scraping sound of the bolt being drawn across the door. She rose from her chair just as the door swung open.

Rolf stepped into the chamber, pulling the door shut behind him. Despite the hours that had passed, he had not changed clothes from the ride. His boots were still covered with dried mud, his tunic rumpled and stained. His eyes were cool and distant and Megan shivered instinctively when his gaze settled fully on her.

"I trust you've been comfortable," he said, striding over to the hearth and holding out his hands to the flames.

Megan nodded wordlessly, wrapping her arms about herself both for comfort and to stop the silly urge she had to tremble. His back still toward her, Rolf bent over and threw another square of peat onto the fire.

Megan twisted her hands nervously in front of her. "Did the rest o' the men get away?" she asked, both dreading and wanting desperately to hear his answer.

Rolf did not reply, instead seeming to take pleasure that for each moment that passed she suffered a lifetime.

"Well?" she prompted anxiously.

Slowly he turned to face her. "We captured no others than the men you treated last night."

Megan exhaled the breath she had been holding, relief flooding through her. "God be praised," she whispered.

"I don't think it is God you should be praising," Rolf said calmly. "In fact, I find it a rather curious matter that two score of injured men so easily slipped through my fingers."

" 'Tis their home, the forest. Once they were in the trees, ye didn't really have a chance o' finding them."

Rolf's eyes narrowed sharply. "I'm afraid I must disagree with you, Megan. Those men were wounded, not able to travel quickly. I am convinced that they could not have done it. Not without help, at least."

Megan blinked in surprise, stunned by his suggestion. Could Robbie and the other men have been waiting on the other side of the castle? 'Twas certainly possible, she mused thoughtfully. Robbie might have gathered the remaining men and come to Castle Kilcraig trying to determine the best way to free the prisoners. What a shock it must have been for Uncle Geddes to stumble across his clansmen, lying in wait in the forest. If it were true, what a stroke of good fortune for them.

Rolf carefully watched a series of emotions play across Megan's face. From her genuine surprise, he was certain she had no prior knowledge that anyone else was waiting to help her men. But that meant the girl was either damn lucky or incredibly intelligent. Either possibility did not sit well with him.

"Quite a remarkable performance by your Wolf," Rolf said with distinct mockery. "He either anticipated your moves or had remarkable faith in your abilities."

For a moment, her startled blue eyes met his. Then she quickly looked away. "The Wolf is very clever," she said softly. "I told ye he still has many tricks up his sleeve."

Rolf laughed, but no humor shone from his eyes. "I'm beginning to think that you are the best weapon he has."

She brushed aside his comment with a careless wave of her hand. "Och, I'm just one o' a great many o' his followers."

Rolf took two strides across the room until he stood directly in front of her. "Somehow, I don't see you as much of a follower."

Megan kept her eyes firm on his, her stomach beginning to churn uneasily. "Then ye are sadly mistaken. I would follow him to the death."

Rolf leaned over until his face was a mere inches from her. Unwilling to cower in front of him, Megan held her ground, keeping her eyes locked with his.

"I don't think the Wolf would let you die, Megan," Rolf said softly, his breath warm upon her cheek. "You are far too intriguing a woman to be so easily dismissed. I think that's why the men were waiting outside my castle wall—not for your clansmen, but for you."

"Wishful thinking, Englishman," Megan replied between clenched teeth. "I know 'twould serve ye well to think ye held such a valuable hostage. But ye are wrong."

Rolf reached out, gently twisting a strand of her raven hair between his fingers. "I suppose you could be right. After all, I am still puzzled as to why you stayed behind while the rest of the men escaped."

"I told ye that I have healing skills. The wounded men needed me."

"And I say that is nonsense. You had no guarantees that I would permit you to attend them."

Megan's eyes flashed angrily. "Ye said I would be allowed to see them."

"See them, yes. But I made no promise that you could treat them."

Megan drew in her breath sharply. "Then 'twas my mistake to believe ye to be a decent man."

Rolf smiled, displaying a row of straight, white teeth. "Perhaps. But it still does not satisfy my curiosity. The men knowingly left you behind. Why? Your argument about Scottish women notwithstanding, I still don't believe the men, including your father, would have abandoned you to a castle full of Englishmen without just cause. There is something you are hiding from me—something I mean to find out."

Megan felt an icy finger of fear slide up her spine. "I think ye are searching for answers where there aren't any. Besides, I haven't hidden the aversion I feel for ye English."

Rolf released her hair, letting his warm fingers lightly brush her cheek. "Do you want to know what I think, Megan? I think you are a very bad liar. I'm certain you don't have an aversion to me . . . or to my kiss for that matter."

She gasped in outrage, but Rolf only smiled. "Have I come too close to the truth for comfort?" he asked.

"Don't flatter yourself," she snapped, her cheeks flushing.

"Then I take it that you do not care to test my theory."

"No' if ye were the last man in Scotland."

"Coward," he murmured.

Megan hastily took several steps backward.

She found to her surprise that her pulse was racing and her breath coming in quick gasps. Whether she was frightened or intrigued by this Englishman, she did not know. She only knew that when she was close to him, she was unable to think properly.

"What do ye mean to do wi' me and the three prisoners ye hold in the tower?" she asked, fighting to gain control of her senses.

Rolf raised an eyebrow. "In the tower, are they?"

Megan immediately realized her mistake. "The men . . . er . . . they were badly wounded and I didn't think they should be moved to the cold, damp dungeon."

Rolf looked at her incredulously. "You mean to say that you ordered my men to keep the prisoners in the tower room?"

Megan jerked her head up defensively. "Well, 'twouldn't be right to say that I ordered it. I simply suggested that ye and I had discussed it earlier and ye hadn't minded the idea."

Rolf shook his head in muted wonder. His men had actually followed an order from a woman—a captive nonetheless! And all because she'd had the audacity to hint that their lord would be unhappy if her command was not carried out.

She was a brazen bit of goods, he mused half in irritation, half in admiration. Damn, but he would have to watch her like a hawk. If he wasn't careful, he was certain she would turn the castle upside down.

"Ye still haven't answered my question," Megan repeated. "What do ye mean to do wi' us?"

Rolf's face grew thoughtful and he absently

stroked his thigh with his long fingers. "I tire of this game of run and chase. I've decided to ask the Wolf for a trade."

"A trade?" Megan echoed.

"Yes, a trade. If he turns himself in, I'll set you and the remaining men free."

Megan waved her hand dismissively. "Then ye waste your time. Your terms will no' be accepted."

Rolf walked over to one of the chairs and sat, leaving Megan standing alone in the middle of the room. "I wouldn't be so certain, Megan. If the Wolf turns himself in, I will also grant a general amnesty to all those who follow him."

Megan drew in a sharp breath in stunned amazement. General amnesty for all the men? It was an astounding offer, but one certain to come with additional terms. Her eyes narrowed as she regarded him warily.

"How could the Wolf be certain that ye would be true to your word?"

Rolf leaned forward. "I could have the papers drawn up beforehand. You would give me a list of the men to be pardoned and I would see that the King's seal is on each one of them. The pardon would take effect the moment the Wolf surrendered himself to me. By forfeiting his own life, he will set the remaining men free, no longer to be hunted by the Crown."

"Ye say that as though it means something," Megan retorted bitterly. "The men would be free to live what kind o' life? A life of abject poverty without land, without homes, is no' much o' a deal, Englishman. Nay, I rather think the Wolf would still no' agree to your terms."

Rolf's eyes sparked with interest. "Then what

if I were to provide land for the men to live on? It would not be large, grant you, but it would be their own. My men would assist them in rebuilding their homes. In return I would require only that they stop following the Wolf and cease their bitter struggle against the English Crown."

Megan raised an eyebrow. "Ye have the power to do this?"

"I do."

"And ye would be the landlord?"

Rolf nodded. "For now. I would give them their rent for free, in exchange for an agreement to cease hostilities against us."

"And after ye are gone?"

"I will see that the provisions remain the same regardless of the landlord."

Megan's mind raced, searching for the deception in such a generous offer. "The Wolf . . . he would still face execution?"

Rolf nodded firmly. "Yes, I will not negotiate on that point. The Wolf must be held accountable for his crimes."

Megan pressed the flat of her hand against her brow. Her thoughts were too jumbled, too unsettled, preventing her from determining the motivations of this handsome Englishman. And she had no doubt that he had some devious motivation in proposing such an offer.

" 'Tis an interesting offer," she said as casually as possible, "but I'm still no' certain the Wolf will trust ye enough to accept them."

Rolf stood, the firelight flickering off his tall frame. "You seem to know his mind better than anyone."

Megan lifted her head quickly. "The Wolf is a

Scotsman. His thoughts are those that I understand."

"But you do not understand me."

"Let's just say that I don't trust ye or your motivations."

A deep-throated chuckle rumbled from his chest. "I've never had my integrity so thoroughly questioned by a woman before."

"Then ye've never known a Scottish woman," Megan remarked dryly.

"Not to the extent that I have had the opportunity to know you. I must admit that I am intrigued."

"Well, I don't know why ye are surprised," Megan said, her voice holding a trace of bitterness. "Ye English have never taken the time to learn anything o' our ways. Ye only kill and conquer without thought, without care to those ways and people ye trample beneath your heavy boots."

Rolf's smile faded and he was silent for a long moment before he stretched out his hand. "Come here, Megan."

Megan looked at him with surprise and not a little bit of alarm. "What do ye want from me now, Englishman?"

"I want you to come and sit by the fire with me," he answered calmly. "I find it absurd and rather uncomfortable that I must shout across the room because you will not share the warmth of the hearth with me. Come. I give you my word that I will not harm you."

Megan hesitated, wary of being near him. Only after realizing he could forcibly move her there if he so desired did she relent and walk over to him. Rolf took her hand, motioning for her to sit in the chair opposite him. The fire radiated heat and Megan's body shivered in welcome response to its warmth. She hadn't even realized that she was so cold.

"I wish to tell you something," Rolf said, still holding her hand. "The King has commanded me not only to capture the Wolf, but to bring peace to this area. You say I know naught of you and your people, and to a great extent, you are right. But I am aware of the fierce pride and remarkable courage of the Scots, and I must say, I greatly admire it."

He paused a moment as if searching for the words he wanted to say. "History is not often fair. Those who are strong will generally conquer the weak, despite the unfairness of it. For people like you and me, Megan, we can only do our part to see that as many people as possible are spared the tragic consequences of war. The Wolf's struggle is honorable, I do not deny this. Your devotion to him is enviable. But the war is over. Scotland has been conquered for five years now and your resistance against us—against me—is futile. You judge us harshly, but you refuse to acknowledge the fact that if the King wanted to end your activities without any regard for life whatsoever, he would have sent a small army of men to crush you. But instead, he sent me. I have come not only to settle this dispute but to find an honorable resolution, a peaceful end, to this bitter struggle. Help me to do it right, Megan. Without any more needless loss of life."

His dark, earnest eyes sought hers. For a moment, Megan measured the man and the sincerity of his words. Her hand felt warm and heavy clasped in his, and she was utterly aware of the strength and warmth of his flesh pressed against hers.

"I cannot speak for the Wolf . . . just now," she said after some time had passed. "Your words and offer must be considered and judged for what they are."

Rolf nodded thoughtfully but still did not release her hand. Oddly, Megan found that she did not mind; his closeness seemed no longer threatening.

"How nice peace would be," Rolf murmured.

"Aye, how nice," she whispered in return.

He began to rub his thumb gently across her knuckles. "You are most intriguing, Megan. I've never met a woman like you."

"There is naught so unusual about me, Englishman," she said, her voice a bit breathless.

"Ah, but ye are wrong," he countered softly. The pulse at the base of her throat was fluttering madly, and Rolf felt a rush of satisfaction that she was not immune to his touch.

Nor was he immune to her allure. The physical attraction between them was almost tangible. Just being close to her had his heart racing and his breathing harsh and uneven. He wanted her—and he wanted her badly.

Had she been an Englishwoman or any score of other women he'd known, he could have relied on his considerable name, position and fortune to impress or seduce her, despite his disreputable reputation and crippling injury. But he knew those things would mean nothing to her, and he would have to rely solely on his wits. A most unusual, if not engaging, prospect.

"Megan, I don't want you to be frightened of me," Rolf said softly. "I want you to trust me."

127

He wanted to kiss her and for a moment, he fancied that she did too. Slowly he leaned toward her, his eyes half-closing. His pulse quickened. She did not move or pull away. Lord, he wanted her. It was sheer madness and bloody dangerous. But he wanted her nonetheless—

*Bam, bam, bam.*

The moment broken, both of them jerked their heads toward the door in startled surprise. Scowling, Rolf came to his feet. "Who is it?" he called out in annoyance.

"My lord, may I have a word with you?" came the voice from the other side of the door.

Rolf strode across the room and threw open the door. "Peter? What in God's name couldn't keep?"

The older man looked into the room to where Megan sat quietly in front of the fire, her hands clasped tightly in her lap. Her cheeks were flushed prettily, but her posture was stiff and uncomfortable. Slowly Peter returned his gaze to his irritated lord.

"Forgive me, Rolf," he said softly. "I wouldn't have disturbed you except that you have a visitor. He insisted he speak with you at once."

Rolf's dark eyebrow raised inquiring. "A visitor at this hour?"

Peter nodded, his gaze straying back to the lovely Scottish lass. "Aye, my lord, 'tis Edwin Farrington to see you."

# *Chapter Ten*

Edwin Farrington was forty-two years of age. He had rather dashing good looks with a full head of blond hair and a finely trimmed mustache. He was built like a tall, willowy tree, his form slender and slightly effeminate-looking. From all appearances he seemed to be a pleasant and quite harmless man.

Yet looks could be utterly deceiving, Rolf thought, as he lifted a glass of brandy to his lips. Beneath that rather ethereal blond head lay a mind as ruthless and cold as he had ever met. From what Rolf knew about the man, Farrington had been disgracefully removed from London by his family because of heavy gambling, drinking and an ugly and illicit incident involving a young servant. Edwin had been granted land in Scotland, primarily because he had an older brother who remained in favor with the King and who wished to stay unscathed by Edwin's scandals. Those involved believed that whatever schemes Edwin hatched in the Scottish Highlands, they would be far enough from the court to shield the remainder of the Farrington family from any more shame.

When Rolf first arrived at Castle Kilcraig, he'd made it his business to find out more about the errant Englishman. He'd soon discovered that Farrington was thoroughly hated by most all his Scottish tenants. Through various discreet sources, Rolf had heard stories of the man's cruelty, that Farrington insisted on exorbitant rents and evicted and burned the homes of those villagers unable to pay—delighting in their suffering.

Rolf was disturbed by these accounts, and even more disturbed by the lurid tales of the rape and brutality that Farrington and his men had allegedly inflicted on the villagers. If it were true, it was no wonder Rolf could not bribe a single one of them into betraying the Wolf. From what he had discovered, the Wolf supplied the villagers with food when Farrington tried to starve them into submission. It was a messy business and one in which Rolf rather wished he had not become involved. But settling tensions in the area was a part of his responsibility and it seemed that, sooner or later, he would have to take on Farrington in one form or another.

But other than the evictions, which Rolf reluctantly acknowledged was within Farrington's rights as a landlord, none of the stories of brutality could easily be confirmed. Regretfully, Rolf realized he would have to become friendlier with this detestable man in order to discover how best to bring him into line with the King's wishes. Swallowing his distaste for the task, Rolf leaned forward in his chair.

"So, Edwin, tell me about this urgent matter that has brought you here at such an hour."

Edwin thoughtfully ran his finger lightly across the top of his glass of brandy, regarding Rolf from beneath pale brows. "I've heard that you've captured several of the Wolf's men. I would like to question them about thirty head of cattle that recently disappeared from my property."

"I'm afraid that won't be possible."

"You refuse me the right to question the heathen?" Edwin said, raising an eyebrow in surprise.

"I refuse you nothing, Edwin. The prisoners escaped last night. I managed to recapture only three of them. They are too badly wounded to be questioned."

"Escaped?" Farrington exclaimed darkly. "Was it the work of the Wolf?"

"Not exactly. That honor goes to a young Scottish lass who slipped past her guard and managed to free the prisoners. I presume the Wolf was lying in wait outside the castle to take them to safety. I recaptured the girl but she refuses to talk."

"Damn," Farrington swore angrily, then paused, considering. "What do you know of her?"

Rolf slowly swirled the liquid in his glass, eyeing at it thoughtfully. "Very little, other than she's apparently one of the Wolf's followers. I made the unfortunate mistake of underestimating her. It appears as if Scottish women are quite unlike English ladies."

"Whores, all of them," Farrington spat out. "She sounds like a woman in need of a lesson. If you really want information from her—turn her over to me."

Rolf's expression abruptly darkened, his eyes hardening. "Your offer is generous, Edwin, but I assure you that I require no help in getting the information I need."

"Of course not," Edwin replied smoothly. "I did not mean to suggest otherwise. And I would like to take this opportunity to express my gratitude for your help in protecting my holdings. I only want it to be known that I am at your full disposal—in whatever capacity I may be of use to you. This includes the questioning of the prisoners. I have proven modestly successful at that, you see."

Rolf took another sip of his brandy and noted the odd gleam in Farrington's eyes. He knew instinctively that the man enjoyed torture. He had seen that same look in other men's eyes after a battle when they roamed the field, taking pleasure in killing the wounded and helpless. Rolf had always severely punished any man he found participating in such activities. But he had been a commanding officer then. Here in Scotland he had no such authority over Farrington and both men knew it. Moreover, Rolf was fully aware that Farrington's respect for him came solely from the fact that he had been sent by the King to protect Farrington and other English landlords in the area. Rolf knew that if he wanted any control over Farrington, he would have to fully exploit that advantage.

Rolf set aside his glass and stood up. "I will make every effort to determine the whereabouts of your missing cattle. I would also like to suggest closer cooperation between the two of us. If you would be so good as to share any information you might come across concerning the activities of the rebels, I would be most grateful. I'm certain the King would be appreciative as well. I will be glad to pass along word of your assistance to him."

Farrington smiled coolly and stood, inclining his pale head toward Rolf. "I am most grateful for His Majesty's concern. Believe me, I am as anxious as you to be done with the illegal activities of these barbaric heathens."

Nodding, Rolf escorted him to the door, calling for Andrew. The young man appeared almost instantly. "See our guest returned to his mount," Rolf ordered crisply before turning to Farrington. "Have you need of an escort?"

Farrington shook his head. "No, I've plenty of my own men with me. I have no desire to be set upon by the Wolf while I traverse the short distance to my estate."

Rolf nodded in understanding and after the men had exchanged a few more polite words, Farrington left. With the man finally gone, Rolf wearily sank into a chair, stretching his muscular legs out in front of him. The events of the past few days were catching up with him. The cleverness of the Wolf, the stubborn, fierce pride of the Scots and the queer gleam in Farrington's eyes as he contemplated torture . . . God's wounds, this was a bloody mess.

And, of course, lest he forget, there was the most intriguing element in all of this—the fiery

Scottish lass who was proving to be a most challenging opponent. One moment he felt like throttling her—the next moment he wanted to drag her into his arms and taste the heady sweetness of her kiss.

Rolf stood wearily, running his fingers through his dark mane of hair. Whatever the mystery behind the intriguing woman with sky-blue eyes, it would have to wait until another day. He was desperately in need of a good night's sleep and, by God, tonight he meant to have it.

The next three days passed uneventfully for Megan. She was permitted to tend the wounded men, surprised but grateful that Rolf had not insisted they be returned to the dungeon.

Thankfully, her clansmen were showing marked improvement. The lad, Lachlan, could now sit up and take broth with his own hand. Megan had removed the bandage from one of Douglas MacLeary's eyes, breathing a sigh of relief when he reported that he still had partial sight in it. The other eye remained behind a makeshift eyepatch after Megan had examined it, fearful he might never regain sight in it. Hugh Graham, the third prisoner, had a broken leg and a deep slash on his neck. Megan had cauterized the wound on his neck with a hot knife the first night he had been brought to her, and then had wrapped it in a warm poultice. Although Megan knew a frightful scar would result, she was relieved to see that it was healing properly.

She was surprised that Rolf had not yet attempted to question the wounded men. Secretly she feared he was simply waiting for them to heal so they could remain conscious under torture. Grimly, she pushed that troubling thought aside. She had not seen him for days, but from what she managed to glean from Abigail, he was leading his men on rounds about the forest, determining a new strategy for capturing the Wolf.

On the afternoon of the fourth day, Megan was sitting in her bedchamber, mending some of her clansmen's clothing, when she heard the bolt being drawn across the door. Thinking it was Abigail, she did not pause nor look up from her sewing.

"Where did you get the needle and thread?"

Megan glanced up, stopping in mid-stitch when she heard the rich timbre of Rolf's voice. He leaned causally against the doorway, dressed in a cream-colored lawn shirt with full sleeves and a tan pair of breeches. His short waistcoat was adorned with finely trimmed braid and worn open.

"Abigail . . . gave them to me," she stumbled, startled by his sudden appearance. "I didn't see any harm in seeking permission to mend a few o' the men's clothes."

Rolf folded his hands across his chest. "So Abigail has fallen under your command now, has she?"

"Don't be ridiculous," Megan countered quickly. "She only responded to a simple request."

Rolf shook his head. "Nothing about you is simple, Megan. But as surprising as it may be, I've not come to argue, but to invite you to take a ride about the grounds with me."

"Take a ride?" she asked. Whatever she had

expected from him, it was not an invitation for a ride.

"Yes, you know, two riders, two horses. Will you join me?"

Megan carefully laid the mending aside and stood, smoothing her skirts down. Folding her arms across her chest in a stance similar to his own, she glared at him mistrustfully. "Somehow I doubt that ye wish just to see me on a horse. What do ye really want, Englishman?"

"Above all, I want you to stop calling me Englishman. My Christian name is Rolf. I give you permission to use it."

Megan raised an eyebrow. "Do ye order all o' your prisoners to call ye that?"

The corner of Rolf's mouth twisted wryly. "In all truth, I find the lack of titles among the Scottish to be quite refreshing. As you have permitted me to call you Megan, it is only fair that I insist you use my Christian name."

Megan shook her head. The thought of calling him by his name made her uncomfortable and implied a far more intimate relationship than she was willing to acknowledge.

"Well?" Rolf repeated when she didn't answer. "Will you join me in a ride or do you prefer to remain here locked in your chamber?"

Megan glanced quickly at the open window. The sun shone brightly, spilling across the wooden floor. The breeze was cool but refreshing. She suddenly had an overwhelming urge to be outside and feel the cleansing wind against her skin.

"I don't have a cloak," she said quietly, turning back to look at Rolf.

"I'll have Abigail fetch one for you."

She paused for a moment more before nodding her agreement. Concealing his grin of victory, Rolf strode to the door, holding it open for her. As they left the chamber, the guard stiffened in attention, nodding sharply to Rolf.

With a firm hand under her elbow, Rolf guided her down the front stairs and left her alone in the entranceway while he searched for Abigail. He returned minutes later with a long black cloak, its collar lined with fur. While Megan stood stiffly, he helped her into it, fastening the pearl clasp at the front. She held her breath but said nothing as he lifted her hair from beneath it, his fingers lightly brushing against her neck and jaw. For a moment their eyes met and then Megan stepped back, unwilling to acknowledge the spark of attraction she felt leap between them.

Rolf did not press the matter either and instead, led her out into the bright sunshine. Once astride a beautiful mare, Megan felt the tension within her ease. It was a beautiful winter day and the sun felt warm on her face despite the cool wind. She had not been outside for days and did not realize how much she missed it. Taking the reins in her hands, she looked over at Rolf.

"Where are we going?"

His head was uncovered and his dark hair gleamed in the sunlight as he leaned toward her. "There is a lake not far from here. I thought we'd ride there and back."

"Alone?" she asked curiously.

Rolf urged his stallion closer. "We won't be completely alone, Megan. My men will be a discreet distance away. So I wouldn't recommend any thoughts of escape or rescue."

She tossed back her head and laughed, her hair tumbling free of her ribbon. "Och, how little ye know o' me, Englishman. I gave ye my word I'd no' escape as long as ye permitted me to treat the wounds of the men. Do ye no' believe me?"

Rolf smiled wryly. "I've learned not to underestimate you. I never make the same mistake twice."

"Then ye have naught to worry about, do ye?"

"Quite the contrary. I'm certain I don't worry enough."

She laughed again, shooting past him and spurring her horse into a gallop. Rolf's momentary annoyance fled as he watched her ride. Despite her cumbersome skirts, she'd managed to fling her leg across the horse, preferring to ride it astride rather than sidesaddle, as he had helped her mount. To his vast amusement, he noticed that a great deal of her stockinged legs were visible and her unbound hair streamed out behind her like a dark, fluttering banner. Entranced by the magnificent sight, Rolf suddenly wondered how it would feel to harness all of that passion and spirit for himself.

Shaking his head, Rolf pressed his thighs against the side of his stallion and galloped forward, soon overtaking her. He raced her, side by side, until they reached the edge of the lake. Pulling hard on the reins, he came to a stop. Megan pulled up alongside. Exhilarated, she brushed the hair from her eyes, her cheeks flushed pink from the ride.

" 'Tis a fine mare ye've permitted me to ride," she said breathlessly. "But your stallion is mag-

nificent." She eyed his horse with such envy that
Rolf could not help but laugh.

"Yes, he's been an excellent mount," Rolf
agreed, sliding off the horse. Stretching out his
good hand, he helped her out of the saddle.

Megan dismounted, her gown bunching up
around her thighs. When she saw him staring,
color flooded to her face.

"I'm no' used to wearing such a fine a gown
when I ride," she said stiffly, brushing down her
skirts. "I forgot how clumsy I am."

Rolf thought her anything but clumsy, but
held his tongue. He didn't want to say anything
that would bring her guard back up, especially
since he was enjoying a rare glimpse of her un-
bridled spirit. Turning, he opened the leather
pack on his saddle and pulled out a large sack.

"What's that?" Megan asked curiously.

"Food, among other things," Rolf replied.
Upon seeing her blank look, he gave her a mysterious smile and indicated with a quick jerk of
his head that she was to follow him.

Puzzled, Megan set out after him, stepping in
the holes his boots made in the snow. She
watched as Rolf approached a large tree and
pulled a blanket from the sack. As he calmly unrolled it and laid it down on top of the snow,
Megan stared in disbelief.

"Have ye lost your mind or is this some kind
o' odd English tradition? A picnic in the middle
o' winter?"

Rolf grinned. "Why not?"

"Well, because it's daft."

Rolf laughed heartily. "I do admit to having
an ulterior motive. I brought you here this afternoon to suggest a temporary truce. For the

time we spend here, I'll ask you no questions about the Wolf or his activities." Grinning, Rolf sat down, opening the sack and rummaging around in it. After a moment, he looked up as if surprised she had not yet joined him.

"Is my offer of a truce accepted?"

Mistrustful of his intentions, Megan opened her mouth to answer in the negative, but he flashed her a smile so boyishly winsome that she felt her suspicion melt beneath its warmth.

"No questions about the Wolf at all?" she asked warily.

"I give you my word."

She studied his face, searching for a hint of deception. When she could find none, she sighed. "All right. I accept your offer o' a truce. But just for now."

"I assure you, I wouldn't dare to ask for more," he replied gravely.

Megan gingerly seated herself on the far side of the blanket, carefully arranging her skirts. Despite the feeling that she was participating in something absolutely ridiculous, she could not shake the lighthearted feeling that was taking root within her. A picnic in the middle of winter? Why it was outrageous, silly and. . . . and a welcome change, she admitted wryly.

In fact, Megan could not stop smiling as Rolf reached into the bag, carelessly tossing a flask of wine, legs of chicken and several oatmeal cakes onto the blanket. She scrambled to catch everything he cast out, giggling at their silliness. Rolf joined her, his own laugh deep, warm and rich.

The food was wonderful and Megan feasted on it with unabashed enthusiasm. She noticed that Rolf, too, seemed to be enjoying himself, eating steadily through a pile of chicken legs and washing it down with wine. She could not help but tease him when he ate seven oatcakes in a row.

"Do all Englishmen eat like ye?" she asked.

"Oh, I've never suffered from a lack of appetite," he said, patting his stomach. "Unfortunately, I'm not always able to eat this well. Today, however, all of this fresh air and stimulating conversation has seemingly made me famished."

Megan smiled. "Aye, there's naught else like the air o' the Highlands, especially wi' the breath o' spring so close. And when spring does come, the whole glen comes alive with the blooming o' the gorse brush, yellow buttercups and purple heather. There's no place in the world as beautiful as the glen in spring." Realizing how enthusiastic her voice sounded, she looked over at him embarrassed. "I should warn ye that 'tis a folly to ask a Scot about his home for he'll speak on and on without end."

Rolf flashed her a disarmingly winsome smile. "There is no need to apologize. I find your description of Scotland to be exceedingly refreshing. It is quite unlike most descriptions usually given of London."

"What is your home like?" she asked curiously.

Rolf reached out and took the flask. "Frankly, I don't spend much time at my estate. I am a soldier by training, as my father was before me. I used to visit home when my father was still alive because I enjoyed his company. But after his death, I found it difficult to return. The estate is mine now, of course, but I still find myself looking over my shoulder as if my father were still there. Without him, the castle seems to have little life of its own."

"Were ye close to your father?"

"I admired and respected him greatly. However, as a child, I saw very little of him. My mother died when I was three. I was raised primarily by the servants and an army of tutors. They ingrained in me the importance of education and training so that the only heir to the St. James estate would be fully capable of serving his sovereign. I know you would dare to disagree with me, but King George is a good man. In all his dealings with me and others in the court, he has always been fair and generous. I owe him a debt of gratitude for that."

"Do ye have many responsibilities at the court?" Megan asked softly.

Rolf grimaced at the reminder, lifting the flask to his lips. After taking a drink, he set the bottle aside, his fingers resting lightly around the neck. "Unfortunately, when I am in residence, I do have responsibilities there. To be truthful, I find it rather unpleasant. The court is filled with a plethora of sanctimonious fools pretending an interest in politics while really plotting ways to undermine the King. Then, when those activities bore them, they gossip incessantly and devise outrageous methods to bed each other's wives. I much rather prefer the military, where a soldier's life is based on a sense of honor and duty."

Seeing the look of surprise on her face, Rolf sighed. "Forgive me, Megan. Had you wish for me to tell you of the dazzling jewels, expensive gowns and extravagant balls?"

She shook her head, loose tendrils of her hair curling alongside her cheeks. "Nay, I just expected ye to boast o' your friendship wi' the King and those at court. I thought something like that would be important to ye."

Rolf leaned over close to her, a lock of his black hair falling across his forehead. "Make no mistake of it, Megan. I do value highly my friendship with the King. But other than the King, I have few friends at court. Most of the time, I despise my social obligations. People can be terribly cruel about things they know nothing about."

Megan immediately thought of the stories she had heard of him, including those that he was the Devil incarnate—a man who enjoyed torturing and crippling his enemies, beating women and small children, and who had even murdered his own wife. At this point, these stories contradicted everything she had seen of him. So far, he had not employed violence against her or her clansmen, although he'd certainly had ample opportunity and cause. Mayhap she had been wrong to judge him so quickly.

"It sounds like a lonely place, this London o' yours," she remarked quietly.

Rolf grunted, taking another sip of the wine, while Megan thoughtfully gathered the remains of their lunch, returning them to the pack. When she was done, she settled back on the blanket, looking up at the sky.

" 'Tis beautiful here," she commented.

Rolf rolled to his side, propping his head up with his hand. "You are beautiful," he said softly.

Color streaked across her cheeks. "Why did ye really bring me here?" she asked, turning her head to look at him. " 'Twas no' just for a picnic, was it?"

Rolf shook his head. "Not entirely. I needed time away from the pressure of hunting the Wolf. And truthfully, I find your company quite enjoyable."

"Imagine that," Megan said cynically. "My company enjoyable to an Englishman."

"Not only enjoyable, Megan. I find myself very attracted to you."

"I don't know what ye mean," she murmured.

"I think you do."

She fell silent, returning her gaze to the sky where drifting clouds had emerged and began to partially conceal the sun. Raising a hand to her brow, she inhaled a deep breath. "Ye know, when I was a bairn, I used to sit in this meadow and dream. As a young lass I had so many hopes for the future. My mother used to tease me about all my grand plans. But 'twas from her that I learned to dream, and 'twas she who told me that dreams bloom like flowers in the heart. When I sat here amid the most beautiful flowers in the world, I had a heart full o' dreams."

"Was your life as a child so difficult that you sought refuge in dreams?" Rolf asked softly, his voice mild but interested.

She frowned. "Nay, I had a loving family. But our life was no' without strife and dying. When I was eight, my mother died. 'Twas the fever that took her, but my da always said 'twas brought on by her grief o'er the loss o' her younger sister. Her name was Ellen and she was killed during a raid by the Chisholms. 'Twas all a horrible mis-understanding in the first place, but it started a feud between our clans that went on for five years. Many o' the people I knew were slain. Thomas, a cousin o' mine, was felled when he was but twelve. I found the body when I went to the forest seeking herbs. At first I thought he was sleeping. I shook his arm trying to wake him— thinking he was teasing me. I even laughed." She stopped for a moment as if remembering the scene, the hand on her brow trembling slightly. "But when I rolled him o'er, I saw the blood. He wasn't sleeping."

Rolf felt his heart squeeze in his chest. "I'm sorry," he said simply.

"Och, 'twas just the first time I saw death closely, but 'twould no' be the last," she remarked, her voice tinged with an aching sadness. "Nay, 'twould no' be the last time by far."

Rolf wondered how she managed to suffer so much heartache and yet keep her pride and dignity intact. He wished to reach over and touch her, but feared he might break the delicate thread that was building between them.

"Do you still come here to dream?" he asked quietly.

Megan started slightly as if she had forgotten he was there. After a moment, she shook her head. "Nay, 'tis little opportunity for dreams now. But once these dreams were everything to me."

Rolf fell silent. "I've had dreams of my own like that," he finally said.

Megan blinked in disbelief. "Ye have?"

"I have. I've been a solider most of my life, but sometimes even I weary of the killing and seek a place where I can find peace."

Megan's brow puckered dubiously. "But your

battles have brought ye wealth and glory. Ye mean to say 'tis no' enough for ye?"

"Would it be enough for you?"

"Nay, but I'm no' English. Surely the titles and estates piled upon ye by the King do much to soothe your conscience."

"It helps," Rolf admitted honestly. "But it is not always enough."

Curious, Megan rolled to her stomach. "Do I detect a hint o' a conscience?"

A dry smile touched Rolf's lips. "Perhaps. Are you so surprised?"

"Aye," Megan replied honestly. "I never thought it possible for . . . well, for an Englishman."

"What exactly do you know of Englishmen, Megan?"

She hesitated for a moment. "Well, I know they are cold, arrogant and cruel to women and bairns. Certainly none have a conscience."

Rolf's eyebrow raised several inches. "I see. I presume you've met many Englishmen on which to base this conclusion."

Megan pressed her lips together uncertainly. "Well, no' many, but I've heard tales from those who know your kind well."

"I'm afraid I don't put much stock in gossip," he said, sitting up. He reached across the blanket, capturing her fingers with his good hand. "And you shouldn't either." He lifted her hand to his lips and pressed a warm kiss on the pulse point of her wrist.

"What are ye doing?" Megan asked, snatching her hand away and pressing it against her breast. She was shocked by his boldness, but even more disturbed by the way her traitorous body leapt eagerly to respond to his touch.

"I'm proving a point," Rolf murmured. "Give me your hand, Megan. I promise you that I'll not harm you."

She thought for a moment and then placed her hand in his. Smiling, he turned it over. As she watched in fascination, his tongue lightly grazed across her knuckles one by one. Megan drew in a breath and held it as her pulse skittered alarmingly.

"So, tell me, Megan, is that the touch of a cold Englishman?" Rolf asked softly.

"Nay," she admitted. "But I also said ye were arrogant."

He chuckled, pressing her hand against his cheek. "Do you really think me arrogant?"

The feel of his rough whiskers beneath her fingertips was so intensely pleasurable that Megan feared it a secret method of English torture. "Aye, I do," she answered unsteadily. Her heart was hammering foolishly in her chest, her flesh tingling from the touch of his feather-light fingertips. "For I have no' given ye permission for such liberties."

He lifted his head to look at her, his dark eyes burning into hers. "Do you wish me to stop? Because if you do, all you must do is say so."

Megan hesitated. Saints help her, but she really didn't want him to stop. It was a dangerous proposition, permitting him to kiss her, but for once she longed to cast propriety to the wind and do something reckless, something wild. Perhaps it was just the beautiful sunny day, the wine, or the warm, but rare feeling of late that came from having a full stomach.

"Nay," she whispered. "I don't want ye to stop."

Closing his eyes, he leaned forward, lowering his mouth. She shuddered in pleasure as his warm lips settled against hers.

"God, Megan, you are so sweet," he murmured.

Megan had no idea what made her yield to the Englishman's caress. It was only that it felt so right. Her body seemed to be made of half ice and half flame as his mouth moved across hers with such tenderness and yearning that she felt like weeping. The sweetly intoxicating scents of leather, smoke and wine thrilled her as his tongue slid lightly across her mouth, coaxing and persistently requesting access. When she finally granted it, his tongue plunged inside with such possessiveness and familiarity that Megan felt faint from the sensual sensations pulsing through her veins.

Welcoming him to her, she wrapped her arms around his neck, her lips clinging to his. Dimly, she realized that he was unfastening her cloak, but could not find it within herself to protest. As it fell open to his hands, she shivered from the cool air.

He moved quickly to warm her, pressing her down against the blanket. His mouth slid down her cheek and jaw, eventually caressing the skin along the neckline of her gown. The first daring dip of his fingers beneath the material sent desire streaking through her. She clutched his arm as he slid his hand lower to cup one of her breasts. He circled and kneaded the soft mound until she arched beneath him, her breath coming in short gasps.

Rolf felt his desire increase tenfold when he heard her soft whimpers. Gently he slid the palm of his hand upward from her breasts, across her neck and shoulders, until it came to a halt beneath her chin. As she trembled in anticipation, he again lowered his mouth to hers. Heat seared through his veins as she clung to him, sighing with pleasure. He intensified the kiss, letting his hands roam across her body, exploring the soft curves and mysterious hollows. He ached to possess her, to strip away their clothes and make slow and pleasurable love to her . . .

"My lord?" a voice called out from nearby.

Rolf jerked his head up swearing, looking around to see from where the voice came. "Lord Almighty, can a man not have a moment of peace?" he exploded in frustration.

Megan blinked at his words, seemingly in a daze. Her cheeks were pink, her lips moist and swollen from their kiss. Rolf felt a sweep of protectiveness surge within him. Gently, he reached over and carefully adjusted the bodice of her gown. She suddenly emitted a small cry of shame and fumbled for her cloak, pulling it tightly about her shoulders.

Seeing her distress, Rolf gripped her chin firmly between his fingers, forcing her to look up at him. "Don't be ashamed for what happened between us. We did nothing wrong to seek a little pleasure amidst all the madness."

Megan could not meet his eyes. "I almost gave my body to an Englishman," she whispered in a choked voice. "To my enemy."

"I'm not your enemy, Megan, and you know it."

"Ye were seducing me," she accused, her

cheeks flushing scarlet. " 'Tis why ye brought me on this picnic, was it no'?"

"I'll not deny that I want you," Rolf answered calmly. "But in all truth, had I wanted just your body, I could have taken it long ago. However, I want more than that and I think you do, too."

"My God," she whispered in shame, her shoulders starting to tremble. "What have I done?"

Her eyes were filled with such remorse that Rolf felt his heart constrict. "No regrets, Megan," he ordered her firmly. "You've no cause to be ashamed. And mark my words, we will finish this later."

With those words, Rolf stood and walked away toward the lake. Andrew saw him and waved, running toward them. "My lord, I'm sorry to disturb you—" he began breathlessly, stopping at the murderous scowl on Rolf's face.

"It had better be damn good, Andrew," Rolf replied icily. "For if your words do not stir me, I will take immense pleasure in strangling you with my one good hand."

Andrew swallowed hard, trying both to catch his breath and calm the pounding of his heart. "F-forgive me," he stammered. "I would not have dared to bother you but the other men insisted that I fetch you at once."

Rolf's frown immediately faded, concern softening his rugged features. "What is it, lad?"

"The Scots' village, my lord," he continued breathlessly. "It's burning to the ground."

# *Chapter Eleven*

"Ye must let me accompany ye," Megan said, running to keep up with Rolf as he strode purposefully toward their horses.

"No."

"But ye must," Megan pleaded.

He stopped, his hand closing over hers. "It's too dangerous," he said quietly.

"Dangerous or no', ye need my help," she insisted. "The villagers will be frightened and ye do no' speak their language. 'Twill only make matters worse if ye and your men go charging in there. Permit me to accompany ye. I'll tell the villagers that ye have come to help, no' to harm them."

Rolf remained silent, considering her words. As Andrew and several other of the men came riding up, Rolf swung up onto his horse. "Agreed, but only if you stay behind me and follow my orders without question. Do I have your word?"

Megan nodded as she pulled herself up into the saddle. Giving a sharp command, Rolf slapped the reins on his stallion's neck, leading the group forward. As they neared the top of a nearby hill, Megan could see thick black smoke rising into the air. Her heart quickened with fear and anxiety.

"Blessed saints," she whispered in horrified shock as they looked down on the village below. Fires raged across thatched roofs, and people and livestock ran screaming and shouting between the huts.

Rolf's face turned black with fury as he kicked his heels into the side of his horse, racing down the hill, the others following. When he reached the center of the village, Rolf quickly dismounted, grabbing Megan's reins as she rode in behind him.

"See what you can do to stop the fires," Rolf ordered his men over the din. They scattered quickly to do his bidding. Grimly, Rolf reached up, helping Megan from the saddle. "Stay by my side," he commanded curtly, gripping her hand.

Black, acrid smoke stung Megan's eyes and throat, causing her to cover her mouth and nostrils. She could hardly see where she was going, but Rolf led her determinedly toward a nearby cottage where one fire had already been extinguished. Flames had ravaged most of the roof and one side of the dwelling. Smoldering wisps rose from the wet timber of the door which had burned slightly but was still intact.

"Is anyone here?" Rolf called out, and Megan repeated his question in Gaelic.

No one answered, but Megan heard a small whimper. Stepping into the cottage, she saw a woman with three children huddling in a dark corner among the debris. All of them had soot-covered faces and tattered clothes. Two of the children were crying softly. The woman gasped and crossed herself when she saw Rolf, while the children simply stared at them with wide, frightened eyes.

As Rolf stepped forward, the eldest of the children jumped to his feet. With a small cry, the lad threw himself at Rolf, his fists pummeling the Englishman's stomach. Rolf reached down for the lad and the mother screamed something in Gaelic, sobbing hysterically.

Megan rushed to Rolf's side, clutching his arm as he pulled the kicking child away from him. "She begs for ye no' to hurt him. P-please."

Startled, Rolf looked into Megan's frantic eyes. "I'm not going to hurt the child, Megan. Tell her to be calm."

Megan hastily repeated Rolf's words in Gaelic. The woman stopped her sobbing, but looked fearfully at Rolf.

"Now ask her what the devil happened here," Rolf ordered Megan.

Megan quickly relayed his question. The woman spoke haltingly between sobs, clutching the remaining children to her bosom.

"She says the Englishman on the hill came down demanding to know who had stolen his cattle," Megan translated. "When no one answered to his liking, he had his men burn the village in retaliation."

"Farrington," Rolf said, swearing softly under his breath.

Megan nodded in confirmation before returning her attention to the woman. "She says she doesn't know where her oldest son is," Megan continued. "Some o' the other young people are missing as well. She thinks Farrington took them to his house."

Rolf's frown deepened as he released the child, giving him a gentle push toward his mother. The boy stumbled a few steps and collapsed into his mother's waiting arms. She gathered him possessively to her bosom, giving Rolf a grateful glance and whispering something.

"She thanks ye for no' harming the boy," Megan reported quietly. "Since he dared to strike ye, 'twas your right to do so, had ye wished."

Rolf stiffened as though she had struck him. "The woman actually thinks it's my right to harm a child?" When she nodded, he swore softly. "Christ's blood, tell her no matter what she has heard about me, I do not harm children."

Megan knelt down beside the woman and spoke rapidly with her. Amazed, Rolf watched how easily Megan soothed the woman by murmuring softly and placing a comforting hand on her arm.

"What did you tell her?" Rolf asked her when she finally stood.

"I told her that you do no' harm bairns."

Rolf pursed his lips. "Surely it couldn't have taken you that long to tell her that."

Megan hesitated for a moment. "I also told her that ye would bring food and blankets for her family," she admitted.

Rolf looked at her in stunned amazement. "You told her what?"

She lifted her chin, meeting his icy gaze straight on. "There are women and bairns in this village who will either starve or freeze to death tonight if they are no' given assistance. 'Tis the fault o' the English that they are in such straits. If ye are serious about bringing peace here, 'twould be a good start."

Rolf's hand shot out and circled around her wrist. With one firm yank, he pulled her to his chest. "Don't you ever give me an order again or I'll—"

"Kill me?" Megan finished for him, her voice hard with bitterness. "Do ye think I care what happens to me? Look around ye. People are suffering needlessly because o' ye and your countrymen. Casting people from their homes and brutalizing them—'tis naught but a game for ye."

Rolf's fingers tightened around her wrist and Megan gasped at the ferocity of his glare. "I didn't do this, Megan, and contrary to your belief, I don't approve of these kinds of tactics."

"But Farrington does," she countered angrily. "And your King has given him the right to do so. Does that make ye feel proud to be an Englishman?"

Anger glittered bright in his dark eyes. "I'd advise you to lower your voice," he ordered, his tone deceptively calm. "You are frightening the children."

A quick glance over her shoulder confirmed that the family was staring at her with terrified eyes, presumably because she dared to raise her voice to the Englishman.

"Don't worry, he won't hurt me," she said reassuringly in Gaelic before glancing up at Rolf's angry face. "I hope," she added in the same breath.

The woman looked at her doubtfully but said nothing. With a firm pull, Rolf led Megan from the cottage toward the village center. Megan saw that Rolf's men had managed to extinguish most of the fires. People were huddled in small groups, crying, moaning and speaking softly to one another. One of the villagers, a young woman, recognized Megan and ran to her, lifting the bottom of Megan's skirts to her cheek. Megan knelt down and gathered the woman in her arms, murmuring soothingly.

"Do you know her?" Rolf asked curiously.

Megan nodded. "Aye, she is a friend o' my family's."

"Why is she treating you like royalty?"

Megan glanced up at him wryly. " 'Tis an odd way o' looking at things, Englishman. Can't ye see that she is frightened?"

Rolf did indeed see that the girl was terrified, but for a brief moment before she had clutched Megan's skirts, he had distinctly seen something else in her eyes. Hope. And as he now looked at the ragged group of villagers, he saw unconcealed looks of relief and expectation.

Rolf thoughtfully returned his gaze to Megan's face. "Do you know many of the people here?"

Megan quickly scanned the tired and frightened faces. "Aye, some."

"Good. I want to find out exactly what happened. Do you think they will speak to you truthfully?"

"Perhaps," she replied, drawing the young woman to her feet. After they exchanged a few whispered words, the woman kissed Megan's hand gratefully and stepped back to the shelter of the crowd.

Rolf frowned, looking down at her. "What did you promise her?"

Megan tilted her head back. "What makes ye think I promised her anything?"

"Megan," he growled warningly.

"Och, all right. Ye have a fierce temper, ye do. I promised her food and blankets as well."

"Damnation, woman" he swore softly. "You are sorely trying my patience."

" 'Tis no' that much o' a sacrifice for ye," Megan countered quickly, realizing that she may have pushed him too far. "But for these people, 'tis a matter o' life and death. Please . . . I ask ye to help them."

Rolf raised his eyes slowly to her face, oddly touched by her sincere request. For a long moment their eyes met and held. Finally Rolf broke the gaze.

"First ask them for an accounting of what happened."

Megan complied, translating Rolf's questions. The villagers repeated stories similar to the one they had already heard. Sickened by their graphic description of Farrington's actions, Megan felt her stomach churn with anger and disgust. Eventually, Rolf raised a hand, indicating that he had heard enough, and went to confer with several of his men.

Left alone, Megan quickly made her way among the villagers, reassuring and comforting as many as she could. Many recognized her and clamored around, begging and pleading in Gaelic for food, supplies and medicine. Overwhelmed, Megan promised to do what she could, asking in return that they not reveal her identity to the English. The villagers nodded with understanding, looking fearfully at the large Englishman with a crippled hand whose dark gaze often rested on her face.

Finally, Rolf returned, pulling Megan aside. "Tell them that several of my men will return with blankets, food and healing salves for the burns. Those cottages that took the least damage will be repaired so at least the children will have a warm place to sleep for tonight. Upon the morn, we'll take stock of the damage and determine the best strategy to help them rebuild their homes."

Megan stared at him in sheer astonishment, blinking rapidly as if she had not heard him correctly. As she hesitated, he took her by the shoulders, gently turning her to face the villagers. "Tell them," he commanded firmly.

Haltingly, Megan repeated Rolf's words. Before she had finished, she was interrupted by an old woman who shouted something and pointed at Rolf. The villagers fell deadly silent.

"What did she say?" Rolf asked curtly.

Megan swallowed, looking up at Rolf. "She . . . she doesn't believe ye."

Rolf strode over to where the woman was standing. The villagers murmured uneasily and Megan held her breath waiting for his explosion of anger. Instead he gazed directly into the old woman's eyes.

"Tell her she is wrong," he instructed Megan. "I give her my word."

Megan exhaled the breath she held, quickly repeating Rolf's words. Murmurs of surprise rippled among the villagers. The woman's eyes widened in disbelief, but she said nothing more.

Rolf gazed out at the villagers once more before sharply turning on his heel, ordering his men to mount. Once upon his own stallion, he motioned for Peter to approach him. The old man guided his horse beside Rolf's, listening rapidly to his lord's instructions. When Rolf was finished, Peter rode directly to where Megan was waiting on her horse. Taking her reins in his hand, he said, "You will be returning with me and several others to Castle Kilcraig. We are to gather the supplies for the villagers. I require your assistance in the preparation of the needed medicines."

Megan looked over at Rolf, who was speaking quietly with a small group of men. "He will no' return to the castle wi' us?"

Peter shook his gray head. "No, my lady, he has other matters to attend."

"Matters?" she inquired, raising an eyebrow.

Peter nodded soberly as Rolf turned his horse around and rode toward the top of the hill. A handful of his men followed, riding quickly to catch up with him.

"Aye, my lady," he replied as they watched Rolf disappear over the hill. "He is quite anxious to have words with a certain gentleman."

Rolf and his men rode up to the stone manor house that sat atop a nearby hill, looking down over the valley from which he had just ridden. Ordering his men to wait for him, he left the reins of his horse in the hands of an astonished stable boy and strode to the front door. Without

159

bothering to knock, he opened the door, pushing past a stammering servant.

"Where is Farrington?" Rolf thundered at a servant who had rushed down the stairs to intercept him.

"I'm s-sorry, sir. My lord is quite indisposed at the moment. Sh-shall I announce your arrival?"

"I'll annouce it myself," Rolf said grimly, taking the steps two at a time. The shocked servant ran after him, babbling in fear. Rolf flung open the first door at the top of the stairs. When that chamber proved to be empty, he systematically opened each door until he came to the last one, now barred by the trembling body of the thoroughly distressed servant.

"I b-beg you, my lord, please do not disturb him."

"Either move out of the way quietly or I'll move you myself," Rolf said in a chilling voice.

The servant swallowed, clearly sizing up Rolf's large form. After barely a moment's hesitation, he stepped aside, just as Farrington opened the door, casually adjusting the belt on his robe.

"Damn you, Farrington," Rolf swore, his voice so harsh, so furious, that he barely recognized it as his own. "What in the hell do you think you are doing?"

Farrington started in surprise at the unexpected intrusion. A mixture of astonishment and rage crossed his face when he saw Rolf, but he quickly composed himself. Backing into his room, he nodded at Rolf. The servant remained at the door.

Farrington walked over to a small table and picked up a crystal decanter. With a small pop, he removed the lid and poured himself a drink. "May I offer you some brandy? It is quite excellent, you know. It's French."

Rolf shook his head coldly. "I wish to speak with you in private."

Farrington glanced once more at the door and then nodded. He swept out of the room, leading Rolf to a small sitting room farther down the hall. Once inside, Rolf shut the door firmly behind them.

Farrington sat himself in a chair by the fire and stretched his bare legs toward the warmth. "Well, to what do I owe this unexpected visit?"

"Curse it, man," Rolf exploded. "Why did you burn the Scots' village?"

Edwin looked at Rolf in surprise. "Is that what this is all about? For God's sake, man, could it not have waited until tomorrow?"

Rolf smothered a curse, straining to control his rage. "I asked why you burned the village," he repeated through gritted teeth.

Edwin shrugged. "I wanted to teach the villagers a lesson. They should understand that if they protect the Wolf, they will pay."

"You bloody idiot," Rolf grounded out contemptuously. "You aren't teaching them a lesson. You are driving them into his arms. The Scots don't fear you—they despise you."

Edwin's eyes narrowed into tiny slits. "Have care how you speak to me, St. James. I've been in the Highlands nearly two years and I bloody well know how to deal with these heathen. They respect strength. In time, they will respect me."

Rolf walked over to the hearth, his good hand gripping the back of one of the covered chairs.

"Respect is earned, not forced, Edwin. Your reckless actions do nothing but inflame old passions and hatred. For God's sake, man, these are people we are talking about, not animals."

Edwin took a careful sip of his brandy. "Ah, but you are wrong. The Scots are nothing but a savage race. I handle them how I would any animals—with force and fear." He laughed, raking a hand through his tousled blond hair. "I'm afraid that you concern yourself needlessly over a few burnt cottages. I know what I am doing."

Rolf laughed harshly. "I presume that is why the King sent me here to protect you and your holdings. You've made a bloody mess of things. Christ, you don't even realize what you have done. You have given the Scots cause to resist us and for good reason. You've shown them nothing but cruelty."

Edwin angrily set aside his brandy and stood up. "I think I've heard quite enough. Just what the devil do you want from me?"

"Stay away from the villagers and let me handle them."

Edwin's eyes narrowed as his fingers played with the cord of his sash. "You? Why should I agree? Those people are my tenants, living on my property. They are protecting people who have stolen my cattle. I have every right to treat them however I choose and you know it."

"Regardless of your complaints, they are not your personal slaves. If I ever catch you harming any of them again, I'll personally see that the King hears of your actions."

A scarlet flush spread across Edwin's face. "Don't you dare threaten me. There are tales of my own I could relate to the King, including some lurid ones involving your dear departed wife. Did you know that the Duke of Holybrook was not her only lover? She had scores of others, including my brother. Rumors can be easily revived, you know."

Rolf shot across the room so quickly that Edwin saw only a blur of color. With a growl of fury, Rolf grabbed the lapel of Edwin's robe with his good hand, nearly strangling the pale man.

"Let me make one thing clear," Rolf spat out. "If you ever mention my wife again, I'll kill you and be damned with the consequences. Do you understand me?"

Rolf's voice was filled with such unspeakable rage that Edwin nodded in fear, his eyes bulging. "I . . . understand," he gasped in fright. "Please . . . release me."

Rolf pressed his forearm tighter against the man's neck before shoving him away with a grunt of disgust. Striding to the door, he said, "I will wait outside with my men for the Scots you abducted from the village today. I will see a thorough accounting for each of those who disappeared today. If I discover that any of the Scottish youths are still missing, I will personally order my soldiers to take apart this house piece by piece until they are found."

"I would warn you not to make an enemy of me," Edwin said, rubbing his throat. "I have the authority to do as I please here."

"Not for long if I have any say about it," Rolf replied grimly. "Now you will do as I ask or I will make good on my threat."

Farrington did not answer, but as he stared at

Rolf, a silent message of hate flared in his eyes. Rolf met Edwin's stare with a contemptuous look of his own before turning sharply on his heel and stalking out of the room.

# *Chapter Twelve*

Peter had not left Megan's side since they returned from the village. Much to her astonishment, he even brought her supper and then asked if he could join her. Nodding mutely, she watched as the stocky, gray-haired man carried the tray to the table and carefully set it down. Dragging up a second chair, he waited until Megan had seated herself before easing himself down across from her.

For a while, they hardly spoke, sipping their wine and eating the thick meaty stew Abigail had prepared for them. Finally, unable to contain her curiosity, Megan pushed the bowl aside, looking at the older man expectantly.

"Did ye wish to speak wi' me about something, Peter? Ye've no' left me alone for a moment since we left the village."

The older man finished chewing the meat he had just put into his mouth and took a long drink of his wine. After wiping his lips with the back of his hand, he opened his mouth to say something and then shut it, looking decidedly uncomfortable.

"Come, what troubles ye?" Megan asked again softly. "Surely ye have more to do than while away the hours wi' me."

Sighing, Peter pushed away from the table and stood. "I'm not certain I should be doing this. I fear I might bring Rolf's wrath upon me. He doesn't approve of people talking about him."

Puzzled, Megan's dark brows furrowed together, but she said nothing, waiting for him to continue. After a moment, Peter unhappily pressed a gnarled hand to his brow.

"What happened today in the village; it didn't set well with me, my lady. I know how mistrustful you are of Rolf and I didn't want you to think that he had anything to do with it. I assure you that he doesn't hold to those methods. I've served with him for ten years and with his father for five and twenty before that. The St. James men are honorable. What you saw today, it is not the work of an honorable man."

Megan remembered the angry expression on Rolf's face when he had seen the woman and her children huddled together in the smoking ruins of their croft. Then she thought of him standing in front of the villagers, promising to bring them food, blankets and wood for rebuilding their homes. She wondered if he were there now, talking with them and distributing food.

" 'Twas still the work o' an Englishman," Megan said quietly.

"Not all Englishmen are alike, my lady. Rolf

wishes to settle this conflict as peacefully as possible. He'd surely not incite the villagers against him."

Megan's lips formed a mirthless smile. "And why would Rolf St. James care what happens to us? As soon as he's captured the Wolf, he'll disappear from this place, leaving all o' his grand promises behind."

Peter leaned forward, his gray scraggly eyebrows drawing together in a firm frown. " 'Tis simply not true, my lady. I've known Rolf since he was a child and never once in all of those years have I seen him go back on his word. Whatever promises he's given you, they've been offered honestly. He'd not deceive you."

Megan stared at Peter with a skeptical look, and the old man shook his head sadly. "I just wanted you to know the truth, my lady. But you needn't take only my words. I ask you to judge the man for what he has done, not what he hasn't." His face reddened slightly as if he'd just realized how wordy he had been. Clearing his throat, he rose abruptly and strode to the door, pausing with his hand on the latch.

"Why do ye care what I think of Rolf St. James?" she asked him softly.

Peter shrugged. "Perhaps I am just a foolish old man, but I've seen that lad go through too many heartaches because people made false judgments about his character. I thought that perhaps once . . . just once . . . I could put a stop to it. Mayhap I was wrong to come. You'll have to decide that for yourself, my lady."

Without speaking again, he opened the door and disappeared into the corridor. The door

167

closed firmly behind him, the sound echoing loudly in the chamber.

Megan sank back in her chair. The grizzled man did not seem the type to willingly deceive her and she knew he was sincerely fond of his lord. Perhaps he was right. Perhaps she had judged Rolf St. James unfairly.

Closing her eyes, Megan leaned back in quiet contemplation. The Englishman was not making this easy on her. Instead of acting with dishonesty and deception, he was somehow proving to be a decent, honorable enemy. Unfortunately, it made her struggle against him even harder to sustain.

"Rolf will see you in the library now."

Megan nodded at Abigail before following the older woman from the bedchamber. She smoothed down her skirts and sighed deeply in resolve. Since Rolf had returned to the castle, he had not made any move to visit her or inform her of the current situation in the village. Unable to bear the wait any longer, Megan had requested audience with him. Now, one hour later, Rolf had agreed to see her.

Megan paused in front of the elaborately carved oak door of her father's former study, waiting as Abigail knocked politely. The older woman pushed open the door when she heard Rolf grant admittance, giving Megan a small push inside. Once Megan had crossed the threshhold, Abaigail withdrew, quietly closing the door behind her.

Rolf was sitting at her father's desk, papers scattered across its smooth surface. He was writing something, his right hand deftly dipping a quill pen into an ink pot positioned to his right. The room was silent except for the scratch of the pen moving across the paper. Megan had no idea how long she stood there waiting for him to look up, but when he did, she noticed the weary lines on his face and the dark smudges of exhaustion beneath his eyes.

"Sit down," he said shortly, motioning to a chair positioned near the hearth. Without another word, he bent back over the paper and continued writing. Megan sat quietly in the chair, watching him. He was clearly upset about something—his hair looked as though he had dragged his fingers through it a thousand times. His mouth was set in a grim line and a muscle in his jaw twitched as his hand moved quickly across the paper. A half-filled glass of brandy sat on top of some papers and he occasionally reached for it, setting aside his pen to take a swallow as he read what he had just written.

Megan wondered nervously if he had discovered her true identity as the daughter of the Black Wolf. It had been a risk for her to appear in the village, and she knew it. She had been instantly recognized by the wives and children of the clansmen from the village who had lived in the camp. Others knew her only as the laird's daughter, still thinking the legendary leader was in command. As they had clamored about her, anxious for news of their loved ones and begging for help, Megan had realized that Rolf's suspicions were growing that she was possibly someone besides just the Wolf's mistress. In fact, she was certain her identity would have been revealed had the villagers spoken to her in English instead of Gaelic.

Yet however dangerous, the visit to the village had also been useful. Megan had asked one of the women to pass on a message to Uncle Geddes, telling him that the Englishman still had no idea as to her true identity and also that she had not been harmed. The unexpected visit had also permitted her to see first-hand Rolf's reaction to Farrington's brutality. His behavior had been intriguing, to say the least. And again he had acted contrary to her expectations of an Englishman. This is a most curious man, Megan thought, staring at the hard, angular lines of his handsome face. Curious and puzzling.

Rolf finally placed the pen aside and stood up. He moved to the front of the desk, leaning back against its solid weight. For a moment, he simply gazed at her. Then he looked away as if remembering something.

"You wished to see me, Megan?" His voice sounded strained and tired.

She nodded, suspecting it was more than just physical exhaustion that made him look so tired. "Peter would no' permit me to accompany him to distribute the medicine and supplies to the villagers. Why?"

"He was following my orders. I told him to keep you here at the castle."

Megan's eyes flashed angrily. "For what purpose? I gave ye my word that I would no' try to escape as long as ye permitted me to treat the wounded. Did ye no' believe me?"

Rolf sighed, reaching behind him for his glass. "That is not the reason I ordered him to keep you here. I did not think you would try to escape. I simply wished to speak with the villagers alone."

170

Megan drew in her breath sharply. A few of the villagers spoke some English. What if he had somehow coerced them into revealing her identity?

"Why did ye have need to speak wi' them alone?" she asked, fearful of his reply.

Rolf cupped the glass in his large hand. "It's simple, really. I wanted to learn more about you."

A wave of apprehension swept through her and she clasped her hands tightly together in her lap. "I see. So, did ye learn more about me?"

"No, I did not," he answered shortly. "In fact, I found the Scots quite reluctant to talk about you at all."

A ghost of a smile played about Megan's lips. "Then mayhap ye are trying too hard. Besides, there is little of any importance to be learned about me at all."

Rolf's mouth twisted into a cynical smile. "Now why don't I believe that?"

"Because ye're a thickheaded Englishman?" she offered helpfully.

He chuckled briefly. "No, because I sense you are hiding something."

Megan quickly looked away from him and into the leaping flames of the fire. "Everyone hides something, Englishman. Sometimes, we even hide things from ourselves."

Rolf pushed himself off the desk and went to sit in a chair across from her. "Yes, I suppose that is true. I don't hold it against you, Megan. I simply mean to find out what those things are."

"I'll no' tell ye," she said, raising her head to meet his gaze evenly. "No matter what games ye play wi' me, Englishman."

171

"I've played no games with you. Everything I've done or promised is the truth."

"Well, I've learned that the truth as ye English know it is much different than we Scottish perceive it."

Rolf didn't answer at once, just continued staring silently at her pensive face. After a moment, he lifted his glass to his lips and took a drink of brandy. "Tonight the villagers were given food, blankets and medicine. My men and I spent several hours repairing the roofs and walls of some of the cottages to give the children a warm place to sleep. We'll spend some more time there tomorrow, and the next day, and as many days after that until the village is back to normal. Is that truth enough for you, Megan?"

Megan's eyes reflected genuine surprise. "Just what do ye hope to accomplish by helping the Scottish?"

He leaned back in the chair. "I've already told you that I have been instructed by the King to bring peace to this area. I intend to do just that. I hope the Wolf will be able to see for himself that I am an honorable man who will bring a peaceful resolution to this senseless conflict."

"But what o' Farrington? Does he share your sentiments?"

Rolf frowned, his eyes level under drawn brows. "I'll manage Farrington."

"What he did to the village was despicable," she argued. "The Wolf will surely seek revenge."

"I am well aware of that. But I have a plan." Rolf watched as an undeniable interest sparked in Megan's eyes. Holding back a smile at her insatiable curiosity, he stood and bent to pick up the fire iron.

"The man whom I questioned in the dungeon—the man by the name Kincaid—is he truly your father?"

A twinge of alarm went through her. "Why are ye asking me that?" she asked warily.

Rolf jabbed at the peat blocks, sending sparks hissing through the air. "My plan depends on my being able to trust you. Is he your father or not?"

Megan swallowed hard, feeling a sweep of regret that she had to lie to him. "Aye, he is my father."

"His loyalty lies firmly with the Wolf?"

"Aye."

"And you, Megan. Does the Wolf trust you?" For this question, Rolf turned around to face her. His dark eyes were hooded like those of a hawk and she could feel his gaze boring into her.

"He trusts me," she whispered softly.

Rolf studied her thoughtfully for a long moment before turning back to the fire. "Then I believe my plan might work."

Megan said nothing, only bowed her head, unable to hold his penetrating gaze. Certain the lie was evident in her eyes as well as on her face, she concentrated on her hands, which were still tightly clasped in her lap. She felt an odd sense of shame for having lied to Rolf, but reminded herself that he was nothing more than an Englishman who had taken her prisoner and killed and wounded several of her clansmen. His good deeds for the village notwithstanding, she could ill afford to trust him. To her knowledge, the English had never in past experience proven to be trustworthy, and she could not risk the future of her people by falling so easily for the polished words of this man.

173

"What do ye want from me?" she asked quietly.

"I've decided to release you if you promise to take a message to the Wolf."

Megan's mouth dropped open in astonishment, utterly unprepared for his announcement. "R-release me?" she stammered, unable to believe she had heard him correctly.

He carefully placed the fire iron back against the bricks and straightened, shaking the dirt from his hand. "Yes. I want you to personally present the Wolf with my offer of general amnesty to his men as long as he turns himself in to me."

Megan snapped her mouth shut, her mind working furiously. After a few moments she found her wits and voice. "What about your promise to offer the clansmen their own land without rent?"

Rolf returned to his seat, stretching out his legs and bracing one boot-clad foot firmly against the leg of her chair. "The offer stands as I stated it to you earlier."

Megan was silent for a long time thinking over his words. "What guarantee do we have that ye will no' simply go back on your word once ye have the Wolf in your possession?"

Rolf shrugged. "What guarantee do I have that the Wolf himself will come and not send another man in his place? Trust has to start somewhere, Megan."

She nodded slowly, absorbing the impact of his offer. For several minutes she was silent, contemplating various aspects of his words. Finally she spoke. "I truly believe the Wolf will take your offer under consideration. But if Farrington continues his brutal actions against the villagers, 'twill be no deal, Englishman."

"I am fully aware of that. In fact when you came in, I was writing a letter to the King about Farrington."

"Insisting that he rescind Farrington's right to the land?" Megan asked hopefully.

Rolf smiled wryly. "One does not *insist* on anything with one's sovereign. However, I am presenting facts that the King may wish to take under consideration when deciding whether or not to take action against Farrington."

Megan nodded as a silent truce seemed to stretch between them. Rolf sat, staring into the fire, his long fingers tapping absently against his thigh.

"Well, what conclusions have you drawn about me now?" Rolf asked after some time had passed. Her eyes were pensive, filled with concern, worry and yet a tiny flickering of hope.

"I promise to see that your offer is fairly considered by the Wolf and his men," she said quietly. "And I will return to give ye an answer to his decision."

"You seem to have remarkable faith that the Wolf will let you do whatever you please," Rolf said with a significant lifting of his brows. "How can you be so certain that he will permit you to keep your end of the bargain?"

Megan lifted her chin, meeting his questioning gaze straight on. "The Wolf is honorable. He will permit me to keep my word."

Rolf thoughtfully stroked his chin as he regarded her. She had an air of dignity and self-confidence that he both liked and admired. In fact, she was the most remarkable woman he had ever met. He felt a stab of regret when he realized that when he released her, there would be no more of their verbal and mental sparing. As his gaze traveled over her face and body, he began to wonder just what it was that he wanted from her.

A soft knock on the door interrupted his unsettling thoughts. Surprised, Rolf rose from his chair. "Enter," he called out.

A servant swiftly entered the room, bowing slightly to Rolf. "A King's messenger has arrived, my lord. He wishes to see you."

"Bring him to me at once," Rolf said as the servant nodded and left the room. Turning to Megan, Rolf extended a hand. She took it and he easily pulled her to her feet. "I apologize, but I'm afraid I need to speak with the man in private."

Megan smiled sweetly. "Och, I could be very quiet and just sit here in the corner. No one would even notice me."

Rolf chuckled, sweeping out his hand toward the door. "I'm certain you would find our conversation fascinating, Megan. But I'm equally as certain you understand my reasons for refusing your request."

"I suppose I do," she said, sighing in resignation. She had just begun walking toward the open door when a tall, elegantly dressed man swept into the room. He was clad in a scarlet coat with long tails made of an oatmeal-colored fabric. His close-fitting breeches and boots matched the color of the tails and his epaulettes were made of gleaming white braid. He wore a powdered wig that was curled just above his ears, and had tucked a fancy black hat beneath one arm. He bowed politely to Rolf and then turned his gaze to Megan. For a moment, their eyes met in shocked recognition. Megan took an involuntary step backward.

"Well done, sir," the messenger said, turning back to Rolf and unbuckling the white pipe-clayed belt that was fastened around his waist. "I can see the King has sent the right man for the odious task of settling things here in the Highlands."

Puzzled, Rolf looked slowly at Megan. Her face had drained of color and she stood motionless, her eyes wide and frightened.

"Just who in the devil are you?" Rolf asked the messenger.

The man stiffened at the harsh tone, his shoulders snapping back smartly. "My name is Owen Rutherford, my lord. I am His Majesty's personal messenger and have often been sent on assignment to this godforsaken land. In fact, this is my third visit to this very castle. I've arrived with a message for you from the King."

Rolf's fingers tightened on the back of the chair where his hands rested. Mixed feelings of dread and anger swept through him. "Do you know this woman?" he asked, dipping his head in Megan's direction.

Owen's bird-like eyes barely glanced at Megan again. "I most certainly do."

Rolf's eyes briefly met Megan's and he saw a look of pleading and desperation in them. He felt his gut clench tightly as he turned back toward the messenger.

"Who is she?" he asked coldly.

Owen looked at him in surprise. "Who is she? Do you mean to say you do not know, my lord?"

"Damnation, man, just tell me who she is."

Owen shrugged. "I met the young lady on two occasions—the most recent being in this very room two years ago when I was conducting negotiations with her father, Robert MacLeod."

Rolf felt as though someone had hit him in the stomach. Abruptly, he clenched his teeth together, biting back the flood of anger that swept through him.

*Her father . . . Robert MacLeod.*

*Megan's father is the Black Wolf.*

Rolf stood very still for several moments, his harsh breathing the only sound in the deadly silent room. After a moment, he strode across the room and took Megan's elbow in a deceptively calm hold.

"I'm afraid you will have to excuse us," Rolf said stiffly, his voice taut with anger. "I shall return shortly to have word with you. But first, I must see Mistress MacLeod safely to her chamber."

"Certainly," Owen said, graciously stepping aside as Rolf steered Megan into the hallway.

As they walked down the corridor in stony silence, Megan stole a glance at him from the corner of her eye. Rolf had a dark and angry look that was unfamiliar to her, even when he had first captured her in the forest. Realizing her situation had just gone from precarious to completely dangerous, she tried not to wince as his grip tightened on her elbow. The entire castle seemed strangely quiet. Yet as they turned the corner of the corridor, Megan was dreadfully certain she could hear the faint laughter of the messenger following them.

# *Chapter Thirteen*

*"You lied to me!"* Rolf thundered, his voice rebounding harshly from the stone walls of her chamber.

Megan fought to keep from cringing at the furious tone of his voice. "O' course I lied. I was trying to protect myself. What did ye expect, Englishman, that I would tell ye who I was and then grovel at your feet while ye ruthlessly trapped my clansmen in a scheme, using me as bait?"

Rolf slammed his fist down hard against a small table. An unlit candle and its metal holder fell to the floor with a crash. "You took me for a fool," he raged, stalking back and forth across the room like a caged beast. "And I played perfectly into your hands. To think I actually believed you had fled to Ireland. I couldn't imagine that Robert MacLeod would permit his only daughter to live in the hills like some kind of . . . of . . ." He let his sentence trail off.

"Animal?" Megan finished for him angrily. "Go ahead, Englishman, say what ye mean. But don't forget, 'tis ye who reduced us to this."

Rolf swore softly under his breath. "God's blood, once again I underestimate the baseness of the Scots. What kind of man would let his daughter live in such conditions?"

Megan clenched her fists at her side, her voice lashing out at him. "Don't ye dare to speak so o' my father. He wanted me to leave but I refused. Scotland is my home, too, and I would no' leave it behind because some rapacious English King took it upon himself to steal land which had belonged to the MacLeod clan for centuries."

"Damnation, Megan, you will speak of your sovereign with respect," Rolf bellowed furiously.

"He is no sovereign o' mine," she shouted back, her eyes blazing blue fire. "Don't expect me to bend a knee to a man who has shown no compassion or fairness to my people."

"No compassion?" Rolf raged. "By God, I've never met a group o' people so stubborn, so bloody thickheaded as the Scots. I almost wish the King had permitted me to bring an army of men to beat some sense into you people. Have you already forgotten everything I've tried to do here?"

Megan spread her hands wide in an angry motion. "Och, and just what have ye done? Raid our camp, kill several o' the men who tried to defend it, and drag the rest o' us to your dungeon. Then ye make promises to help us while behind our backs your fellow countryman burns our villages to the ground."

"For God's sake, I am not Farrington and you know it."

"Well, how do we know that ye don't secretly approve of his tactics? Did ye really think we would so easily trust ye?"

Rolf took three long strides across the room, grabbing Megan by the shoulder with his right hand and shaking her once, hard. "I thought you would trust me, Megan. I foolishly thought we had established an understanding—a promise of good faith to each other. But you lied to me from the beginning, mocking my words—mocking my attempts at bringing a peaceful settlement to this dispute."

She struggled to free herself from his iron grip. "Don't make yourself out to be all that honorable. Ye were only using me to trap the Wolf. Well, I'm no' simpleminded. Ye tried to seduce and confuse me . . . use any method ye could to extract information from me so ye could destroy my people. Ye never once planned on keeping your end o' the bargain."

Rolf's fingers tightened angrily on her flesh. "Blast it, woman, you are wrong. I had every intention on keeping my word. You were the one who wove a web of deceit: pretending to be nothing more than the Wolf's whore. A part you played exceedingly well, I might add. Lord, what a jest."

Megan stiffened in his grip, crimson flames streaking across her cheeks. Seeing the stricken look on her face, Rolf abruptly released her, stalking over to the window. With a hard yank, he shoved aside the heavy velvet drapery and stood staring out at the starlit sky. A chilly silence throbbed between them. When Rolf finally spoke, his voice was flat and emotionless.

"I apologize. That remark was unfair."

Megan's teeth were clenched together so tightly, she could not open her mouth. Hot tears swam in her eyes and she held them back fiercely, not willing to let him see how deeply his words had shamed her.

Rolf exhaled, willing himself to a calm state, and turned to face her. When he saw the bright glitter of tears in her eyes, he abruptly slammed the flat of his hand against the stone wall. "Damnit, Megan, I'm not a man who takes well to being made a fool. King George will surely roll with laughter when he hears how his trusted lord was deceived by the daughter of the Black Wolf himself. It will provide fodder for the court gossips for months." Scowling blackly, he returned his gaze to the open window.

Megan felt a twinge of guilt that she had brought him such embarrassment, yet she angrily reminded herself that she owed him nothing. He was her enemy and her actions had only been in defense of her people. Taking a small step forward, she lifted her chin.

"Now that ye've discovered who I am, I wish to know what ye mean to do wi' me and the other prisoners."

Rolf did not answer immediately, and kept his gaze focused on the night sky. His fingers drummed restlessly against the stone. "That man Kincaid, whom I held in the dungeon—he was not your father, was he?" he finally asked.

Megan's profile stiffened against the flickering light of the fire. Rolf's mouth twisted with exasperation. "I have only to ask the messenger for a physical description of your father for the answer."

"Then ask him," she snapped.

Rolf folded his arms across his chest, turning to face her. "I'd rather hear the answer from you. I want to know if it is possible for you to speak any words without employing deceit."

Megan jerked her head up angrily, her dark hair spilling over her shoulders. "I didn't lie when I said I would present the Wolf wi' your offer. Nor was I lying when I said I'd return wi' his answer."

"Do you really expect me to believe that your father would let you walk back into the hands of his enemy?"

"He would if he were convinced ye were an honest man."

"I sincerely doubt that, Megan."

"Then we have returned to where we started. Neither o' us believes the other."

Rolf was silent for some time, staring at this proud, stubborn woman who still dared to defy him. "All right then, answer me this. Despite the fact that I was forced to trap you in a raid and take prisoners, have I ever given you reason to believe that I would rescind my promises? Don't answer with your anger, but think about what I've said and done since we have met."

Surprised by the bluntness of his question, Megan hesitated. Rolf St. James was her enemy, a man who represented everything she despised. Yet, in all the time since she had met him, he'd remained true to his word, permitting her to treat the wounded clansmen and refraining from torturing them when they were at their most vulnerable. He had also kept his word to provide food and medicine for the villagers, even helping them to construct shelter for the children. As much as it dismayed her to admit it, he had shown unusual compassion and justness for an Englishman.

"Ye have been true to your word so far," she replied reluctantly. "But I don't trust your motivations."

"Then you judge me unfairly."

"Unfairly?"

"You have yet to give me the benefit of the doubt."

She exhaled in frustration. "Why do ye continue to pretend that ye wish to help us? Ye have a valuable hostage in your possession. Why no' just torture me for information? Finish what ye came to do, Englishman. Beat me and the rest o' my people into submission. 'Tis what ye do best, is it no'?"

"Somehow I doubt that even torture would force you into submission," Rolf remarked dryly.

A soft gasp escaped her, blue eyes flashing disbelief. "Ye wish to jest?"

Rolf sighed. "You have no need to fear torture from me, Megan. Despite my rather disreputable reputation among you Highlanders, I do not harm women or children. I genuinely want to find a way to settle this dispute peacefully. The offers I have given you in regard to your father's people—they still stand. I intend to put a stop to the strife in this area."

"Wi' the English as our conquerors," Megan added, her voice bitter.

"As your landlords . . . for now," Rolf corrected her gently. "I do not dictate the forces of history and neither do you, Megan. Let's simply do our best to see that another generation of children are not sacrificed because of this senseless feuding."

Surprised, Megan realized his words held no hint of triumph or vindication. She heard only the slightest tinge of sadness and weariness, as if the bitterness and deceit of their contention had touched him deeply. Her emotions in a jumble, she walked over to one of the chairs by the fireplace and sat down, folding her hands tightly in her lap. After a moment, Rolf came up behind her, placing a hand on the back of her chair.

"The man who called himself Kincaid," he repeated again quietly. "He is not the Wolf."

She hesitated for a moment and then shook her head in resignation. "Nay, he is no' my father."

Rolf knew it was but a small admission—one he could easily prove or disprove. But to hear it come from her lips was a step forward, a tiny spark that might keep the doors open between their two peoples. And for now, it was all he could hope for.

"You must realize that I cannot release you to take my offer to your father," Rolf said, moving around the chair to face her.

"Because I am too valuable a hostage," she remarked bitterly.

"Yes," he admitted honestly. "And because it is my duty to inform the King of your capture."

Megan nodded wordlessly, his announcement coming as no surprise to her.

Exhaling heavily, Rolf dragged his fingers wearily through his hair. "I'm sorry, Megan. If there was any way to change things between us, I would do it."

She was silent for a long moment. "At least ye've been honest wi' me," she said finally. "I am certain the Wolf . . . my father . . . will still consider your words. He would give more than just his life to save his people."

"Does that include his daughter?"

She looked up quickly. "I would willingly sacrifice my life for the clan. He would understand that."

"Would he really?" Rolf murmured. "I'm afraid I don't believe that."

"Because ye don't understand us," she replied softly. "And mayhap ye never will."

Rolf felt a strange twinge in his chest. Hell and damnation, she was actually causing him to have regrets about having to carry out his responsibilities to King and country.

"I will capture the Wolf, Megan," he said firmly, shaking off his unsettling feelings. "But I won't lie to you. The more I come to know you, the more the task of capturing your father has become damnably distasteful. But that is the way it must be. I have no choice."

"Ye are wrong, Englishman," she answered softly. "We all have choices. But ye've already made your choices and I've made mine. Now we have but to live wi' it."

"What are we going to do, Da?" Robbie exclaimed, thrusting his hands beneath his plaid and striding anxiously back and forth across the snow-covered ground. "We canna just sit here day after day while the Englishman holds her prisoner."

Geddes watched his son's frantic movements, fighting to keep his own concerns from hindering his ability to think clearly. Deliberately, he arranged a calm expression on his face, holding out his hands to the warmth of the small fire. " 'Tis little choice we have and ye know it. The Englishman's raid cost us heavily. The men are in no condition to ride, let alone plot a rescue. We canna act rashly and besides, we've no evidence that Megan's been harmed. The villagers said she appeared well and dared to stand up to the Englishman, even raising her voice to him. We both know that Megan is no fainthearted lass. She'll no' waste the time she has wi' the Englishman. Instead, she'll learn all she can about him and bring that information back to us. 'Tis her way."

Robbie stopped in his tracks, whirling to face his father. "Da, are ye listening to what ye are saying? Meggie is being held by a man who murdered his own wife."

Geddes closed his eyes. "I'm fully aware o' that. But I still dinna think she's been harmed. The Englishman thinks she is my daughter, naught more than kin to a simple man. As soon he discovers there is no information to be gained from her, I'm certain he'll release her to the village like he did wi' the other women and bairns."

Robbie looked at his father incredulously. "How can ye expect him to act so honorably?"

Geddes rubbed his temples wearily. "Haven't ye heard o' his actions? The Englishman and his men have been in the village for the past several days distributing food and clothes and helping the villagers rebuild their homes. 'Tis even said that he confronted Farrington at his own home, warning him to leave the villagers alone."

Robbie spat on the ground. "Lies and deception, all o' it. Ye saw what he did to our camp. 'Tis only some kind o' ruse to lure us into trusting him."

"Mayhap ye are right, but we must consider that he might genuinely be seeking peace wi' us."

"Peace?" Robbie spluttered. "Saints above, Da, I canna bear to hear ye talk so. When did ye become so soft? That English bastard holds Meggie captive—the woman who will be my wife."

"She's a lot more than that, Robbie. By all rights o' our law, that woman is still our laird until she marries or is replaced. Ye know that, son."

"By all the saints, I know that better than anyone," Robbie replied bitterly. "But most o' the men think she is only acting as her father's proxy, no' as our laird. Haven't ye heard the talk about the camp? The whisper grows louder wi' each passing day that the Wolf is dead and we have no one to lead us. We canna keep up the deception much longer, Da."

Geddes sighed unhappily. "Aye, 'tis so. We'll have to tell the rest o' the men o' Megan's deception and soon. I dinna know what will come o' it, other than 'twill make the men certain to seek her release at any cost."

" 'Tis what I've been saying all along."

"Ye are speaking wi' your heart and no' your head, lad. The last thing we want to do is draw attention to her. Besides, ye know full well that we canna storm a well-fortified castle with men who can barely ride or lift a sword. 'Twill only cost more lives. Megan would no' approve o' that."

Robbie swore softly with frustration, hearing the truth in his father's words. His cheeks blazed angrily and his fists clenched helplessly at his side. "Damned and bedamned, Da, 'tis an intolerable situation. I should have never permitted her time to think o'er my proposal. By God, as soon as I see the lass, I'll drag her before the kirk whether she is willing or no'."

Nodding sadly, Geddes crouched in front of the fire, flexing his cold fingers out in front of him. " 'Tis my fault for agreeing to go along wi' Megan's scheme in the first place. But she has a strong mind and all the wit and cunning o' her father. I should have brought the deception to an end a long time ago." Robbie walked over to his father and put a hand on his shoulder. Snow swirled around them like a soft white cloud.

"Dinna fash yourself, Da," Robbie said. "I'll get her back somehow. Ye can rest assured that I'll no' leave her in the clutches o' the evil Englishman for much longer."

# *Chapter Fourteen*

Rolf stood by the open window, letting the cool wind refresh him by lifting the unbound hair from his shoulders. The light in the library was dim and soothing; a single lamp burned softly on his desk and the flickering glow of the fire sent shadows skittering across the leather-bound books in the tall bookshelves. Earlier he had studied the titles, impressed by Robert MacLeod's taste in literature. He wondered again about the clever mind of the Black Wolf and how unfortunate it was that ruin had come to this brilliant man and his family.

As he thought of Megan, the muscles in Rolf's jaw tightened and his fingers drummed restlessly on the windowsill. What an irony. He held his enemy's most valuable possession in his hands, but found himself reluctant to use it to his advantage. Perhaps he was growing old . . .

or just weary of a challenge he had once relished.

The shuffle of footsteps in the corridor interrupted his thoughts. Crossing the room, he pulled open the door just as Peter was reaching for the latch. Megan stood behind him and Rolf quickly ushered her in, motioning with a slight glance of his head that Peter was to wait outside. The older man nodded and took up a stand outside the door.

"Ye summoned me?" Megan asked as Rolf shut the door behind her.

"Yes. I want to speak with you."

Concern flitted across her face, but she said nothing as Rolf guided her to a chair, indicating that she should sit. He did not join her, however, and began to walk slowly across the chamber, his face drawn, his hands clasped behind his back.

"I've asked you here because it is time to inform your father that I am aware of your identity as his daughter. However, I also intend to give him my word that you will not be harmed."

Megan wondered fleetingly what Geddes and Robbie would think when they heard that her true identity had been discovered. More than likely, they would be frantic with concern. She only hoped that they would keep calm and not incite the others into doing anything foolish.

"Therefore," he continued, "I need to know whether there is someone else other than your father to whom I should direct my message."

"Someone else?" Megan repeated blankly. "I don't know what ye mean."

"Curse it, Megan," Rolf exclaimed in frustration. "You aren't making this easy for me. I'm trying to ask you whether you are unwed or with husband."

Megan gasped, staring at him in stunned amazement. Again this unpredictable man had completely caught her off guard. Gathering her wits and voice, she murmured, "Why would such a thing be o' importance to ye?"

Rolf stopped his pacing and stood directly in front of her. "Because if someone held my wife captive, I would be beside myself with concern. It's my duty to reassure your husband, if he exists, as well as your father, that I have no intention of harming you."

Megan searched his face for signs of deceit, but found none. A wayward strand of dark hair had fallen forward onto his forehead. For a fleeting moment, she had the strangest urge to reach up and sweep it aside.

"Well, are you going to answer me," he demanded, "or do I order my men to seek out every church in the area and search their records? I will do it, if it becomes necessary."

Seeing the determined look in his eyes, Megan shook her head. " 'Twill no' be necessary, Englishman. I am unwed."

Rolf felt relief surge through him. Exhaling the breath he didn't know he held, he sat down heavily in the chair across from her, his long legs brushing against hers. "Forgive me for asking. You cannot know how greatly it pained me to think I may have compromised you in some manner."

To his astonishment, she laughed. "Ye were no' so concerned about my virtue when ye thought I was no more than a man's mistress. Why should I believe ye now?"

Rolf refrained from pointing out that it was she who had misled him in the first place. "Because I don't want to see you harmed," he said calmly. "Frankly, I'd like us to try to start over. Honestly."

His voice was so sincere that an unexpected wave of guilt swept through her. She was still continuing to deceive him, leading him to believe that her father was alive. Yet she could see no alternative course of action. She could hardly reveal herself as the Black Wolf and forfeit the promises he had made of pardons and land grants to her clansmen. Given the disastrous consequences of his raid against their camp and Farrington's subsequent actions against the villagers, she had come to believe that Rolf's offer was the best way to resolve this matter peacefully. The only difference was that it was her life, not her father's, that would end. She had no other choice than to preserve her secret until they had the pardons and land grants in their possession.

"Your actions are no' those I expected from an Englishman," she remarked quietly.

"I know. We can't keep behaving in this manner with each other, Megan."

"In what manner?"

"Refusing to work together to end this matter without further bloodshed. We can't keep making truces and then breaking them. Continuing the deceptions and mistrust between us."

Megan opened her mouth to reply and then shut it, staring down at her hands. Rolf took a deep breath. "I understand you have little reason to trust me. Generations of hatred cannot be eased in a few days, months or even years. For all we know, it may take a century or two. But by God, Megan, right here at Castle Kilcraig, I would like it to start with us."

A series of perplexing emotions raced though Megan. "Ye expect me to aid ye in ending the life o' my father and then speak o' peace in the same breath?"

"There is nothing I can do about your father, Megan, and you must know that. But I can protect his daughter and his men. Would he rather have it another way?"

"I'd rather have it another way," she retorted sharply. "I want the English to leave us alone forever."

Rolf sighed deeply. "I'm sorry. But you also know that is not possible. Some things are beyond even my control."

Megan unclasped her hands in her lap. Her anger was evaporating, leaving only weariness from the weight of her responsibilities. "I know. Ye are right, though. My father would give his life for that o' the clans. So would I."

"I'll stand by my promises, Megan. I've given them to you and your father in good faith."

She looked at him curiously. "Your honor is terribly important to ye," she observed. " 'Tis why it pains ye when others misunderstand your actions or judge ye unfairly."

"Why do you say that?"

"Because I suspect 'tis the truth. And because Peter told me it was so."

Rolf smothered a half-curse. "Peter has been talking with you? God's teeth, the man is far too interested in my personal affairs to please me."

A soft smile touched Megan's lips. "He cares for ye greatly. Like a father, perhaps."

"Like an old woman who enjoys gossip," he retorted crossly.

" 'Twas no' something he did easily," Megan responded quietly. "He feared it would bring your wrath upon him."

Rolf nodded grimly. "Aye, and it might still."

"Don't cast your anger on him. He couldn't bear the notion that I might think ill o' ye or your actions against my people."

"Peter has an ungainly habit of attaching too much nobleness to what I do."

"He admires and trusts ye. I see that same admiration and respect in the eyes o' the rest o' the men that serve ye as well. Ye treat them justly and with honor. In our country, 'tis just the traits we look for in a laird."

Startled by her compliment, Rolf inclined his head slightly. "I am honored that you think so."

Megan flushed slightly, not knowing why she had permitted herself to compliment him. It was a dangerous game she was playing; each passing day her feelings for him were becoming more confused. Many of his actions reminded her of the noble way her father conducted himself with friend and foe alike. Whether she wanted to admit it or not, Rolf St. James *had* proven to be a man of his word. Although this realization dismayed her, the harder she tried to ignore the truth, the more it persisted.

Pensively, she stood and moved toward the hearth, reaching out to touch the edge of the mantle with her fingertips. She let her hand trail lightly across the dusty surface. "Did ye know that the MacLeods have been living at Castle Kilcraig for o'er three hundred years? 'Twas my grandfather's home, and his father's before that, and so on for centuries. Here in my da's library, over this very mantle, hung the treasured MacLeod claymore. When we were forced to leave the castle, my da bundled it up and gave it to Jamie. My brother was terribly honored to have that sword. I remember the fierce light in his eyes as it passed from my father's hands to his own. It meant everything to him . . . to us. 'Twas the last symbol we had left o' our heritage." She paused, her blue eyes brimming with unshed tears at the memory. "Jamie was carrying it the day he was killed by Farrington. My da buried that sword wi' my brother. He couldn't bear the thought that even in death, Jamie would be parted from it."

Rolf gazed at her proud, dark profile and the unbound hair cascading down her back in long, thick waves. Coming to his feet, he reached out, taking her shoulders and turning her to face him. "I'm truly sorry, Megan," he said softly. "I wish there was something I could do to change what has happened between our people."

She sadly tucked a strand of her loose hair behind her ear. "I suppose ye have made a start, Englishman. Mayhap ye are right and 'tis time to put aside our pride and hatred and seek a solution that will bring no more bloodshed to this land . . . to my people."

Rolf nodded, his gaze sweeping across her face. Her pale cheeks were flushed from the emotion of their discussion. He longed to reach out with his fingers and touch the softness of her skin, and was suddenly aware of a strange tenderness inside him. With a jolt, he realized that he had come to care for her greatly. He didn't know whether it was because of her unsettling loveliness or her remarkable wit and courage. Whatever the reason, he had the damnedest feeling that for once in his life he was dealing with a woman who had shown herself to be fully his equal.

Yet she was also his captive. Megan MacLeod held the key to his success in the Highlands and he knew he would never leave this place without her father. He had given his word to the King that he would deliver the Black Wolf to London and he was bound by his duty and honor to that promise. But the thought of bringing harm to Megan's father filled him with more regret than he cared to admit.

"Can we put aside our differences and try to resolve this matter together?" he asked, surprised that his words sounded almost tentative, as if he were testing the idea.

She hesitated for only a moment before nodding, her eyes filled with a mixture of pain and sorrow. "Aye, we shall try. But there are things I will no' tell ye, Englishman, nor will I knowingly betray my people. Secrets will still remain between us. However, I'm willing to take those first steps, if we can both agree that 'twill be for peace."

Rolf marveled that she was able to look both strong and fragile. "I'll not ask you to divulge anything that would place your clan in greater danger," he said. "And I give you my word that no harm will come to you."

"Don't make promises that ye may no' be able to keep," she warned softly, gazing sadly into his eyes. "There is still much ye do no' know about me."

Seconds ticked past and they stood silently regarding each other—he marveling at her eyes of blue Scottish fire, and she judging the character of a man she hoped desperately she could trust. Finally, Megan broke the gaze and lifted her skirts, intending to move past him. Rolf raised his good hand to stop her.

"Just one more thing, Megan. I will release one of the prisoners to personally take word of your safety and my offers of pardons and land grants to your father."

She took a moment to digest the information. "Have ye already chosen a man?" she asked.

"The one-eyed man you call Douglas. Other than the wound to his eye, he is fit to ride."

"What guarantees do we have that ye will no' have him followed?"

"He'll be released to the village. For all we know, he may send word to your father through another of the villagers. We cannot follow everyone."

Megan nodded thoughtfully, her mind weighing his offer. "Aye, 'tis true. But I wish to speak privately wi' him first. He'll no' trust your words, Englishman, but he'll trust mine."

Rolf regarded her intently from beneath dark brows. "You will not try to compromise my offer in any way?"

"I give ye my word."

He nodded satisfied with her promise. "Then you may meet with him. But I will first make an announcement to the villagers, telling them I know of your identity but will not harm you."

She looked at him in surprise. "What purpose do ye think that will serve?"

"I wish the villagers to know what I am offering. We both know that they look to your father for protection. When he is taken from here, I want them to know they can come to me for assistance."

"And when ye are gone, Englishman? Who will protect them from Farrington and others like him?"

Rolf exhaled deeply. "I will insist on provisions that will keep Farrington's actions limited when it comes to the villagers."

She thought for a moment. " 'Tis generous, but I don't believe that is the only reason for your announcement to the villagers. I think ye hope to put additional pressure on my father by adding the villagers' voices to those who might wish him to accept your offer."

The corner of Rolf's mouth twitched into a smile. "You are indeed a worthy opponent, Megan. Yes, I do admit to hoping the villagers will help convince your father to accept my offer. But it is not so simple. I do truly wish for everyone to clearly understand the terms of my offer."

" 'Tis odd, but for some reason I believe ye."

The lines on Rolf's face softened. "I'm glad."

Thinking that their conversation was over, she waited for him to move out of the way. When he did not, she looked at him, puzzled. "Is there something else?"

Rolf hesitated as if searching for the appropriate words, then shook his head regretfully. "No, not really. I wish only to say that . . . well, I may not agree with everything you have done, but I understand it. If the truth be known, I myself wouldn't have done anything differently had I been in your position. You've conducted yourself with a dignity befitting your people."

"And ye, Englishman? Have ye made your people proud?"

Rolf shrugged. "I would not presume to judge my own actions. However, I do believe it takes decent people on both sides to put a stop to senseless killing. I'd like to think that here at Castle Kilcraig, the end of this conflict started with us."

She considered his words before nodding. "I'd like to think that, too," she agreed softly.

After a moment, Rolf stepped aside. Megan moved past him, opening the door. "Good night, Englishman," she said quietly.

"Good night, Megan."

After she left, Rolf stood at the open window, welcoming the cool breeze. Finally he extinguished the lamp and left the library, returning to his bedchamber. Once there, he cast off his clothes and stretched out on the bed. He did not embrace sleep at once. Instead he let his thoughts drift back through his conversation with Megan.

From the first moment he had found her in the forest wrapped in the pelt of the Black Wolf, he had sensed something unique about her. Nonetheless, he had never expected such deep emotional feelings to surface concerning her. As astonishing as it was, for the first time in his life, he had met a woman who matched him in intelligence, spirit and passion. And in spite of everything he had done, who he represented, and all the rumors of his misdeeds and his crippling injury, she still did not fear him. Instead, Megan MacLeod was a special and rare woman, drawing her own conclusions, looking beneath the surface and judging him for the man he really was. In doing so, she had somehow awakened a fierce desire within him to know her intimately and gain her confidence and friendship. Never before had he sought such things from any woman—even his first wife. That he would wish for them now, and with the daughter of his sworn enemy, was at the same time frustrating and ironic.

Murmuring a curse, Rolf rolled over to his stomach, ignoring a painful twist in his gut. He had to remind himself that this would soon be over. If all worked out as planned, he would shortly ride away from Castle Kilcraig, leaving Megan MacLeod far behind him. Resolutely he closed his eyes, commanding himself to sleep. But slumber eluded him and instead, visions of a spirited Scottish lass filled his thoughts until dawn.

Rolf knew it was hopeless.

He couldn't stop thinking about her.

# *Chapter Fifteen*

Two weeks passed at Castle Kilcraig with little
incident. Rolf and his men spent most of their
time at the village, helping people rebuild their
homes. Megan was not permitted to accompany
them. Instead, she watched each morning from
her small window seat as he and the others rode
out of the courtyard, not returning until long after dusk. Occasionally she was allowed to take a
walk about the gardens with Andrew, who had
obviously been instructed to keep a close eye on
her. She was also permitted to treat her injured
clansmen, but a guard was always present, preventing them from talking.

Rolf carefully avoided her for most of that
time, until one night he appeared at her door
with a chessboard beneath his arm. Megan
looked at him with surprise, but after a moment
permitted him entrance. Wordlessly, he set up
the chessboard on a small table near the fire.

When all was prepared, he motioned with his hand, inviting her to sit. They played only one game before Rolf took his leave, the two of them saying almost nothing to each other.

In this non-threatening manner, they began a nightly custom. As the evenings flew past, Megan felt herself become more accustomed to him, more comfortable with him. As players, they were evenly matched, although her daring and reckless moves kept him unbalanced and challenged. More than once, she managed to lure him into a foolish move, causing him to lose the game. Surprised, Rolf told her he admired her unorthodox and spirited style.

Yet during their games, Rolf never spoke of the Wolf or of his efforts to find her father. Their conversation instead drifted to neutral subjects such as art, literature and science. Rolf admitted that he was astonished by her intelligence and delighted by the knowledge that she even spoke a little French. After some encouragement, she hesitantly conversed with him in the language. Fascinated by her quick mind, Rolf could not help but wonder how she had become so well educated. One night, he asked.

A smile flitted across Megan's face at his question. " 'Twas all the fault o' Jamie. I adored my brother and followed him about constantly from the time I was a wee bairn. Whatever Jamie did, I wanted to do, too, only better. My mother indulged me while I was young, but after she died, there was no one to guide me toward more womanly pursuits. 'Tis no' to say that no one tried—poor Janet Glennie spent two years teaching me embroidery and weaving. But even she lost patience, throwing her hands up in despair and telling my da that I had more talent wi' horses and the sword than I did wi' a thread and needle. She was right at that. 'Twas much more fun to be riding outdoors wi' Jamie than staying inside wi' a group o' somber women who did little other than complain o' their ailments and gossip about the servants. Nay, 'twas no' a life for me."

Rolf smiled, imagining her as a young woman, stubbornly insisting on remaining by her brother's side. A free and untamed spirit, indeed. Unbidden, the image of her riding toward the lake, her hair streaming out behind her, leapt to his mind.

"So your father permitted you to study with your brother," Rolf commented.

Megan nodded, reaching up to absently finger a strand of her long dark hair. "Aye, but 'twas an awful scandal. My da forbid it at first and Jamie thought I had gone completely daft. Ye see, Jamie didn't take to learning too well. But I told my da that I would just listen verra quiet and no' interfere wi' Jamie's studies. He wasn't too keen on the idea but he finally permitted me."

For a moment, Rolf watched as her remarkable blue eyes lit up happily with the memory. He felt his heart stir. It was no wonder her father refused her little. Had she begged him with that same intensity in those sky-blue eyes, Rolf was certain his resolve would crumble to dust as well.

"But you just didn't sit there quietly, did you?" he inquired, leaning back in his chair.

"Och, 'twasn't hard to win o'er our tutor, old Francis Tosh. He didn't have many friends o' his own as Francis was a Lowlander. Many o' our clansmen believed he was too friendly wi' the English because he had studied in Edinburgh under the tutelage o' an Englishman." She shrugged, her hand dropping to her lap. "But he taught us our lessons well, so the clan tolerated him. And my da paid him well, so he tolerated us. All in all, 'twas a satisfactory arrangement."

"And you excelled in your studies," Rolf remarked.

She laughed. "Jamie used to get so angry wi' me. He didn't care much for science or geography. He was much more interested in history and military strategy. But I liked those subjects, too. We spent many fruitful hours in front o' this very fireplace discussing politics and law. Jamie always had a keen sense o' what was right. He would have made a good laird o' the MacLeod clan. He was sometimes a hothead and a wee bit reckless, but one of the kindest and fairest persons I ever knew. I loved him wi' all my heart." Her voice caught slightly with emotion and she leaned over the board, picking up one of her chess pieces, clutching it tightly in her hand. "I miss him terribly."

After a moment of silence, Rolf leaned across the board, placing his hand over her fist. "I'm sorry, Megan."

To his astonishment, a tear slipped down her cheek. "Damn ye English," she whispered angrily. "How could ye take the life o' a young man so full o' life and passion?"

Rolf felt his heart tighten with emotion, feeling utterly helpless for one of the few times in his life. "I wish I could have met him."

Megan quickly drew her hand away from his, dashing the tears from her cheeks as if embarrassed. "He would have killed ye on the spot. He did no' have much o' a fondness for the English."

"Hatred can be overcome."

Megan permitted herself a small laugh. "Ye didn't know my brother. 'Twouldn't have been that easy, Englishman."

"I didn't say it would be easy."

Megan slowly unclenched her fist, studying the board and then placing her piece down deliberately. "Have ye any brothers or sisters o' your own?"

Rolf studied the board for a moment, analyzing her move before making his own. "No," he said, setting down his own piece. "After my mother died, my father never remarried. It wasn't necessary as he already had a legitimate heir to the St. James estate. Besides, he knew well that a mistress is far less trouble than a wife."

Megan lifted her head in surprise at the note of bitterness in his voice. "Ye don't sound as if ye have much respect for the union of matrimony."

"I'm afraid my experience with this matter has been less than satisfactory."

"So I've heard," she said, the words slipping from her mouth before she could stop them.

There was a moment of strained silence before Rolf spoke, his voice sounding cool and aloof. "And what exactly did you hear, Megan? That I rid myself of my wife?"

"Did ye?" she asked softly.

Rolf laughed harshly, but Megan saw no humor grace his eyes. "Well, it makes for a magnificent tale and did wonders for my reputation. The ladies of the court found it titillating gossip, indeed. The men, on the other hand, secretly feared me, wondering what kind of man would ruthlessly murder his wife and be damned with the consequences."

"Ye didn't answer my question," Megan repeated quietly. "Did ye do it?"

Rolf's eyes hardened. "Would ye believe me if I told you I didn't?"

She thought a moment before nodding. "Aye, I think I would. I've seen how kindly ye've treated the bairns and women o' the village. And ye've raised no hand in violence against me, though ye've had plenty an opportunity."

He cocked a dark eyebrow mockingly. "Your evaluation of my character surprises me. Am I not a detestable Englishman capable of nothing more than murder and deceit?"

Megan smiled faintly. "Ye may be many things, Englishman, but I don't see ye as a man who would knowingly murder his own wife."

Rolf stiffened, the muscle in his jaw clenching tightly. "Well, I'm afraid you are wrong about me, Megan. I did kill my wife."

Megan gasped in shock, her face paling. "Ye did?"

"Yes, I did." Abruptly pushing himself up from the chair, Rolf stood in front of mantle, his back to her. "Caroline was very young when I married her. Naive, fragile and beautiful. She needed a husband, not a soldier who was rarely home. One summer when I returned to London after more than a year on campaign, I found her five months with child. She'd had an affair, numerous affairs to be exact. I don't know who the child belonged to . . . I don't know if she even knew. She confessed everything, overcome with guilt and heartache. To say the least, I was furious, enraged. I accused her of shaming our family and making a mockery of our marriage. I swore to banish the bastard child from our estate forever."

He turned to face her, the look in his eyes dark and tormented. "That same night, she threw herself out of the tower window. I killed her and the babe as surely as if I had pushed them myself."

Megan drew in a sharp breath. "Mary, Mother o' God, I'm sorry."

"I'm not asking for your pity," he said bitterly.

"I do no' offer it. 'Tis a great tragedy."

He closed his eyes. "Then condemn me like everyone else. I don't blame her for seeking companionship elsewhere. When I married her, I was a whole man—yet I came back from battle a cripple. She was horrified, frightened by my injury. I could see in her eyes that she didn't want me to touch her. It soon became quite evident that it was better for both of us when I was away."

For some time Megan simply stared at him gravely. Then she spoke. "Your injury does no' change the man ye are on the inside," she said softly. " 'Twas a great misfortune that it affected everyone so deeply. But ye'd do best to put the past behind ye and start wi' the healing. Ye can't change what has happened, but ye can make a difference wi' the future."

Rolf looked down at his maimed hand. "Are you saying that this abomination does not offend you?"

She shrugged. "I've seen men recover from far worse wounds. 'Tis no' the hand that pains ye, Englishman, but 'tis what's inside. Ye mistakenly view yourself as less than a man. And unless ye rid yourself o' this misconception, ye'll never make yourself whole again."

For a long moment, Rolf looked into her steady blue eyes, wondering how it was that this simple Scottish girl could reach into his ravaged soul and comfort it. At once he became aware of a hunger for companionship and understanding that he had never known before. It was a frightening moment for he realized that somehow it had rendered him vulnerable to her.

"You are a remarkably wise woman, Megan MacLeod," he said stiffly. Abruptly he stood, leaning over the chessboard and sweeping the wooden pieces into the velvet bag. "However, I'm afraid I must concede the game. I find myself weary and in need of a stiff drink."

After he left, Megan stared at the empty chair where he had sat only minutes before. "Ye are a strange man, Rolf St. James," she whispered, watching as the fire cast dancing shadows across the wall. "A very strange man, indeed."

# *Chapter Sixteen*

"The King's messenger has just arrived," Peter announced, walking into Rolf's bedchamber.

"At this hour?" Rolf asked in surprise. When Peter nodded, Rolf closed the book he was reading. He had already undressed for bed, and sat near the fire in a loose dressing robe, warming his bare feet. "Splendid. Take him to the library. I'll be with him as soon as I am dressed."

Peter nodded and shut the door. Rolf stood, untying the robe and casting it carelessly to the bed. Quickly, he strode across the room, reaching for his breeches and pulling them over his legs. Perching on the edge of the bed, he drew stockings over his calves, fastening them to his breeches with a small buckle. He then thrust his feet into a pair of boots before standing and tugging on a long-sleeved shirt of white linen. As he headed for the door, his hand paused over the neckcloth he despised. After a moment, he left the cloth where it was, damning convention and fashion.

In minutes, he entered the library. The messenger was already there waiting for him, standing at the hearth where the fire had been rekindled. He turned quickly to face Rolf when he heard the approaching footfallls.

"My lord," he said politely, dipping his head.

Rolf nodded a greeting, noticing that this messenger was far younger than he had expected. Dark circles of exhaustion beneath his eyes were evident, as was the paleness of his skin. It appeared as if the journey through the Highlands had been a difficult one for him.

"Please sit," Rolf said, motioning to a chair and then seating himself.

The young man looked at him gratefully. "Thank you, my lord. It was a most tiring journey. I'd s-swear that there were evil spirits in the forest, watching me as I passed through. It was most . . . unsettling."

Rolf smiled, remembering that on arrival in the Highlands, he too had felt as if someone were watching him. More than likely, though, it had not been evil spirits but instead the Highlanders themselves, clad in colorful but forbidden plaids, blending into the landscape.

"You traveled alone?"

The young man shook his head. "No. I had an armed escort of Scotsmen from Edinburgh. These Lowlanders are loyal to the King. It was a rather unusual experience, but I arrived safely."

"Have you a message for me?" Rolf asked eagerly, leaning forward.

The messenger nodded, reaching into a small

pouch on his leather belt and pulling out a rolled parchment. He handed it over to Rolf, who examined the seal. Satisfied that it was genuine, he rose to his feet.

"My men will see that you and your escorts have something to eat and a place to rest. I may have wish to send a reply, so I require you to remain for at least another day."

The young man came to his feet quickly. "Aye, my lord."

Moving over to the door, Rolf opened it and called for Peter. The older man appeared almost instantly. "See that Abigail prepares the men something to eat," he instructed. "Then return as quickly as possible. I wish to have a word with you."

Peter nodded, motioning for the young man to follow him. As soon as they had disappeared down the corridor, Rolf stepped back inside the library, shutting the door firmly behind him. Taking the parchment, he sat behind the desk, clearing the top of papers with a single sweep of his hand. Then, with a swift pull, he broke the seal on the parchment and unrolled it, smoothing the edges down with the flat of his hands. Dragging the lamp closer, he began to read.

He had no idea how long he sat there, reading and then re-reading the message, as if he couldn't believe his own eyes. He was reading it for the fourth time when Peter knocked on the door and then entered.

"Rolf?" he asked softly when his lord did not lift his head from the parchment. "Has something happened?"

Rolf jerked his head up angrily, his eyes a mixture of rage and unhappiness. "Yes, something has happened. Everyone in London has gone bloody mad."

Peter was taken aback by the look of sheer fury on Rolf's face. "What is it?" he asked alarmed. "Has the King denied you the right to grant pardons and land?"

Rolf's eyes glittered darkly. "No, of course not. He had already given me permission to do so before I left. But he has insisted that I must see Megan wed to Edwin Farrington."

Peter blinked at Rolf in shock, his weathered face draining of color. "Wed to Farrington? Good God, whatever possessed him to command such a thing?"

Rolf angrily released the parchment from beneath his forearms and the paper bounced once before curling up again. "King George cites her father as a traitor to the crown and therefore claims Megan as his ward. He believes her union with Farrington will secure English authority in the area."

Peter stared at Rolf in stunned horror. "But it will do little more than goad the Wolf into acts of greater violence."

"Damnation, man, do you think I do not know this?"

Peter's legs suddenly felt wobbly and he reached out for a chair, lowering his stocky frame into it. "Perhaps the lass is already wed," he offered hopefully.

Rolf scowled fiercely. "She isn't. I spoke with her about that very matter just a few weeks ago. And now she is certain to think I had something to do with this."

"Her opinion matters to you?"

Rolf pushed away from the desk, coming angrily to his feet. "What difference does it make now? We both know that such a wedding will settle nothing. Farrington is unstable, detestable and fiercely hated by all who know him."

Peter raised a shaggy eyebrow at the unexpected emotion in Rolf's voice. "Still, you know it's not an unusual request. Enemies are often wed to secure peace."

"But to wed her to Farrington is unthinkable."

"Unthinkable for you, Rolf. Apparently not for the King."

Rolf crashed his fist down on the desk. "It would destroy everything I've tried to do here. I won't permit it."

"Your sentiments about the girl are noble, but we have little choice. We must do as the King commands."

Striding angrily across the room to the window, Rolf pulled aside the drapes and gazed moodily at the dark courtyard. "Blast it, he knows how I feel about Farrington. What game is he playing with me?"

Peter reached up to rub his aching temples, already feeling a dull throb behind his eyes. "Would you like some advice from an old man? Don't question the actions of a King."

"I can't just turn her over to Farrington, and you know it."

The older man sighed deeply. "It's not hard to imagine what life would be like for her if she were to wed such a man. I also know that you have come to care for her, Rolf. She is a most . . . unusual woman."

Rolf's face remained grim. "Unusual, indeed. She has lied to me about her identity, misled me to believe she was a common whore, single-handedly injured one of my men while releasing Scottish prisoners held under my control, and damn near skewered me with a blade. Yet I find myself drawn to her, as I've not been to any other woman."

"I suppose we can't blame her for trying to protect her father and her clansmen. She appears to be fiercely loyal to those she cares for."

"I know it, but damnation, there must be something we can do to extricate ourselves from this situation honorably."

When Peter did not answer, Rolf began his lengthy strides back and forth across the room. "What could George be plotting? He knows that I admire her. For Christ's sake, I couldn't have made it any clearer in my letter. He would have realized that I'd be opposed to such a suggestion."

"He must be quite anxious to see matters here settled once and for all," Peter said quickly. "Don't forget that Farrington is destined to live his life in the Highlands. He's a petty nobleman with no future in London. Perhaps the King wishes to forge something permanent here. I suppose this could be accomplished by a union such as he proposes."

Rolf suddenly stopped his pacing and turned to Peter. "I have a better idea. I could petition the King to allow me to wed Megan instead of Farrington."

Peter's mouth dropped open in stunned amazement. "Y-you?" he gasped, clutching the side of the chair in shock. "Have you gone mad, Rolf?"

"If the King wishes to secure this area under English rule, what better way than to have his one of his most trusted lords wed the girl?"

"But it would mean living in the Highlands . . . indefinitely."

"Megan and I could divide our time between London and Castle Kilcraig. It would be no loss for me. You know full well that ever since Caroline's death, London and the court have been intolerable for me."

Peter stood agitatedly, spreading his hands in dismay. "But certainly the King never believed that you would actually wish to live here."

"Perhaps he did, Peter," Rolf murmured distractedly. "He knows how blasted miserable I am in London and he's been urging me to marry. I did speak quite highly of Megan in my letter. Possibly, in his own crafty way, this is George's method of prodding me into action—testing me to see how much I care for the girl."

"God preserve us," Peter exclaimed, throwing up his hands. "Now I am certain you have gone mad. Do you really think the King would want the only heir to the St. James estate to wed nothing more than a penniless Scottish girl?"

"She's not really penniless, Peter, at least not in the eyes of the Scots. She is the daughter of the MacLeod laird—the most powerful laird in this area. Her claim to that land, and thus mine if I were to be her husband, would be fully legal within the boundaries of their laws. I'm certain the King would approve."

"For God's sake, I urge you to think about what you are proposing," Peter argued strenuously. "This land already belongs to England. You do not need to wed her for it to be legal in our laws."

Rolf sighed patiently at the distressed tone of

Peter's voice. "I am not concerned with our laws, Peter. If we want to soothe tensions here, then we must learn to respect the customs of the Scots. By taking Megan as my wife, I would settle two very important issues. First, in their eyes, I would have the strongest claim to the lairdship. It doesn't matter that I already inhabit Castle Kilcraig. If I were to wed Megan, they would finally see me as having acquired it legally. Second, Robert MacLeod would certainly find some measure of satisfaction that his only daughter would return to Castle Kilcraig as its mistress. He would also be assured that her future is secure. I believe it to be an honorable solution to all parties involved."

Peter shook his head, his face a mixture of concern and disbelief. "Even if the King were to agree to your proposal, you can't expect the girl to accept it. Farrington may have slain her brother, but you are seeking to end her father's life. What makes you any better in her eyes?"

Rolf winced at the truth of his statement. "Presumably nothing. But I'll not harm her as Farrington would. You know that, Peter."

"Aye, *I* know that, lad. But you'll have the devil of a time convincing *her*."

"Yes, I know. But we both know that I don't need her permission." Rolf walked over to Peter, placing a hand on his shoulder. "Come now, man, don't be so anxious for my future. You worry over me like a nursemaid to a babe."

"Are you certain you really want to do this, Rolf?" Peter asked, still sounding unconvinced. "Sacrificing yourself like this? I'm not certain your father would approve."

Rolf clapped him firmly on the back. "On the

contrary, old friend. Although I can't say that I look forward to the event, it is time for me to take another wife and provide an heir to the St. James estate. By wedding Megan, I will solve a problem for the King as well as for myself. My father always encouraged me to put duty and service above all. What more could he want for me than to marry for the good of England?"

Peter shook his gray head doubtfully. "I just hope you know what you are doing. I'm not convinced the King will agree to your proposal."

"Somehow, Peter, I am certain he will. In fact, while I await his reply, I believe it's time I made myself more familiar with the glen, the villagers, and the woman I plan to make my wife."

# *Chapter Seventeen*

Spring was in the air.

Megan lifted her nose to the wind, letting the reins of her mount rest lightly between her fingers. It was her personal rite of spring—seeing if she could detect the first scent of the yellow buttercups, blue harebells and wavy purple heather.

The scent was not yet full blown, but Megan could already observe the first signs of the season in the glen. The sun had all but melted the most stubborn patches of snow, revealing scattered patches of rich, fertile Highland soil. The grass had begun to sprout from the earth and sun warmed the soft green moss. The hills were on the verge of bursting into the full colors of spring—lush green, cheery yellow, stunning purple and rich browns.

Megan could hardly believe that spring had arrived in Gairloch and she had been held a prisoner by the English for several months already. Yet that time had not been wasted. A foundation for peace had been laid, if only she could convince her people to accept it.

She glanced over at Rolf, who rode beside her. He had been in remarkably good spirits for the past three weeks, whistling cheerfully and jaunting about the castle as if he had not a care in the world. Today he had appeared in her doorway, his eyes twinkling merrily, and invited her to accompany him to the village. She had not been there since the day Farrington had burned it down, and wondered what had prompted his sudden decision to permit her to come with him now. When she questioned his unusual invitation, he only smiled mysteriously.

Warily she climbed on her horse and rode to the village with him. Peter, Andrew and several other men also accompanied them. Much to her astonishment, when they reached the village, people ran out of the crofts to greet Rolf, smiling and waving buoyantly. Megan's mouth dropped open in stunned amazement. Had the villagers forgotten that he was an Englishman?

Rolf stopped his horse at one of the crofts where a middle-aged man sat out in front, whittling a piece of wood with a sharp knife. Megan immediately recognized him as Dugald Faegen, the village woodcarver. Built like a small tree trunk, Dugald had been one of the best raiders her father had. Unfortunately, he had been lamed in one leg during a foray. Her father had insisted he return to the village where he could better serve the people who needed his skills. Dugald had done so reluctantly, but had served as a source of strength to the villagers ever since.

When Dugald saw Rolf, he put aside his knife and wood before rising. Rolf dismounted and strode toward him in a few short steps. Megan quickly slid off her horse as well, watching with growing curiosity as to what Rolf would do next.

To her stunned amazement, Dugald reached down beside his chair and tossed Rolf a long wooden pole. Rolf caught it easily in his good hand as his men crowded around him. Megan gasped as Dugald picked up another pole and held it in front of him.

"Are ye ready, Englishman?" the wood carver called out.

More villagers began to emerge from the huts, greeting Megan excitedly, but quickly turning their attention to Dugald and Rolf. Before Megan could ask what was going on, Rolf had unfastened his light cloak, letting it fall to the ground.

"I'm ready," he announced.

"Saints above," Megan gasped when she realized what was about to happen. "Ye must stop this. He can't fight Dugald," she whispered furiously to Peter.

Peter put a hand on her shoulder, quieting her. "Have ye forgotten that Rolf has only one hand? He'll not harm the old man."

" 'Tis no' Dugald I'm worried about," she hissed back.

Peter smiled. "Hush, my lady, and watch. It is quite a sight."

Megan looked on in dismay as Dugald moved forward, raising his pole. Rolf stepped forward to meet him, holding the stick in his good hand. Dugald gave a small cry and the two sticks crashed together with a loud crack. The force of

Rolf's hit was jarring, but Dugald cleverly feinted sideways, slipping behind Rolf and clobbering him on the back with a loud thud. Rolf grunted in pain and stumbled sideways, but managed to turn around and get his stick up in time to deflect the next blow.

"Well, now, ye are improving a wee bit, lad," Dugald taunted, a broad smile crossing his face. "Two weeks ago, ye'd be on your arse."

Rolf moved forward a step, taking a swing at Dugald's left shoulder. "Well, I assure you, I have no intention of finding my arse on the cold, hard ground today."

Dugald blocked the stick with his own, but the force of the blow caused him to back up a few steps. "Ye've a lot o' fancy words, Englishman. But let's see what ye can really do."

Rolf grinned, swinging his stick again. Megan held her breath as Dugald easily met it and thrust at Rolf's exposed side. But Rolf had anticipated the attack, leaning into the blow instead of away from it. The stick hit Rolf's shoulder with minimal force. Rolf seized the advantage of his close proximity by thrusting his own stick firmly against Dugald's arm. Dugald managed to hold on to his stick but was not fast enough to counter Rolf's next blow. Moments later, the older man went sprawling face-first in the dirt.

Gasping in surprise, Megan rushed forward to help him, but Peter grabbed her arm, holding her firmly in place. As she watched in stunned astonishment, the villagers cheered their approval as Rolf tossed aside the club and stretched out his good hand to help Dugald to his feet.

"You don't know how badly I've wanted to do that," Rolf said, grinning as the older rubbed his shoulder ruefully.

"Ye are a damn quick learner, Englishman. Even if ye only have one hand."

"Well, you are not so bad for a lame man yourself."

The two men laughed and slapped each other on the back. As Megan watched in openmouthed surprise, several pretty young girls from the village ran forward, giggling and talking shyly with Rolf. Outraged, Megan yanked free of Peter's hold and stormed over to Dugald.

"What the devil is going on here?" she demanded furiously in Gaelic.

Dugald shrugged. "The Englishman asked me to teach him to fight like a Scotsman. He's been working hard at it for two weeks now. 'Twas but a spot o' honest fun, lass."

"Fun?" Megan spluttered indignantly. "Have ye lost your senses? Need I remind ye that he is an Englishman—our enemy. How could ye teach him our ways?"

Dugald massaged his shoulder thoughtfully. "He's no' like other Englishman, Megan. He's a good man, even helping us to rebuild our homes wi' his own hands. And he brought me back my young Duggie. Farrington took him to his house after his men burnt the village. I owe him a debt, lass. One I dinna think I can ever really repay."

Exhaling a deep breath, Megan clenched her hands at her side in frustration. Rolf glanced her way and disengaged himself from the circle of young girls.

"How did you like the joust?" he asked, smiling. His dark hair was tousled about his shoulders, his face flushed red from the physical activity and the cool air.

She stared at him angrily. "Just what do ye think ye are doing? Trying to become one o' us so ye can better figure out ways to kill us? Ye may have fooled them, Englishman, but ye canna fool me. I know what ye plan for us." Turning sharply on her heel, she strode off toward her horse, her unbound hair swinging furiously.

Rolf watched her go, the flush of victory fading from his face. Seeing the frown on his face, Dugald put a hand on Rolf's shoulder. "Dinna fret, lad. The lass has a sharp tongue, but she's had a difficult life at the hands o' the English. She's very protective o' us, much like her father."

"So I'm discovering," he murmured.

"Ye have an eye for her, do ye no', lad?" Dugald asked.

Rolf looked at the man in surprise. He was still not used to the way the Scots spoke to him with such familiarity. "I'm not certain what you mean."

Dugald guffawed. "Och, I may be lame, but I'm no' blind. I see the way ye look at her. But be warned that she's far more than just a comely lass."

Rolf said nothing but returned his gaze to Megan, who was standing near her horse, speaking rapidly with one of the village women.

"Ye're no' the first to fall under her spell," Dugald continued. " 'Tis many a lad who wished to claim her. Most simply fell by the wayside, too daunted by her sharp wit, too awed by her courage. 'Twill take a man strong in character and possessing o' much patience to match her spirit."

"It is most curious that her father has never insisted that she wed."

"Most o' us thought she would eventually wed Robbie. Poor lad's been in love wi' her since he was a wee bairn."

"Robbie?" Rolf questioned sharply.

"Aye, her cousin. A bit o' a hothead but a good man, he is."

A dark frown crossed Rolf's face and Dugald chuckled. "Och, is that the green-eyed devil I see? Well, if 'tis her heart ye want, ye'd better woo it like a Scotsman. By learning our ways, ye'll learn hers, too."

Rolf turned to look at Dugald curiously. "Why are you being so kind to me? Do you not harbor any of the suspicion she holds for me?"

Dugald stroked his beard, regarding Rolf pensively. "One thing I've learned is that 'tis possible to judge an honest man by his actions. Ye may be an Englishman, but at least ye have acted like one wi' honor."

"You have remarkable faith in your judgments."

Dugald nodded. "Perhaps. But we also know how ye stepped in to protect us. Besides, ye haven't harmed Megan, even though ye've learned her identity as the laird's daughter. The Scots are no' ones to forget a kind turn."

Rolf looked back over to Megan, who had already mounted and sat glaring at him. Dugald followed his eyes, his face breaking out into a broad smile. "Och, dinna be intimidated by that fierce look. I saw how unhappy she looked when ye were talking and laughing wi' those pretty lassies. Mayhap she's a bit touched by the green-eyed devil as ye are. Megan may be hot-tempered, but she is still a lass. Ye'd do well no' to forget that, lad."

A slow smile rose to Rolf's lips as he walked back to his horse. As he passed Megan, he flashed her a grin, ignoring her frosty stare. Then with a jaunty wave to the villagers, he swung up into the saddle. Slapping his reins lightly on his horse's neck, he led the others toward home.

"How long have ye been doing that?" Megan demanded furiously, her foot tapping relentlessly on the stone floor of her chamber.

Rolf leaned back in his chair and regarded Megan silently. Spots of anger blazed red in her cheeks and enchanting wisps of her dark hair drifted around her face.

"Doing what?" he asked innocently.

"Ye know what I mean. Learning sticks wi' Dugald and making friends wi' the villagers."

The fact that she was angrily accusing him of being kind to the villagers almost brought a smile to his lips. "Well, let's see. I've been learning the rather interesting technique of the sticks for about two weeks now," he said, studying his nails with interest. "As far as making friends with the villagers, I can't ever remember making a conscious effort to do so. I presume it just happened from working side by side, helping them to repair their homes."

"Ye are trying to trick them into trusting ye," she nearly shouted at him.

Rolf rolled his eyes in exasperation. "I have no need to resort to trickery and you know it. A man's actions speak louder than his words."

"Now ye sound like Dugald," she snapped.

Rolf laughed. "Yes, perhaps I do."

"Why are ye doing this?"

Surprised by the anguished tone of her voice, Rolf leaned forward, frowning. "What is really bothering you, Megan?"

Her slender hands twisted anxiously in front of her. "I canna bear to see the villagers harmed again. Please, don't do this, Englishman."

"Then listen to me carefully, Megan. I have no quarrel with the villagers. I seek only the Wolf. If you fear your father's loss of influence on the villagers, then at least you may rest assured that I will not harm them."

Megan swallowed with frustration and looked away. It wasn't her father's loss of influence she feared, it was her own. Yet, if he discovered that she was really the Black Wolf, all her bargaining power would be gone. He would simply drag her off to London and be damned with his promises to her and her people. She could not . . . *would not* . . . let that happen.

Now she only awaited word from Geddes. Before Douglas MacLeary had been released to the village, Megan had spoken at great length with him, instructing him to urge her uncle to accept Rolf's terms. She was certain that by now Uncle Geddes had informed the Chisholms, Mac-Donnells and the other clans that her father was no longer alive and she had been acting as laird in his absence. She only hoped that the men would be willing to look beyond their anger at her deception and do what was right for their people. She'd accept Rolf's truce and then reveal herself as the Wolf. Her life for the lives of all the clansmen and their families. An honorable trade.

"Megan?"

She lifted her dark head quickly. "Aye?"

"Will you have supper with me tonight?"

After her dark thoughts, such a request came as a surprise. "Ye wish to sup wi' me?" she repeated blankly.

"Yes. Tonight, I prefer to face you over a table instead of a chessboard. And I wish to speak to you about something."

She looked at him warily. "Why wait till supper to talk? Ye have my full attention now."

Rolf looked about the room. "Frankly, this is not the setting I had in mind. I would prefer something . . . well, more intimate." When she hesitated, he took a step toward her. "I've given you my word that I'm not going to harm the villagers, Megan. I think you know that I am telling the truth. Please, leave your reservations behind and join me for supper. It's important."

Megan stared at him. "Ye are the most contrary man I've ever met."

"I wish you would call me Rolf," he said softly. "It's not such an unreasonable request. But I'll not hurry you. You'll say it when you are ready. But come now, will you accept my invitation to supper?"

She sighed. "Ye won't stop asking, will ye?"

He smiled. "I've been told that persistence is one of my more honorable traits."

"I suppose 'tis rather useful in pursuing one's enemy."

"You are not my enemy, Megan."

She rubbed her temples. "I wouldn't be so certain o' that if I were ye. But if ye insist, I'll join ye for supper."

His dark eyes lit up. "Splendid. I'll have Abigail fetch one of the trunks that I presume contains more of your clothing. Since you're going to be here a bit longer, you might as well dress comfortably." Turning jauntily on his heel, he left the room, leaving Megan staring after him in surprise.

"What are ye plotting now, Englishman?" she whispered under her breath.

She walked over to the window and pulled aside the draperies. A dazzling spring sun was shining and there was nary a cloud in the sky. Still, the cheerful weather could not raise her spirits or cast off her nagging doubt that something terrible was about to happen—beginning with supper this evening. Rolf St. James was plotting something and Megan had a dreadful premonition that she wasn't going to like it one bit.

# *Chapter Eighteen*

Rolf not only sent Megan a trunk filled with her clothes, but he also instructed Abigail to help her dress.

" 'Twas foolish for him to bother ye," Megan protested as Abigail held up a gown of sapphire blue velvet and lifted it carefully over Megan's head. "I'm perfectly capable o' dressing myself."

"O' course, ye are, my lady," Abigail said, deftly smoothing the material over her petticoats. "But it would have taken some time and, in my humble opinion, I wouldn't keep a man both waiting and famished."

Megan couldn't help but smile, wondering what had made the older woman so talkative this evening. Usually, she brought Megan her food or bedding and left, engaging in only minimal conversation. But tonight, the normally staid housekeeper seemed different. She was lively, cheerful, and her gray eyes sparkled with excitement. "Nay, still 'tisn't quite right," she murmured, fussing with Megan's bodice.

Self-consciously, Megan looked down at the gown, noticing that it hung sadly on her frame instead of clinging to her tightly. "It used to fit better through here," she said wistfully, touching her waist. "But truthfully, I never thought to wear any o' these gowns again. They bring back too many memories."

Abigail clucked softly. "Well, if ye would eat what I fixed, ye'd gain at least two stone in a fortnight or two. But ye eat as little as a bird. A shame, I say."

Megan's eyes saddened. " 'Tis no' the food, Abigail. Ye are a wonderful cook. I simply don't feel like eating when many o' my people are going hungry."

Abigail paused, her hand hovering over Megan's shoulder. "Ye have a good heart, my lady. I wouldn't have expected it from ye, being Scottish and all."

Megan sighed. "I can see that prejudice and mistrust runs deep on both sides. 'Tis most difficult."

The lines on Abigail's face softened. "Well, I've learned a lot about ye people since I've been here. In many ways ye are rather similar to us." She glanced up quickly at Megan. " 'Twas a compliment, my lady, that was."

Megan smiled. "I know that ye meant it as such."

The woman nodded as she stepped back, critically surveying the off-shoulder deep décolletage of the gown. "Aye, ye look right lovely," she said with satisfaction, reaching out to fluff up the petticoats.

Strangely pleased by the compliment, Megan twirled around, feeling the soft swish of the material around her stockinged legs. "Why all the bother for a simple supper? I might have just as easily decided to wear the same gown I've worn for the past several weeks."

Abigail shook her head disapprovingly. " 'Tisn't right for a lady like ye to wear the same gown day after day. Besides, it's only fitting that tonight ye wear something special."

Megan looked at the older woman in surprise. "Tonight? Why? What is happening tonight?"

Abigail shrugged, lowering her voice to a conspiratorial whisper. "To tell ye the truth, my lady, I'm not certain. But I haven't seen my lord look so . . . er . . . happy in a long time. He's had the kitchen in an uproar for hours and even instructed the servants to polish the silver. Then he asked me to lay out his finest clothes and see that ye are dressed in a proper gown. Now I may be an old woman, but I have my suspicions as to why he'd want to put on such a show for a pretty lady. I think he wants to impress ye."

Megan felt her cheeks warm. "Ye must be mistaken."

"I'm not," Abigail said, ushering her to a chair. "No one knows the lad like I do." Picking up a brush, she began to pull it through Megan's long, thick tresses.

"Abigail," Megan said softly, wincing as the woman found a snarl. "Does your lord treat all o' his prisoners this way? I mean, inviting them to supper and such?"

"I promise ye that Rolf doesn't make a practice of holding young women prisoner. 'Tis only in your case, the circumstances having been rather odd. Imagine his shock when he discovered that ye were the former mistress of this castle."

"I don't need to imagine it," Megan remarked wryly. "He nearly throttled me, he was so angry."

Abigail waved her hand dismissively. "Oh, men are always angry about one thing or another. Ye have naught to fear from him, my lady. I know in my heart that he's a good man and I have yet to see him raise a hand against a woman in all my years with the family."

"How many years have ye been with the family?" Megan asked curiously.

"Let's see, 'tis nearly two and thirty years now. I practically raised young Rolf by myself."

"Really?" Megan said with genuine interest. "I suppose that means ye must have known his wife, Caroline, as well."

Abigail immediately ceased her strokes. Megan turned around in the chair, looking up at the older woman apologetically. "Forgive me if I tread upon a forbidden subject."

The older woman sighed, pushing a strand of gray hair from her forehead. " 'Tis not a forbidden topic, just a painful one. Lady Caroline was . . . well, she was very young. She loved beautiful gowns, handsome lords and dancing until midnight. She wasn't at all suited for a man like Rolf, even before the horrible injury to his hand."

"I'm sorry to hear that," Megan said sincerely, turning back around as Abigail resumed the slow, rhythmic strokes through her hair. "Her death seems to have pained him greatly."

"Ach, 'twas a horrible tragedy. And if that weren't enough, the gossip at court was most cruel. There was even a trial. Those who accused him said he pushed her from the window. But I know he didn't have anything to do with her death. I myself saw him go into his bedchamber moments before she fell. I don't wish to speak ill of the dead, but Lady Caroline brought it on herself, I say."

" 'Tisn't right to lay blame on anyone," Megan said gently.

"O' course, my lady, ye are right," Abigail agreed, lifting Megan's hair off her shoulders. She twisted it deftly around Megan's head, securing it with a gold comb. "There," she said, stepping back to survey her work. "Ye do look a fair sight."

Megan stood, smoothing down her skirts. Gently she laid a hand on Abigail's arm. "Thank ye for your help," she said softly. "I know 'tis no' required for ye to act this way toward me."

The housekeeper shrugged. "I'll not lie to ye. When I first heard that ye'd tried to harm my lord . . . well, my mind was made up that I wasn't going to like ye. But over the past several weeks, I've seen a decency and an honesty about ye that has caused me to change my mind. I can see ye are just trying to help your people and do what is right. I suspect Rolf knows it, too. Ye know, it brings a bit of gladness to my old heart to see him smile again. And 'tis ye who brings it to him."

Megan was touched by the woman's words. Quietly, she folded her hands in front of her. "I don't deserve your kindness, Abigail, but I appreciate it. Thank ye."

The older woman gave Megan a comforting pat on the arm and then withdrew from the room. Minutes later, Andrew arrived to escort her to dinner.

As they reached the great chamber, Andrew left her abruptly at the entranceway, disappearing quickly down the dark corridor. Taking a deep breath for courage, Megan entered the room. What she saw caused her mouth to drop open in astonishment.

The chamber appeared to have been scrubbed from top to bottom. The stone floor was brushed clean of dirt and refuse and the long oak table shone from a recent polish. A beautiful, lace tablecloth adorned one end of the table near the hearth and was set with delicate plates and gleaming silver utensils. Two crystal wine glasses shimmered and sparkled in the candlelight.

Rolf rose from behind the table, his dark eyes sweeping over her bare shoulders and the visible swell of her breasts at the dip in her gown. "You look magnificent," he said softly.

Megan blushed. " 'Tis Abigail's work."

"Yes, I can see that, and I'll have to have a word with her." He took her elbow. "God's teeth, I'm not a saint," he added to himself under his breath.

Megan caught the inference and blushed as Rolf led her to the table. He graciously permitted her to slide onto the bench before slipping in beside her. At his close proximity, Megan was intensely reminded of their last dinner together at this table. Except somehow, tonight seemed different. The tension of their first confrontation was gone and in its place was an uneasy but standing truce.

As Megan looked around, her spirits could not help but be lifted as she saw this great room restored to its grandeur. Why he had gone to such trouble to set her at ease, she did not know. She only knew that this unpredictable Englishman never ceased to amaze her.

Covertly, Megan stole a glance at him, marveling at how impeccably he had dressed. Clad in a dark blue waistcoat that fit snugly across his shoulders and a ruffled white shirt, he was devastatingly handsome. His gleaming black hair had been brushed back from his face and neatly tied at the base of his neck with a velvet ribbon. He even wore an elegant silk neckcloth, although he repeatedly pulled on it, clearly uncomfortable with the fit of the fabric around his neck. A smile rose to Megan's lips at the thought that this formidable man could be bothered by a simple piece of material.

"Why all the formalities tonight?" she asked. "Ye do look a wee bit restless in your finery."

Rolf's hand froze over his neckcloth before he broke out in laughter. "You have a sharp eye. I'm afraid that I have never been one for fashion. But you, on the other hand, look absolutely enchanting."

His gaze on her face was warm and appreciative, yet his eyes held an emotion she could not read. Flushing slightly, she brushed a stray strand of hair from her brow. "Och, well despite your discomfort, ye look rather grand yourself, Englishman."

Rolf grinned at her and the awkwardness between them lessened. "I would like to propose a toast," he said, reaching for the wine and pouring it into their glasses.

Megan looked at him curiously, accepting the glass he handed her. "To what?"

"To peace."

For a moment, their gaze locked and held before he lifted the glass to his lips and took a sip. After a moment, Megan did the same.

"To peace," she murmured softly.

At that moment, Abigail and two young men entered the room, carrying several trays. Abigail set one of the trays on the table and lifted the cover, displaying a rack of roast venison.

"Absolute perfection," Rolf commented as she held it close for his inspection. "As usual."

Megan nodded in anticipation, her mouth watering from the delicious aroma. "Aye, 'tis one o' the few times I can say that I completely agree wi' ye, Englishman."

Abigail beamed as she bustled about, piling their plates with food. "Now see that ye eat some of this fare," she instructed Megan firmly. "Ye'll offend my pride if ye leave anything on your plate."

Rolf looked over at Megan and winked. "I'll warn you in advance that it is not wise to offend Abigail's delicate sensibilities."

Megan saw the bright twinkle in his eye and smiled. "Somehow I sense that ye may well have done that once or twice in the past."

Abigail glanced affectionately at Rolf. "Ach, my lady, he was a lively child. He was curious, reckless and always chasing after something. It put an awful strain on my old heart, it did. 'Tis a wonder I lived to see him grown."

Rolf chuckled. "Don't believe her, Megan. She put the fear of God in me with her stern frown and an occasional threat of the switch. But it's God's truth that I never missed a meal."

Abigail and Megan both burst into laughter. Sweeping up an empty plate, Abigail gave Rolf a fond pat on the shoulder and withdrew, taking the two young men with her.

As soon as she was gone, the two set hungrily upon the meal. Megan savored every bite, remembering the nights she could only dream of such fare. Rolf filled both wineglasses twice as he steadily worked his own way through the pile on his plate. Finally, he set aside his knife, sighing with pleasure. Leaning his elbows on the table, he studied Megan's face as she tore off a piece of bread and put it in her mouth. Her face reflected sheer delight as she chewed. Rolf smiled in response, finding pleasure in watching a woman enjoy a meal as much as she did.

"Abigail seems to have taken to you," he commented.

Megan looked up at him in surprise. "Do ye really think so? I'm afraid she didn't like me much at first."

Rolf laughed. "It's not terribly surprising, considering you tried to skewer me like a roast pig."

Megan smiled sheepishly. "I suppose I can't blame her. She does seem to be quite fond o' ye."

"She is as close to a mother as I have," he said, unexpectedly reaching across the table and covering her hand with his. "I implicitly trust her judgment, especially on women."

Megan blushed, actually enjoying the warm clasp of his fingers. " 'Tis much she doesn't know about me."

Rolf smiled. "She knows enough . . . as do I." He squeezed her hand. "Have you ever wanted to see London, Megan?"

"London?" she repeated, surprised by his quick change of thought. "Why would ye wonder about such a thing?"

Rolf shrugged. "Simple curiosity, I suppose."

Megan thought of the gallows that awaited her there, and her fingers reached up to touch her neck. "I don't know. Perhaps under certain circumstances, a journey to London might be considered interesting."

Rolf saw the troubled expression on her face and thought he understood her concern. "Do you worry that I'll force you to view your father's execution?"

"I never know what to expect from ye next, Englishman."

"I would not put you through such an ordeal, Megan. I've become rather fond of you."

At his unexpected confession, Megan carefully withdrew her hand from his and placed it on her lap. " 'Tisn't wise to reveal such things to your opponents, Englishman."

Rolf took a sip of his wine, staring at her thoughtfully. "I have decided that I no longer wish for us to remain opponents."

She flashed him a puzzled look as he slid out from behind the table and stood. His dark brows drew together in concentration while his fingers toyed with one of the flap pockets on his waistcoat. As he stood there, a sudden draft of air swept through the chamber causing the fire to flicker madly behind him. Shadows danced eerily across the stone walls and the chill sent goose flesh skittering across Megan's bare neck and shoulders.

"There have been some rather unusual developments since my discovery of your identity as the daughter of the Black Wolf," he said slowly.

Megan stiffened, fear and anxiety knotting inside her. "What kind o' developments?"

Rolf's eyes became sober and serious. "Frankly, I'm not certain the best way to tell you this, Megan. I know it may come as a bit of a surprise, but the King has declared you his ward."

Megan stood up hastily, nearly knocking over her half-full wineglass before removing herself from the bench. "His what?" she exclaimed, her blue eyes blazing with disbelief and the first flickers of anger.

Rolf frowned, trying to decide the best way to lessen her ire. "I know this seems rather frightening, but it is actually rather a reasonable move on the part of the King."

"Reasonable?" she cried out, her voice raising a notch. "Ye tell me that I've suddenly gone from being your prisoner to a ward o' the King and you expect me to view this as reasonable?"

"As your father is engaged in illegal activities against the Crown, you have been left without proper protection or guidance. You should be honored that the King has taken an interest in your welfare."

Megan's fists clenched at her side, the color heightening in her cheeks. "How dare your King presume to know what kind o' protection and guidance I need."

Rolf's voice hardened at the disrespectful tone of her voice. "He has the right to presume whatever he wishes, Megan. Moreover, he has instructed me to go forth with certain plans for your future."

Megan took a startled step backwards. "What kind o' plans?" she asked warily.

"He has commanded me to wed you to Edwin Farrington."

Megan managed to gasp once before a hand seemed to close around her throat, choking off the air to her lungs. All color drained from her face and a tremble shot through her body.

"Nay, no' Farrington," she whispered in horror. "I would rather die first. He is the vile man that murdered my brother." *And my father*, she added silently.

Rolf moved forward as she began to shake uncontrollably, gripping her firmly by the shoulders. "Ease yourself, Megan," he ordered her calmly.

She only stared at him with large, horrified eyes until he shook her again, this time hard. "Listen to me. If you do not wish it, I will not force you to wed Farrington. Do you hear me?"

Megan closed her eyes, forcing herself to take a deep breath. "Ye would dare to disobey your King?" she asked in a small voice.

Rolf sighed, shaking his head. "I'm afraid it's not that simple. However, I have petitioned him for another course of action. Today, I received word that he approves of my request." He reached into his pocket and pulled out a rolled parchment.

Megan's heart began to beat erratically as she opened her eyes and focused onto the curled paper in his hand. "Wh-what request?"

Rolf tapped the parchment against the top of his gloved hand. The sound beat a dreadful tune in step with the fierce pounding at Megan's temples.

"It is rather simple, really," he answered calmly. "I've asked the King for permission to wed you in place of Edwin Farrington. He has graciously agreed to my proposal."

241

Megan's mouth dropped open in sheer astonishment. She stared at him as if he had lost the last vestiges of sanity. She gasped as if trying to say something, but found her voice frozen in her throat.

At her shocked expression, Rolf's lips formed a wry smile. "I can see you are overcome by emotion at my proposal. However, I urge you to think calmly about what I've said and not reach any hasty conclusions."

"Ye? Marriage to ye?" she finally gasped out with difficulty. " 'Tis impossible."

Rolf took her arm, steadying her as she visibly swayed on her feet. "It's not only possible, it's advisable. If you refuse to marry me, I'll have no choice but to see you wed to Edwin Farrington."

Rolf helped her to her seat on the bench. Kneeling down in front of her, he took her cold hand into his. "You must marry me, Megan. It is the only way."

" 'Tis no' the only way. Please, we must wait until we have an answer from my father. 'Twill be soon, I'm certain o' it. Then there will be no need for any more talk o' marriage."

The lines around Rolf's mouth tightened. "The King's command has nothing to do with my offer of amnesty and land to your clansmen. He wants you wed in order to secure English authority in this area after your father is gone. He thought that by having Farrington wed you, English claim to the land would be perfectly legal in the eyes of the Scots. He believes it would help settle tensions here."

"If I were forced to wed Farrington, 'twould only set off a bloody feud within my own clan as well as those neighboring our land," Megan contested hotly. "Ye are right to believe that the man who marries me will have the strongest claim to the lairdship, but the people would never recognize Farrington as their laird, even wi' me as his wife."

"I know," Rolf answered calmly. "But they might recognize me."

"Ye?" Megan echoed in astonishment, the soft sound drifting away on the air. When he nodded, she pressed her fists against her temples. "God preserve me, but I've been such a fool. 'Twas all part o' your grand plan, wasn't it, Englishman? First ye tried to seduce me. Next ye discovered I was unwed. Then ye befriended the villagers, luring them into trusting ye. When ye had accomplished all that, ye made bold offers o' land and pardons, handing out promises ye never meant to keep. Now ye make your bid for MacLeod land by threatening me wi' a marriage to Farrington unless I wed ye. 'Tis a most brilliant plan, Englishman. I'll at least give ye that."

A sudden anger lit Rolf's eyes. "Do you really think that this is some kind of game, Megan? That I've created a magnificent scheme to trick you and the others into trusting me so I could collect a piece of land in the Highlands?"

"I don't know what to believe anymore," she said bitterly.

"Damnation, woman," Rolf said, his voice grating harshly. "Need I remind you that this land and Castle Kilcraig already belong to me? I don't need to wed you or anyone else to have legal claim to it. Besides, the King's motives are far grander than that. He really does intend to bring peace to this area and I've offered to be his instrument in doing so."

"Och, 'tis a noble sentiment, Englishman, but your fancy trickery won't work wi' me."

Rolf's jaw hardened. "I don't need your permission to marry you, Megan. If I must, I will drag you bound and gagged before a man of the cloth, whether it be with me or Edwin Farrington."

She stiffened, her eyes blazing. "Ye wouldn't dare. I'd no' recite the vows."

"Your spoken acceptance of such a union is of little concern to me. Your mere presence would suffice."

"I find your threats to be most vile, Englishman."

Rolf's eyes darkened seriously. "They are not threats, Megan, but promises. Now, you can either agree to marry me or I will offer your hand to Edwin Farrington. Which shall it be?"

Megan saw the hard determination in his eyes. Anxious, she sought another method of discouraging him. "Please, I beg o' ye no' to insist on this mockery. I am certain my father will soon accept your terms."

Rolf folded his thick arms across his chest. "I've already explained that your father's decision regarding my offer has no bearing on the King's insistence that you wed. In spite of that, I can understand why your father might resist your wedding Farrington. However, I can hardly see why he would object to a union between the two of us. Other than the obvious drawback of my English heritage, you can't tell me that he wouldn't find some measure of comfort knowing that his only daughter would be well provided for once he is gone. Moreover, he would have the satisfaction of knowing that a MacLeod woman is once again mistress of Castle Kilcraig."

Megan tossed her head angrily. "Have ye considered that I may object to marrying the man who seeks to end the life of my father?"

"Your father knew the risk of engaging in illegal activities against the crown. Now he must pay the price. I do not make the laws, Megan. I seek only to ensure that his death will not be in vain. This is for your sake, as well as for all the innocent people in that village."

Megan pressed a hand to her brow, trying to think above the pounding ache from behind her eyes. " 'Tis more complicated than that, Englishman. I can't explain it now, but ask only that ye wait until we have settled this matter wi' the pardons and the land grants. I give ye my word that at that time, all issues will be resolved without a need for a hasty joining."

Rolf gripped her chin firmly in his hand, forcing her to look directly into his eyes. "Why do you really hesitate to accept my proposal, Megan? Am I so loathsome to you?"

His earnest question was an unexpected stab in her heart. "Nay, ye are far from loathsome," she said softly. "But ye must trust me when I say that if ye wed me, 'twould be a terrible mistake ye'd be making."

"Why?"

"I can't explain, at least no' yet. But I promise ye that if ye insist on wedding me, ye'll live to regret your decision for the rest o' your life."

"Nonetheless, I intend to wed you just the same."

"Och, why are ye being so bloody stubborn?" she cried out, throwing up her hands in despair.

"Ye barely know me, yet ye wish to sacrifice yourself and your entire future? What do ye really want?"

Rolf's eyes darkened. "Let me make something perfectly clear. I am by no means sacrificing my future, Megan. On the contrary, I am strengthening it. The King was most pleased by my offer, confident that affairs in this area will finally be settled under my command. And now that I will again take a wife, the matter of providing an heir for the St. James line will be resolved as well. I've made no secret of my attraction to you and I am certain that in time, you'll come to look upon me as something other than your enemy."

She looked at him in astonishment, crimson flames streaking across her cheeks. "Heir? How dare ye suggest such a thing. I will no' be some kind o' breeding mare for ye or your precious family line."

"My wife will share my bed," he replied firmly.

"Well, I won't be your wife," she retorted, her eyes flashing daggers.

For a moment, they simply glared at each other, neither wanting to be the first to look away. Finally Rolf took a step back.

"I presume you would give Farrington the same answer," he asked softly. Megan shuddered in reply. Exhaling a deep breath, he rose to his feet, clasping his hands behind his back.

"Then, from what I can determine of this conversation, you will not consent to a wedding until this matter with your father is settled."

She looked up hopefully. "As soon as we have his answer, ye'll realize how foolish this entire conversation has been."

"Tell me, Megan. Why are you so certain that the Wolf will accept my offers of land and pardons in exchange for his life?"

Keeping her gaze on him steady, she raised her chin. "Because no one knows the Wolf's mind as I do. I am certain he will accept your offer."

Rolf studied her thoughtfully for a moment before turning and walking over to the hearth. For some time he stood there in silence, staring into the flames. When he finally spoke, his voice was flat and distant.

"I'm afraid you don't know your father as well as you think, Megan. Two days ago, I received word from the Wolf. He rejected my offers and demanded your immediate release. Therefore, I have decided to proceed with the wedding. As honor will not permit me to turn you over to a man like Farrington, I will wed you myself."

Megan gasped in stunned disbelief as her hand groped at the table for support. "R-rejected?" she stammered, her mind whirling madly. "Ye must be mistaken."

Rolf turned to face her, an aloofness showing in his face. "Sadly, I am not."

She shook her head in dazed shock, as if she could not believe what she was hearing. How could Uncle Geddes have refused to carry out her instructions? It meant either he had lost control of the clan or someone was unduly affecting his decisions. Abruptly the answer came to her with the full force of a heavy blow to the stomach.

*Robbie. God's mercy, it had to be Robbie.*

"Oh, nay," she gasped in anguish, thinking of all she had lost. "What has he done?"

247

Rolf's jaw hardened at her words, thinking she referred to her father. "What he's done, Megan, is seal your fate. Whether you like it or not, you will be wed to me by the end of next week."

# *Chapter Nineteen*

"This is intolerable," Megan muttered, pacing anxiously back and forth across her bedchamber. "There must be a way to put an end to this madness."

She had been repeating the same phrase for days, yet no matter how she tried, she couldn't think of a single reasonable settlement. Nearly a week had passed since Rolf's shocking proposal. And although it was utterly inconceivable—unless a miracle happened—tomorrow she would be the new wife of English nobleman Rolf St. James.

It was sheer insanity.

Saints help her, how had everything become so hopelessly tangled and confused? She no longer had control of the clan nor their actions. Peace had been almost within her grasp. If only Uncle Geddes and Robbie had obeyed her, she would already have the signed land grants and pardons in her hands. Once they were distributed to the men, she would reveal her identity as the Black Wolf and the senseless fighting would be over. The villagers and the clan would be protected.

But now she was left helpless and at the mercy of the English. How could she possibly wed Rolf St. James? If he uncovered her true identity and discovered it was she who plotted the raids against Farrington, would he still be honor-bound to execute his own wife?

Megan clasped her hands anxiously in front of her. Events were spiraling out of her control. There had to be a way to stop the ceremony. Pleading had not worked and reasoning with Rolf had been unsuccessful. From the very beginning, he had taken charge of the situation, making preparations and sending word to the village of his intentions. Several times Megan had almost blurted out the truth, hoping that he would still honor his word to provide amnesty and land to the men. But at the last minute she had held her tongue, hoping that somehow she could extricate herself from this situation without giving away her secret and the only real advantage she had left with which to maneuver.

"Oh, please, God," she prayed softly. "There must be some way to end this peacefully. I ask for ye only to show me the way."

As if in answer, a sudden knock sounded on the door. Whirling around in surprise, Megan stared at it for several seconds before finding her voice. "Who is it?" she finally called out.

" 'Tis me, my lady," Peter answered. "May I enter?"

"Aye, o' course."

The bolt was drawn from the outside of the door and Peter entered the chamber. Behind him followed the unmistakable form of Douglas MacLeary.

Megan's eyes widened when she saw the Scotsman. "Douglas," she breathed.

Douglas turned slightly to look at Peter. The older man dipped his head slightly and withdrew, leaving the two of them alone.

When the door was shut, Megan launched herself into Douglas's arms. "By God, Douglas, 'tis good to see ye. How did ye manage to get permission to see me, and alone nonetheless?"

The older man pulled away from her, adjusting the patch over his bad eye. "The Englishman granted our request to be permitted to see ye and know for ourselves that ye have agreed to this union of your own free will."

"My own free will?" she exclaimed. "Why, the Englishman threatened to see me wed to Edwin Farrington if I did no' accept his proposal. I would hardly say this constitutes free will."

A dark frown crossed Douglas's face, his voice lowering. "Then 'tis imperative that we remove ye from this situation before 'tis too late."

Megan gripped his arm. "Why did Uncle Geddes refuse to accept the Englishman's offers o' land grants and pardons? If he had only agreed to them, none o' this would be taking place."

"Your uncle no longer has control o'er the clans. When he told the men o' your father's demise and that ye had been acting as the Black Wolf in his place . . . well, the Chisholms were furious and the MacDonnells were none too pleased either. Still, I'm certain that all o' them were secretly impressed wi' your skill in leading the clans. 'Tis said that now the Chisholms' eldest son wishes to take ye for his wife. Understandably, Robbie has angrily protested such a union, insisting that 'tis your wish to be betrothed to him. 'Tis an awful mess, lass, and no one seems to be in command. As far as I know, three separate plans for your rescue are being plotted. All o' which have their own goals in mind."

Megan sank into a chair, her hands covering her face. "Saints above, Uncle Geddes warned me o' this very thing and I didn't listen. I should have wed long ago, but my pride and stubbornness prevented me from doing so. Now look what I've done. I've torn asunder the union o' men I fought so hard to bring together. Instead o' standing together against the threat, we are split and weakened. If only Uncle Geddes had accepted the Englishman's offers, none o' this would be happening. As soon as I had the pardons and land grants in my possession, I would have revealed myself as the Black Wolf. Then the Englishman would have had his prize and our people a new beginning. How could it have gone so terribly wrong?"

"Ye should have known that Robbie would no' have allowed him to accept such terms."

"I am Robbie's laird," she countered angrily. "He has no right to disobey me nor put my welfare above that o' the clan."

Douglas put a gentle hand on her shoulder. "A lad in love is likely to think wi' his heart, no' his head. And your uncle is no' one to stop him. He feels guilty that he left ye behind while he and the other men made their escape."

" 'Twas no' his decision. I ordered him to do so," she replied fiercely.

"It does'na change anything and ye know it."

Her anger evaporated. Wearily she pressed her hand to her brow. "Was it Robbie who was waiting for them outside the castle walls?"

Douglas nodded. "Aye, and ye can well imagine his surprise when the men practically fell into his arms. Ye saved many lives that day, Megan. The men have no' forgotten that, nor will they let ye die for them. 'Tis no longer a matter of orders, lass, 'tis a matter o' pride. Ye gave them back their lives. Now they wish to do the same for ye."

Megan threw up her hands in despair. "But I don't want them to risk their lives for me. Please, Douglas, ye must convince them to give up this mad effort to rescue me. If they but harm one o' the Englishman's men, he will be so enraged that any more efforts for a truce will be futile. My life simply isn't worth it. Peace is within our grasp, we have only to take it. Ye must convince my uncle and Robbie that accepting the Englishman's offer is the only way."

Douglas's face was grim. "I canna help ye wi' this, Megan. Robbie's mind is made up. He will no' permit this wedding to take place. And even if he fails, there will be others seeking to remove ye from the Englishman's hands."

Megan looked at him pleadingly. "Ye must do something."

"Even if I could convince Robbie, I couldn't reach the Chisholms or MacDonnells to stop their efforts. 'Tis out o' my hands now, just as it is out o' yours."

"Please, Douglas. I need your help."

The old man sighed. "I'll tell Robbie o' your wishes, lass. But I fear he will no' listen. Nor can I blame the lad." He patted her cheek lightly. "Megan, the Scots have never been ones for an easy solution and ye know it. We will do what we must. Just be careful, for the plan may unfold at any time. Godspeed to ye, lass."

"Are you certain that this is what you want to do, lad?"

Rolf turned from the window where he had been observing the wedding preperations. "Yes, Peter. For the hundredth time, I'm certain I wish to wed Megan. Cease your tireless worrying and be happy for me. It is my wedding day, after all."

The older man sunk into a chair, straightening the fabric on the sleeve of his best shirt. "I am happy for you. But I'm concerned about what you have planned for the ceremony. The Wolf has proven to be frustratingly clever. What if the girl gets hurt during the skirmish?"

Rolf's features hardened. "No harm will come to Megan. I promise you that."

"Still, I urge you to be exceedingly careful with her. She is a strong woman who will not easily divide her loyalties. Even when she is your wife, you cannot expect her to give up her fealty to the clan. We don't know how she will react."

"You leave Megan to me. In time she'll come to see that this is the proper course of action. I only hope that after I have captured her father she will find it in her heart to permit us to start anew. We shall see." He jerked his head toward the open window. "Are the men ready?"

Peter nodded. "Everyone is in place. The villagers have begun arriving for the ceremony and your bride is being readied. As you expected, Farrington sent his regrets, although I sincerely doubt anyone will miss him. And Abigail reports that Megan has been remarkably quiet since the visit from her clansman yesterday."

"Undoubtedly MacLeary warned her to be ready for a rescue attempt," Rolf replied wryly. "She probably thinks she will be safely in the arms of her father by sundown."

Peter chuckled lightly. "Imagine her surprise when she finds herself in the arms of her husband instead."

Rolf could not help but smile at the thought. "Yes, indeed," he said softly. "Imagine it, indeed."

Megan stood by her open window, looking down onto the courtyard. The weather was surprisingly beautiful for spring: bright sun without a hint of rain in the air. Rolf's men moved about, clearing the area and preparing for the ceremony. Fresh rushes were being arranged like a small carpet leading to the center of the courtyard. A small wooden altar had been constructed—an altar at which she would bind herself to the Englishman unless a miracle happened. Or unless he got himself killed first.

Megan shook her head in frustration. Had Rolf St. James any strategic sense at all? Didn't he realize that by holding the ceremony outdoors, it permitted her clansmen greater maneuverability? Didn't he understand that his gesture of goodwill by inviting the villagers to the celebration would also provide cover for her men?

Megan closed her eyes. As much as she wanted to escape this fate, she had no wish to turn it into a bloodbath. Nor could she bear the thought that Rolf might get hurt. And even if she did manage to escape and Rolf survived, he would have no choice but to strike back at them with deadly force. Her men would be ruthlessly hunted down, with no mercy shown. The offers of land grants and pardons would be gone forever. The fighting would begin again and the never-ending cyle of attack and retaliate would continue. God help her, but she had to put a stop to it somehow.

Abigail broke her concentration by entering the room carrying a black tray with tea and toast. "I've brought ye a bite to eat and some tea to calm your nerves," she said briskly. "Then we'll see ye into your gown."

Megan looked at the tray, her stomach churning. "Thank ye, Abigail. But I cannot eat. I fear even a bite would make me ill."

"Nonsense," Abigail said, putting a hand on Megan's shoulder. " 'Twill be hours again before ye can eat. Come now, try something. I know that all brides are nervous, but Rolf is a good man. You have naught to fear from him."

" 'Tis no' Rolf I fear . . . at least no' now." Suddenly a new determination flashed in her eyes. "Abigail, do ye think there is a chance that I may speak to him . . . before the ceremony?"

The older woman looked appalled at the suggestion. "Ye wish to see Rolf a scarce two hours before ye are to wed? Do ye not know that this is bad luck?"

Megan grimaced wryly, thinking that at this point bad luck was the least of her concerns. "I know 'tis a most unusual request, but 'tis most urgent. Please, Abigail, would ye be so kind to tell him I wish to see him? I wouldn't ask if 'twasn't important."

"My lady," she breathed in horror. " 'Tis sacrilegious, I say."

"Please, Abigail. His life may depend on it. I don't want him to get hurt."

Abigail frowned in dismay. "I still say 'tis not right. Are ye certain that ye must do this, my lady?"

"I'm certain."

The older woman sighed. "I don't know if he'll see ye, but I'll give him your request just the same. God forgive my soul if I start ye both off with cursed luck."

Megan let out a breath of relief. "Bless ye, Abigail," she said softly. "And please, don't worry. I promise that ye'll no' regret it."

# *Chapter Twenty*

"An ambush against me and my men during the ceremony?" Rolf repeated, raising a dark eyebrow speculatively. He sat inclined in the leather chair behind his desk, his booted feet propped casually on top of the desk.

Megan felt her frustration rise when she realized that he didn't look the least bit concerned. "Aye, 'tis so," she repeated firmly, clasping her hands behind her as she paced back and forth across the library floor. "And if ye don't put a stop to this ceremony at once, there will be unnecessary bloodshed. Everything we have worked for will come to naught."

"Everything, Megan?"

She stopped her pacing to look at him. "Why do ye keep answering me wi' a question? The solution is quite simple. Ye must put a stop to this wedding at once."

"I'll not do that."

She gasped in surprise. "Did ye no' hear what I just said? They mean to kill ye. Ye do no' fear for your life?"

Rolf unfolded himself from the chair and walked around the desk to face her. "What do you expect me to do, Megan? Quake in my boots with fear?"

"I expect ye to listen. I promise ye that this 'twill no' be a feeble attempt. Many lives will be lost today, mayhap even your own, if ye do no' heed my words. Is this what ye want?"

Rolf leaned back against the desk, folding his arms across his chest. "Is that what you want? To see me dead?"

She shook her head vigorously. "O' course I don't want to see ye dead. 'Tis why I am here, telling ye this. I want to work together for peace. But ye must stop this ceremony. 'Twill only make matters worse."

"I'm afraid matters could not get much worse," Rolf said, shrugging. "It is clear to me that your father has no intention of turning himself over in exchange for the land grants and pardons. So by wedding you, I'm taking a different approach toward that peace."

"And I'm telling ye honestly that this approach won't work," she pleaded earnestly. "Please, ye must listen to me. I have a new plan. I'm ready to accept those pardons and land grants on behalf o' my father."

Rolf looked at her in a moment of stunned amazement before breaking out in laughter. "*You?* You want to accept my offers for your father and the clan?"

"I do," Megan replied, holding her chin up proudly.

Rolf ceased his laughter, rubbing his chin in disbelief. "Really, Megan, do you expect me to believe that the clan would accept the word of a woman over that of their laird?"

"Aye, 'tis what I'm asking ye to believe. Please, at least give me the chance to show ye I am right. Postpone the wedding and let us discuss the matters at hand."

Rolf chuckled. "You are the most outrageous woman I've ever encountered. But I'm afraid I can't do as you ask. I intend to wed you this afternoon, ambush or no ambush."

"Ye'd risk your life to wed me?"

Rolf raised a dark eyebrow in surprise. "Could that be a hint of concern I hear in your voice?"

"Concern that ye may be casting away our last chance at peace."

"I had rather hoped it was concern for my well-being."

"I can't believe that ye jest wi' me when your life is at stake. Ye're as stubborn as a Scotsman."

"Why, I do believe your opinion of me is improving."

She sighed in exasperation. "Will ye at least heed my warning?"

Rolf unfolded his arms from his chest. "You concern yourself needlessly, Megan. I've already taken precautions. Your father's attempt to rescue you today has been well anticipated. It won't succeed, but it might finally put an end to this senseless fighting if I am able to capture him."

Megan's eyes widened with surprise before a look of anger crossed her face. "Ye knew," she accused him furiously. "Ye've known all along. 'Tis why ye decided to have the ceremony outdoors and that's why ye invited the villagers.

Ye've set some kind o' trap, using me as the bait."

Rolf shrugged. "I won't deny it. We both know it's time for me to come face to face with your father. I intend to have the Black Wolf in my hands by this evening."

"And if ye don't? Will all o' your grand plans be dashed?"

"Your father can't hide from me forever. Whether or not I catch him today, I will wed you. It's time for all of us to put an end to this fruitless confrontation and start healing our wounds."

"This is no' the way," she cried.

"This is my way. We will be wed, Megan."

"They will kill ye first."

Rolf sighed. "I appreciate your warning, Megan. I know that it cost you much to tell me this. And I hope that after the wedding you will give me . . . us another chance. It's time to end the bitterness and deceit that still lies between us."

Megan felt her anger disappear. "Ye ask far too much o' me, Englishman. There are secrets . . . things I cannot reveal to ye. No' yet, at least."

"I'm not going to ask you to betray your people."

Megan lowered her gaze. " 'Tis a wise decision, for I would no' do it, even as your wife."

Rolf strode across the room, resting his hand lightly on her shoulder. "Return to your chamber, Megan, and prepare yourself for the ceremony. We have many things to work out between us. But if God is willing, we shall have the time to do so in the future."

She lifted her eyes to meet his. "There is naught I can say that will change your mind?"

"I'm afraid not. I've made my decision."

"Aye, I can see that ye have," she said sadly. "I only hope that ye'll be able to live wi' it."

"Oh, I will," he said confidently. "And so will you, Megan. You might just be surprised."

Megan stood at the window, forcing herself to swallow her panic and think rationally. The villagers were gathered in the courtyard below, jostling about in good cheer, seemingly undisturbed by the unusual union about to take place. God in heaven, how had she permitted this to happen?

She admitted to herself that Rolf had been clever to gain the villagers' trust and respect. They were simple people, understandably anxious to put an end to their suffering. Lest she forget, Rolf had protected them from Farrington in ways that Megan and her father had been unable to do. It was only natural that they would turn to him for help . . . and hope.

Megan sighed deeply. She couldn't blame the villagers. After all, she'd had the same feelings herself. Only as their laird, she was responsible for so much more. These were her people. Their fates were hers to decide. Weren't they?

Anxiously she reached up to wind a curl of hair about her finger. It was too late to do anything about it now. She was already dressed in a long, flowing wedding gown of white linen with a high lace neck. To provide warmth from the cool spring air, a soft cloak of white with a fur collar had been draped loosely around her shoulders. A veil of lace streamed down her back and was held to the top of her head by two large wooden combs. Her hair had been pinned up beneath the veil and small ringlets framed her cheeks. She wore no jewelry, nor had she wanted any. Abigail had agreed, stating the simplicity of the look suited her. Megan only hoped she wouldn't retch all over herself or others before the ceremony.

She exhaled deeply, her eyes nervously sweeping the courtyard for the hundredth time. What was happening down there? She had not seen any sign of Uncle Geddes, Robbie or the men of the other clans. Were they disguised as simple village folk? And where were Rolf's men? Except for the handful that stood scattered about the courtyard, the majority of them seemed to be missing.

Rolf had not yet made his appearance either. Presumably he was late or—if she dared hope—had changed his mind about marrying her. Or mayhap Robbie had discovered a way to steal into the castle undetected and kill Rolf before the ceremony.

Closing her eyes to the grim possibility, Megan chided herself for such a thought. It was true that Rolf St. James was an Englishman and she wished him and his kind gone from Scotland forever. But the notion that he might be slain in a deceitful attack somehow sickened her. Continued deception and dishonesty from either side would only lengthen this confrontation, not settle it. And the truth of the matter was in some strange way, she had come to care for the Englishman.

Megan pressed her hand to her stomach, hoping to settle it. Better not to think such traitorous thoughts. Besides, she didn't know how much longer she could maintain this masquerade of calm. She was almost relieved when Abigail entered the room, announcing that it was time for the ceremony to begin. Taking a deep breath for courage, Megan silently followed the woman out of the room and down into the courtyard.

The sun was blinding and Megan paused in the entranceway for a moment to let her eyes get fully adjusted. As she stepped outside, she was immediately met by Peter and Andrew, both of whom tightly escorted her through the crowd.

As Megan passed the guests, her eyes scanned rapidly for any sign of her clansmen. Most of the crowd did not look at her and kept their faces covered and gazes averted. Instinctively she knew that many were her own men and those of the MacDonnell and Chisholm clans. Only one man, a clansman named Allan Grant, looked at her directly. He was dressed like a peasant and his expression was grim, as if sending her a warning. Swallowing hard, she quickly shifted her gaze to the altar where Rolf patiently awaited her.

She gasped as she took her first good look at him. Clad in a splendid coat of burgundy and a crisp white linen shirt, he was nothing short of magnificent. His long, dark hair was pulled back at the nape of his neck with a velvet ribbon and he wore dark gloves on both hands. A gleaming shortsword hung around his waist from a leather belt.

Realizing that the sword was little more than ceremonial, Megan glanced up at his face, puzzled. Surely, he couldn't mean to leave himself unprotected, especially after the warning she had given him. Dismayed, she frowned at him.

Seeming to have read her thoughts, Rolf

smiled reassuringly and offered his arm. Megan took it, surprised to find herself trembling. He gently led her a few steps forward until they directly faced an English vicar and a local kirksman from a nearby village.

With a sinking heart, Megan realized that Rolf had most likely arranged to have the kirksman at the ceremony to give legitimacy to the marriage in the eyes of the villagers. Yet at the same time, it also served to make the marriage all the more real to her. If she took these vows in front of a kirksman, it would bind her to Rolf forever.

She swallowed hard, glancing at him from the corner of her eye. He had left no stone unturned. Whatever happened between them today would be irreversible. She understood that now.

The vicar began to speak, but Megan could barely hear the words over the thundering of her heart. Any moment she expected a cry to sound and a battle to begin. She was amazed that Rolf seemed so calm. Twice he smiled at her, squeezing her hand reassuringly. Megan fumed inwardly at his arrogance, wondering if he might not get them all killed.

As the cleric droned on, Megan felt increasingly ill. Her vision began to swim sickeningly and she felt hot and suffocated in her gown. Feeling herself starting to swoon, she tried to brace herself against Rolf's solid form, but instead swayed forward into the kirksman.

As Rolf moved to catch her, all choas broke loose. A primal cry arose from the crowd and the sounds of steel being drawn filled the air. Dazed, Megan watched as Allan Grant threw back his hood and jumped toward Rolf, brandishing his sword. She opened her mouth to scream, but

Rolf had already anticipated the attack. He stepped sideways, depositing her into Peter's arms and neatly catching the sword Andrew drew from beneath his cloak and tossed him. In seconds Rolf and Allan were engaged in a furious swordfight.

Megan was instantly surrounded by a protective circle of four of Rolf's men, including Peter and Andrew. Anxiously, she tried to look over their broad shoulders to discover what was happening. From what little she could see, Rolf's men seemed to be materializing from everywhere. Fully dressed in light armor and with deadly weapons, they cleverly cut off the only escape from the courtyard and methodically herded the fighting men into a tight circle. With a gasp of dismay, Megan saw that Rolf intended to trap her men inside the gates of the castle until he could effectively disarm them.

"Och, my God," she whispered under her breath in dismay.

"Meggie, where are ye? Meggie!"

Megan whirled around, recognizing the voice immediately. "Robbie," she screamed as soon as she saw the unmistakable red hair and beard of her cousin. "Look out behind ye."

Robbie turned just as one of Rolf's men swung at his unprotected back. The big Scotsman managed to step out of the way of the deadly arc and bury his sword in the Englishman's shoulder. An agonizing scream spilt the air. Shouting a curse, one of her guards stepped forward to engage Robbie. At the same moment, Robbie danced sideways, coming within an arm's reach of Megan and tossing something at her. Surprised, she barely caught it, fumbling with the object until it was secure in her grasp. She had but a moment to meet Robbie's determined gaze before he turned to engage the English guard.

"Use it," he hissed over his shoulder.

Looking down at her hand, Megan saw that he had thrown her a dagger. Gasping, she quickly thrust it into the folds of her gown just as Peter grabbed her and pushed her behind him for safekeeping. She didn't think anyone had seen the exchange. Anxiously she tried to follow Robbie's progress, but he and his opponent were quickly swallowed up by the crowd until she was no longer sure where they had gone.

She frantically looked about the courtyard for any sign of a familiar face, including that of Rolf St. James. But all she could see was an occasional flash of the Chisholms', MacDonnells' and McLeods' plaids amid a sea of gleaming blades. Unarmed villagers ran about shrieking in fright while trying to stay clear of the fighting. At the same time, Rolf's soldiers were steadily making headway by tightening the circle and leaving the Scotsmen little room to maneuver.

Too late, Megan realized the crux of Rolf's plan. In addition to trapping the Scots in the courtyard without permitting them a chance to retreat and regroup, he was also forcing them to swing their heavy claymores in an increasingly confined space against men who were fully protected in armor and carried shorter and lighter swords. Even worse, none of the clansmen seemed to have a unified strategy, and they all were reduced to fighting single battles instead of combining forces to defeat the English. Rolf had known them better than she had thought possible. His strategy had been well planned and brilliantly executed.

She, like the rest of her men, had once again underestimated him.

"Saints above," she murmured in despair. "'Tis truly the end."

Numb, she watched as the fighting ebbed until there were but a few clanging swords. Rolf's men began rounding up the Scotsmen, until they were all disarmed and stood hostile and dejected inside a well-armed circle of Englishmen. Those that were wounded lay were they fell. Megan turned away, unable to bear seeing the defeated and pained looks on the faces of her countrymen.

A silence fell on the courtyard as the crowd parted and Rolf emerged. His burgundy jacket had been ripped in several places and he had blood spattered across his shirt. His hair was no longer tied back neatly at the nape of his neck, and instead hung in a disheveled heap about his shoulders. Behind him, he angrily pulled a man. A gasp of dismay escaped her lips when she saw who it was.

"Geddes," she murmured, leaning weakly against Andrew.

"Come here, Megan," Rolf ordered when they reached the altar.

When she didn't move, Andrew took her by the shoulders and pushed her unceremoniously toward Rolf. As she stumbled forward, Uncle Geddes raised his head to look at her, his eyes weary and defeated.

"This is the man who called himself Kincaid, and you his daughter," Rolf said in a short, clipped tone. "Who is he really to you, Megan?

I'd advise you not to lie to me again."

Megan exchanged a long glance with her uncle before gazing at the hostile English faces of those who surrounded her. "He is my uncle," she said softly. "My mother's brother. I beg ye no' to hurt him."

"And what would you have me do with him?" Rolf asked angrily. "He just tried to kill me."

Megan raised her chin proudly. "He is my kin and was trying to rescue me. If the tables were turned and your niece was captured, would ye no' see it as your duty to try and help her?"

"I would have never permitted my niece to be captured in the first place."

"Mayhap your niece is no' as stubborn as I am," she countered. " 'Tis no' fair to hold him accountable for my sins."

"Then who shall I hold accountable? Your father, perhaps?" He turned to the huddle of hostile and captured clansmen. "Step forward at last, Robert MacLeod, and I shall spare your kin."

A surprised murmur sounded among the Scotsmen, but no one moved forward. His jaw tightening, Rolf turned back to face Megan. "So what else can I expect from your father, Megan?" he said icily. "He refuses to save his daughter and hides like a coward behind his men to save his own skin."

" 'Tis no' so," she shot back furiously, her cheeks flushing with anger. "The Wolf hides behind no one. He has no' come forward because he is no' among the men ye hold there. 'Tis God's truth."

Peter took a step toward Rolf. "Some of the Scotsmen did escape," he said in a low voice.

"Perhaps the Wolf was among them."

Rolf's scowl deepened as he glared at Megan. "How long does your father intend to play this game of run and hide? Is he a coward now that he is without his magical cloak?"

A red flush of anger crept up her cheeks. "What have ye done wi' my father's cloak?" she demanded.

"It's gone, destroyed, just like your foolish struggle against us. It's time to put these useless ideas of resistance behind you and start working for the future. Summon your father to come forward and face me like a man."

Megan matched his angry stare. "The Black Wolf will come forward when the time is right and all o' our conditions are met."

"And what conditions might those be?" Rolf asked acerbically. "A knife in my back? Another ambush? Or perhaps a slit throat while I sleep in my bed? The Wolf has already rejected my offers of peace—what else does he possibly want? By God, woman, I should force the answer out of you."

"Nay," Geddes cried out. "Dinna harm the lass. She knows naught."

Megan threw her uncle a stern warning glance. "I can speak for myself, Uncle. My father's concern for my welfare has adversely affected his judgment in regards to this situation. I am fully ready to make peace wi' ye, Englishman, on behalf o' my father and all the clansmen here, if ye agree to live up to your promises o' land grants and pardons. We can start the process today."

An interested murmur rippled through the crowd as the villagers pressed close to hear more. The captured clansmen stood deathly still as if hanging on to each word.

"And why should I believe you now?" Rolf replied coolly. "Have you been nothing but deceitful with me? You were part of this planned ambush, weren't you? Swooning just as your men jumped forward so that my hands would be full?"

Megan looked at him incredulously. "Ye think I did that on purpose?"

"Didn't you?"

"Nay, I did no'," she snapped back. "I swooned because it was preferrable to retching all o'er ye. 'Tis no' every day that a woman faces the man she is to wed, knowing all the time that behind her is a crowd full o' armed and angry men ready to slay him. Can ye really blame me?"

Rolf studied her face and the heightened color in her cheeks. By God, it was madness, but he was beginning to believe her. "So you weren't part of this all along?"

"O' course I wasn't," she replied softly. "I tried to warn ye . . . to tell ye o' the folly o' such a ceremony, but ye didn't listen to me."

"I'm listening now," he said quietly.

She nodded, moving toward him when Andrew suddenly lunged at her, grabbing her elbow and forcing her hand out from beneath her gown.

"My lord, 'tis treachery, it is," he shouted. "She has a dagger." He pressed painfully on her wrist until her hand opened and the dagger fell to the ground with a sickening thud.

Rolf looked in amazement at the dagger and then brought his disbelieving gaze to Megan's face. "By God, woman, will your deceit never cease?"

Megan flushed, a stricken look crossing her face. "Nay, 'tis no' as ye think. One o' my clansmen . . . he threw it at me to protect myself."

Rolf took a step forward, bending over and picking the dagger up off the ground. He looked at it for a long moment before flipping it over in his hand and thrusting it toward her handle first.

"Very well, Megan, then take it. If you wish to kill me, have the courage to do it while I watch. For I'll not have you planning any more deceit or murder in our home."

Andrew gasped and moved forward, but Rolf threw him a dark, thundering look that froze the young man in his tracks. "I said take it," he ordered, turning his attention back to Megan. When she did not move, Rolf pushed the dagger into her hand, firmly closing her fingers over it. Keeping his eyes on her face, he grasped the front of his shirt, ripping it open and revealing his bare chest.

A murmur of surprise rippled through the crowd. Uncle Geddes stared at Megan with wide eyes, while Andrew's hand tightened on his sword. Everyone in the courtyard seemed to be holding their breath.

"Come now, Megan," Rolf said softly. "What are you afraid of? Let's settle this matter between us once and for all."

Megan took a shaky step forward, lifting her hand with the knife. She kept her eyes firmly on his face, amazed that he neither blinked nor moved a muscle. He simply watched calmly and waited for her to do what he expected her to do.

Kill him.

Megan's hand began to tremble. Exhaling a deep breath, she abruptly tossed the dagger aside.

"I'll no' kill ye, Englishman, and ye know it. I wish for peace between our people. Let us work toward that end and no' engage in any more senseless killing."

Rolf held her gaze for a long moment. "Are you saying then that you, Megan MacLeod, will take the vows to wed me in good faith?"

She again looked over at the captured clansmen. She started as Robbie suddenly burst forward from the prisoners, knocking one of the English guards to the ground.

"Nay," he shouted, lunging toward her. "Dinna do it, Meggie."

One of Rolf's men tackled Robbie from behind. The big Scotsman went sprawling facefirst to the ground. Megan screamed when one of the guards raised his sword, intending to use it against her cousin.

At the same time, Geddes shouted, rushing toward his son. Peter neatly stepped in front of the old man, forcefully stopping him with a firm hand on his chest.

"Stop!" Rolf commanded loudly, putting an abrupt stop to the spectacle. "Bring that man to his feet," he ordered, pointing at Robbie.

It took four men to drag Robbie from the ground. The flame-haired Scotsman stood, arms pinned behind his back, glowering at Rolf.

Geddes looked wildly at Rolf. "Please, dinna harm him, I beseech ye," he pleaded with Rolf. "He is my son."

"Dinna beg him for naught, Da," Robbie

growled in rage. " 'Tis time he and I faced each other, man to man."

Rolf looked back and forth between the Scotsmen before crossing his arms against his chest and studying Robbie thoughtfully. "So, you are Megan's cousin," he commented with interest.

The big Scotsman spat on the ground and then glared at Rolf with hate blazing in his eyes. "Ye sully Megan's by speaking it on your tongue," he snarled. "Dinna say it again."

A dark scowl crossed Rolf's face. "Megan," he enunciated clearly, "is going to be my wife."

"She'll never belong to ye or any o' to your kind," Robbie shouted.

"You are wrong about that."

"Then show me just how wrong I am. Fight me, Englishman," Robbie challenged recklessly. "Just the two o' us. Let's end this quarrel right now."

"Nay," Megan implored Rolf, clutching his arm as he reached for his sword. "Ye don't have to fight anyone. Please, I will wed ye peacefully, Englishman."

Rolf looked at the imploring expression on her face, and his grip on the hilt of his sword eased.

"Dinna give in to his threats, Meggie," Robbie protested angrily. "I'll no' let ye wed him."

"I'm afraid you are in no position to stop us," Rolf stated. "Megan will be my wife within the hour and we both know it."

"Ye black-hearted bastard," the Scotsman shouted, lunging toward Rolf. "I'll kill ye if ye dare to touch her."

Rolf neatly sidestepped the lunge, grabbing Robbie's arm and twisting it behind his back. Using a trick he had learned in hand-to-hand fighting on the battlefield, he aimed a savage kick at the back of the kneecaps, rendering the big Scotsman flat on his back in one fluid movement.

Robbie scrambled to get up, but froze when Rolf pressed the tip of his sword to his throat. Megan flew to Rolf's side, grasping his arm.

"Nay," she cried. "Don't hurt him."

"Och, let the knave kill me," Robbie spat, never taking his eyes off Rolf. "I'd rather be dead than see ye wed to the likes o' him."

"As you wish," Rolf replied, shrugging and pressing the point tighter against his neck.

"Don't do it," Megan said softly, pulling on Rolf's arm. " 'Twas ye who wanted an end to the senseless killing. If 'twas true, then show me that ye truly meant what ye said."

Rolf paused for a long moment before lifting the sword from Robbie's throat. "Take him away," he ordered his men coldly. "Then see to the injured and take the rest of the prisoners to the dungeon. We shall finish the ceremony now."

"Nay," Robbie shouted. "Meggie, dinna wed him."

"God forgive me," Megan whispered as her cousin was dragged away. Tears slipped down her cheeks.

"Come, Megan, let us complete the matter at hand," Rolf said evenly, putting his good hand beneath her elbow to help steady her.

Megan took a deep breath, determinedly brushing the tears away from her cheek. She had to pull herself together—try to make some good of the spectacle that had just happened.

"First, I want ye to know that even if I pledge

275

myself to ye, I'll no' knowingly betray my people," she said firmly. "Even for ye as my husband. 'Tis only fair ye understand that now."

"I understand."

"And what do ye mean to do wi' Robbie, my uncle, and the rest o' the men ye hold prisoner? I'll no' see them harmed."

"The men will be questioned, but I assure you they will not be hurt. When I am done, I will set them free."

"And those who are injured?"

"They will be treated and then they will also be released. Does that allay your fears?"

"It does," Megan answered softly.

"Then so shall it be. Now let us continue." He took her arm, leading her to the base of the altar where the visibly shaken vicar and kirkman stood.

"Where were we?" Rolf asked.

The vicar fumbled with his leather book and then hastily asked them to recite their vows. A few tense minutes later, Megan found herself legally bound to Rolf. Her life as she had once known it was now over.

Rolf turned to his wife, releasing his hold on her arm. "You will return to your room where you will be permitted to rest before the celebrating begins," he ordered her briskly.

"Celebration?" she gasped.

"We have just been wed, have we not? It is a momentous occasion and we will celebrate it fittingly."

"Ye must be in jest," she said, her blue eyes widening in disbelief. "Ye can hardly expect us to celebrate after what has happened."

Undaunted, Rolf lifted her hand to his mouth,

grazing her knuckles with his warm lips. "Oh, but I assure you that I do. Go on now, Megan, I have a few matters to settle before we begin."

Megan opened her mouth to reply, but Rolf gently pressed a finger against her lips. "For once don't fight me. Just be ready when I come for you. For now, it's really all I'll ask of you."

# *Chapter Twenty-one*

Megan sat numbly at the banquet table, not even managing to summon a smile as the boisterous English soldiers lifted their goblets in toast after toast to the bride and groom. She suspected their good cheer was partly because Rolf's trap for the Scotsmen had been executed so effectively, and partly because Rolf put no restrictions on the wine and ale that flowed into their cups. Whatever the reason, the noise in the room was deafening and the mood buoyant. Megan thought it to be little more than a nightmare from which she could not escape.

For the hundredth time that evening, she stole a quick glance at Rolf. He also appeared to be in unusually good spirits, despite the fact that he believed the Black Wolf to have slipped through his fingers again. He had changed his clothes and sipped his wine in a relaxed manner while talking with Peter and several of his men about the day's activities.

In fact, he had barely given her a glance all evening. Megan wondered if this was an indication of how their marriage would be. He had wooed and seduced her until he had what he had wanted—a legitimate claim to her and her lands in the eyes of the Scots. Now his bargaining position was stronger and more secure than ever. What he didn't know was that she still had one more card to play. She was the Black Wolf, the quarry he so desperately sought, the prize he had promised to his King. She had not given up hope that she could still play that card. And once she had possession of the promised land grants and pardons, she'd reveal herself as the Wolf. But until then, she would have to make her moves carefully. *Very* carefully. She knew that deceiving an enemy was one thing. But she suspected that deceiving a husband was something else entirely different.

Megan felt a tightening in her stomach. She could raise no suspicions about herself. This meant she had to do her best to play the docile wife of Rolf St. James—both in and out of his bed—until the time was right.

*His bed.*

Megan pressed her hand to her brow, feeling faint at the thought. How could she have been so foolish to think that his kisses were warm and exciting? Now that she understood there was nothing behind his ardor but cold, hard ambition, the thought of lying in his arms held no attraction. In fact, as she glanced around the table at the faces of the English soldiers, she began to feel increasingly ill. Had she made a terrible mistake by wedding this man? Should she not have had the courage to plunge the knife into his breast?

She shook her head. No matter how distasteful the thought of lying with this man, it was a sacrifice she would make for her people. She had done the right thing. Now, she had only to pray for strength. The bedding act—it couldn't be that horrible. After all, women had been doing it for centuries and still managed to survive. No matter how terrible it was—she would just have to bear it bravely in order to save her people.

Megan's eyes were suddenly drawn to the door as Abigail discreetly stepped inside the chamber and stared at Rolf. Curiously, Megan followed her eyes and saw Rolf nod briefly at the older woman. At once Abigail moved directly to Megan's side. Lightly she placed a hand on her shoulder.

"Come, my lady. 'Tis nearly time."

Megan started violently, nearly knocking over her goblet of wine. "Time for what?" she asked in a hollow voice, her lips cracked and dry.

Abigail bent down near Megan's ear. "Come now, my lady. 'Tis naught to fear."

Megan stole another glance at Rolf, but he was speaking with Peter and did not even glance her way. Swallowing hard, she stood and let Abigail guide her from the room, feeling like a lamb being led to slaughter.

When they reached Rolf's chamber, Megan stood on the threshold, feeling a sweep of bitter irony that she would spend her wedding night in the same chamber her parents had once shared. What a mockery that this night she would suffer horribly in the bed where two people had once loved so deeply. God help her, could the humiliation go any deeper?

"Let me help ye," Abigail said, untying the back of Megan's gown and lifting it off over her head.

Megan did not resist or move, only stood staring dumbly at the hearth where a roaring fire blazed. The room was dark except for the glow of the fire and a few scattered candles. The scent of hot spiced wine wafted from two goblets on a small table near the fireplace. In any other circumstances she might have found it cozy and inviting, but now she wished with all her heart she were anywhere other than this room.

*God, give me strength*.

"Well, that's finished," Abigail said, pulling the shift over Megan's head and leaving her naked save only her stockings and shoes. "Sit down, and I will remove your stockings."

Megan slowly walked over to the bed, where she perched on the edge. Abigail made quick work of her shoes and stockings before handing her a white woolen nightdress. Megan quickly slipped it on, thankful that the gown had a high neck and long sleeves. Fingers trembling, she buttoned it all the way to her throat.

Abigail clucked her tongue sympathetically. "I know that this is probably not how ye imagined your wedding day. But Rolf is a good man and all will be well. Ye'll see, my lady. Have faith."

Megan swallowed, fighting back the tears that had threatened to fall all day. " 'Tis no' just that, Abigail. Rolf is an Englishman . . . the subject o' a King who cruelly drove my family from our home and has the blood o' my clansmen on his hands. He seeks to slay my father and took me as his wife only to further his ambitions. How can I participate in this marriage in good faith?"

Abigail firmly took Megan's cold hand in hers. "Now ye listen to me. Rolf is a good man and he cares for ye, no matter what ye may think. He could have forced ye to wed a brutal man the likes of Edwin Farrington, but he did no'. Instead, he chose ye for himself. I think he did so because he believes ye both have a chance at happiness if only ye would put the past behind ye. 'Tis a lot more than many marriages begin with." She patted Megan's hand encouragingly. "I wish for happiness for ye both."

Her words were interrupted by a noise at the door. Megan went a shade paler as Rolf appeared in the entranceway, his arms folded lightly across his chest.

Abigail rose. "The girl is readied, my lord."

Rolf nodded, and Abigail turned to give Megan's hand a final pat before she disappeared from the room. Rolf closed the door after her.

Megan sat deathly still on the edge of the bed, keeping her eyes trained on the floor. The silence in the room was deafening until Rolf strode across the room, removing his jacket and neckcloth. Draping both over a chair, he sat down near the hearth and lifted the goblet of wine to his lips.

"Come join me, Megan," he said softly.

After a moment of hesitation, Megan rose from the bed and slowly walked toward him. Rolf watched her without comment, wondering how it was possible that her simple and demure nightdress seemed so seductive. He thought perhaps it was the way the soft fabric clung to her slender arms and waist, or the way her bare toes peeked out enticingly from beneath the hem. Whatever the reason, he found the effect erotically provocative.

Now, though, she looked frightened half to death. Her blue eyes were round and afraid, her mouth drawn in a tight line, her face as pale as a sheet of parchment paper. As she came closer, her hand unconsciously clutched the material at the collar of her nightdress. God help him, but he would have to take this slowly. He did not want her to be frightened.

"Have some wine," he said, pressing the goblet into her hand as she sat. When she held it to her lips, Rolf saw her hand tremble uncontrollably.

"To us," he said softly, raising the goblet in a salute. "And to putting the past behind us. No more lies between us, Megan. No more deceit."

At his words, Megan lowered her gaze and the goblet, staring miserably into the wine. She would not further compound her deceit and meet his toast . . . she couldn't. Not while she still held the secret of her identity from him.

When she did not raise her cup in agreement, Rolf felt his hopes for an easy transition to the bed fading. Taking a large swallow of his wine, he stood up determinedly. Drawing this out would only make it harder on both of them.

Holding out his good hand, he took the goblet from her hand and set it on the table. After helping her to her feet, he began gently pulling the pins from her hair. Thick dark strands tumbled down her back and around her shoulders.

"Much better," he murmured.

She didn't move, standing as still as a statue, unmoving and cold. Slowly, he slid his hand down from her hair to her cheek, lingering on her shoulder and then her breast. When she shivered, he lifted his hand to her chin, nudging it up until she looked at him.

"Are you cold, Megan?"

"N-nay," she said, her teeth chattering slightly.

Rolf let his knuckles graze her cheek. "There is a draft in here. I think it best if we retire to the warmth of the bed."

"I'm no' yet tired," she said so softly he barely heard her.

"Hmm . . . it wasn't sleep I was thinking about," Rolf said, fingering the top button of her nightdress and watching as a flash of panic shot across her face.

"I would like some more wine," she said hastily. "It might warm me."

"I can think of another and more pleasurable way to warm you," he replied, his voice low and husky. "Come now, Megan, don't you think it's time to remove this gown?"

She gasped audibly as his fingers unfastened the top button of her collar and began to lightly caress the skin at her throat. "I . . ." she began unsteadily, and then cleared her voice. "I think 'twould be better if I kept it on. Besides, as ye said, there is a wee bit o' a draft in here."

Rolf's dark eyebrow shot up in amusement. "Are you saying that you wish to conduct our lovemaking within the layers of this woolen gown?"

"Aye," she said quickly, and then looked up at him with a questioning look. "I mean, if 'tis possible to do so."

Rolf smiled in amusement. "All things are possible, Megan. But I assure you that your gown would only be in the way."

"But why must I remove my gown when ye are still clad?" she protested.

Looking down at himself, Rolf nodded. "So I am," he agreed. Pulling his shirt over his head, he cast it carelessly to the chair. "There, I've taken off my shirt. Does that make you more comfortable?"

Quickly averting her gaze from his muscular chest, Megan shook her head. "Nay, no' really."

Sitting down in the chair, Rolf pulled off his boots one by one, followed by his stockings. Barefoot and bare-chested, he stood in front of her, his hands on his hips. "Now?"

Megan looked over at him, and shook her head again. "No' yet."

Sighing, Rolf unfastened the ties at the front of his breeches and stepped out of them, leaving them on the floor. Spreading out his arms, he gave himself up to her inspection. "Now?"

Megan slowly lifted her gaze, drawing in a sharp breath. She had half-expected Rolf St. James to be rendered vulnerable by his nakedness, but it was exactly the opposite. Instead of being embarrassed or self-conscious, he stood easily in front of her. His skin was bronzed and taut, and the corded muscles in his arms and legs revealed a strength of body that she had not fully realized. A dark whorl of hair covered his chest and spiraled down to the flat of his stomach to where it cushioned his manhood and spread out across his thighs and legs. He was every inch a man.

Megan bit her lower lip uncertainly. It was not the first time she had seen a man unclothed—she had long been responsible for treating the injuries of her clansmen. But for the first time in her life she was looking at one in a different light. This man who stood in front of her was her husband . . . someone with whom she would share a bed. Stunned, she realized that the thought of lying with him was not such an unpleasant prospect after all. He was a magnificent specimen of a man.

After some time had passed and she had not spoken, Rolf cleared his voice. Megan started guiltily, her cheeks flushing red. "I'm sorry. I didn't mean to stare," she confessed in embarrassment.

Reaching out his good hand, Rolf lifted her chin until she looked at him. "I don't want you to be afraid of me, Megan. There is nothing wrong with what we are about to do as husband and wife."

"I know," she replied, wringing her hands together in front of her. " 'Tis just . . ." She fell silent.

"Just what, Megan?"

Her brow furrowed worriedly. "Well, I know ye married me to gain legitimacy in the eyes o' my people and secure a stronger foothold for the English here in the Highlands. But ye could have just as easily seen me wed to Edwin Farrington without a stain to your reputation and still achieved your goals. So why did ye really wed me?"

Rolf moved his hand from her chin to wind a strand of her dark hair about his finger. "It's true that was part of the reason I wed you. But I also married you because I wanted to. It's the damnedest thing, but I've been attracted to you from the first moment I saw you huddled in the snow, wrapped in that black wolf pelt. You are not like any woman I've ever known, Megan. Somehow it became inconceivable that I might leave here, never really knowing what happened to you and what it would be like to share that remarkable spirit of yours."

"Then ye do care . . . for me?" The words came slow and haltingly, as if she were afraid to speak them aloud.

"Certainly enough to hand you a knife with which to kill me. I pledged my life to you today, Megan. If you wish to take it, there will certainly be a time when you would be able to do so."

"I would never willingly harm ye," she replied quietly. "But things between us are so complicated—so hopelessly tangled—that sometimes the truth is hard to find."

"I'm not going to let anything come between us anymore."

"I wish ye wouldn't say that. There's much ye still don't know about me."

"I know that you are my wife. Right now, that is enough for me."

She smiled tremulously. "I care for ye, too. There may be things that will happen between us to give ye cause to doubt it, but 'tis true. I don't know how it happened, but I do know that ever since I've met ye, ye've kept your word to me and acted wi' honor."

"Is that really the only reason you care for me, Megan?"

She exhaled a deep breath. "Nay, I suppose 'tis no' the only reason. Sometimes when we are together, I feel different. It's as if I can't quite seem to catch my breath and my stomach flutters like it is full o' butterflies. But other times, like tonight at the banquet, I feel as if ye are a cold, aloof stranger."

"Tonight? At the banquet?" Rolf repeated puzzled.

She nodded. "Aye, 'twas like I was no' there. I thought that mayhap now that ye got what ye wanted, ye no longer wished to bargain with the Wolf to provide my clansmen wi' pardons and land grants."

"I gave you my word that I would."

"But those same men tried to kill ye today. No one would blame ye if ye decided to rescind your promises."

"I don't go back on my word, Megan," he said firmly. "Ever."

Megan sighed, absently tucking the wayward strand of hair behind her ear. " 'Tis still hard for me to accept the word o' an Englishman. Ye canna blame me for that."

Rolf placed his hand on her shoulder, turning her to face him. "I'm not just an Englishman anymore. I am your husband. And if you must know, the true reason I paid you scant attention at the banquet was to keep from sweeping you off to my bedchamber before an acceptable amount of time had passed. I've done a lot of thinking about this night, Megan."

She blushed deeply at the implication of his words. "But I've no' been wi' a man before. What if I disappoint ye?"

"You will not disappoint me, Megan. And I'll not force you to do anything you don't want to do. I want to make this a pleasurable experience, not a frightening one."

" 'Tis why ye have disrobed in front o' me. Ye wish to set me at ease."

He grinned. "Yes. Do you realize we've been standing here talking for some time and I am completely unclad? Are you comfortable yet with what you see?"

Megan stepped back from him and then shook her head. "Nay," she said softly. "For I've no' seen all o' ye." She glanced at his left hand, which was still gloved and hung loosely at his side.

Rolf followed her gaze, frowning. "I don't normally remove it. It's not a pleasant sight, Megan."

"But I want to see all o' ye," she repeated firmly. "I must."

"I don't think it wise."

"What are ye afraid o'?" she asked him quietly. "That I'll recoil from ye as Caroline did? Ye've no need to fear such a reaction. I'm your wife now. If we are to bare our bodies to each other, we must also bare our souls."

Rolf met her steady gaze for a long time, as if weighing the sincerity of her words. Finally he reached down and began peeling the leather glove from his hand. The material stuck slightly on his little finger and he pulled it off with a yank, wincing in pain.

Silently Megan stepped forward, bending in front of him on one knee and taking the maimed hand in hers. It lay frozen in a clench, the fingers curled and stiff from disuse.

"There, Megan," he said tightly. "You have seen all of me. Are you disappointed I am not a whole man?"

To his surprise, she leaned forward, her dark hair spilling like a river of silk over his arm. With agonizing tenderness, she pressed her lips to his lame hand.

"Ye are beautiful," she whispered softly. "All o' ye."

Rolf's breath caught in his throat. "Oh, God, Megan," he murmured as her lips moved across his fingers to touch the vein that pulsed at his wrist.

"Thank ye for trusting me enough to show it to me," she whispered, lifting her head to meet his gaze.

Bending over, Rolf lifted her into his arms and carried her to the bed. Settling her back against the pillows, he joined her, rolling onto his side and resting a hand on the curve of her hip.

"You are the most extraordinary woman I've ever met," he said softly. "If only our joining could have been under different circumstances. I never wanted to cause you any pain."

Megan reached up to touch his cheek. "Have ye heard the saying 'A wise man lives in the present'? Well, I think 'tis good advice. I want only to think o' now and what we can make o' this moment. I won't ask more o' ye, if ye will no' ask more o' me."

Rolf took her hand, holding it firmly against his cheek. "I won't lie to you, Megan, I do want more from you. I want to be more than just your husband in name. I don't want to repeat the same mistakes I made with Caroline. I know it will be difficult for you to accept me for who I am, especially after all the pain I have caused you. I want you to know that if I could spare the life of the Wolf, I would. But I can't, and we both know that. My responsibilities lie heavy upon me."

Megan looked at him, surprised by his confession. "Aye, we must both live out our destinies, Englishman," she said softly. "But for tonight, let's put all other thoughts aside except what we feel for each other right now. For neither o' us knows what tomorrow will bring."

Tenderly smoothing back a strand of hair from her face, he brought his mouth down over hers. The feel of her soft moist lips beneath him ignited a flame of desire he had long thought extinguished. His tongue glided sensuously across her lips until she opened her mouth to him. Gently he plunged inside, stroking and kissing her soft crevices with his tongue. His desire increased. She felt so good, so right against him.

Slipping his hand down to her waist, he pulled her nightdress up around her hips. Lightly he drew his fingers in small circles around the inside of her thighs and across the flat of her stomach until she moaned and shifted restlessly against him.

"Perhaps now would be the appropriate time to remove this gown," he murmured in a hot breath against her cheek.

She smiled and nodded in agreement as he slipped his arm behind her back, lifting her up as he pulled the woolen gown over her head. When she lay naked in from of him, he drew in his breath sharply.

"My God, Megan, you are lovely," he said in a hushed voice.

Hesitantly, she reached up for him. "Kiss me again," she whispered. "Help me to forget everything except being here with ye."

Rolf drew her closer, his hand sliding beneath

her neck. His own passion mounting, he tilted her head back and molded his mouth to hers. She kissed him back awkwardly at first, and then with a growing eagerness that ignited a burning ache inside him. Feeling his need begin to spiral out of control, he pulled away slightly, trying to slow down.

"Easy, Megan," he murmured, reaching down to caress her bare breasts. "You're so damn beautiful, it's a miracle I've been able to resist you for so long."

She grasped his shoulders. "Nay, don't stop. Please."

Rolf smiled, staring down at the passionate dark-haired beauty beneath him. He still couldn't believe that this remarkable woman was his wife. Her fire boiled his blood; her passion mirrored his own. Never before had he met a woman more suited to him. The knowledge both thrilled and stunned him. Never before had he had so much to lose with a woman, and so much to gain. He wanted everything to be just right for both of them. This time he would do everything right.

"I'm not stopping," he said, nuzzling her neck. "Before God, I couldn't stop if I wanted to. I think I'm in love with you."

Megan's eyes snapped open as she heard his words. *Love*? God in heaven, he couldn't possibly. If he truly did love her, it would make her betrayal all the more devastating. She cared about him too much to let that happen. Frantic, she tried to sit up, but was pressed down by the weight of his body.

"Wait," she said, but her cries were silenced

by his hungry mouth covering hers with urgent need.

"Lie still, Megan," he murmured lifting his mouth from hers and planting his knee between her legs. "When you move like that beneath me, it takes all I have to control myself."

"Nay," she said, panic starting to grip her.

Rolf shook his head, misunderstanding her fears. "Don't be afraid, Megan. It will hurt only for a minute. I promise you." Before she could protest further, he eased her legs apart, poising himself between her hips. "The first bit is the hardest. But after that, I assure you that it gets easier." Lifting his hips up, he thrust forward toward her damp core. He felt a brief resistance and then he was inside. Shaking with need, he took a deep breath, managing with supreme effort to still himself.

"Are you all right?" he inquired through gritted teeth.

"Is it over?" she asked in a small voice.

He made a sound between a groan and a laugh. "No, not yet."

"What's next?"

"Just relax for me, love," he whispered. "It will be good, I promise."

Slowly he began to move inside her, and Megan felt a delicious quiver of expectation tingle in her abdomen. " 'Tis nice," she said softly. Looking up at him, she saw his eyes were closed and the expression on his face one of pain and concentration.

"Does it hurt ye, too?" she asked curiously.

"Yes . . . no," he gasped, between thrusts. "I want to go slow, but I'm not certain how much longer I can hold out. I want you, Megan."

Instinctively, she arched against him in an inexperienced manner, drawing him deeper inside her body. "Then ye don't have to go slow," she said softly, moving her hands across his back and the hardness of his spine. "Do what ye must."

Rolf groaned in response, his heavy body pressing down against her. "It . . . feels . . . so . . . good," he panted. "I want you to . . . feel it . . . too."

"Help me then," she whispered back.

Moving his mouth near her ear, he began whispering hot words of sensual promise. All the while, his hand slid seductively down her bare hip and the smooth roundness of her buttocks. He kissed her, slowly at first and then roughly, wildly, barely reining in a burgeoning passion. Need crashed over him like a tidal wave. He'd never wanted a woman like this. It was if his entire body were on fire—every pore screaming for release.

Forcing himself to slow down, Rolf lifted a scant inch to look at her. Her hair was in a tangled disarray about her shoulders, her lips red and swollen from his kisses. "Do you feel it now?" he murmured against her cheek.

Megan wanted to answer, but she couldn't. Her breath was all but gone as he touched her everywhere, knowingly, intimately and without pause. She felt as if an explosive force had gathered in her stomach and threatened to explode.

"Megan?" he inquired again softly.

"Something . . . something is happening to me," she gasped in a terrified voice.

At her words, desire roared in his ears, snapping the last of his control. "Hold on, love," he whispered hoarsely. A groan ripped from his throat as he sank deeper and deeper into her.

Megan arched hard against him, straining toward him and toward something else . . . something elusive and just beyond her grasp. The pressure in her stomach built and increased. Both frightened and exhilarated, she grasped his shoulders so tightly, her nails dug into his skin. When the force finally exploded within her, she stiffened and then moaned with pure delight.

"Rolf," she gasped.

Rolf heard her call his name, and his own consciousness faded before he burst inside her. She still clung to him, her hair plastered against his damp chest. Sweat trickled down from his temples and he shuddered once before collapsing on her in a heap.

Slowly, he felt reality return piece by piece. The flicker of the candle, the rough feel of the quilt beneath his knee, the warm, sensuous scent of their lovemaking. For a moment, he simply held her close, savoring the exquisite pleasure he felt in her arms.

"Are ye all right?" Megan asked timidly, reaching up to stroke the damp hair at the base of his neck. She could feel the rapid pounding of his heart against her breast. Holding him close, Megan felt a curious sense of tenderness. God help her, but was she falling in love with him, too?

Lifting himself up on his elbows, Rolf looked down at her, their bodies still joined. He gently kissed her forehead. "I don't think I've ever been better. But I'm sorry I had to hurt you."

"Och, 'twas only a wee bit. And what came afterwards . . . well, 'twas worth it."

Grinning at her honesty, he rolled to the side,

pulling her with him into a tight embrace. "Do you know what I liked best?"

She snuggled into the crook of his arm. "What?"

"You called me by my Christian name for the first time since I have met you."

Megan laughed softly, blushing at her moment of pure abandon. "Well, if that was the best part for ye, then I fear I have failed miserably in my efforts to please ye."

Rolf tipped her chin up until she was looking directly at him. "No, Megan, you didn't fail. You've more than exceeded my expectations in all ways."

Sensing a deeper meaning behind the words, she looked away, not ready to face his emotions . . . or her own. "Well, mayhap we'd better do it again until I get it right," she said lightly. "Another lesson, perhaps."

Rolf chuckled, his hot breath fanning against her cheek. "I've created a wanton wench. Well, dear wife, just give me a minute or two, and I assure you that your wish is my command."

# Chapter Twenty-two

Rolf dressed quietly in the cool chill of the morning air as the sun streamed in through the window, sending light dancing across the stone walls and floor. The fire had long burned out and there was a faint chill in the air.

"When will I be able to see my uncle?" Megan asked suddenly, clutching a blanket to her bare chest.

He hadn't known she was awake. Turning around slowly, he saw her sitting up in the middle of their bed, her hair tumbling over her shoulders, cheeks flushed pink from sleep and a long night of lovemaking. In fact, she looked so innocently enchanting he had to fight the urge to join her under the covers again.

"Soon," he promised, calmly tucking his shirt into his breeches. "I only need some time to speak with him alone."

"Ye . . . ye won't harm him?"

Rolf walked over to the bed and lifted her chin gently. "When will you learn to trust me, Megan? I gave you my word I will not harm him."

She nodded uncertainly, the intimacy of what they had shared last night still too fragile to withstand examination in the harsh light of day. "I know. 'Tis just that I can't help but worry about him."

Rolf sat beside her on the bed, lightly brushing her dark, heavy hair from her shoulder. "It's time I met your father, Megan. I want your uncle to convey a message to him. He and I are now kin whether or not he likes it. I'm offering to meet him alone, without the threat of capture or trickery. I want only to convince him, face to face, that surrendering peacefully is the best solution for all of us."

"Ye wish to meet my father face to face? I don't think 'twill be possible."

"It is not an unreasonable request."

"I know," she agreed. "But he is a very cautious man. Would ye instead consider meeting wi' a proxy who has been given the right to act on his behalf?"

"Why are you so certain that he'll reject my offer? We are now family after all."

" 'Tis just a feeling I have. I don't think he'll agree to meet wi' ye."

Rolf frowned. "Do you really think your father fears me so much? This doesn't sound like the behavior of the legendary Black Wolf."

Megan looked away quickly, fearful that her face would betray too much information. "I know our ways seem odd to ye. But my father is a very prudent man. Mayhap he would simply deem it wise to have someone else act on his behalf."

Rolf stood slowly, walking over to the hearth, where he picked up his leather glove and began pulling it onto his crippled hand. His expression was thoughtful and grim. "I'd be disappointed if the Wolf refused to meet with me," he said finally. "But I suppose I might consider discussing matters with a proxy, if that is what it would take to put an end to the fighting and convince your father to turn himself over to me."

"Any proxy?" Megan asked quickly.

Rolf raised a dark eyebrow. "Why do you show such interest?"

Megan flushed, shrugging with as much nonchalance as she could summon. "Och, I was just wondering."

Rolf picked up his jacket from the back of the chair and thrust his arms into it. "Well, don't wonder too much. All of this is out of your hands now. However, if I were you, I'd encourage your uncle to cooperate with me. We both know that drawing this situation out is not beneficial for either side. And make no mistake about it, Megan. If there is another attack like the one yesterday, I will not be so forgiving."

Megan stared at her husband wordlessly as he strode across the room to brush a kiss across her forehead. "Don't worry," he said, softening his tone. "I'm sure that your father is a reasonable man and all of this will be settled with due haste. Then we can finally get on with our lives. I ask you to trust me. That's not too much to ask now, is it?"

Megan managed a tremulous smile. " 'Tis harder than ye think. But I'll try."

Rolf stood, giving her soft cheek a final caress. "Good. Because I look forward to the day when we no longer must face these unpleasant issues. I want a resolution to this problem and I want it soon."

After he left, Megan fell back onto the bed with a thump, taking the blankets with her. "That resolution will be sooner than ye think, Englishman," she whispered softly, pulling the covers up to her chin. "Far sooner than ye think."

"Uncle Geddes," Megan exclaimed as Peter led the older man into the small sitting room. "Thank God ye are finally here. Have ye been harmed?"

Geddes shook his head and stood quietly as Peter removed the strips of cloth that bound his hands behind his back.

"Rolf said to permit you a few minutes alone, but no longer," Peter said briskly, looking as if he did not approve of their meeting. When she nodded in acknowledgment of his words, he withdrew from the room, leaving the two of them alone.

As soon as he was gone, Megan threw herself across the room and into her uncle's arms. "Och, Uncle, 'tis good to see ye. Are ye certain ye are no' hurt?" Her eyes filled with concern. "Mayhap ye should sit for a spell." Firmly, she steered him toward one of the chairs in the small sitting room.

Geddes lowered his large frame into it with a sigh. "I'm not hurt, Megan. In fact, none o' us have been harmed and many o' the men have already been released. The Englishman's been true to his word. But how have ye fared, lass?"

Megan blushed deeply, thinking of their long night of lovemaking. "I'm well, Uncle."

Geddes breathed a sigh of relief. "I feared greatly for ye, lass. But dinna fret. 'Tis still a chance we might have the marriage annulled."

Megan looked up in surprise. "Annulled? Why, 'tis impossible. I took the vows in front o' a kirkman."

"Ye were coerced. Even the kirkman could see that."

"Aye, 'tis true to a point. But don't forget that the Englishman could have forced me to wed Edwin Farrington. Instead, he offered me a bargain. 'Twas one I reluctantly accepted, but accepted nonetheless. We both know I took those vows willingly . . . at least as willingly as can be deemed possible under the circumstances."

"Willingly is no' a word that comes to mind," Geddes protested, clearly surprised by her resistance. "We both know ye sacrificed yourself for the clan. Even the Englishman knew that. He blackmailed ye into wedding him."

"It still doesn't change the fact that I agreed in principle to this marriage. The reasons behind my consent don't matter. I stood in front o' the kirkman and God and said my vows. There'll be no annulment."

Geddes stroked his bearded chin with his fingers, his face deepening into a frown. "Do ye understand what ye are giving up, lass? What about your life wi' Robbie?"

She sighed deeply. "I love Robbie wi' all my heart—ye know that. We grew up together as bairns; we helped each other through our deepest pains. But I fear our union 'twas simply no' meant to be. He'll find someone else—there are many women who would be honored to have him."

"He's never wanted anyone but ye."

Megan's blue eyes filled with sadness. "I know. But he will find someone else. He deserves happiness and I pray that he finds it. How is he faring in the dungeon?"

Geddes lifted his hands wearily. "Och, he's as angry as a trapped bear, but none the worse. The Englishmen are still questioning him, but he's no' been harmed. Ye have naught to worry about wi' Robbie or any other o' the men. No one has revealed anything about the death o' your father . . . nor what we've done since his demise."

She nodded gratefully, clasping her hands behind her back. "What about the Chisholms and MacDonnells? Are they keeping silent about the Black Wolf as well?"

"For the time being. They need to determine how your marriage to the Englishman will affect them. I suspect, however, that they'll no' honor Rolf St. James' claim to the lairdship in this area."

"Och, 'tis naught but bluster," Megan grumbled, starting to pace the chamber, the skirts of her blue gown swishing with the rapid pace. "We both know they have little choice in the matter."

"Aye, 'tis so," Geddes agreed. "But 'tis the MacLeod clan that will prosper from a deal wi' the Englishman, no' them. Ye canna blame them for being wary."

Megan whirled around quickly. " 'Tis no' only the MacLeod clan that will prosper. I intend to bargain for land grants and pardons for all the clans in Gairloch. That includes the Chisholms and MacDonnells."

Geddes's eyes widened in surprise. "Have ye lost your senses, lass? What makes ye think the Englishman will agree to such broad terms?"

She exhaled a deep breath. "Truthfully, I don't know that he will agree. But I've come to see him as an honest man. He's told me that he intends us to live at least half the year at Castle Kilcraig and govern the area personally. Frankly, I believe him. 'Twould be in his best interest to bring peace to as much o' the land as he can."

"Do ye really trust him to keep his word, Megan?"

"I do."

" 'Tis still a lot to expect o' the man," Geddes said doubtfully. " 'Twill take much persuasion, I fear."

Megan lowered her head. "Mayhap no' as much as ye think," she said softly. "He's said he's in love wi' me."

Geddes choked on the breath of air he had just taken, the color draining from his face. "Good God, Megan," he spit out. "Do ye realize what ye are saying?"

"O' course I do. And it doesn't make it any easier for me."

"Is this part o' your plan?" he asked hesitantly. "Because if 'tis so, 'tis terribly dangerous."

" 'Tis no plan, Uncle," she said quickly. "And I swear on all the saints that I didn't do or say anything to make him feel this way."

"Yet ye refuse to consider an annulment," Geddes said, frowning. "Tell me the truth, lass, what do ye feel for this man?"

Megan lifted her face quickly, her expression

troubled. "I don't know, Uncle. Sometimes I can't stop thinking about him. And when I'm no' wi' him, I find myself wondering what he's doing and if he's thinking o' me. When he smiles at me, I can feel my heart beat faster. I know he's an Englishman and 'tis wrong, but 'tis God's truth that I've come to care for him."

Geddes pressed a hand to his temples as if to calm the visible throbbing there. "Saints preserve us, this does complicate matters. But mayhap 'tis for the best. If he does love ye, 'twill make it easier for him to accept the word o' Cameron McCandie."

"Cameron McCandie?" Megan repeated blankly. "What does Cameron have to do wi' any o' this?"

"Now dinna argue wi' me, Megan."

Megan's blue eyes narrowed angrily. "Don't argue wi' ye about what? Just what are ye plotting, Uncle?"

"Cameron has agreed to forfeit his life and come forward as the Black Wolf. 'Twill be the best solution for all o' us."

Megan's mouth hung open in shock. "Wh-what?" she gasped.

Geddes put his hands firmly on her shoulders. "Listen to me. I'd do it myself, but ye have already foolishly revealed me as your uncle."

"I'll no' agree to it," Megan declared firmly. "So ye might as well put it out o' your mind."

"Now ye listen to me, lass. We both know the Englishman will never agree to any bargain unless the Wolf turns himself in. Cameron is the same age as your father and is fairly similar in appearance. Once ye make the deal for the land

304

grants and pardons, he'll come forward as part o' the deal."

Megan angrily shook her uncle's hands off her shoulders. "I am the Wolf, no' Cameron. And I will reveal my identity as soon as the pardons are distributed."

"The Englishman will no' believe ye."

A stubborn glint flashed in her eyes. "Aye, but he will. I'll explain to him in great detail each and every raid and strategy we've employed since my father's death. I'll even tell him how I brought together the clans. I can give him information that no one except the Wolf could possess. I promise ye that by the time I'm finished, he'll have no choice but to believe me."

"It does'na matter," Geddes replied, raising his voice heatedly. "We both know that he won't let ye die as the Wolf. Ye're his wife, for God's sake. He'll insist on another to take your place."

" 'Tisn't so. Rolf St. James is a man o' honor," Megan countered fiercely. "He'll have no choice but to tell his sovereign the truth. And there will be no more talk o' another standing in my place. 'Twas I who assumed my father's identity, no' Cameron. I'll no' let another man suffer for my deeds."

"What if the Englishman is angered by your deception?" Geddes shot back heatedly. "He might just take back everything he has given us. 'Tis too much to risk."

"I believe he'll no' rescind on his promise. Besides, 'tis too late. Have ye forgotten that he now owns the land by both decree and marriage to me? We both know 'tis irrelevant whether I live or die. Naught will change here. So ye can tell

Cameron that his offer is noble, but I'll no' let him stand in my place."

"Megan," Geddes growled in warning.

She shook her head in firm resolution. " 'Tis my final word, Uncle. I'll no' compromise on this, no matter what ye say. I'm the last surviving MacLeod. 'Tis my responsibility."

"Ye are the most stubborn woman I've ever known," Geddes exclaimed, throwing up his hands. "Ye've yet to listen to reason. Do ye really think the Englishman will permit his own wife to be executed?"

" 'Twill no doubt be painful for him, but necessary. 'Tis his duty to bring his King the Black Wolf. I am the Black Wolf."

Geddes growled with frustration. "God forgive me, but I should have put a stop to this madness long ago."

"Now listen to me, Uncle. If it hadn't been for our activities, we'd have never caught the eye o' the King and maneuvered ourselves into a bargaining position. I can end the feuding, if ye'd just let me. For God's sake, I beg ye to let me finish what we started. 'Tis the only way."

"I'm no' going to let ye die, Megan."

"Well, mayhap ye won't have to. The truth o' the matter is that I don't know what will happen when I reveal my secret to the Englishman. Perhaps my life might be spared. But ye and the clan must be ready to face the consequences if I am to be taken to London. Think o' it this way— my life for the all the lives o' our clansmen, including their wives and bairns. Don't throw away our only chance. Go tell the clansmen what I intend to do. Then return to Castle Kilcraig and inform the Englishman that I have been chosen to speak on behalf o' my father. Tell him also that the Black Wolf has given his word to come forward when all matters are settled and the land grants and pardons are distributed."

Geddes began pacing the room agitatedly. "And what if the Englishman will no' agree?"

"He'll agree. Ye have only to trust me."

"Trusting ye is what got us into this misfortune to begin with. I dinna like this plan. I'll no' let ye sacrifice yourself."

"But ye'd have another sacrifice his life in my place? Listen to me, Uncle. Cameron McCandie has a wife and six bairns. I'll no' let him take my place and that's my final word on the matter. Besides, if his deception is discovered, it could cost us everything."

"Och, and what o' your deception?" Geddes shot back. "Have ye thought carefully o' that, Megan? No' every man is reasonable once he discovers the woman he has confessed to loving has betrayed him."

A troubled expression crossed her face. "I know. 'Tis a matter that must be settled 'tween me and the Englishman. Yet I believe he'll punish only me when he learns o' my deception. Undoubtedly he'll be in a rage, but he is a fair man."

Geddes stopped his pacing. "God save us from your innocence, child. Ye know far too little o' men, Megan. 'Tis a dangerous a game ye play."

"Mayhap 'tis so, but I'll take that risk. Please, Uncle, we've come this far and are so close to peace. Don't ruin it out o' some misplaced effort to save me. 'Tis too late for that and we both know it."

"I dinna know anything o' the sort."

Megan put a gentle hand on her uncle's shoulder. "Aye, but ye do. I am already wed to the Englishman and he's agreed, at least in principle, to deal with a proxy o' my father's as long as the Wolf gives his word to turn himself in. 'Tis my belief that we are but days from witnessing the end o' the feuding in Gairloch. 'Twill be my greatest accomplishment as a MacLeod."

Geddes frowned, the lines on his weathered face deepening. "Ye are far too noble . . . much like your da, Megan. Why couldn't ye have gone to Ireland for safekeeping like he asked?"

Megan gazed directly at her uncle. "Because running away is no' the way o' the MacLeods. Ye know this to be true. When my da died, the legacy was mine to continue. I'm no' sorry for what I have done, nor would I have done anything different."

Geddes sighed deeply. "Do ye really trust the Englishman to live up to his promises?"

"I do."

Geddes threw up his hands in the face of her certainty. "God's blood, I canna believe I'm even considering this. My mind must truly be affected by all this madness."

"I know ye'll do what's right."

"What's right is to stop ye from throwing away your life."

"What's *right* is to save our people."

Geddes exhaled a frustrated breath. "There is no guarantee that this plan o' yours will work."

"There's no guarantee that it won't."

Geddes was silent for a long moment. "I'm no' blind, Megan. I know we have a lot to gain if this plan actually works. 'Tis only that the cost is too high."

"Och, now ye are speaking wi' your heart and no' your head."

"I'll no' deny it. Ye are like a daughter to me, Megan, I love ye wi' all my heart. I canno' in good faith let ye trade your life away."

"We *must* put the clan first."

Geddes sighed deeply. "Saints forgive me, but I know. 'Tis what pains me so much." He closed his eyes wearily. "And as much as I dinna want to admit it, your argument does have merit."

"Then let us end the bloodshed now, Uncle."

Geddes opened his mouth as if to protest, and then shut it. "Again events have moved out o' my control. All right, Megan, I'll agree to cooperate wi' ye, but only on one condition. Ye'll no' stand alone in front o' the Englishman. I'm as much responsible for this scheme as ye are. If ye insist on revealing yourself as the Wolf, I will also insist on facing the punishment wi' ye."

Megan shook her dark head vigorously. "Don't be foolish. There's no need for both o' us to give our lives. Besides, the clan will need ye more than ever once I'm gone."

He folded his arms stubbornly across his chest. "Either ye tell the Englishman that I'm as much responsible for this deception as ye or I'm no' going along wi' your plan. Ye canna have it both ways."

"B-but—"

"No more arguments, Megan," he interrupted firmly. "Either agree or I walk out o' here."

Frustrated, Megan met her uncle's unwavering stare. "All right," she finally agreed. "But I don't like it."

Geddes snorted. "Well, if the truth must be known, I dinna like it much either. I only hope the Good Lord will forgive me for all the mis-steps I've made wi' guiding ye."

Megan exhaled a deep breath, reaching out to place a hand on her uncle's shoulder. "If ye don't mind, while ye are talking to Him, would ye mind asking forgiveness for my sins as well? I'm afraid I've made far too many missteps o' my own and fear He isn't even listening anymore."

Geddes shook his head sadly. "Ye are impossible, Megan."

She smiled at his words, absently tucking a strand of hair behind her ear. "Aye, I guess that I am, Uncle. Mayhap 'tis just in the MacLeod blood."

# *Chapter Twenty-three*

Rolf impatiently paced the drawing room of Edwin Farrington's house, where he had been waiting for nearly half an hour. He had anticipated a delay, as his visit was unexpected, but he suspected that Farrington was deliberately taking his time. Swallowing his frustration, Rolf paused at the window and pulled aside the heavy drapes, staring out at the Scots' village below.

The view was magnificent and Rolf drew in his breath sharply. It was another beautiful spring day in the glen and not at all what he had expected. He had been told that Highland springs were wet and miserable, but the gorgeous weather of the past several days were proving all the naysayers wrong.

The village itself was a quaint sight, snuggled between two large hills. Faint wisps of smoke rose lazily from the huts and people moved about the village paths, carrying baskets filled with wood, peat and other assorted necessitites. A small distance away on a grassy hill, two men and a dog herded sheep.

Rolf shook his head in wonder. This peaceful setting was a far cry from what he had expected to find the day after the chaotic events of the wedding. In fact, he had been surprised when his men had informed him that all appeared calm in the village. Had violence and chaos become such a part of their lives that they were so easily able to shrug it off? If so, it was a pity and only strengthened his resolve to see a peaceful end to the conflict. God help him, but these honest and good people deserved better.

"My sincere congratulations on your wedding."

At the sound of Farrington's voice, Rolf turned slowly from the window, letting the draperies fall back into place. Edwin stood causually by the hearth, the picture of an impeccable English gentleman. He was dressed in a pale gold jacket and matching breeches, white stockings and gold buckled shoes, his fair hair brushed neatly to the nape of his neck and fastened with a gleaming gold clip.

"I must say, however, that your announcement came as rather a shock," he continued. "I still can't imagine what possessed you to marry one of the heathen."

Rolf stood perfectly still. He had to maintain control, at least until he finished his business here. "My reasons are my own," he said tightly.

"Of course they are," Edwin replied smoothly. "And she appears to be a pretty wench, indeed. I hope you received my regrets about the wedding. I sincerely apologize for missing the grand event, but I've been feeling rather ill lately. I'm certain you understand."

"Perfectly," Rolf replied shortly.

Edwin smiled, his thin lips stretching apart in what almost appeared a grimace. Striding across the room, he lifted a glass decanter from the table and poured the amber liquid into a glass. "May I offer you a glass of whiskey in celebration?"

"No. What I'd like is a moment of your time to discuss a rather new arrangement."

Edwin replaced the glass stopper on the decanter and turned around to face Rolf. His eyes flashed with curiosity. "A new arrangement, you say? By all means, you have my fullest attention."

Rolf lifted his elbow and leaned it lightly against the mantle. "I came here to tell you that as a result of my wedding yesterday to the daughter of Robert MacLeod, things in Gairloch have changed. Substantially."

"Changed?" Edwin inquired warily. "In what manner?"

Rolf shrugged. "It's quite simple really. I now own this land."

"You?" he gasped in stunned disbelief.

"I'll have you know that I'm not an unreasonable man," Rolf continued, ignoring the shocked look on Edwin's face. "I will permit you to continue the day-to-day supervision of the village and let you conduct whatever business you have in this area as long as it is done in a legal and just manner. But you will answer to me and you should be aware that your tenants have a right to complain. They will be afforded due process of those complaints—complaints which will ultimately be heard and judged by me. My word in these matters will be final."

Edwin looked at him stupidly, his mouth hanging open. When Rolf met his gaze calmly, Edwin set his glass down on the table with a loud thump, the liquid sloshing over onto his hand.

"Have you utterly lost your mind?" he spluttered in outrage. "I'll have you know that the King himself has given *me* jurisdiction in all matters relating to this area. If you think that your marriage to that Scottish harlot changes things—think again. You are nothing more than a soldier sent here to protect me and my holdings from the heathen. Just who in the devil do you think you are?"

Rolf stood up slowly, the lines at his mouth tightening with anger. "Frankly speaking, as of this moment, I'm your landlord. And despite your fondest wishes, I'm no longer just a temporary presence in this area. The King has permanently granted me Castle Kilcraig and all her grounds in an effort to bring peace and stability to this area. Of course, he asked me to permit you to stay here and conduct your dealings in the area. I graciously agreed on the condition that you do not act against my wishes. However, I'm giving you fair warning that if at any time I deem your behavior to be inappropriate, I will have you removed from this property at once."

"Don't you dare threaten me."

Rolf smiled coldly. "I'll do whatever I damn well please."

"We'll see about that," Edwin said, his mouth narrowing with anger. "I'll bring this up with the King personally if I have to."

"That is certainly your right," Rolf said calmly. "However, I suggest you familiarize yourself with this document first." Reaching beneath his jacket, he pulled out a rolled parchment and tossed it onto the table. "It's the King's instructions. You'll find your position here explained in great detail."

A red flush of anger crept up Edwin's neck as he clenched his hands at his side. "Damn you. You'll rue this day, I promise you. My brother has the ear of the King. He won't stand for this. He'll make the King see the folly of his ways."

Rolf laughed. "You're pathetic, Farrington. Do you really think I fear your brother's influence with the King?"

"If you don't, you should. These lands rightly belong to me and so do the heathen. You've gone too far this time."

Rolf strode across the room, disgusted by Farrington's behavior. "I've given you a warning, Farrington. One warning. I'll not give you another chance. If you disobey me, you'll regret it."

"Get out," Edwin shouted, his face turning purple with anger. "Get out of my house at once."

Rolf looked at him with contempt. "Just heed my words for you've had your warning." He strode to the door, pausing momentarily in the doorway. "Oh, yes, and one more thing. If you ever call my wife a harlot or a heathen again, I'll kill you. In fact, I believe I'd damn well enjoy it." Without waiting for comment, he left the room, letting the door swing shut behind him.

Swearing, Farrington picked up his drink, his fingers tightening around the glass. "Crippled, pompous bastard," he spat out. "I'll show you

what happens to people who dare to cross me."
Tilting back his head, he threw back the rest of
the whiskey. Coughing from the fiery liquid, he
wiped his mouth with the back of his hand and
hurled the glass at the door where Rolf had disappeared. The goblet smashed into the wood
with a shattering crack, scattering shards and
fragments across the floor. Moments later a servant timidly peeked his head around the door.

"Is everything all right, my lord?" he asked in
a small voice.

"Get someone in here at once to clean up this
mess," Edwin snapped angrily. "And then bring
me my pistol. I've a personal matter to attend
to."

"Ye're finally back," Megan said sighing a
breath of relief as Rolf walked into the bedchamber. "I've been waiting all day here alone in this
room. How much longer are ye going to treat me
like a prisoner?"

Rolf unwound the neckcloth from around his
throat, tossing it on a chair. "I'm sorry, Megan.
It won't be much longer. Just remember that this
is for your protection as well."

Megan walked over to the window and pulled
aside the drapes, staring moodily out into the
courtyard. The dusk of evening had already
crept across the landscape, shrouding the trees
and shrubs in gray shadows. "Well, 'tis awful."

Rolf sighed, walking over to her and massag-
ing her shoulders. "I know that it has been difficult. But perhaps it will cheer you to know that
the rest of your clansmen have been released,
including your uncle and Robbie. Perhaps one

of them will soon bring word from your father."

Megan turned to face him, her expression serious. "I haven't yet thanked ye for releasing them. I know ye could lawfully punish them for possessing weapons and wearing their plaids. 'Tis great restraint ye showed. I wanted ye to know how much it means to me."

Rolf placed his forefinger under her chin, caressing it gently. "I did it for us, Megan. Because I want us to start trusting each other. But I won't lie to you. If your father rejects any more of my attempts at compromise, I'll have to employ force to end this standoff."

"He'll cooperate," she replied softly. "This time I am certain o' it."

"I hope you are right." Impulsively, Rolf drew her to him and held her tightly to his chest. "Damn it all to Hell and back, I wish this detestable business was finished. Every day that passes only causes you more pain. Why must it be me who always brings it to you?"

Megan felt her throat constrict at the tenderness of his embrace. "I don't blame ye. 'Tis simply our fate."

"Well, I'm going to change that fate. Things will work out for us, Megan. I promise you that. I'm not going to repeat the same mistakes I made with Caroline."

"Ye are a good man," she whispered. "But 'tisn't wise to make promises that ye may no' be able to keep." A sob caught in her throat.

Frowning, Rolf pulled away slightly. "What's wrong?" he asked in concern. She looked away in embarrassment. " 'Tis naught."

Determinedly, Rolf took her by the shoulder, propelling her to a chair and sitting her down in it. Kneeling in front of her, he took firm hold of her hand.

"I want you to talk to me, Megan. Tell me what is bothering you."

She shook her head. "Ye wouldn't understand. Naught is wrong and yet, everything is wrong."

"How can I help you if you won't talk to me?"

"I'm no' the woman ye think I am," she whispered. "Ye deserve someone better."

Rolf looked at her in amazement before laughing softly. "Forgive me, Megan," he said when she looked at him in astonishment. "It's just that no woman has ever said such a thing to me. Most women would be satisfied with my fortune or titles. But you are the only one who has ever been concerned about my heart."

"I oft wish things could be different 'tween us."

Rolf's expression softened. "I know our problems seem difficult, even insurmountable. But I promise you that when all of this is finished, we'll start over. We can still make it work, Megan. I know we can."

She smiled sadly. "Ye know so little about me."

"I don't need to know more."

"Och, but I'm afraid ye do, Englishman."

A surprised look of hurt flashed in Rolf's eyes. "We're back to 'Englishman' now, are we?" he said, his voice deepening with a trace of anger. "What happened to that passionate woman who shared my bed last night and called me by my Christian name?"

"She existed only for the night," Megan said softly. " 'Tis all she really ever had."

Before he could reply, a sharp knock sounded on the door. Dismayed by the interruption, Rolf jerked his head toward the sound. "Who is it?" he called out irritably, rising to his feet.

" 'Tis Peter, my lord. The man who calls himself Geddes Kincaid has returned. He said he brings word from the Wolf."

Rolf glanced swiftly at Megan, who looked up at him anxiously. Bending over the chair, he put a hand on her shoulder. "We'll finish this coversation later," he said in a low voice. "I intend to find out what is bothering you."

For a moment something flickered deep in her blue eyes. "Ye are wrong to care so much about me," she said softly. " 'Tis almost the end for us."

Rolf shook his head determinedly. "You're wrong, Megan. It's only the beginning. Now think about that while I hear what your uncle has to say."

# Chapter Twenty-four

"You knew your father would choose you to be his proxy," Rolf said angrily, throwing open the door to their bedchamber with a loud thump.

Megan rose slowly from the chair, pulling her white woolen robe tighter around her shoulders. Her dark hair was loose and hung to her waist in a thick, heavy curtain of black silk. Rolf thought she looked like an angel of the night amid the dim and flickering light of the fire. It only heightened his anger that she looked so soft and innocent.

"Aye, I knew," she said quietly.

Slamming the door behind him, Rolf walked across the room until he towered above her. "Hell and damnation, Megan. How did you know that?"

Calmly she looked up at him. "My da trusts me and my negotiating skills. I knew he would choose me to work wi' ye regarding the pardons and land grants. But I also knew ye had to hear it from him before ye would believe it."

His expression darkened. "There's something more you aren't telling me."

"Aye, 'tis so, but I told ye I'd no' betray my people, even as your wife."

Rolf's eyes narrowed. "Do you know what I'm beginning to think? I think that there is no such person as the Wolf."

She paled at his words, but lifted her chin stubbornly. "Don't be absurd," she answered. "Do ye think ye fight a ghost?"

"I don't know who I'm fighting, but I'm beginning to believe that your father is not the man he has been made out to be. How else can I explain his cowardly actions?"

"The Wolf is no coward," Megan answered quietly. "Did he no' promise to turn himself o'er to ye once the land grants and pardons are distributed?"

"Frankly, I no longer believe in his promises."

Megan reached out and took Rolf's hand into her own. "Then believe in me. I give ye my word that the Wolf will reveal himself as soon as we are finished with the business at hand. Please, 'twill be as I say."

Rolf raised an eyebrow. "How curious, Megan. You want me to trust you, but you won't trust your own husband to have your best interests at heart. Is that not a lot to expect of me?"

"I know 'tis a great leap o' faith. But please, I beg ye to take it. For me."

Moving away from her, he walked about the room, his hands clasped behind his back. Finally, he stopped to look at her. "You've asked for a leap of faith and I'm willing to grant it to

321

you. But only if you agree to trust me. I don't want any more lies between us."

She gazed at him solemnly. "I promise ye, Rolf St. James, that after this business is finished and the Black Wolf has turned himself in, there will be no more deception or lies between us. I give ye my word as both your wife and as a MacLeod."

Rolf stared at her for a long moment, weighing the sincerity of her promise. "All right, then," he finally said. "I'll accept you as your father's proxy. I'd like to put an end to this as quickly as possible."

"Let's start tonight," she said quickly.

"Tonight?" He raised a dark eyebrow. "The hour is late."

"I know, but I'll no' be able to sleep, knowing that peace is within our grasp. Please, let us begin now. 'Twill no' be a moment too soon."

He looked at her curiously and then sighed. "All right, I'll go to the library and bring up the papers."

"Thank ye," she said softly. "Ye don't know how much this means to me."

Edwin Farrington was furious. In fact, he could not remember when he had been so angry. He wanted to punish someone for the injustice that had been done to his person; he needed to vent his rage. And he knew exactly how he would do it.

Scowling, he bent low over his horse. There was no moonlight, but the small covered lantern he dangled in his hand shed just enough light to see the path. Impatiently, he glanced over his shoulder, urging the handful of men that accompanied him to make haste. His excitement heightened as he saw the faint glow of several small campfires in the near distance.

"Onward," he shouted eagerly, digging his heels into the side of his horse. He and his men thundered into the first cluster of village huts which lay less than two miles from his estate. Edwin pulled back hard on the reins, ordering his men to stop. The villagers came running out of their huts in surprise, warily regrouping when they saw who it was. Several of the men formed a protective circle in front of the women and children, who stood huddled wide-eyed and frightened in the doorways of the huts.

Two of the village men stepped forward, one of them holding a pitchfork in his hand. Edwin eyed them disdainfully from his perch on his horse.

"What do ye want o' us at this hour?" the villager asked, holding the pitchfork out in front of him.

Edwin slid off his horse and motioned for a few of his men to follow suit. He set his lantern aside and approached the man slowly.

"I've come at this hour because I've decided to evict you," Edwin announced softly. Then in an abrupt tone of voice, he bellowed, "You will leave at once!"

There were gasps of surprise and shock among the villagers. Several of the women clutched the children closer, pulling woolen wraps more tightly around their shoulders.

"We aren't going anywhere," a villager shouted from the back of the crowd. "Ye canna make us. Ye are no' our landlord anymore."

Edwin stepped forward, the glow of firelight

glancing off the sharp edges of his pale face. "I'll do whatever I please," Edwin replied, raising his voice a notch. "And I assure you that I can make you do what I want . . . unless you do something to appease me."

The villagers fell silent until one man stepped forward from the back of the crowd, coming to stand beside the man with the pitchfork.

"What is it that you want from us?" he asked Edwin, crossing his arms against his chest. Edwin studied the man with interest. The villager was an older man with a heavy red beard tinged with gray. He was dressed as commonly as the others, but he had an air of authority about him that made Edwin slightly uneasy.

"And just who are you?" Edwin asked, frowning.

"My name is Geddes," the man answered. "Geddes Kincaid."

The name meant nothing to Edwin, but the fact that this large man spoke to him in such a non-deferential manner infuriated him.

"I would suggest, old man, that you step aside. You can't help here."

The Scotsman did not move. "I beg to differ," he replied calmly. "Mayhap I can assist ye. There is no need for anyone to be harmed here."

Edwin's mouth dropped open in astonished shock. How *dare* the old man speak to him in such a fashion.

"I . . . I simply can't believe your impertinence," he spluttered. "Get out of my way."

"No' until ye tell me what ye want from us."

"I want you to obey my orders," Edwin said dramatically, "or someone will get hurt." As if on cue, one of Edwin's men darted forward and roughly grabbed a young boy standing by by the fire, dragging him back to where the Englishmen stood.

The young boy yelped in surprise, flailing his arms and trying frantically to free himself from the vicious hold. Geddes and several of the villagers leapt forward to intervene, but Edwin immediately drew his pistol and pointed it directly at Geddes's chest.

"If anyone moves," he warned, "I'll shoot him."

The villagers froze in place and the young boy fell silent, trembling in fright.

Lifting his hands slowly, Geddes spoke. "Let the lad go," he said slowly.

Edwin laughed. "You would dare to defy me? You—a pitiable old man? Have you really such a strong wish to die?"

Geddes shook his head, stepping forward until the pistol nearly touched his chest. "Ye are no' going to hurt us any longer, Farrington," he said firmly. "Shoot me, if ye may. But be warned that I'm no' just any villager. I'm kin to Rolf St. James's wife. If ye shoot me or the boy, he will seek retribution. I promise ye that."

There was a murmur of surprise from Edwin's men. Edwin's pale face contorted with anger, the light dancing eerily off the curved planes of his face.

"You are kin to the low-bred MacLeod strumpet?" he said, his voice rising a notch in disbelief.

Geddes calmly crossed his arms against his chest. "Insults about me or my kin will no' waver my resolution," he said.

Several of the village men stepped up beside Geddes, forming a solid line beside him. They were unarmed, but their faces were determined and strangely unafraid. Edwin felt the first twitch of panic.

"Get back, I say," he warned, waving the pistol. "I'll shoot this man, I swear I will." Suddenly the young boy wrenched himself free from Edwin's man with a frightened squeal. The sound of tearing cloth filled the air as the boy left his shirt behind in the hands of his stunned captor. As he darted into the crowd, several of the Scotsmen stepped in front of him to form a protective barrier.

Furious, one of Edwin's men swung his sword flat-bladed, sending one of the villagers sprawling to the ground, screaming in pain.

A bellow of rage sounded from the villagers as they abruptly rushed forward. Geddes swung his fist, aiming for the pistol in Farrington's hand. Just as he made contact with the metal, Edwin fired the pistol. Geddes swayed on his feet for a moment in shocked surprise and crumpled to the ground.

Edwin scrambled for his horse, swinging up into the saddle. "Retreat," he shouted. He pulled back on the reins of his horse while at the same time kicking out savagely at one of the village women as she tried to set his breeches on fire with a burning torch. He laughed as she shrieked in pain.

Bringing the reins down against his horse's neck, he shot forward. Riding frantically from the village, he dared a glance backward and saw that chaos had broken loose.

Throwing his head back, he laughed wildly, feeling a sudden rush of satisfaction. He had killed the marriage kin of the despicable Rolf St. James. That would teach him to think twice before crossing Edwin Farrington again.

# Chapter Twenty-five

The sound of running footsteps down the stone corridor of the castle jolted Megan from a deep sleep. Rolf had already leapt out of the bed and was thrusting his bare legs into a pair of breeches by the time she sat up.

"What is it?" she asked him in alarm, frantically searching the bedcovers for her robe.

"I don't know," he replied, snatching his shirt from the back of the chair. "But stay here and bolt the door behind me."

He grabbed his sword and headed for the door just as someone pounded heavily on it. Rolf slowly lifted the latch with the tip of his sword and kicked open the door, holding his sword out in front of him.

Andrew gave a frightened squeal, jumping back to avoid the deadly blade. "My lord," he gasped.

"That will teach you to identify yourself before

you pound ceaselessly on my door," Rolf snapped, pulling a shirt on over his head. "Would you care to tell me what the devil is going on?"

"It's the villagers, my lord. They've risen up and are making their way to Farrington's estate. Word is that they are going to burn it to the ground. It seems Farrington wandered into the village completely sotted and demanded the people leave. A few of our men were there and witnessed the entire spectacle. One of the villagers stood up against them. He was shot."

Andrew swallowed hard, his glance moving from Megan to Rolf. "It was her uncle, my lord."

"My uncle?" Megan gasped in horror, the color draining from her face. "Geddes?"

When Andrew nodded in confirmation, Rolf swore fiercely under his breath. "The damned idiot. He's gone too far this time." Expression darkening, he grabbed his boots, thrusting his feet into them. "Have my horse readied and see that at least thirty of the men are saddled," he instructed Andrew. "Then return here and make certain that Megan remains safely under your protection."

Megan rose from the bed, her face drawn but angry. "No' this time," she said quietly. "I am going wi' ye."

"Don't be foolish, Megan. It's far too dangerous for you to acompany me. I promise that I will deal with Farrington properly this time."

"My uncle needs help. He is injured."

Andrew cleared his throat uncomfortably. "I'm sorry, my lady. Your uncle . . . I'm afraid he . . . well, you see . . . oh, curse it, there is no easy way to say it. He didn't survive. Farrington shot him dead." The young man looked down at his boots miserably.

Megan stilled in shock. "Dead?" she repeated dazed.

Exhaling a deep breath, Rolf strode across the room, gathering her in his arms. "Oh, Megan, I'm sorry."

She buried her head in his chest, her shoulders starting to shake. "Oh, God, no' Uncle Geddes," she moaned in despair.

Rolf tightened his embrace. "I'm not going to let Farrington get away with this, Megan. I promise you that he will be justly punished."

She lifted her head from his chest, a deep-seated grief etched on her face. " 'Tis too late now, Rolf."

He cupped her cheek gently. "I won't kill him in cold blood, but I will see that he stands trial, Megan. Some of my men witnessed the murder. This time he won't get away with it."

She shook her head. "Nay, ye don't understand," she whispered. " 'Tis no' ye I fear will kill him. 'Tis Robbie. He'll kill Farrington for this. Or die trying."

Rolf frowned. "If your cousin kills Farrington, *he'll* face a sentence of death for the murder."

Megan's eyes clouded with worry. "He won't care. 'Twill be too much for him to bear. We must stop him."

"I must stop him."

"*We* must stop him," Megan repeated firmly. "I'm going wi' ye to Farrington's."

"You aren't going anywhere," Rolf repeated. "You will remain here."

Megan slipped from his embrace and picked up her blue gown from where it lay over the back of a chair. "Ye won't be able to stop him, Rolf. He won't listen to ye."

"I'll make him listen."

"Ye can't, Rolf, and ye know it. But he might listen to me. Now don't argue any more wi' me about this. I'm coming wi' ye."

Rolf growled in frustration. "I don't like this, Megan."

She turned to face him, her eyes weary and grieved but determined. "I've lost my brother and now my uncle. I'm no' going to lose my cousin, too. I just couldn't bear it. Now if Andrew would give me a moment o' privacy, I will put on my garments and we can leave at once."

Rolf gritted his teeth in frustration and then jerked his head at Andrew. "Leave us," he ordered curtly.

The boy quickly withdrew. Rolf strode over to Megan, laying his hand on her shoulder. "You can accompany me, Megan, but on one condition. You must stay close to me and do exactly what I tell you, regardless of what you want."

She hesitated for a moment and then nodded, her dark hair tumbling softly about her shoulders.

"I give ye my word, Rolf St. James," she answered.

Megan rode double with Rolf, her arms wrapped tightly around his waist. The night was cold and she shivered beneath her cloak.

"Take several of the men to the village and secure it," Rolf ordered Peter over the galloping of the horses. "I want to make certain Farrington and his men don't try to double back and burn the entire place down. I'll take the rest on to Farrington's estate."

Peter nodded, veering off to one side and motioning for a half-dozen men to follow. Rolf continued straight up the steep hill in front of them.

When they reached the top, Rolf paused, aghast at the spectacle in front of him. Clearly the villagers had already reached the outskirts of the estate. Farrington's stable and a few other assorted buildings were already on fire. Flames licked up toward the sky like a bright orange tongue, casting an eerie yellow glow over the entire area. Horses that had been released from the stables whinnied in fright and stampeded unhindered about the grounds in panic. Piercing screams and angry shouts split the night air.

"My God," Megan breathed from over his shoulder.

"Hold on to me tightly and keep your head low," Rolf ordered, digging his heels into the side of the horse and rushing toward the house.

The fighting was sporadic, but fierce. Rolf carefully guided his stallion among the clashing men. Several were engaged in hand-to-hand combat, using swords, knives and clubs. A few of Farrington's men had pistols, and Rolf could see that they were firing indiscriminately.

Rolf whistled under his breath. This scene was far worse than he had anticipated. If he didn't act soon, he'd have a damn massacre on his hands.

Wheeling his horse around, Rolf manuevered sideways just as a musket ball whizzed past his head.

"That's it," he said between clenched teeth.

Urging the horse away from the action, he dismounted near a tree, handing Megan the reins. "Stay here," he ordered her. "I must get this situation under some kind of control."

With those instructions, he headed for Edwin's house. Nearing the structure, he saw one of Farrington's men raise his pistol and take aim at a villager. Sprinting across the grass, Rolf grabbed the man by his shoulder and hauled him to the ground. The pistol fired aimlessly into the air and they both hit the earth with a heavy thud.

Frantically the man tried to escape, but Rolf kept him on the ground with a savage blow to his midsection. "Stay down," he warned, pressing his forearm into the man's windpipe. "My lord," the man gasped in shocked surprise as he recognized Rolf. "I'm sorry, I didn't know it was you."

"You're damn fortunate for that," he growled, rising and pulling the man to his feet. "Where is Farrington?"

The man looked nervously over his shoulder, his face black from the smoke. "He's in the house. We were told to stay out here and protect the estate."

"By attacking unarmed villagers?"

"They have torches and clubs, my lord. They mean to burn the place down."

"It's no wonder after what Farrington did—shooting defenseless old men. Damn, are you all fools?"

"I was just doing as I was ordered," the man said sullenly.

"Well, you have new orders now. Inform your men that I've ordered the fighting to cease at once. I'll do my best to get the villagers under control."

When the man hesitated, Rolf gave him a push. "Get to it, man. Are you deaf?"

"N-nay, my l-lord," the man stammered. "I'll do your bidding at once."

He scurried off toward the manor, shouting and waving his arms. Rolf turned, intending to return for Megan when a dark shape stepped out in front of him.

" 'Twas my life ye just saved."

Rolf recognized the villager as Dugald, the lame carver with whom he played sticks.

"Then consider yourself lucky," Rolf replied, brushing the dirt from his sleeve. "It's a bloody chaotic spectacle here."

" 'Tis what Farrington deserves."

"I won't argue with that, but burning this place will serve nothing. Have you people lost your senses?"

Dugald straightened his shoulders. "Ye should know, Englishman. There comes a time when a man must finally take a stand. 'Tis no longer that we'll let Farrington terrorize us ceaselessly."

Rolf's jaw twitched angrily. "You still don't realize what this means," he exploded.

"Farrington may be a bastard, but he is still an English subject. Actions like these will only infuriate the King. If you persist in such behavior, even I will not be able to protect you."

Dugald looked at him steadily. " 'Twas our beloved Queen Mary that stood before her English judges and said, 'Remember that the theater o' the world is wider than the realm o' England.' The Scots are a proud people, Englishman. Know ye that there is more behind the actions o' the Scottish than just retaliation for what ye English do to us."

Rolf exhaled heavily, raking his hand through his hair. "Christ, Dugald, I don't blame you for what you have done. Just see if you can stop the villagers before any more damage occurs. I'll take care of Farrington myself."

"I'm afraid that Farrington is no longer a concern for ye, Englishman."

Rolf eyes narrowed. "What do you mean?"

"I mean 'tis a matter for young Robbie now. 'Tis his justice that will be served to Farrington, no' yours."

Rolf swore fiercely. "Damnation, Dugald. He'll only end up paying for Farrington's death with his own life. It's not worth the price he'll pay."

Dugald placed a hand on his shoulder. "But 'tis the way it shall be. Robbie is in the house. I fear 'tis already too late for Farrington."

"Not if I have anything to do about it," Rolf said grimly, moving away.

"Wait," Dugald called urgently, stopping Rolf in his tracks. " 'Tis one more matter for us to settle, Englishman. Ye have proven to be a man o' honor and have saved my life and the life o' my son. In return, an old man would like to give ye a piece o' advice."

Rolf cocked his eyebrow with interest. "Such as?"

"Give up your search for the Wolf. Ye may not like what ye find."

"That is your advice?" Rolf said bitterly. "If you must know, I hold the Wolf responsible for all of this. If he had come forward long ago, none of this would have happened."

Dugald hunched his shoulders against the cold. "Mayhap he's already come forward, but ye canna see him. Try thinking like a Scotsman, no' an Englishman. Perhaps then ye will find your Wolf."

"Must the Scottish incessantly speak in riddles?" Rolf snapped impatiently. "Hell and damnation, where is he, Dugald? Let me put an end to this now."

Dugald sighed. "Ye still do no' understand us. The Wolf is no' just a person. 'Tis much more than that—an emotion that feeds our spirit and renews our hope for the survival o' our people amid your oppression. The Black Wolf is a legend created by one man, but he need no' live for the spirit o' his struggle to live in all o' us."

Rolf stilled. "What are you saying? That Robert MacLeod is dead?"

"I'm simply saying that he need no' live for his legend to continue."

Rolf hit his forehead with the palm of his hand. "Good God, I've been such a fool.

Robert MacLeod is dead and that is why he hasn't come forward. But how can that be? How do you account for the raids, the organized resistance, the brilliant negotiating strategy? If MacLeod hasn't been leading the clan all this time, who in the devil has been doing it for him?"

When Dugald didn't answer, Rolf fell pensive, rubbing the gloved knuckles of his maimed hand. "Well, it couldn't be just anyone. Whoever has been leading the clan possesses a keen wit, a bold spirit and a damnable amount of stubbornness to have forced me into such generous terms for your people," he mused. "Not only would it take a person of immense courage to have accomplished what has been done, it would require someone who has been involved in the process from the beginning and could fully understand and direct the intricacies of the negotiations and—"

Rolf abruptly stopped in mid-sentence, looking at Dugald with a stricken expression on his face. "God's teeth, it's Megan, isn't it? Blast it, she's been the Wolf all along. How long has MacLeod been dead?"

"He died four months before ye even came to

Gairloch. 'Twas Megan herself who brought the other clans into the fold. Her da would have been proud o' her."

Rolf started to pace, swinging his arms back and forth. "Christ, I'm an even bigger fool than I thought. Of course, it all fits into the puzzle. That's why the Wolf seemed to know my every thought. And that's why Megan didn't want us to wed. She knew I'd be honor bound to reveal her identity to the King. God Almighty, what have I done?"

Dugald shrugged. "Just remember, ye can present your sovereign with the Black Wolf, but ye will no' silence the legend. The legend will live on forever in the hearts o' the Scots. If your quest is to quell the resistance o' the Black Wolf and the legend's followers, ye must find another solution."

Rolf stopped his pacing and turned sharply to face Dugald. "Such as?"

"That, lad, is for ye to decide. Ye must find a way to satisfy your honor without renewing the flames o' hatred 'tween our peoples."

Rolf stared at the old woodcarver for several minutes before laying his good hand on the man's shoulder. "You've given me a lot to think about, Dugald. Consider your debt to me repaid."

Dugald nodded. " 'Twas only a matter o' time before Megan's identity was revealed. I told ye this, Englishman, not to bring harm to Megan, but to help ye find a way to save her."

"I know," Rolf replied quietly. "And you can rest assured, I'll do my damnedest to find a compromise."

# Chapter Twenty-six

"Where in the devil are ye, Rolf St. James?" Megan breathed in frustration, patting the side of the stallion's neck impatiently.

It seemed as if she had been waiting for hours. Several times she'd had to fight back the urge to cast Rolf's instructions to the wind and ride up to the house. Part of her yearned to extract her own revenge on Farrington, while another part worried about Robbie and what might be happening in that house while she dallied out here in the dark.

"Blast it all," she muttered under her breath. "Why did I give him my word?"

"Because I made you," the answer came from the dark.

She gasped in surprise as Rolf materialized from the dark, leapt onto the horse and took the reins. His hair was disheveled, his shirt torn, and he had a grim look on his face.

"Ye've been fighting," she observed.

"You could say that," he answered. "But don't worry, the other fellow looks worse than me."

"Ye wish to jest?"

He shook his head. "Not particularly. Look, we don't have much time," he said, urging the horse into a gallop. "From what I understand, your cousin is already in the house."

"Robbie," she gasped. "Och, blessed saints. Are we too late?"

"I hope not. I've ordered Farrington's men to cease their attack on the villagers. Dugald will urge the villagers to do the same. I think we'll have a temporary truce shortly. However, that might change if anything happens to either your cousin or Farrington."

Megan pressed her face into Rolf's back, tightening her arms around his waist. "Please hurry," she urged him.

Although the fighting seemed largely to have stopped at the far perimeter of the estate, the scene close to Farrington's house was still in chaos. Several people were engaged in fierce personal battles on the front greensward.

Swearing, Rolf drew his stallion to a halt and dismounted, bringing Megan down after him. "Stay close," he warned, gripping her hand.

As they approached the house, Rolf could see that it had been severely damaged. Several windows had been shattered and small fires had been set and then extinguished all along the west side. One shutter hung drunkenly from a sill.

Shouting came from inside the house. Rolf hastened his step to the front door, stepping back in surprise as one of Farrington's men staggered out, clutching a bloody middle. He collapsed against Rolf and then slid to the ground.

"Stop them, my lord," he whispered in a ragged voice. "They will kill us all."

"Where is Farrington?" Rolf demanded, kneeling beside the man.

"Upstairs," the man answered weakly. "In his ... bedchamber. They ... went ... after him." He gurgled once and then lay still, his bloody hand falling to his side. Megan pressed her lips together and quickly turned her head to the side.

Rolf straightened and then gently lifted her chin until she looked directly at him. "Are you certain you want to do this?" he asked softly. "There may be things inside you will not wish to see."

She drew in a deep, steadying breath. "I know. But I must go. We have to stop Robbie."

Setting his mouth in a grim line, Rolf took her hand. "All right, but stay beside me," he said. Giving her hand a squeeze, he stepped across the threshold and into the foyer.

The house had been thoroughly ransacked. Rugs and tapestries had been slashed, furniture and paintings smashed, and glass and broken porcelain lay in broken pieces across the floor.

"God's teeth," Rolf said under his breath. They moved forward, walking past the sitting room.

Rolf glanced inside, his blood running cold at the sight. Two of Farrington's men lay sprawled on the floor dead. Their throats had been cut.

Rolf quickly stepped in front of Megan to block her view of the grisly sight. "We'd better hurry," he said darkly, propelling her toward the staircase. He took the stairs two at a time, pulling Megan close behind him. "I'm afraid we don't have much time, if any."

Surprisingly, the upstairs was deathly quiet. Rolf moved forward noiselessly, his concern deepening when he saw the door to Farrington's bedchamber was closed.

"Stay here," he whispered to Megan, pressing her against the side wall. She nodded, her eyes wide.

Carefully drawing his sword, Rolf lifted the latch on the door and kicked it open with his boot. Lunging into the room, he stopped cold at the scene in front of him.

Farrington, dressed in a white silk robe, was on his bare knees in front of the hearth, his hands clasped behind his back. He was sobbing pitifully, blood dripping onto his robe from a nasty gash on his neck. Megan's flame-haired cousin stood behind him, holding a dagger to the Englishman's ear.

Two other Scotsmen, lounging against the wall, leapt forward in surprise, drawing their swords when they saw Rolf enter the room.

"Drop the sword, Englishman," Robbie warned. "Or I'll kill him instantly."

Edwin began to sob, his entire body trembling with fear. "Oh, God, he intends to kill me," he sobbed. "You must stop him."

"Ye're a bloody coward," Robbie said in disgust, yanking back on Farrington's hair. "Ye delight in killing others, but canno' face your own death like a man. But I'm no' going to make this easy for ye. Nay, I'm going to make it so painful that ye will beg me for death." He pressed the blade against Farrington's neck, drawing blood. Farrington screamed in fright.

"Let him go," Rolf said calmly. "I can't permit

341

you to murder him no matter how much he deserves it."

"He killed my da and now I'm going to kill him," Robbie replied. "So, drop the bloody sword or I'll slit his throat this instant."

Rolf looked from Robbie to the other Scotsmen before casting aside his sword. One of the Scotsmen scurried to pick it up while the other circled behind Rolf, grabbing his arms and pinning them behind his back.

"I'll let ye watch if ye want," Robbie growled. "Farrington will finally get the justice he deserves."

"Indeed, he will," Rolf countered. "But let's do this legally. If you kill him now, you will only forfeit your own life as well. It's the law."

" 'Tis your law, Englishman, no' ours. We Scots believe in an eye for an eye, a tooth for a tooth. In this case, Farrington's life for the life o' my da's."

"Farrington will answer for the murder of your father. Some of my men witnessed it. The case against him is strong."

Robbie laughed bitterly. "Och, and ye expect me to take the word o' an Englishman just like that? Ye'll never punish your own kind and I know it. Killing him is my right—my revenge. He'll die now, by my hands, for all the pain and suffering he has caused." He lifted the knife and Farrington sobbed in fear.

"Don't do it, Robbie," Megan said, stepping into the room and pushing the hood of her cloak from her head.

"Meggie," Robbie exclaimed, his mouth gaping open in astonishment. The two Scotsmen also started in surprise. "What in all the saints' names are ye doing here?"

"I came to stop ye before ye made a terrible mistake. Don't kill him."

Robbie shook his head in disbelief. "Dinna kill Farrington? Have ye gone mad, Megan Mac-Leod? He's the man who killed your family and who knows how many o' our clansmen. And now he's killed Da." A mixture of grief and rage crossed his face. "Och, Meggie, he's killed Da."

A sob escaped her lips. "I know," she said in a choked voice. "Saints above, I know. And I understand exactly how ye are feeling. I used to lay awake at night and dream o' cruel and unmerciful ways to end the life o' this vile man. He has taken from me everyone I've ever loved. But I'm no' going to let him do it again. I couldn't bear losing ye, too, Robbie. Please, I ask ye to put the knife down."

Robbie threw a distrustful glance at Rolf. "And ye think this man will help bring Farrington to justice? I dinna trust him and ye shouldn't either. Let me do what I must and then I'll take ye away from all o' this. We'll start anew, Meggie. We'll reunite all the clans in Gairloch and build up our strength again. We can still fight the English. I know we can."

Megan glanced over at the two Scotsmen. "Clarence and John, leave us at once," she ordered firmly. "This is a matter to be settled 'tween Robbie and myself."

Clarence shook his head in disbelief. "Have ye gone mad, Megan? What about him?" He jerked hard on Rolf's arms.

"Ye may release him," she stated quietly. "He is my husband. He will no' harm us."

Clarence murmured doubtfully, but looked to Robbie for an answer. The flame-haired giant kept his eyes locked on Megan's. After a moment, he jerked his head sideways.

"Let the Englishman go," he said curtly.

"But, Robbie—" Clarence started in protest, but Robbie abruptly cut him off.

"Do as I say," he roared. "And get out o' here. Both o' ye. I'll take care o' this myself."

Clearly shaken, Clarence released Rolf and the two men quietly withdrew from the room, shutting the door behind them.

Megan stepped forward. "There is no more need to fight, Robbie," she said quietly. "We began signing the land grants and pardons last night. It's over. There is no more need of bloodshed in Gairloch."

Robbie scowled. "'Tisn't so, Meggie. Your Englishman still seeks the Black Wolf."

She nodded somberly. "I know. But rest assured that the Black Wolf has accepted his fate, just as ye must accept yours. Don't throw it away for rabble like Farrington. Ye have your whole life in front o' ye."

Robbie's scowl deepened. "Do ye really expect me to simply abandon ye to this fate, Meggie?"

"'Tis what is best for the clan."

"I dinna care anymore what's best for the clan."

"I don't believe that, and I don't think ye do either," she answered quietly. "I've made my peace wi' this, Robbie. Ye should, too."

"How can ye be so trusting after all the English have done to us?" Robbie exclaimed. "He's no different than Farrington."

"That's where ye are wrong. He is different. He

has kept all o' his promises to me. And I know he will keep his promises to the clans o' Gairloch, whether I am alive to see it or no'. He is an honorable man."

"He's a cursed Englishman."

"Who is trying to save your miserable life, might I add," Rolf interjected, taking a step forward. "Look, I've been patient long enough. You'd be wise to listen to her. Now put the dagger aside and let Farrington go."

Robbie pressed the knife tighter against Farrington's neck. "Dinna come any closer, Englishman," Robbie warned. "I'll slit his throat from ear to ear, I promise ye that."

"Don't be a fool, Kincaid," Rolf said quietly. "The truth is that this man is not worth one minute of your life. Let the court deal with this and we can all walk away from this honorably."

Robbie shook his head vigorously. "No' this time. All my life the English have cheated me from what I wanted. Well, no' any more. I want justice for my da, for Megan's father and brother and for all the friends and kin o' mine that this vile man has murdered. This time I'm going to take what I deserve."

"Please, Robbie," Megan pleaded. "Rolf is just trying to help."

"Rolf?" Robbie repeated astounded. "Is that what ye are calling him now? Saints above, Meggie, dinna tell me that ye have actually come to care for the Englishman."

Megan met his eyes evenly. "I love him, Robbie.

Rolf looked at her in surprise and wonder. It was the first time she had said those words.

Robbie laughed in disbelief. "Love? Och, Englishman, ye are good," he said harshly. "How hard was it to seduce an innocent like Megan?"

Megan gasped at the bitterness in his voice. "Robbie," she breathed in shock. "How can ye say such a thing?"

Rolf scowled deeply. "You know, Kincaid, you are making it very difficult for me to want to save your skin."

"I dinna need your help, Englishman."

"Stop it, both o' ye," Megan cried, her cheeks staining red. "Rolf has been good to me, Robbie. 'Tis but jealousy speaking for ye now. Can't ye see 'tis time to put all o' our hate and mistrust behind us? I'm asking ye to do so as my kin and my friend."

Robbie froze, and Megan drew a deep and steadying breath. "Please listen to me. Killing Farrington is no longer the answer. We've finally a chance at a future, a peaceful one, for all the people o' Gairloch. For ye, too, Robbie. Don't let this horrible man steal the last o' your dreams."

Robbie looked painfully at Megan before his eyes softened. "All I ever wanted was ye."

Megan swallowed back the tears. "But don't ye see? I'm giving ye another chance at life—a life ye can fill wi' new dreams and wee bairns o' your own. I beg ye to see reason, Robbie. Put down the knife and let Farrington go. He'll be served his justice in the court, and ultimately in the eyes o' God."

Robbie kept his eyes on her face for a long endless moment. Then he abruptly cast the dagger aside with a sharp flick of his wrist. It clattered against the stones of the hearth and lay still.

Farrington gave a broken sob of relief, looking

over his shoulder at Robbie as if he couldn't believe it was over. Then he rose to his feet, steadying his trembling legs by placing both hands on the mantle. Blood still oozed from the gash on his neck, dripping onto his robe.

"I did that for ye, Meggie," Robbie said softly. "For a new beginning."

Before she could answer, Farrington suddenly whirled around. Horrified, Megan saw he held a pistol in his hand.

For an instant he aimed it at Rolf, smiling. Then he turned and aimed it at Robbie. "You wretched heathen," he screeched. "How dare you hold a knife to my throat." With a twisted snarl on his face, he fired the gun.

"Nay," Megan screamed in horror as smoke from the pistol spread across the room.

Robbie staggered back one step and then crumpled to the floor with a startled look on his face. Farrington waved the pistol in the air, cackling in laughter. From the maniacal expression on his face, Megan realized the man had likely gone completely mad.

With a howl of anger, Rolf lunged forward, slamming into Farrington and sending them hurling to the floor. They landed atop a small table near the hearth, crushing it to splinters and sending candles and papers scattering across the room.

With a screech, Farrington smashed the pistol into the side of Rolf's temple. Rolf grunted in pain as blood steamed from the gash and into his eye. Furious, Rolf swung his fist, connecting with Farrington's jaw in a bone-thudding crunch.

Snapping out of her shock, Megan flung herself to Robbie's side, cradling his head in her lap. She sobbed in relief when she saw he was still breathing.

"Hold on, Robbie," she breathed, pressing her hand against his cheek. "Ye are going to be all right."

She heard Edwin shout a curse, and looked up just in time to see his hand close over the handle of Robbie's dagger.

"Rolf," she screamed. "He's got Robbie's dagger."

Rolf rolled sideways, grappling for control. Megan could see he was at a disadvantage because Edwin had the knife in the hand directly opposing Rolf's crippled appendage. Rolf could only press down with his forearm, trying to keep Edwin from lifting his arm. Both men's faces were twisted in pain and concentration. Megan knew at once she had to get help.

Sobbing, she set her cousin's head gently on the floor and ran to the door. Lifting the latch, she flung it open.

A blast of heat and smoke slammed into her, taking her breath away. Coughing and gagging, she slammed the door shut.

"Och, my God, Rolf," she shouted, tears streaming down her face. "The house is on fire."

At that exact moment a piercing cry filled the room. Horrified, she stared in shock at the two men, an invisible hand clutching her heart. Rolf and Edwin lay in a heap of bloody and tangled limbs. It was impossible to determine where one man started and the other ended.

"Rolf," she whispered, staggering forward a few steps. "Rolf, are you all right?"

Afraid of what she might discover, she

dropped to her knees beside the men. She heard a groan, and then saw Rolf struggle out from underneath Farrington. His clothes were ripped and blood dripped down his face from the cut over his eye. But he was alive.

Sobbing, she flung herself into his arms, pressing her tear-stained cheek against his face. "Och, Rolf," she cried. "I feared that I had lost ye."

He held her tightly to his chest. "I'm all right, Megan. But Farrington is dead. It looks like he found his justice after all."

"Meggie?" a small voice said.

Megan lifted her head in concern. "Robbie," she exclaimed, untangling herself from Rolf's embrace. "Don't move," she said, crawling to his side. "We are going to get ye out o' here."

"Meggie . . ." he said hoarsely. "I . . . I . . ."

"Don't talk," she said, gently smoothing back the hair at his temple. "Save your strength."

"I won't be going anywhere," he said, grimacing in pain.

"O' course ye will. As soon as we get out of this godforsaken house, I'll get a healing salve and ye'll be feeling like yourself again in no time."

"Nay, Meggie . . . no' this . . . time," he whispered hoarsely. His hand fell limply from his abdomen.

Megan gasped in horror at the gaping wound near his stomach. The blood was gushing out from an ugly ragged hole, staining crimson the material of his white shirt.

"Och, nay," she cried in stricken horror, pressing her hand against the wound to stop the bleeding. "We've got to get ye some help right away."

"I fear 'tis too late this time, Meggie."

"Nay," she countered fiercely. "I'm no' going to let ye die."

He smiled weakly. "Ye were always . . . tending . . . to my hurts."

"And ye always came out the better," she replied, holding back the tears. "This time 'twill be no different."

He coughed and then winced in pain. "I fear . . . 'twill be different this time, Meggie. What happened . . . to Farrington?"

"He's dead," she answered in a steely tone. "He won't hurt anyone ever again."

"I wanted . . . so much . . . to kill him."

A tear slid down her cheek. "I know," she said softly. "But ye are no' a murderer, Robbie. Ye are a kind and gentle man."

He managed a weak smile. "The Englishman . . . mayhap I was wrong about him. He can't be that vile . . . if ye love him . . . so."

A sob caught in her throat. "Aye, he's a good man, Robbie," she whispered. "I've been honored to know two such men."

Robbie grimaced, his face twisting in pain. "Then 'tis one more matter . . . to be settled. Tell the Englishman . . . to come closer."

Megan looked over at Rolf with a stricken expression. Rolf rose and stepped closer until he was standing above the Scotsman.

"I'm listening," Rolf said.

"Ye should know . . . that I am . . . the Black Wolf," Robbie said, wincing in pain from the effort of speaking. "Robert MacLeod is dead. I . . . took his place. Ye have . . . vanquished . . . me."

Megan gasped in shock at his words. "Nay, Robbie," she cried. "Don't say so. 'Tisn't true."

Robbie reached up and grasped her hand with surprising strength. "Dinna argue wi' me, Megan MacLeod. Let me give ye . . . one last gift."

Tears began to spill down her cheeks in earnest. "Och, God, Robbie, don't do this."

His breath was labored, but he managed to squeeze her hand. "I'm doing it for ye, Meggie . . . for us. For our . . . dreams."

"Och, Robbie," Megan breathed, holding back the sobs forming in her throat. "Ye never gave up your dreams. 'Tis what I always loved best about ye."

A spasm racked his body and his face turned ashen. "Meggie," he said so softly she barely heard him. "Do ye think . . . I'll be able . . . to dream in Heaven?"

She nodded, bending her head down near his face. "I'm certain o' it," she whispered against his cheek. " 'Twill be a beautiful place."

He looked up at her, and for a fleeting moment she saw the young and innocent boy he had once been.

"Be good . . . Meggie . . . *mo graidh*," he breathed. He squeezed her hand once more and then it fell limp and slipped from her grasp.

For a moment, Megan could only stare at his still, unbreathing form. Then, uttering a heart-shattering cry, she threw herself on his body. "Nay, Robbie," she sobbed. "Ye can't leave me."

"Megan," Rolf said, grabbing her under the arms and lifting her to her feet. "We have to leave at once. The house is burning."

Megan saw with alarm that smoke had begun to drift into the room from the cracks around the door.

"I can't leave Robbie here," she cried, looking

at him with a panicked expression on her face. "Please, Rolf, don't make me leave him."

Rolf looked down at Robbie's body and then nodded. "All right, I'll take him. But first you must climb out the window. Hold onto the drape and I'll lower you to the ground."

She looked at him puzzled, but he offered no explanation and instead quickly propelled her to the open window. He tossed one end of the heavy velvet drape he had torn from the wall out the window and grabbed the other end firmly.

"Hold on to the drape and climb down," he ordered, bracing his booted feet against the wall beneath the sill.

"But how will you get out?" she protested.

"I'll think of something," he replied sharply. "Go on now, Megan. We don't have time to argue."

Seeing the grim look on his face, she swallowed her doubts and began her descent. When she reached the bottom, she tugged twice on the drape. She felt him respond with a pull, and then it went slack in her hand.

Moments later an explosion came from the room. Looking up, she saw smoke pouring from the window.

"Rolf," she screamed. "Where are ye?"

After an agonizing minute, Megan saw him appear in the window. She gasped when she saw he had Robbie's body slung over his shoulder. Wobbling unsteadily, he sat on the edge of the window and then hoisted himself down, hanging from the sill with one arm. After swinging precariously for a moment, he let go, dropping to the ground.

Megan raced to his side, sobbing in relief

when she saw him sit up, ruefully rubbing his backside. His clothes and face were black with soot and he was nearly unrecognizable. But he was alive.

"Och, Rolf," she said, throwing herself into his arms. "Thank God, ye are all right. Do ye know how much I love ye?"

He coughed and then drew her close with one arm, wincing as she leaned heavily against his rib cage. "Despite all of this, we are going to be all right, Megan MacLeod," he replied, wearily resting his chin on top of her head. "Just as I promised you."

# Chapter Twenty-seven

Dusk had fallen by the time Rolf finally returned to Castle Kilcraig. There was still much to be sorted out, but first, the injured required attention and the dead needed burying. After that, it would be up to him to see that the healing process began in Gairloch. But for now, he needed to settle some unfinished business of his own.

On his way back to the castle, Rolf had stopped at the lake for a quick dip to cleanse himself of soot and blood. The water had been damn near freezing, but it was also invigorating and helped to clear his mind. He definitely wanted a clear head when he faced Megan.

Entering their bedchamber, he found her sitting alone in front of the hearth. She was staring into the fire, her expression sad and pensive. He detected a new but weary maturity about her. A white wool blanket lay loosely draped about her shoulders and she clutched one edge of it between her fingers.

He saw that she, too, had bathed. The blood was gone from her hands and her dark hair lay shiny and unbound across the blanket. She looked up at him when he entered, but said nothing.

Unbuckling the sword belt from his waist, he set it aside and walked over to the hearth. Kneeling, he added several squares of peat to the fire, stirring them until they caught. When he finished, he stood quietly, holding out his hands to the warmth.

"Do you wish to discuss what has happened?" he asked her quietly.

He heard her draw a heavy breath. "Aye," she replied softly. "Sit down, Rolf."

"First, I want to give you this." He walked over to a small wooden trunk and knelt down on one knee. From a small pouch around his waist, he pulled out a key. Inserting it into the lock, he opened the trunk and lifted the lid.

Megan gasped when she saw what he held in his hands. "The cloak o' the Black Wolf," she whispered softly. "Ye kept it after all."

"Yes, I kept it. A part of me longed to destroy it, but something held me back. Now I'm beginning to understand that this cloak is more than just a symbol of Scottish resistance. It is a part of your heritage, perhaps much like the sword your father buried with your brother."

A tear slipped down her cheek as he placed the cloak in her hands. "There will be no more killing in Gairloch," he said softly. "I know that no matter what I do, the legend your father created will live on. We must now find a way to reconcile that legend with the opportunity for peace."

Megan lifted the cloak to her cheek and closed her eyes. Her hair tumbled over her face, shadowing the tears that now fell freely. Rolf knelt down beside her chair.

"Megan, I'm truly sorry about what happened," he said quietly. "If only I had stopped Farrington earlier, both Robbie and your uncle might still be alive."

She brushed aside a tear with her fingertip. " 'Tis no' your fault, Rolf. I don't blame ye for what happened."

"I still can't help wishing there had been a different outcome," he said with a deep sigh. "There was no need for a further loss of life. Megan, you've lost your entire family. What can I possibly say that will make you feel anything except bitterness toward me . . . toward my countrymen?"

She lifted her head to look at him, her eyes grieved and brimming with tears. "I will learn to live with my pain. We all make decisions that affect our lives. 'Twas Geddes' decision to stand up to Farrington, 'twas Robbie's to seek his revenge, and 'twas mine to become what I've become."

"Megan—" he began, but she interrupted him.

"Don't stop me now, Rolf. 'Tis time to bring the truth out into the open. To finish the unfinished 'tween us. There is something ye must know about me."

He put his fingers gently against her lips. "If this is about the Wolf, Megan, you can consider it a closed matter."

She reached up, grasping his fingers and pulling them aside. "Ye once asked me to speak only the truth wi' ye. Well, Robbie lied for me as he lay dying. 'Twas no' him who became the Black Wolf after my da died."

Rolf abruptly stood, walking over to the hearth and leaning his elbow atop the mantle. For a long moment he stood there silently before he turned to face her. "Do you know what happens to people who admit to treason, Megan?" he asked abruptly.

She glanced up at him, clearly surprised by the new crisp tone of his voice. "What do ye mean?" she asked.

He kept his gaze steady on her face. "You should know that I am duty-bound by my honor to report those who confess to treasonous activities against the crown. Robbie Kincaid has done such a thing by admitting that he became the Black Wolf after the death of your father. Now that he is dead, the resistance has no leader, no rallying point. My duty to bring the Black Wolf to justice has been fulfilled. As far as I am concerned the matter is closed."

"But—" she started to protest.

"I said the matter is closed," Rolf repeated tightly. "The Black Wolf is dead. There will be no more Scottish resistance in Gairloch nor will there be another dishonorable English landlord to disturb the peace. It all begins anew right here, right now. With us."

Megan stood slowly, the blanket slipping from her shoulders. Her thick dark hair hung in graceful curves over her shoulders. "Ye know, don't ye?" she asked.

Rolf reached out, placing his hand gently on her shoulder. "What I know is that as the last surviving MacLeod, you will act on behalf of your deceased father and for the clan by agreeing to accept the land grants and pardons in exchange for the cessation of all hostile activities against the crown. My search for the Black Wolf has ended."

She regarded him with disbelief. "Have ye no wish to punish me for my actions?"

"You acted with honor and courage, putting the welfare of your clan above your own life. There is no shame in that. And there is no shame in what we feel for each other."

She glanced back at the fire, the fringe of her lashes casting shadows on her cheeks. "But everything is so helplessly tangled wi' us," she said softly. "Betrayal, deception and lies. 'Tis what we've based our relationship on."

"Did you lie when you told me you loved me?"

She shook her head vehemently. "Nay, 'twas no lie."

"I love you, too, Megan. We'll start with that. It will give us a chance at a new beginning. I won't pretend that it will be easy. It won't. We need to give ourselves time to heal—to forgive each other for what we have done and to learn to trust each other. But when we are ready, we'll have something to build on—a foundation of love and respect."

They sat in silence for some time before Megan finally turned to him, leaning forward in her chair. Slowly she held out her hand.

Rolf took it, his warm fingers circling around hers. It was a gesture of peace—Scottish to English. Now they could move forward.

"Will ye promise me something, Rolf St. James?" she asked quietly, the expression on her face both tender and wistful.

He squeezed her hand gently. "What is it, my love?"

"Will ye promise that when we have put this all o' this behind us, that ye'll go wi' me to the meadow where as a child I used to dream? I want to try to find some of those dreams again."

Rolf rose from the chair, pulling her to her feet. He drew her into his embrace, holding her snugly against his chest.

"I can easily keep that promise," he murmured, feeling the soft brush of her hair against his cheek. "I think, my love, that it's long past time we start making your dreams come true."

# DESPERADO

## SANDRA HILL

Major Helen Prescott has always played by the rules. That's why Rafe Santiago nicknamed her "Prissy" at the military academy years before. Rafe's teasing made her life miserable back then, and with his irresistible good looks, he is the man responsible for her one momentary lapse in self control. When a routine skydive goes awry, the two parachute straight into the 1850 California Gold Rush. Mistaken for a notorious bandit and his infamously sensuous mistress, they find themselves on the wrong side of the law. In a time and place where rules have no meaning, Helen finds Rafe's hard, bronzed body strangely comforting, and his piercing blue eyes leave her all too willing to share his bedroll. Suddenly, his teasing remarks make her feel all woman, and she is ready to throw caution to the wind if she can spend every night in the arms of her very own desperado.

_52182-2                        $5.99 US/$6.99 CAN

# BETRAYAL Evelyn Rogers

## By the Bestselling Author of
### *The Forever Bride*

If there is anything that gets Conn O'Brien's Irish up, it is a lady in trouble--especially one he has fallen in love with at first sight. So after the Texas horseman saves Crystal Braden from an overly amorous lout, he doesn't waste a second declaring his intentions to make an honest woman of her. But they have barely been declared man and wife before Conn learns that his new bride is hiding a devastating secret that can destroy him.

The plan is simple: To ensure the safety of her mother and young brother, Crystal agrees to play the damsel in distress. The innocent beauty has no idea how dangerously charming the virile stranger can be--nor how much she longs to surrender to the tender passion in his kiss. And when Conn discovers her ruse, she vows to blaze a trail of desire that will convince him that her deception has been an error of the heart and not a ruthless betrayal.

___4262-2                                    $5.99 US/$6.99 CAN

# CATHERINE HART

# Ashes & Ecstasy

## The smoldering sequel to the blazing bestseller
### *Fire and Ice*

Ecstatically happy in her marriage to handsome gentleman pirate Reed Taylor, Kathleen is never far from her beloved husband's side—until their idyllic existence is shattered by the onset of the War of 1812. Her worst fears are realized when she receives word that Reed's ship, the *Kat-Ann,* has been sunk, and all aboard have perished.

Refusing to believe that Reed is dead, Kathleen mounts a desperate search with the aid of Jean Lafitte's pirate band, to no avail. The memory of the burning passion they shared is ever present in her aching heart—and then suddenly an ironic twist of fate answers her fervent prayers, only to confront her with evidence of a betrayal that will threaten everything she holds most dear.

___4264-9 $5.99 US/$6.99 CAN

# Connie Mason
# The Dragon Lord

Renowned for his prowess on the battlefield and in the bedroom, the Dragon Lord has no desire to wed an heiress he has never seen, but he has little choice. When given the option of the three Ayrdale women, he has no taste for the grieving widow or the sharp-tongued shrew, so the meek virgin it must be.

High-spirited Rose knows she is no thornless blossom waiting to be plucked. Her gentle twin longs for a cloistered life, whereas Rose has never been known as a shrinking violet and is more than capable of standing up to a dragon. A clever deception will allow her sister to enter a nunnery while an unexpected bride awaits her unsuspecting husband for the most unforgettable deflowering of all.

___4932-5 $5.99 US/$6.99 CAN

# Viking!

## Connie Mason

The first time he sees her she is clad in nothing but
moonlight and mist, and from that moment, Thorne the
Relentless knows he is bewitched by the maiden bathing in
the forest pool. How else to explain the torrid dreams, the
fierce longing that keeps his warrior's body in a constant
state of arousal? Perhaps Fiona is speaking the truth when
she claims it is not sorcery that binds him to her, but the
powerful yearning of his viking heart.

___4402-1                                        $5.99 US/$6.99 CAN

**Dorchester Publishing Co., Inc.**
**P.O. Box 6640**
**Wayne, PA 19087-8640**

Please add $1.75 for shipping and handling for the first book and
$.50 for each book thereafter. NY, NYC, and PA residents,
please add appropriate sales tax. No cash, stamps, or C.O.D.s. All
orders shipped within 6 weeks via postal service book rate.
Canadian orders require $2.00 extra postage and must be paid in
U.S. dollars through a U.S. banking facility.

Name_____
Address_____
City_____State_____Zip_____
I have enclosed $_____ in payment for the checked book(s).
Payment <u>must</u> accompany all orders. ❑ Please send a free catalog.
       CHECK OUT OUR WEBSITE! www.dorchesterpub.com

# Pure Temptation
## Connie Mason

Spirits can be so bloody unpredictable, and the specter of Lady Amelia is worst of all. Just when one of her ne'er-do-well descendants thinks he can go astray in peace, the phantom lady always appears to change his wicked ways. A rogue without peer, Jackson Graystoke wants to make gaming and carousing in London society his life's work. And the penniless baronet will gladly damn himself with wine and women—if Lady Amelia gives him the ghost of a chance. Fresh off the boat from Ireland, Moira O'Toole isn't fool enough to believe in legends or naive enough to trust a rake. Yet after an accident lands her in Graystoke Manor, she finds herself haunted, harried, and hopelessly charmed by Black Jack Graystoke and his exquisite promise of . . . Pure Temptation.

___4041-7                                    $5.99 US/$6.99 CAN

**Dorchester Publishing Co., Inc.**
**P.O. Box 6640**
**Wayne, PA 19087-8640**

# THE LION'S BRIDE — CONNIE MASON

## Winner of the *Romantic Times* Storyteller Of The Year Award!

Lord Lyon of Normandy has saved William the Conqueror from certain death on the battlefield, yet neither his strength nor his skill can defend him against the defiant beauty the king chooses for his wife.

Ariana of Cragmere has lost her lands and her virtue to the mighty warrior, but the willful beauty swears never to surrender her heart.

Saxon countess and Norman knight, Ariana and Lyon are born enemies. And in a land rent asunder by bloody wars and shifting loyalties, they are doomed to misery unless they can vanquish the hatred that divides them—and unite in glorious love.

_3884-6                                                $5.99 US/$7.99 CAN